Random Violence

Also by the Author
Stolen Lives
The Fallen
Pale Horses

Random Violence

Jassy Mackenzie

To Dion—now, always and forever

Published by
Soho Press, Inc.
853 Broadway
New York, NY 10003

Library of Congress Cataloging-in-Publication Data

Mackenzie, Jassy.
Random violence / Jassy Mackenzie.
p. cm.
ISBN 978-1-61695-218-1
eISBN 978-1-56947-887-5
1. Women private investigators—Fiction.
2. Police corruption—Fiction.
3. Johannesburg (South Africa)—Fiction. I. Title.
PR9369.4.M335R36 2010
823'.92—dc22
200904401

10 9 8 7 6 5 4 3 2 1

I

Annette arrived home in the dark. Her car's tires crunched on the sand driveway and the brakes squeaked as she pulled to a hurried halt outside the tall metal gate. The heater's fan was on maximum and the eight o'clock news was starting on the radio, but she didn't have time to listen. Stopping at night was risky. Getting out of the car was even more dangerous, but she had no choice. Pulling the keys from the ignition, with the useless gate buzzer dangling from the bunch, she climbed out.

She hunched her shoulders against the cold, hugging her flimsy work jacket around her as she hurried over to the gate. She passed the "Sold" sign, rattling against the metal stakes that held it in the ground. The wind was blowing hard, hissing and whistling through the long dry grass that flanked her driveway. The growth swayed and parted and she peered at it suspiciously. For a moment it looked as if somebody was crouched inside, trying to hide.

Her head jerked up as she saw movement ahead of her. Four large dogs rushed towards the gate, their shadows stretching out behind them in the beams of her car's headlights. The lead Alsatian snarled at his followers, defending his position as the others crowded too close. Leaping and wagging their tails, the dogs pushed their noses through the bars in welcome.

Annette smiled in relief, leaning forward and scratching their coarse fur. "Hey, boys. Just a minute and I'll be inside."

She fumbled with the bunch of keys, searching for the right one, her breath misting in the icy air. The giant padlock was easy to open because it was new, but it was difficult to remove because of its size. It was wedged into the thick steel rings between the gate and the gatepost. She struggled with the stubborn metal, so cold to the touch it seemed to burn. She glanced behind her at the lonely road while the dogs whined and shoved their muzzles against her hand in encouragement.

Finally the padlock jerked free, pinching a fold of skin on her finger as it came loose. She swore, cradling her hand against the pain. She would have a blood blister tomorrow, to add to the one from yesterday.

"Got to get that gate motor fixed," she told the dogs.

Her keys dug into her palm as she wrapped her hands around the bars and shoved her shoulder into the heavy gate. The sand and rust clogging its runners made it a swine to slide open, especially at the start. Once it had been forced to get moving, it was easier. But as she started to push, her dogs tensed and one of them barked. Spinning round, she squinted into the blackness beyond her little Golf. She saw another vehicle pull to a stop in the road. It had approached silently, headlights off. Its dark body gleamed faintly red in the glow of her taillights.

Annette stared in disbelief as the driver climbed out and strolled round the front of the car towards her, as casual and relaxed as if he was a friendly neighbor stopping to give her some help. But she lived on two hundred acres of land and spoke to the neighbors two or three times a year about fencing and firebreaks. If they drove past her place at night, they would have their headlights on full and their feet on the accelerator, gunning their car down the dark ribbon of tarmac, counting the minutes until they reached home.

This man wasn't a neighbor. And he certainly wasn't friendly. Once he was clear of the car, he turned to face her. With a heart-stopping rush of terror, she saw the shape of a gun in his hand.

"No, please, don't. Oh Jesus. Help me!"

Her first instinct was to run. But the dark car blocked the road ahead of her, and there were deep drainage ditches in the overgrowth on either side. She turned back to the gate, pushing with panicked strength against its stubborn weight. If she could let the dogs out, she'd have a chance. It moved a few inches and then jammed, just as it had done the night before. The dogs were all barking now, hurling themselves at the gap in their efforts to protect her. Their noise was a solid force that pulsed against her face, but they couldn't get through to help her. Sobbing from the effort, her shoulder in agony, she knew she had no more time to try.

She turned back to face her attacker.

"Do you want my car? Here, take it." Her voice sounded thin and high and the keys jingled in her unsteady hand as she held them out towards him.

The shadows on the man's face deepened. He shook his head. He took another step forward and raised the gun.

Above the clamor of the dogs, Annette heard a metallic clicking sound. She didn't know much about guns but there was only one thing this could mean.

The safety catch was off.

Her legs wouldn't move. Her arms dropped to her sides. She wanted to plead, to beg him for her life. But what good would it do? He had already refused her car. And her throat had become so dry, she doubted whether she could speak at all.

Her fingers brushed against the pepper spray on her key ring. It was her only chance, even if it was a hopeless one. She fumbled with the metal canister. Quickly now. Lift and spray. Aim high, go for the eyes. Praying for a miracle, she raised her hand.

The man fired twice. The first shot got her square in the chest, slamming her back against the gate. As she began to slide to the ground, the second shot caught the side of her neck, ripping it open. Gushing blood, she collapsed onto the stony surface.

The killer watched her die, and then moved over to the open door of her car, where the heater was blowing and the newsreader was telling listeners about the price of gold and the strength of the rand against the dollar. With gloved fingers, he removed her handbag from the passenger seat. As quietly as it had arrived, the black vehicle moved away. At the gate the dogs continued to bark, their eyes brilliant in the glow from the headlights, their muzzles now crimson with blood.

2

The highway from Johannesburg's airport was busier than Jade remembered. More cars, more taxis, queues of trucks and lorries. Forests of billboards advertised insurance and cell phones. Smog and dust smothered the city like a dirty blanket, trapped by the temperature inversion that would only lift when the summer rains came.

Road signs loomed above them and David changed lanes, forcing a BMW to veer out of the way. The driver blasted his horn and gesticulated furiously through his tinted windows.

"What's his problem?" David asked.

Jade eased her foot off an imaginary brake pedal. "Nothing, I'm sure. Carry on with what you were saying. And watch out, because there's some slow traffic ahead."

Not everything had changed, she thought. David's driving was as bad as ever. She'd hoped that in the ten years she'd been away it might have improved a little.

"Like I was telling you, I got promoted a month ago. You're talking to Superintendent Patel now. I head up an investigation unit at Johannesburg Central."

"Congratulations. That's great news."

David grimaced. "I thought so too at first. Then I realized I've landed in one hell of a mess."

"What kind of a mess?"

"My predecessor died. Heart attack. He left me with a case backlog longer than a Sandton traffic jam. I found a knee-deep pile of dossiers in his office. Literally. Stacked up on the floor. Old cases, cold cases, priority cases. I've seen three affidavits in there already that everybody thought had been lost. It took nine years of his inefficiency to create that bloody heap and now I'm getting saddled with the blame."

Jade could easily imagine what David's reaction must have been. When it came to his work, he was a perfectionist. His desk was always immaculate. In the morning it would be piled with reports and case files, their edges set square. By the evening, it would be clear. The paperwork would have been dealt with, or filed away. She'd called him a magician. He'd said it was easy. She wondered how long it would take him to sort it out. Perhaps he already had.

"How did he get to that position if he was so inept?"

"He's not the only one, Jade. You won't believe how the

police force has changed. We're swamped with incompetents. If your father was here today, he'd be after half the new personnel with a sjambok, whipping them into shape."

Jade hadn't thought much about her father since she left. It had taken considerable effort, but she had managed. Back in Johannesburg she knew she'd be reminded of him constantly. Especially when she was with David. He had long been like an older brother to her. Now she couldn't look at him without imagining Commissioner de Jong hovering in the background, gazing at both of them with fatherly affection while keeping a stern eye on David to make sure he didn't transgress any of the unspoken rules regarding his daughter.

She took a deep breath and forced the image of her father firmly out of her mind.

"You mentioned a problem case when we spoke on the phone. Is that part of the backlog?"

A couple of days previously, Jade had been almost deafened by David's delighted bellow when, after a moment's pause, he'd realized who was on the long-distance line.

"Jadey! Where the bloody hell have you been?"

"I'm in the UK. But I'm coming back to Jo'burg," she'd told him.

"When do you arrive? Give me your flight number and I'll fetch you from the airport. Do you need somewhere to stay? Oh, and while you're here there's a case you can help me with, if you have time."

She hadn't been able to suppress her delighted grin. David sounded exactly the same as he had ten years ago, barking out instructions, organizing everything down to the last detail in the time it took the average person to draw breath.

Damn, it was good to see him again. Good to be back in the crazy boomtown energy of Johannesburg, too. She hadn't realized how much she'd missed the feel of the city. She'd just completed a surveillance job in the muggy heat of an English summer. The firm had offered her another assignment but she'd turned it down. It was time for her to return to South Africa.

David swung the car into the fast lane, glanced at the road ahead, and turned his full attention back to Jade. "No. I need your help with a new case. A woman was murdered a few nights ago, on a smallholding just north of here. Shot as she arrived home. It looks like a car hijacking that went wrong."

"What happened?"

"We think some guys pulled off the road and threatened her. Opportunistic crime. But she had a pepper spray in her hand when we found her body. Seems she tried to resist them instead of saying 'Yes, sir' and handing over the keys."

"She tried to use pepper spray? With a gun aimed at her?"

"Maybe she panicked. Acted without thinking."

"And what did they do?"

"Seems they also panicked. Shot her dead, snatched her bag from the car, then took off."

Jade shook her head. She was back in South Africa all right.

"Any evidence?" she asked.

"First person on the scene was a minibus taxi driver. According to his report, one of his passengers saw the body and shouted at him to stop. So he reversed and they all got out to go and have a look. Eighteen people and one goat."

"A goat?" Jade glanced at David to see if he was joking. He wasn't. He was looking straight at her, his eyes worried and serious in his brown-skinned face. She hurriedly transferred her gaze back to the road, ready to warn him if he strayed into the path of an oncoming tanker.

"One goat and eighteen people," he repeated. "If there was any evidence nearby, it was history after the time that taxi stopped. When the flying squad got there, all they found were eighteen different footprints. And goat droppings."

"Any leads so far?"

David shook his head. "Not a clue."

"No informers?" Jade was watching the steering wheel. He wasn't touching it and the car was drifting to the left. Couldn't he see?

"Nope. We're working on it. But in the meantime there are complications." David slid his hands over the wheel and the car straightened up.

"What complications?"

David turned off the highway and accelerated onto a road going north. Jade saw brand-new office parks surrounded by raw earth and piles of sand, and acres of townhouses where she remembered trees and open space.

"Her ex-husband Piet. He's decided the best way to speed up the investigation is to contact every newspaper and radio station who's prepared to speak to him, and create the biggest media circus since Zuma's rape trial."

"That can't be helping you."

He shook his head. "I've got journalists pestering me every time I turn on my cell phone. And Commissioner Williams is on my back wanting to know how hotshot new Superintendent Patel has managed to create more negative press in one week than the old one did in nine years."

"That could be career-limiting."

"It is already. Williams doesn't like me. I wasn't his choice for the job. He's already said he wants to take me off the case. I'd be out of the department altogether, if he had his way."

David made a few more turns, and drove down a sand road so rutted and potholed that Jade felt her teeth being rattled loose in her head.

"Where are we going?"

"To your hotel."

"Down this road?"

A couple of minutes later he stopped the car outside a gate and pressed a remote control button to open it. The thatched cottage behind it was enclosed by a palisade topped with six strands of electric fencing.

David turned to Jade and smiled. "It's next door to where I'm renting. It's secure, and best of all, it's free. I did a favor for the landlady a while ago. Her boyfriend got drunk and started threatening her with a knife, so I did the neighborly thing and arrested him. When she heard I had a friend coming, she offered it to me for you. It's yours for a month."

Jade climbed out of the car and breathed in. The fresh, cold air had a tang of wood smoke blended in with other scents that made her think of vegetation—not green, not rotting, but concentrated and crisp and dry. She could imagine staying here for a month. Perhaps even longer.

❖

Jade had spent most of her childhood in Turffontein, south of the city. Not the best area in the world. She hadn't needed to look at the calendar to know when it was the weekend, because the couple next door would start drinking and fighting at eight in the morning, instead of waiting till five thirty in the afternoon when work was over.

She used to sit in her bedroom studying her textbooks with her fingers in her ears. It didn't stop her from hearing the screaming and swearing, and the occasional smashing sound as one of the tall brown quart bottles of beer was dropped or thrown. The broken bottles were piled up outside the house in cardboard boxes every Monday, the day the rubbish collectors came round.

Her father was a highly respected police commissioner. Despite his senior position, he couldn't afford to live anywhere else. Jade knew she needed a career that paid better than police work, so she'd decided to study law at varsity. One day, she would be a wealthy attorney and live in a huge house. When her father retired, she'd build him a luxury cottage.

Then, when Jade was in the second year of her law degree, David transferred from Durban to Johannesburg to join her father's unit, and rented a house in the next street.

"This is David Patel—my new assistant," her father had told her when she'd arrived home one day to find the two of them drinking coffee in the kitchen. The young man, dressed in a neatly ironed white shirt and black tie, unfolded himself from the wooden chair and walked over to shake her hand.

David Patel. What kind of a name was that? Jade looked up at him. And further up. He was so tall his black spiky hair brushed against the glass shade of the ceiling lamp. His expression reminded her of a hawk. But his eyes fascinated her the most, because they were the lightest gray she'd ever seen. They looked almost colorless, like water.

"When I retire, he's going to be the best detective in the whole of the South African police force," her father continued proudly. Jade blinked, surprised by her father's announcement. He didn't usually make mistakes about people, but she wasn't sure about this man. He didn't look like a detective at all. He looked like he should be out fighting with mercenaries in an exotic and dangerous location, a machine gun strapped to his back.

David looked down at her with his strange eyes, so oddly pale in his brown-skinned face. He took her hand in a gentle grasp. And then he smiled.

At that exact moment Jade changed her mind about him.

With David there, Turffontein didn't seem like such a bad place after all. And when she spent time talking to him about his job, Jade thought she might have been wrong about a career in the police force, too. Crime-fighters were heroes. At least, David made it sound that way. But when she'd told him she had changed her mind about being a lawyer, he discouraged her from joining the police.

"As a woman you'll be limited, Jadey," he told her. "You'll be kept in an admin position for so long you'll start to grow mold. Why don't you become a private investigator? That way you can be your own boss. Run your own show, work with the cops."

Jade liked the idea of working with David. And she had never wanted to grow mold. So she took his advice.

❖

David walked into the well-tended garden with her. Now that she wasn't trying to watch the road for him, she had a chance to look at him properly.

She had expected that time would have stopped while she was away, that David would look the same as when she'd last seen him. He didn't.

His face was thinner and careworn, his forehead furrowed, his body more solid. Looking closely, she saw white strands gleaming in his dark hair. He still reminded her of a mercenary, but now it looked as if his fight had been harder and his victory more narrow.

She saw he was staring at her, too. She wondered what he was thinking.

"You haven't changed a bit, Jadey," he said. "You still look so damn good."

He was being kind, she knew, although she was encouraged by the unbrotherly tone of the compliment. She was thirty-four now. She had smile lines and tiny crow's feet around her eyes. Her hair was darker brown than it had been; she'd started dyeing it last year when she'd spotted the first evidence of gray. She was still slim and wiry though. Like her father she had a ridiculous metabolism that allowed her to eat whatever she wanted and stay that way.

She smiled up at him.

"You haven't changed, either," she said.

She could be kind, too.

They strolled over to a railway-sleeper bench in the shade. He thumped his weight down on the wood, and patted the seat next to him. Jade joined him. The bench was punishingly hard on her backside, still numb from the eleven-hour flight.

David gazed at the view. She thought he looked puzzled, as if he couldn't believe that it was as real as the crime and brutality that he saw in his working life.

"The case. Could you help me with it?" he asked.

"Of course."

"I can't pay you. We've got no budget."

"You can owe me." Jade watched a bird with a luminous turquoise breast hop along the grass towards the bench. It stared at them, inquisitive. Then David bent to adjust his shoelace. Startled by the movement, it flew up to a safe perch on the branch of a syringa tree.

"If you were thinking of coming back permanently, it would be a good kick-start for your career," he added.

"Yes, it would."

"Why the hell did you disappear, Jadey?" He looked at her, his pale gray eyes keen and sharp under his elegant brows. "I've often wondered. You left the country so suddenly, you didn't tell anyone where you were going. What happened?"

Jade chose her words carefully. Not because David was a top-notch investigator who might pick up the slightest whiff of falsehood. But because he was her friend. She didn't want to lie. Equally, she couldn't tell him the truth. Not now. Not ever.

She settled for saying, "It was to do with my dad, mostly."

He nodded, as if he'd been expecting her to say that. She was worried he'd question her further, but to her relief he looked at his watch and stood up.

"I'd better get going now," he said. "Or else I'll be in more trouble."

They went back to the car. David took her suitcase out of the trunk, together with a beige folder containing a slim sheaf of papers.

"This file contains everything on the case so far."

"Thanks. I'll look at it now."

He slammed the trunk shut. "And this car is for you. I hired it on your behalf. It's a good choice, I think. Inconspicuous."

Jade ran her hand along the hood. "Great choice, David.

Thank you very much." It was small and white, so inconspicuous she didn't know how she would ever find it again if she walked away from it in a car park.

She buzzed the gate open for David and watched him jog the short distance to the house next door. He ran up a flight of outside stairs to a room above the garage, reappearing a minute later with a tie in his hand, climbed into the unmarked vehicle in his driveway and headed down the road, honking as he passed her cottage.

She hefted her bag into the bedroom. The cottage was furnished, although the décor was too chintzy and frilly for her taste. She drew the line well before heart-shaped scatter cushions and lacy toilet-roll holders. But it had what she needed. Steel security gates, burglar bars on all the windows and an alarm system that was linked to an armed response company.

Jade walked outside to her car.

She'd get to the case file as soon as she could. But first she had more urgent business, on the wrong side of town.

3

The industrial section nestled behind Johannesburg's inner city had boomed in the early 1900s during the gold rush, and slumped into seedy decay when the last of the surrounding mines had closed. Now, Jade discovered, it was back in business again. The traffic was worse than she remembered. Streams of hawkers threaded their way in between the queues of cars selling newspapers and squeaky toys, beanies and sunglasses, batteries and replica perfumes. Jade wound down her window and bought a bottle of mineral water from a dreadlocked man wearing a Coca-Cola T-shirt.

The place she was looking for used to be a warehouse with a sad empty plot lined with vicious-looking weeds on one side and a dilapidated building on the other. Now it was one of twenty warehouses. Jade recognized it just in time.

She stamped on the brakes and honked in front of the big metal gate. A faded sign outside read "Auto Parts." She guessed it hadn't been repainted since she was last here.

A man wearing dirty blue overalls came out to meet her. He was tall and gangly, with a dark olive complexion. The black peppercorn curls on his head had been bleached orange-blond. The effect was garishly amateur. Beneath it, his nose showed the signs of a botched re-setting, and his eyes were hard and wary.

She got out of her car.

"Robbie."

"Jade." He wiped his oil-stained hands on his overalls before giving her a hug. "Good to see you."

They walked into the warehouse.

Jade looked around. It was so cold her breath steamed in the air. A receptionist was sitting at the table inside the door. She had long dark hair and was wearing tight pink jeans and a fluffy hooded jacket that zipped up. The zip wasn't pulled up very high, and she didn't seem to be wearing anything under the jacket. She looked like the prize performer at an Eskimo strip club.

"That's Verna," Robbie said.

"Hi, Verna," Jade said.

Verna smiled back at her. Jade thought she probably smiled even wider for men.

Inside the place was surprisingly clean and tidy. The steel shelves were stacked with parts. She wondered how many were new and how much came from cars that had been stolen. There was a strong smell of oil in the air.

Robbie's office was at the back, protected by a sturdy security gate. He took out a set of keys and unlocked it.

"How's business?" Jade inquired.

"Never been better."

"I'm sure Verna is good for sales."

Robbie smiled. "She's good for lots of things. And for sales."

He pulled up a chair for Jade and punched a button on a CD player. Whitney Houston came crooning out of the loudspeakers. Jade was pretty certain that the CD player was stolen, and if the album had been anything else, she would have guessed it was pirated, because that was Robbie's way. But why anyone would want to pirate Whitney Houston was beyond her.

"Coffee?" he asked.

"No thanks. I had some on the plane." She hadn't forgotten the taste of Robbie's coffee. It left a lasting impression. She wasn't willing to gamble on the possibility that he might have learned how to make a better cup since they'd last seen each other.

Social obligations over, they got down to business.

"So. Same again?"

"Same again."

Robbie nodded. "Thought so." He pulled open the desk drawer and took out a gun. He winked at her. "This is the best I've got."

It was a Glock 19. Compact, black, stubby and functional, with a simple but brutally efficient design that always made her think of a shark. Her fingers closed around the ridged grip and she felt it nestle into her palm. It felt hard and cold and familiar. She looked at it more closely. It was very familiar. It had a C-shaped nick on the barrel that she'd been in the habit of running her fingers over the last time she owned it.

"Robbie."

"Yes?"

"This is the same gun."

"Am I good or what?"

She frowned at him. "You promised to get rid of it. You said nobody would ever be able to find it."

"What's your problem, Jade? Nobody did find it. That's why it's here now. I kept it safe for you. Oiled, that sort of thing. Nobody's used it since then, I'm not that daft." He ran a finger over the barrel. "It's a good piece and I didn't want to get rid of it. You know, for me, a Glock is a cultural weapon. One of my grandfathers was Austrian, which I'm sure I've told you before. That's where my white genes come from. The Nazi side of the family."

"You told me your grandfather was Irish."

"Oh. Well, I was trying to get into your pants then. Irish sounded better."

Jade sighed. "What if the Scorpions had raided you?"

"They didn't. I haven't had a problem with any of the cops recently. And if they had, they wouldn't have found it. I didn't keep it in the damn desk drawer the whole time, you know."

Jade ran her fingers over the nick again.

"You were supposed to throw it away for me."

"In a week or so you can do what you like with it. Go out on a paddle ski and chuck it in the middle of the Vaal Dam. Bury it on a mine dump. Whatever."

Jade looked down at the Glock. The grip felt cold and clean in her hand, as if it had never been exposed to the hot sweat on her palms that left wet streaks on the hard black plastic the last time she had touched it. The gun had done its job. Afterwards, she'd never wanted to see it again. She felt uneasy holding it now.

"Robbie, I don't want this one again. It's too risky. I'd prefer another piece."

"You think I know the history of everything that comes in here? You want me to sell you something that was used to shoot some bloody kid in a robbery? If they don't catch you, nobody'll be any the wiser. In any case, it's the only suitable one I have right now."

He grinned, and yet again Jade was reminded of a shark. "There's too many people dealing in guns. It's not a profitable business any more. Or a safe one. So I don't do it much. I've got a damaged piece I wouldn't sell to you, and the only other one's a Desert Eagle. You can have it if you want, but you won't even be able to get your hand around the grip."

Jade shook her head. "That's not an option, then."

"I won't charge you for the Glock. You bought it off me once already. I won't even charge you storage." He slid a cloth bank bag across the desk. "Give me five hundred rand and you can have this lot. Holster, extra mags and a stack of ammo. If you run out, it's because you've pissed off too many people. Not because I short-supplied you."

Jade counted out five notes. The currency felt unfamiliar in her hands. She saw a blue line drawing of a gloomy-looking buffalo head on the topmost note. Then Robbie's fingers covered it as he swept the money towards him and shoved it into the drawer.

"There we are then. Done deal. You can smile, you know.

Be happy. You got your old weapon back. It'll work for you again. You watch."

She picked up the bag of ammunition, feeling its weight.

By sitting here with Robbie, holding an illegal, unlicensed firearm in her hand, she knew she was betraying David. But unless she went through with what she planned to do, she couldn't help him with the case. It would be too dangerous. Because Viljoen would learn she was back.

Viljoen, the convicted murderer who'd spent the last ten years of his life locked away in a high-security prison cell while Jade roamed the world. She'd timed her return perfectly—he was due to be released in a couple of days.

She snapped a magazine into place. In his own way, Robbie was right. There was nothing that made this gun different from any other. It was a machine designed to kill people. No more, no less. In a few days it would be able to fulfill its function and get rid of somebody who'd deserved to die a long time ago.

"So." Robbie continued, drumming his fingers on the table in a frantic rhythm that bore no relation to the slow love song playing in the background. "Plan's going ahead?"

"Yes. As soon as Viljoen's out. Do you still want to help?"

"I promised. I always keep my word."

The way he said it reminded Jade of the first time she'd met him, ten years ago, in the cigarette reek of the Hillbrow nightclub. They'd sat on a cracked leather sofa, their faces almost touching. They must have looked as intimate as lovers. She shouted in his ear over the pounding music. Who she was, what she wanted, why she was on the run. Why she was desperate.

When she'd finished, he shifted back on the couch and

looked at her for a long moment. Then he leaned close and shouted, his lips against her ear.

"I don't think you're a cop, OK. The cop chicks I've seen are all pig-ugly Afrikaans women. But I'm giving you one chance now. If this is a set-up, walk away. Because if I find out you're trying to screw me around, I'm going to come after you and I'm going to kill you. That's a promise. And you'd better believe it. I always keep my word."

She had stayed. And she believed him then, just as she believed him now. She didn't know if Robbie always kept his word. But she knew he did when it came to killing people.

4

Jade jerked awake in the early hours of the following morning, gasping for breath and scrabbling under the pillow for her gun. Her heart was hammering, and in spite of the room temperature being uncomfortably cold, her hair was damp with sweat.

She sat up in the dark, her fingers curling around the grip of the gun as her nightmare dissolved. The feel of the hard plastic didn't reassure her. It was a stark reminder of what she had done, and why she was back.

Jade swung her legs off the bed and stood up. Was it the dream that had woken her? Or something else?

She could hear the trill of crickets, and the far-off rumbling of heavy trucks on the highway, travelling through the night. Closer to home, she heard dogs barking. Why were they barking in the small hours of the morning?

She unlocked her bedroom door and walked towards the kitchen, the cold tiles stinging her bare feet.

The security light outside the kitchen window cast dark shadows onto the floor. Jade padded over to the window and looked out. She could see the gleam of the metal body of a car. It was parked on the road outside her house, headlights off. Somebody was watching her.

She tensed, and dropped down to her knees. If she could see the vehicle outside, could the driver see her?

While she was crouching on the floor, she heard the scrunch of wheels. The car was moving off. Straightening up, she saw it pull away, the shadows patterning its side.

She took a deep, shuddering breath. It could have been opportunistic criminals checking out a newly arrived resident. She didn't think so, though, but she didn't know why.

Jade turned on all the lights and checked the cottage thoroughly. The front door was secure. The alarm was armed. The battery box that fed the electric fence was beeping quietly, its green light flashing.

She got back into bed and lay there listening until the traffic noises grew louder and the birds began to sing and the sky turned from black to gray.

❀

Annette Botha had died almost immediately after the first bullet hit her. According to the coroner's report, her chest had been penetrated by one of the two .45 caliber bullets that hit her. It had burst the aorta, causing a massive rupture. The gush of her blood had flooded her heart, stopping it instantly.

The other shot, to her throat, had torn open her carotid artery. That would have been fatal on its own.

Jade had set up a temporary office in the kitchen, where she could see the road outside. Even with an oil heater next to the table, the room was freezing. Chilly air seeped through the gaps in the door and window frames, dispersing the heat as soon as it was produced.

She turned the page and took a sip of coffee. She'd found bread, butter and cheese in the fridge. And two bottles of Tabasco in the cupboard. David's contribution, she was sure. She was having cheese on toast for breakfast, liberally dotted with Tabasco.

The two bullets had been fired from an estimated distance of around six meters. So, Annette's killer knew how to shoot. There were plenty of gun-carrying criminals in South Africa who didn't. They only used them for show, to scare. To be certain of killing somebody, they'd have to fire from point-blank range. At six meters, in the stress of the moment, somebody unfamiliar with guns would've probably missed the target completely. A random hit would have been a lucky shot.

Annette had clearly been murdered by an experienced shooter. Someone cool and calculating, with a steady hand. Someone who had fired twice, a swift and deadly double-tap, placing the bullets where they would kill. Jade looked up from the file and considered the distance. From six meters, she could have put the bullets side by side in the woman's head.

She read in David's report that Piet Botha had been in Cape Town, where he lived, when the murder took place. On the evening that Annette was shot, he'd been giving an art class to his night students.

"Still a suspect," David had written. "Could have organized it. Inherits everything. Won't assume he's innocent until cleared beyond doubt."

Later on, when Jade phoned Piet she discovered he was in

Jo'burg, packing up the house where his ex-wife had died. She got directions from him and said she'd be round in half an hour.

Paging through the map she'd bought at the airport, she was amazed to see that Jo'burg and Pretoria had practically merged, woven together into a megalopolis by a spidery network of streets, highways, businesses and residential developments.

Jade remembered her history teacher telling the class that Johannesburg's earliest settlers had harnessed up their ox-wagons and travelled for days to reach the city. There were many who were eager to make the trip, despite the fact that their destination was little more than an arid, treeless desert. Almost every other city in the world had been built near a plentiful supply of water. Johannesburg had sprung into existence because of the huge gold-bearing reefs that lay deep below the hilly surface of the ground. The resulting gold rush had caused the original shantytown to explode in size. The original buildings that formed the city of Johannesburg had been crammed into the only triangle of land in the Witwatersrand basin where there was no gold to be found.

Jade had been enthralled to hear that when the city center was laid out, the street blocks were deliberately designed to be as small as possible. This created the maximum number of sought-after corner stands, so that the government could increase its takings when the land was auctioned off to buyers. Imagine the short-sighted greed that sentenced an entire city to a century of traffic gridlocks, all for the sake of cashing in at the start.

Since then, the city hadn't stopped expanding. The gold-rush mentality that had driven the earlier fortune seekers to the city was alive and well in modern Johannesburg. And certainly, short-sighted greed was still a strong driving force.

Annette had lived out of town in the far northwest, right at the edge of Jade's map. She saw long roads and enormous sections of land, and tracts of white space on the page. She expected it to be out in the deepest countryside. She was right.

Annette's property was on a narrow road with lighter squares where the tarmac had been patched, and darker areas where holes had been filled. The area looked forgotten, as if the land surveyors and developers with their transits and theodolites had overlooked it in their search for prime residential land. But she was sure they would come back.

The only movement she could see was the wind tugging at the brittle shrubs and grasses that lined the verges. Jade tried to imagine what it would be like here at night for a woman arriving home alone. Frightening, she decided.

When she pulled up outside the house, four Alsatians raced to the gate. They leaped up, pawing the metal bars as if they wanted to break through. Shiny white teeth snapped in their open mouths. The gate rattled on its runners.

Jade climbed out of the car and walked over to them. She loved dogs. She'd had two jobs protecting the two consecutive girlfriends of a Greek shipping tycoon. Both women had been blond, model-gorgeous and terrified of the guard dogs that roamed the grounds. Jade couldn't blame them. Rottweilers were intimidating animals, although these two had been friendly and well trained. She'd taught each of the women to be confident, stand still, and show no fear. In the end, they'd both ended up getting on a lot better with the dogs than they did with the Greek tycoon. The first girlfriend stormed out after a month. The second left in hysterical tears after six weeks. Then the tycoon was single again, and Jade was temporarily out of a job.

She smiled down at the Alsatians. "Hey there," she said.

The barking stopped. They sniffed the air. One of them wagged its tail.

"Good dogs," she added.

There was more tail-wagging in response. One dog shoved his nose through the gate. Jade let him lick her hand.

Then a squat, gray-haired man walked around the corner and whistled. Jade guessed he was Piet. The dogs ignored him. They started barking again, and leaping up at the gate.

He attached a lead to the collar of the biggest dog. It tensed and growled, retreating reluctantly and forcing him to drag it across the brown grass. The others barked at the gate for a few more moments and then bounded off, following their leader.

Piet returned without the dogs and pushed the gate open. It looked heavy, and it squealed on its runners.

"The motor still isn't working," he said. "The bastards tried to steal it, you know. The day before she died. They broke it, although they didn't take it. If that motor had been working, she might still be alive. She wouldn't have had to get out of her car to open it."

Jade shook Piet's hand, looking at him curiously. He was wearing a tattered jersey, a pair of jeans with old paint stains in all colors of the rainbow, and green socks under sandals with Velcro straps. His wiry gray hair was tied back in a ponytail and his face was deeply tanned. His eyes were a watery blue. For his size, his hands were surprisingly large and their grip firm.

"Thank you for coming, Jade."

"I'm so sorry for your loss," she said. "Whatever I can do to help, I will."

He opened the door of the house and she followed him in.

"I'm finishing the packing. She'd already started to sort everything out. Her things. Her brother's old stuff. She was going to move to Cape Town next month."

He turned and swung the security gate shut. Jade looked around the cottage's interior.

She saw a framed photo of Piet smiling proudly with his arm around a woman who she supposed must be Annette. The photo must have been taken a while ago, because Piet's hair was brown not gray, and there was a lot more of it on his head. Jade was surprised by how striking Annette had been. Flawless bone structure, icy blue eyes, platinum hair. She could see how the woman had attracted Piet's artistic eye.

There were two golf trophies next to the photo. Silver, shiny and sparkling clean. The name engraved under the trophies was Adrian Muller. Who was Adrian? She'd have to ask Piet.

A newspaper lay on the coffee table, open at page three. "Artist Devastated by Family Tragedy," the headline screamed. Jade scanned the story. According to the writer, Annette's murder was brutal, senseless and typical of the new South Africa. Piet had been quoted as saying, "The police have done nothing so far. They haven't brought my ex-wife's killer to justice."

She could see why David needed her help.

Next to the newspaper was a scattered pile of Piet's business cards. Ready to hand out to more reporters, she supposed.

He sat down opposite her and pushed his tough, gnarled fingers together.

"So you're a detective?"

"Yes. A private investigator."

Piet's knuckles shone in patchy red and white.

"Those bastards took her away from me. Annette was my life. She was all I had." He was silent for a while. Jade listened to the rhythmic tick of the clock on the wall. "We were going to be together again. That's why she was moving. So we could give it another chance." He unlaced his fingers and pulled at a rip in his jeans. His gaze strayed to the photo and back.

"You're lucky to have Superintendent Patel in charge of the case. He's one of the leading investigators in this province."

Piet continued as if he hadn't heard her. "Annette's brother Adrian was killed a few years ago." Jade glanced at the golf trophies on the wall unit. "Stabbed while he was withdrawing money from an ATM. They never caught the guys. I saw what that did to her. He was the last family she had, and she never saw his killers brought to justice." He stared at the photo, jaw working, eyes watering.

Jade wondered just how upset he was. He had an unbreakable alibi. But had he planned the crime? She had assisted with a case where the victim's wife had been openly traumatized after her husband was shot during a botched bank robbery. The heartfelt eulogy she had given at his graveside had reduced friends and family to tears. A couple of weeks later, she'd been convicted for organizing his murder. Spouses were top of the list of murder suspects. You just never knew.

She leaned forward and spoke gently. "This property was sold recently. I saw the sign outside."

Piet nodded. "She put it up for sale when she decided to move."

"Did she get a good price for it?"

Piet dragged his gaze away from the photo to look at her. "How would I know? I'm no good with money. I'm an artist. She wouldn't discuss the sale of her property with me."

"How often did you speak to Annette?"

"Every few days. We had a lot to talk about, with her moving to Cape Town."

"Did she mention anything unusual to you in the last week or two? Anything she'd noticed? Any cars near her place, any people outside watching her? Any strange incidents?"

Piet buried his bristly chin deep in his hands and stared ahead. Jade watched him closely. He started to speak, then stopped himself and shook his head. She wondered what he had decided not to say. Then he straightened up and turned to her. "There was something, yes. I don't know if it's important or not, but she did ask me an unusual question a couple of weeks ago. She wanted the number of a private detective."

Jade put the newspaper back down on the table and turned to Piet. "Did you tell the police?"

He spread his hands. She noticed his fingers were stained brownish-yellow on the tips. Paint, perhaps. Or nicotine.

"I forgot about it till now."

"It could be important."

"I suppose so. I'm sorry."

"Who was she trying to contact?"

Piet rummaged in his pocket and pulled out a battered pack of cigarettes. He put one in his mouth. He didn't light it. He spoke with the cigarette in his mouth. It moved up and down, punctuating his words.

"She wasn't trying to get hold of anyone special. She just told me she needed a private detective."

"Do you know why?"

"She never said why. I didn't ask. That's what I learned from being married to her. She didn't like to be quizzed. She'd tell you when she was ready."

"What did you tell her? Did you give her any names?"

He shook his head. The cigarette followed the motion. "I told her she should look in the Yellow Pages. She said she didn't know if she would be ripped off by a person from the Yellow Pages. She was like that. Careful with money."

"Did she mention it again?"

Piet's cigarette waggled to and fro. "No. She never spoke about it again."

"Did she sound scared or worried when she asked you?"

He thought for a minute.

"She sounded the same as always. Curious, maybe. If she'd sounded scared I would have been worried. But she didn't, so I forgot about it."

He patted his pockets, looking for a lighter. Finding none, he took the cigarette out of his mouth and put it back in the packet.

After Piet had pushed the gate closed behind her, he walked over to the yard and let the dogs out. They bolted for freedom. One of them lunged at him as it ran past, forcing him to leap aside.

Jade shook her head as she pulled out onto the lonely road. She had a feeling that the dogs preferred women to men. Which was unfortunate for Piet.

5

Jade drove back to the cottage and rechecked the information in Annette's file. There was one other avenue that she wanted to explore.

She had to sign an entrance register before the security guard allowed her to park outside Annette's workplace. The building was a mishmash of steel, glass and face-brick. She supposed the architect had been aiming for a modern industrial effect. She wondered if he'd burst into tears when he viewed the finished result.

She asked the receptionist to call Yolandi Storr, Annette's colleague.

Yolandi was a small, frail-looking woman with a mop of badly dyed hair and a stooped posture. Her face looked as if, over the years, it had been etched into a permanent expression of dread.

"Come through, please," she said. She pushed open the security door that led to the offices.

Jade followed her down blue-carpeted corridors, listening to the hum of the air-conditioning and the muted noise of phones ringing and business being done. She wrinkled her nose at the strong camphory scent of Yolandi's perfume. They passed a pair of men in dark suits and striped ties striding along importantly. Jade thought they must be managers. They had that look.

"This cold is terrible, isn't it? Just unbearable." Yolandi pushed open another security door. Without waiting for an answer, she continued. "I can't give you much time. We're all going into a meeting at two."

"What business are you in?" Jade asked.

"We manufacture plastic kitchen goods."

"And Annette worked in accounts?"

"Together with me." Yolandi turned her distraught face to Jade as she unlocked an office door. Her hands were trembling.

If Annette had worked with state secrets or been involved in the manufacture of weapons of mass destruction, Jade might have wondered if her murder was linked to her job.

However, managing accounts for a firm that made bowls and scrapers didn't seem to be a high-risk occupation.

"I do hope that you manage to find the people who killed her," Yolandi went on. "We've all been shaken by this. It's a dreadful thing. But then, crime in this country is out of control, isn't it? My two daughters are both in Canada where it's safe. They worry about me here. I get phone calls from them almost every day. I'd go too, but it's so expensive to emigrate and I just don't have the funds."

Presumably, in Canada the cold wasn't terrible or unbearable. For an uncharitable moment Jade wondered whether her daughters had emigrated to find a better life, or to get away from their mother's complaining.

"This is our office." Yolandi pushed open the door and Jade followed her in. The room contained two desks, two high-backed office chairs and two flimsy steel chairs for visitors. One desk was piled high with papers. A computer keyboard and monitor were wedged into the remaining space. The other desk was empty.

"How long had Annette worked for the company?"

"Twelve years."

Jade took the seat that was offered to her. It was the kind of chair that made people glad to be standing. It was like sitting on gravel. She faced Yolandi across the cluttered desk and wondered what it must be like to spend twelve years of your life working for one company, in one place.

As a child, she had traveled with her father wherever his investigations had taken him. When Commissioner de Jong spent time away from home, his daughter went with him. Jade had spent long hours in planes and cars watching the landscape speed by and listening to the detectives discussing whatever case they were busy with. She was used to being locked in a hotel room with a selection of books, a box of biscuits, and firm instructions not to open the door to anyone unless it was her father.

She had to crane her neck to see Yolandi over the towers of paper. "Did you know Annette well?" she asked.

Yolandi adjusted the clasp on a string of plastic beads that hung around her drooping neck. "As well as anyone. She kept to herself. I considered myself her friend, you know. We'd worked together for years. You'd think there'd be no secrets between us. I'm an open book, myself. But Annette hardly ever spoke about her personal life."

"Did you notice any change in her behavior in the last month or so?"

Yolandi thought for a while. She stared at a spot on the wall so intently that Jade looked too, to check whether she had noticed something interesting. She hadn't.

"No change, really. She was stressed about the move. Preoccupied. But that's natural when you're packing up house, isn't it? And she was working hard. Working late some evenings. This was going to be her last month here. She wanted to get everything finished before she left for Cape Town." Yolandi glanced at the empty desk.

"Her husband told us she was looking for a private investigator a couple of weeks before her death."

Yolandi nodded. "Yes. I knew about that."

"What did she say?"

"She asked me if I could recommend anyone."

"And could you?"

"Well, I used an investigator during my divorce. To prove my husband was cheating. I gave her his number."

"Who is he?"

"He's a man named Dean Grobbelaar." Yolandi's face pulled down into a more extreme expression of defeat. "Not a nice person. But then, divorce isn't a nice business. He was reliable and he did the job. And he didn't charge the earth for it."

"Do you know why Annette needed a detective?"

Yolandi sighed. "She never said. I asked, but she wouldn't tell me." She looked up at Jade. "I knew, of course."

"Why?"

"Her husband."

"Piet? What about him?"

"He was having her followed."

Jade edged the chair closer to the desk, and leaned forward. Her elbow pushed against the biggest pile of paper and it tee-tered sideways. She withdrew her arm hurriedly.

"Piet was having her followed?"

"She never said it was him. But he'd done it before, a year or two ago."

"How do you know that?"

"Annette was a clever woman. She noticed things. She found him out. And he admitted to it. Then last week, she said she was being followed again."

"Did she tell you she suspected her ex-husband?"

The lines on Yolandi's face deepened and she twined her fingers together.

"No, no. She didn't tell me anything, as such. I happened to overhear her conversation. I walked into the office unex-pectedly while she was on the phone."

"I see," Jade said. She would have bet a substantial amount of money that Yolandi had been eavesdropping behind the door, since Annette was so secretive.

"Who was she speaking to?"

"I don't know. I just heard her say, 'I know I'm being followed.'"

"You think it was Piet?"

"I think that he was having her followed again. And that she hired the private detective to try and catch him. Probably, Piet had her killed too. She was a wealthy woman. And he's just a bum. But you didn't hear that from me."

Yolandi gave Jade a small, satisfied smile. Then she lifted a page off the tallest stack of documents, blew the dust off it, and turned her attention back to her work.

6

The trunk of the car was heating up in the morning sun. The car turned off the tarmac and bumped along a rough road. Branches swished and scraped over its roof.

The man in the trunk was pouring sweat. His white golf shirt was drenched and clammy and no longer white. He could smell his perspiration and the stench of his own terror. For hours he had twisted and writhed, flinging himself against the carpeting on the sides and against the hard metal shell above his head.

The car had been parked somewhere overnight. At one stage, when he'd stopped struggling, he'd realized how cold it was. He'd curled up and shivered. He hadn't slept. The long minutes had passed, quiet and deadly slow.

Then the car had started up and begun to move again. He'd renewed his efforts to make a noise, to produce some motion that might attract somebody's attention. But the car was too big and heavy. Its new, springy shocks simply absorbed the impact of his rolling body. He had a gag in his mouth, but he hadn't let that stop him. He'd grunted and bellowed, putting all his effort into getting his voice past the obstruction in his mouth, in the desperate hope that somehow, somebody might hear.

The gag was one of his own socks, ripped off his foot and secured in his mouth with sticky brown packaging tape. He could taste the sour sweat and dirt from his foot and his shoe. The sock's coarse cotton fibers pushed against his tongue.

The man who'd gagged him had wound the tape round and round his head, covering his mouth and chin in a brown bandage. In the back of his mind, he thought that the gag would be agonizing to take off. It would rip out the two-day growth of stubble and his graying buzz cut. Then he realized how stupid he was to think that. Because if the gag ever came off, it would be a miracle. He would be glad of the pain.

He was a strong man and, although he was pushing fifty-five, still a tough man. He'd thought he was too hard, too experienced to fall victim to an attack like this. But he'd been taken by surprise because it had been slick, so slick, and completely unexpected. Done with military precision. He'd done a few years in the army way back during apartheid. He knew training when he saw it. He'd been outnumbered. And he was familiar with the brutal intent these men showed.

They'd handcuffed and gagged him. They'd yanked his laptop from the power supply and taken his cell phone. Then they'd searched his files. He'd shaken his head and shrugged. Whatever they wanted, he wasn't going to point it out to them. An operation like this, he was in deep shit anyway. He'd recognized the signs.

The tall man had shouted at him and punched him in the

stomach with an iron fist, so hard that he'd doubled over in agony. He'd braced himself for a brutal beating, but the man with the gun had intervened.

"Leave him. Not here, not now."

"We could take the gag off and question him."

"And if he shouts?"

"We need the info."

"It's recent. Probably nothing's been filed yet. Anyway, he's all we need. And this." He indicated the laptop.

Then they'd marched him down to the car and, at gunpoint, forced him into it.

Slowly, fighting the gag, he'd screamed his voice away. Now his throat felt ragged and he could taste blood in the back of his mouth. Even if the gag was removed, there was nothing he could do now. He'd been stupid. He had wasted his voice.

The cable ties that bound his hands behind his back had been too tight to begin with. His hands had swollen now, which made the thin plastic even tighter. His wrists throbbed with a hard hot rhythm in time to the panicked beating of his heart. Every time he moved, a bolt of pain shot up his arms. He wondered if he'd ever be able to use his hands again. Then he realized that was the least of his problems.

He always instructed his clients to try to loosen the carpeting on the inside of their car's trunk so that they could kick out a rear light if they were held captive in a hijacked vehicle. The carpeting in this vehicle was sturdy. In the darkness, it took him a long time to work out where the lights were. Eventually he followed the curve of the trunk's lid and found the area by feel. He tried to grab the edge of the carpet with his swollen fingers and yank it away.

It didn't work. He lost a nail. The red, tearing agony as it ripped out of his finger squeezed a flood of tears from his eyes. His nose blocked and he sobbed in desperation, fighting for breath as the gag threatened to choke him. Deep in his gut he knew that this was it. You didn't get let out and set free when you were tied up in the back of a car. Only worse would happen.

The car stopped. The heat pulsing through the metal above him reduced just a little. The engine was switched off. In the shade, he thought, with odd clarity. They had stopped in the shade.

Then the lid was flung open.

He shrank away from the light that burnt his eyes, filtered only by a thin layer of dry leaves and twigs from the tree above him.

Blinking in the low rays of the sun, he looked up at the man who stood there. The tall man. The one with the cold, empty eyes.

He could only watch. The man lit a cigarette.

"Get out."

He sat up, knocking his head on the top of the open lid, and a wave of dizziness caught him. The world spun, and for a moment he thought it would spin away. Then it righted itself. With legs that trembled so violently they could hardly work, he wriggled up until he was sitting on the rim of the trunk. Then he pushed himself over. He lost his balance and fell head first onto the stony ground.

"Get up."

He swung onto his knees and staggered to his feet. His bare feet, bruised from kicking and struggling during the journey. The stones hurt his soles. They were soft, used to shoes. He stood bowed, swaying and snuffling through the gag.

"Walk."

The other man climbed out of the passenger seat and trained the gun on him. There was nothing he could do. He stumbled into the trees. They were somewhere out in the bush, far from anywhere. Tears welled in his eyes as he walked. What had he done to deserve this?

"Stop."

Trees were all around him. Their long trunks stretched up to a winter sky. Birds twittered in the branches. His feet were planted in a carpet of leaves.

The man shoved him backwards against a tree trunk. He had more cable ties with him. Long enough to stretch around the tree. Two were tightened around his neck. Another two pulled his ankles back against the rough bark.

He couldn't speak, but his pleading eyes asked questions. The tall man laughed.

"You might be wondering what we're going to do to you now." He waited for a moment with his head on one side, as if expecting an answer.

"Nothing."

The two men turned and walked away. He couldn't move his head, only follow them with his eyes. They reached the car. Were they going to leave him on his own?

He closed his eyes for a moment, wondering if anyone would find him or if he would die slowly, strangled by the cable ties when his exhausted legs finally gave way.

He heard scrunching on the leaves and strained his eyes sideways again. The tall man was returning. He was wearing a full-length protective mackintosh, the sort of coat that might keep you dry in a monsoon.

The man smiled. "Before I go, I think I'll cut a little wood.

It's always nice to have freshly chopped wood in winter, for the fireplace."

His eyes grew wide in horror and he struggled with all his might, bucking and fighting the cable ties.

The man had produced a heavy-looking, long-handled axe from under his raincoat.

The forest was still for a moment, seeming to hold its breath. Then the first blow of the axe landed. A shower of dry leaves fluttered to the ground and, in the tree above him, the birds took fright and wheeled away into the air.

7

Dean Grobbelaar had a hoarse, grainy voice. It sounded as if he had been chain smoking for decades. Jade couldn't ask him if he had though, because he wasn't answering his landline or his cell phone. Each time she phoned, she got the same rasping growl of his voicemail. She left yet another message asking him to call her back. She'd just have to wait.

Jade clenched her fists in frustration. She didn't want to wait. There was too much to do. She wanted to have this investigation finalized as soon as possible. Preferably before Viljoen was released from prison.

Thinking of Viljoen made her even more restless. She decided not to go back to the icy cottage. Instead, she drove to a shooting range for an hour of practice.

❖

Her father taught her to shoot the day she turned thirteen. It was a rite of passage. When he'd turned thirteen, his father had taken him shooting for the first time. Jade was his only child. He'd told her he didn't see why he should make an exception for her just because she was a girl. Besides, Jade played football and took judo lessons and fought with the other kids in the area, just as she would have done if she'd been a boy. Maybe more, because being a cop's daughter in a poor neighborhood wasn't easy. Jade was as tough as any boy, and he wasn't going to treat her any differently when it came to her first shooting lesson. Not when she was looking forward to it, pestering him about it every day.

That very morning he took her to a shooting range in Upington, where they were based for a few weeks. It was a place where daily temperatures regularly broke the forty-degree barrier and the distant mountains shimmered in the waves of heat. Her dad's service pistol was boiling hot from the short trip in the car. The heat baked her feet in their thin sandals and billowed up from the ground onto her bare legs. Her baseball cap shielded her eyes from the worst of the glare, which meant she was able to see the owner of the range glowering down at her.

"How old is this child?"

"She's thirteen today," her father replied proudly.

"Well, she's too young to be shooting on my range," the owner said. "Fourteen years and over, that's the rules here. I don't want the police on my back, thank you very much."

Commissioner de Jong didn't tell the owner he was, in fact, the police. And he wasn't discouraged. His daughter was going to have a shooting lesson for her birthday. They'd set their minds on it.

They ended up at a game reserve on the outskirts of the Kalahari desert. The game ranger there was an old friend of her father. Jade knew that because he called her father Rooinek and her father called him Doppies.

Doppies led Jade onto their range, which was just a long dirt track sloping down into a valley and up the other side.

He stopped to point out a large bird with rusty-red feathers on its head. It was perched in a wizened-looking tree.

"Do you know what bird that is?"

Jade shook her head. "No, sir." She wasn't going to call him Doppies.

"Red-necked falcon. We don't often get them here. They like those camelthorn trees."

Jade took another look. It looked just like any other bird to her.

"Come on," her father said. "Enough about birds. Let's get on to what we came here for."

"She can have a go with this." Doppies passed what he called an elephant rifle to her father. Jade looked at it in amazement. It was almost as tall as she was.

"It's not an elephant rifle," Jade's father corrected him, shaking his head at the folly of a man who could think that species of birds were more important than types of gun. "That's what he tells the ignorant tourists," he said to her. "This is a Musgrave 30-06. Locally-made barrel. If you're shooting lighter bullets at targets far away, you'll kill a small buck with it easily. Close up, with heavier ammo, you'll get a kudu or a gemsbok. I know people who've taken lions down with them at close-range. Now then, this one's a bolt-action. What does that mean?"

"It means you operate it by hand." Jade had swotted up on her gun knowledge in preparation for her big day.

"And is it more accurate than a pump-action shotgun?"

"Yes, it is. And it's more powerful."

"Good girl."

Doppies watched this exchange. He muttered something that Jade thought sounded like "Jesus Christ help the child."

Her father showed her how to lie prone on the dusty track. Doppies put his jacket over a ridge on the ground and rested the barrel of the gun on it. Jade hefted the gun in her hands, her left elbow wedged into the ground for support. She pressed the butt of the gun against her cheek.

"If you do that, you'll break your jaw," the ranger told her, pushing the gun away from her face. "These guns have a massive recoil. Hold it against your shoulder, or you'll be sorry."

Jade didn't want to break her jaw. Her nervousness and the weight of the gun made her arms start to shake. She looked through the telescopic sight. Far, far away through the milky glass, she could see a Coke can propped upright on the ground. It was on the track on the other side of the valley. It was so distant that if she took her eye away from the sight, she couldn't see it at all.

The can seemed to be circling in a large orbit that took it way outside the crosshairs of the sight. She knew the can wasn't moving. Her trembling arms were causing the rifle to circle. If it moved like that, there was no way she would hit her target.

Jade took a deep breath and steadied the rifle. She stared at the target and tried to calm her nerves. The circles became smaller. She pulled back on the trigger, feeling resistance. Now she thought it was ready to fire.

She focused on the target. It still moved in tiny circles. There was nothing she could do about that. She didn't have the strength or experience to hold the big gun still. But she could judge the circles. The crosshairs moved in a pattern. Up, around and down. Up, around and down. As they came down, they passed straight over the blurry outline of the can.

As the hairs came down, Jade squeezed the trigger.

The gun exploded in her arms and bucked against her shoulder, thrusting her backwards along the dirt. She clutched the barrel and closed her eyes against the dust.

Doppies took the rifle from her. "Well done, my girl. Well done. Let's go and see if that Coke can took any damage."

She could sense he was humoring her. But she didn't care. The proud smile her father gave her was enough. She had tried. She'd dared to do it.

They walked down the path, all the way to the bottom of the valley. Then they walked up the other side.

The ranger started looking anxious. He couldn't see the can in the dirt ahead of them. He shaded his eyes and peered into the distance. He shook his head. He knew where he had put the can. There was no point in walking any further. Then he looked over at the grass on the left-hand side of the track. Jade looked, too. A glint of red and white caught her eye.

Doppies picked up the can. The impact of the bullet had flung it off the track and into the grass. There was a hole directly through its middle. The bullet had pierced it twice. Once on the way in and once on the way out. He held it up and shook his head in disbelief. The sun flashed at Jade through the double hole her bullet had made.

"Keep shooting like that, you're going to be a dangerous woman when you're older," Doppies said, stunned.

And Jade kept shooting like that. Straight enough to beat

her father's score when they practiced together. Accurate enough to win the provincial combat pistol-shooting championships three years in a row.

Since then, she'd never gone more than a few weeks without practicing, because that was another rule of her father's.

The practice range she chose while she waited for Dean Grobbelaar to return her call was owned by one of Robbie's contacts. He was a no-questions type of guy, which suited Jade fine. She didn't want a friendly type who would engage her in conversation, request a copy of her identification, ask where she was from and where she'd got that handsome gun. Robbie's friend was the exact opposite. He actually looked pissed off to see a customer, as disoriented as if he had just surfaced from a heavy freebasing session. He had dark shadows under his eyes, and wore a string vest that defied the cold and showed off his substantial belly.

She reloaded with lead-tipped ammo and spent an hour firing off a hundred rounds, ducking and diving, sprinting and crouching. She clicked fresh magazines into place on the run, double-tapping the metal targets and hearing them clang onto the uneven ground as they fell. On every target, she pictured Viljoen's face. When she spun and fired, she imagined him behind her. Would she be fast enough when the time came?

By the end, she was sweating under her long-sleeved shirt. Her hands and arms were sore from the gun's recoil and her ears rang despite the protective earmuffs.

She got back to her car to find that Grobbelaar still hadn't returned her call. Just what kind of an investigator was he?

She thumbed the last of the lead-tipped bullets out of her gun's chamber and inserted a magazine of copper-jackets.

Real targets needed penetration and stopping power, not loud noise and surface splatter. Especially real targets that stopped their car outside her house in the middle of the night, engine idling and lights off.

She shivered as she thought about that nighttime surveillance. How had Viljoen known she was back in the country less than twenty-four hours after her flight had landed? While he was locked up in prison, serving the last few days of a ten-year sentence which he surely wouldn't want to jeopardize.

There were only two possibilities. Either Viljoen had uncanny instincts and a network of contacts second to none. Or she was wrong and somebody else was watching her. If so, she had no idea who it could be.

❀

She'd been home for about half an hour when she heard honking at the gate. It was David, in an unmarked vehicle, on his way home from work. He wound the window down and shouted at her.

"You don't have a bloody doorbell! The only way I can get your attention is to honk."

Jade could see his breath fogging in the cold. She pressed the button on the remote control and opened the gate.

"You could have phoned," she said as he got out of the car and slammed the door.

"Bloody airtime. Costs a bomb. It'll bankrupt me."

David's large presence and angry mood filled the small kitchen.

"Tough day?" she asked.

"I've come round to see if yours was as crap as mine." He

slumped down onto a chair. It creaked ominously under his weight.

"I thought you were here to scrounge dinner."

"That too. Same as always. And a beer if you have one. We can talk about the case afterwards. I'm too damn hungry and thirsty right now." He glanced around the cottage, and looked at her. His mouth twitched in a smile. "Feels like we last did this yesterday," he said. "You, me and your dad. All around the table in that tiny bloody house. Those were the good times, Jadey."

She put a beer in front of him and poured herself a glass of wine. She'd gone shopping on the way home and the fridge and cupboard were now stocked with an optimistic selection of healthy food. Vegetables, lentils, brown rice, chicken breasts. That would have to stay where it was for now.

Jade took two giant pepperoni pizzas out of the oven. She knew that when David said he'd be round to discuss the case that evening it was a thinly disguised request for junk food and beer. Cop food, he called it. He was addicted. She had never seen him eat anything healthy.

He grabbed the biggest piece of pizza and crammed it into his mouth. The cheese stretched into long strands that snapped halfway and coiled around his chin.

He started talking before he had swallowed. "If you'd stayed here, we'd have made a good team. Remember. We were going to open the first ever multi-racial, bisexual detective agency in South Africa."

"Not bisexual. Multi-gender. There's an important difference," Jade corrected him.

"Whatever. We had it all planned."

She nodded. "I remember." Planned was an exaggeration.

But they had talked about it. It had been a dream for her. Perhaps it had been a dream for him too.

She'd ordered a small tub of chopped chili with the pizzas. She spooned a large pile of the oily green substance onto her slice.

"We'd be making a fortune now," David said. "Easy work. Cheating husbands and debt dodgers. Good money. None of these politics. All I've been dealing with today is red tape and paperwork. The whole bloody day."

"We could still do it."

David lifted the beer bottle to his lips. He put it down again, empty, a minute later. He wiped a hand across his mouth, looking glum. "We wouldn't be the first any more."

Jade took another beer out of the fridge and passed it to him. She watched his hands as he took the bottle. They were surprisingly elegant, with long fingers and short, neat nails that shone against his dark skin.

"Every year, I tell myself this is my last in the police service," he said. "Then I think to myself, if I leave, who the hell else is going to get the job done? It's not like we don't have the numbers. We do. But nobody's halfway competent. That's the problem. Case files, evidence, reports go missing all the time." He rubbed his chin with the back of his hand.

"There is a paper napkin. There, by your knife."

"Oh." David looked at it suspiciously, as if it was a piece of evidence that didn't match a crime scene. "You see, Jade, transformation is good and necessary. Don't get me wrong." He glanced up and saw her frowning. "Transformation. Getting more black people into the workplace. In places where white people used to have nice cushy protected jobs. The police service, for instance."

"But?"

"But it's been too much, too soon. Most of the officers with knowledge and experience were told thank you and goodbye. Or they got their backs up because of all the changes and left. Either way, they never had a chance to pass on their skills. So now we've got a crowd of semi-educated and inexperienced workers trying to do some bloody demanding jobs. They're not coping. You want to know what the police suicide rate is right now? If anyone in my team doesn't pitch up for work, I phone them straight away to check they haven't shot themselves with their service pistol."

Jade started on her third piece of pizza. She was matching David slice for slice, but she wasn't confident about this situation continuing much longer. For one thing, the chili was almost finished.

"You can't help it if your staff are inexperienced. You're doing the best that can be done. You always have."

"Tell that to Commissioner Williams."

"Is he still on your back?"

David shook his head. "Jade, I don't know what the hell this guy has against me. He's making me believe I can't do the bloody job."

Jade frowned. Williams had been a competent investigator, according to her father. Perhaps he was a poor manager, promoted past his level of skill. Then she had another idea. "You mentioned transformation. Could he have an issue with race? He's an old-school white Afrikaner. He's been in that position ever since my dad died. Perhaps he's angry he's got a non-white guy working below him now."

"Yes. I'd say that also. It would be my first thought. Except the last superintendent was a colored man, and he didn't have a problem with him."

"The one who had a heart attack?"

He nodded, taking another slice. "The one who left things in a complete bloody mess."

"Maybe he was good at blaming his inefficiency on other people."

"If so, I'd better start learning how to do that in a hurry."

"David." Jade leaned towards him. She wanted to touch his arm, squeeze his shoulder. Hug him. Do something comforting. She wasn't great with physical contact. Never had been. And she was worried that he would interpret it the wrong way. Or rather, if she was honest with herself, the right way.

David was like an older brother, friend and protector combined. She'd liked him ever since the first time he smiled at her. A few months after that, when her father was out of town, David had come round for supper and they'd shared a couple of bottles of wine. They talked, with increasing incoherence, about life and love and everything in between. She'd told him how hard it had been to grow up as a policeman's daughter in a rough neighborhood. "Pig's kid" was what the other children had called her when her father wasn't around. When things had been really bad, she'd taken a knife with her to school, just in case.

In return, David had told her about his childhood. It had been difficult for him, too. He had an Indian father who lived in Durban and a white mother who lived in Port Elizabeth. When he was old enough to understand, his mother explained that she'd divorced his father when David was very young. It took him a few more years to work out that she'd lied to him, and that although she'd given him his father's last name, his parents had never been married. He told Jade he was illogically ashamed about this for many years. And he had never fit in. Not with the white people, not with the Indian community. He was a half-breed, an outcast. Bloody lonely, he'd told her. Just like her.

When David had finally staggered out of the house that night, after kissing her on the cheek and cracking his head against the door lintel, Jade had realized that she was hopelessly in love with him. But what could she do about it? He worked under her dad. She could imagine how difficult it would have been for him to confess to stern Commissioner de Jong that he had romantic feelings for his daughter.

Worse still, perhaps he'd never felt anything for her beyond simple friendship. So she'd bitten her tongue and said nothing.

Now, looking at him across the pizza boxes in the little cottage, all her old shyness returned in an unwelcome rush. It was ridiculous, when she thought about it. After all, she had suffered her share of rejection since then. Taken it and doled it out. Mended her heart and moved on. But David was different. He made her feel like an awkward teenager again, not somebody who'd been involved with other men in other countries. She didn't want to think about having him look her in the eye and explain with uncharacteristic and humiliating gentleness that he'd never felt the same way about her.

So she leaned towards him without touching him and said, "You know you're not inefficient. You're a details man. And a fantastic cop. Ten years ago you were the best investigator in the whole precinct. Everyone knew you'd be promoted fast and that you'd do the best job. Why should anything have changed?"

David's face softened and he stretched out his hand across the table.

Jade sat immobile, her heart racing. Perhaps he did feel exactly the same way about her. She waited for his hand to touch hers, imagining how his fingers would feel laced through her own for the very first time.

It never reached her. He pulled her pizza box towards him and lifted out a slice.

"You don't mind sharing, do you, Jadey? These things are bloody tiny. A whole one gone and I'm still hungry."

"Of course I don't mind." Jade resisted the temptation to run outside and howl like an abandoned dog. Instead she got up and poured herself another large glass of wine. She felt she deserved it.

After David had eaten the last piece of pizza, they started discussing the case.

He told her they'd found no prints on the gate motor. The lid of the motor had been levered off from outside the gate and two fuses had been broken. The gate had been effectively disabled. He strongly suspected that Annette's killer had jimmied the motor a day or two earlier, so that she would have to get out of her car when she arrived home.

"Makes it much easier to hijack a vehicle if the owner isn't in it," he said. Jade moved her chair closer to the heater. David slung his arm over it and put his feet up on the table. She could have reached out and touched his legs. Put her hand on them. But she didn't. They sat together in silence.

She couldn't hear any cars on the bumpy road outside. Only the muted beep of the electric fence power supply.

That didn't mean she felt safe. Jade never felt safe. Not in cottages, not in hotels. It was laughably easy to gain access to a hotel room. She'd done it before when she needed to.

A plausible story at the reception desk, a swift bribe slipped to the right person. Or better still, a hurried entry into the room as the turndown service was being done, with an apology to a chambermaid who wouldn't think twice about it. Jade never opened a hotel room door without wondering if somebody was inside, waiting for her.

The cottage was more difficult to penetrate. But it was still possible in spite of the reassuring electric fence. She'd seen gaps under the palisade fencing where people could crawl through. Then her attackers would have the advantage. They could break in or they could wait for her to step out of the front door.

Forcing back the troubling thoughts, she told David about her day.

He frowned. "So Annette's work colleague claims her husband had her followed? That doesn't sound good. What's your impression of Piet?"

Jade thought that over for a moment. "Before I spoke to Yolandi, he wasn't my first choice of suspect."

"Why not?"

She struggled to find the words to describe the weathered little man. "Not because of motive. He benefits from her death. More because he's so unworldly. I feel sorry for him. He can't control Annette's dogs. I can't imagine him being able to deal with a Pekingese. He couldn't manage to light a cigarette while I was talking to him. He got distracted and then just gave up on the job. If he'd arranged a successful hit, which would surprise me, there's no way he could do it without leaving evidence behind. That's my first impression of him, anyway."

"Let's find out what he's up to, then. But if the evidence

points any further towards him, I'm going to have to bring him in and ask him some tough questions. Maybe handcuffs and a night in a cell will get the truth out of him."

"I'll talk to the private detective tomorrow. See if Annette contacted him, and why." Jade stood up. She bent the empty pizza boxes in half and pushed them into the dustbin.

David took his feet off the table and rocked forward on the chair. "Yell if you need anything. Thanks for supper, and all that." He got up and walked towards the door. She followed him, but he stopped suddenly and turned back to her. They were so close they were almost touching. He gazed down at her.

"You know, Jade, it's bloody cold in here."

"Yes. I know."

He turned and left, closing the door quietly behind him.

8

"Always check your facts, Jade," her father used to say. After she'd told him she wanted to become an investigator, he spent many hours talking to her about the profession. Usually they'd sat at the kitchen table and drank coffee. Often she took notes, and sometimes he wrote them out for her. During these informal training sessions, she'd felt closer to her father than she ever had before.

"Check and double check. People lie. If you're a cop they might lie to you just because of the uniform you wear. Sometimes they'll lie for other reasons, especially to a pretty girl like you. Maybe they're trying to impress you by making out they're more than they actually are. Or maybe they're jealous."

"And what if they lie because they're guilty?" she asked.

"That happens. Those are the biggest lies of all. And the hardest to catch out, because the people who tell them have the most to lose. So you have to keep digging away to uncover the truth. And remember that the minute you try to find something out, there will be people who'll try and stop you. So never make yourself vulnerable. Trust your gut feeling. And always watch your back, or have somebody watch it for you."

Her father's words echoed in Jade's head as she drove into the center where Dean Grobbelaar had his office. The shopping center was small. The entrance was in a quiet minor road and it didn't look like it was doing too well. The parking lot was deserted, the gutters littered with cans and crisp packets. The tarmac was cracked in places where grass, now withered, had pushed through.

Jade wound down her window and checked it out. She saw a row of three shops. Two of them looked closed. The windows were dusty and dull, the spaces beyond were bare except for empty shelves and discarded cardboard boxes. One, at some past date, had been a hairdresser, if the peeling poster hanging from the door could be believed. Another had been a hardware store. The glass in the shop front was cracked, as if somebody had thrown a stone at it.

Only one shop was operational, the little general store on the corner. The aproned shopkeeper stood outside leaning against the doorframe, his face turned to the sun. She saw two black domestic workers approaching the store, chatting and shrieking with laughter, their voices loud in the stillness. Roused from his reverie, he hurried inside to serve them.

Jade parked next to the general store just as the two women walked out with bulging shopping bags, still talking at the tops of their voices.

She watched them go, wondering how far they had to plod up the road with their heavy bags while drivers whizzed uncaringly past them. She felt sorry for Jo'burg's poor, who had to walk vast distances to reach crammed and dangerous taxis. Nameless, faceless, they were ignored by the rich people speeding past in the air-conditioned cocoons of their fast and expensive cars.

Turning away from the women, she noticed an open doorway at the side of the building. A staircase led up to the first floor. The steps looked ancient, dips worn into the middle of each tread.

Jade walked up and reached a landing with an open window that looked out over the back of the building. She leaned out and saw another dilapidated parking lot. An old Toyota occupied one of the spaces. It was parked at an angle in the shade and its windows and windshield were still covered by a thin layer of ice.

The Toyota looked like a typical police unmarked. Like the kind of vehicle that a cut-rate private detective might drive.

Jade's fingers brushed against the shape of the gun under her jacket. She trusted her gut, just as her father had always told her to do, and it was telling her that something was wrong. The car clearly hadn't been driven anywhere since the frost came down, which would have been well before sunrise.

She reached the top of the second flight of stairs and started down the corridor. Her shoes clacked on the linoleum. The walls were dirty. They needed a scrub and a fresh coat of paint.

She shivered. The corridor was like a wind tunnel, channeling cold air along its length.

The first office door was protected by a security gate locked with a rusty padlock. The metal was also dusty. It had been a while since anybody worked in this room.

The next door had a sign on it, handwritten on a piece of cardboard that curled at the edges. "Alliance Finance." It, too, was locked from the outside. Jade wouldn't have trusted a finance company operating from premises like these, or with a sign like that. Presumably the clients had felt the same.

The door of the third office was closed. But the security gate was ajar.

D. GROBBELAAR INVESTIGATION was printed on a laminated piece of cardboard and attached to the door with four brass drawing pins. Compared to the signage on the previous door, Dean had chosen the luxury option.

Jade knocked on the door. There was no answer.

She lifted her elbow—she didn't want to leave fingerprints—and pushed the door handle down. Hinges squeaking, it swung open.

She stepped inside and almost tripped over a pair of shoes. They were placed side-by-side, facing the door, as if somebody had decided, on a whim, to leave their footwear behind when they'd left the office.

The shoes were big and heavy, with battered leather uppers and thick tough soles. She thought they probably had steel toecaps. A gray woolen sock with a hole in the heel lay next to one of the shoes.

At the back of the office was a large wooden desk. Behind it was a leather-covered office chair. Two other chairs stood opposite, set squarely in place. Jade could see a blotter, a fax machine and printer, and a telephone on top of the desk. A fluorescent strip light on the ceiling flickered occasionally.

A wooden filing cabinet with three drawers stood in the corner nearest the desk. Its top drawer was open a few inches.

Jade stepped closer. Something else, in the corner of her vision? She looked down. A black cable and adaptor for a laptop computer lay like a coiled snake on the floor.

She walked over to Grobbelaar's desk. When his phone rang, where did he write his notes? Could she find any clues to his current whereabouts?

Not on the blotter. That seemed to be reserved for detailed and explicit drawings of naked women. Jade frowned down at them. Presumably he met with his female clients in a more savory location.

She opened the top drawer. Inside were some loose pens, a pink highlighter, a camera battery charger and a USB cable.

The second drawer contained an empty box for an electronic listening device and three Peppermint Crisps.

Under a copy of *Hustler* in the bottom drawer were some lined sheets of paper with "Grobbelaar Investigations— Client Sheet" printed at the top. She moved over to the filing cabinet to see what happened to all these client sheets once he had filled them in.

A handwritten label pasted onto the top drawer read "Clients A–M." His filing system looked haphazard. Folders were dog-eared, names scrawled on the cardboard. She couldn't see a file for Botha. She wondered if there had been one before the drawer was opened.

Pulling her jacket sleeve over her hand so there could be no confusion over prints, she pulled out the second drawer, labeled "Clients N–Z." She saw a file labeled "Storr–Yolandi." It looked old and battered.

She closed it again. The bottom drawer was labeled simply: "Pending." Perhaps she would find the folder she was looking for in here.

As she bent down to check, a sound from the doorway startled her. She spun round, an apology on her lips, expecting to see an irate building superintendent standing there, or perhaps even Grobbelaar himself.

Two black men in bulky duffel jackets shouldered their way into the office. The taller one was hefting two plastic jerry cans filled with pale fluid. His partner was carrying a gun.

9

The two men paused when they saw Jade. In a heartbeat, she assessed her predicament. It couldn't be worse. There was no time to draw her weapon. She was outnumbered. And cornered. She'd walked into a dangerous situation without backup. Investigating a run-down office block in broad daylight might not be a high-risk activity in Britain, but this was South Africa. She should have been more careful.

Jade's gut constricted as the Beretta's barrel swung towards her. She dived to the floor behind the desk, scrabbling under her jacket for her own gun, her heart banging against her ribs. As she fell, she heard a deafening report from the Beretta's muzzle. Plaster scattered to the floor.

Her finger curled round the trigger of the Glock. She could hear the men speaking in rapid voices. An African language. She couldn't understand the words.

Heavy footsteps stomped towards the desk. Jade crouched

under her wooden shelter, waiting for the man to come into view. They didn't know she was armed. If she was fast enough, she could have the advantage.

One of the men shouted, his voice urgent. The footsteps stopped and then retreated.

Jade waited, listening. He didn't speak again. Moments later she heard a trickling sound and the acrid fumes of gasoline filled the air.

Dread curdled her stomach. The men were planning to torch Dean's office and all its contents, including her. They weren't going to bother to shoot her first. In any case, gunfire was out of the question now. The tiniest spark—or a muzzle flash—would ignite the vapor into a deadly inferno. She was certain of that. But she wondered if the two thugs handling the gas were up to speed on its volatility.

If she ran, would the gunman shoot and risk trapping them all inside a giant fireball?

Jade knew she didn't have a choice. If she tried to escape, death would be possible. But if she stayed where she was it would be a certainty.

She tensed, ready to sprint to the door from her precarious shelter, sure that when she left the desk she would see the tall man bent over the jerry cans and his partner facing her, his finger tight on the trigger.

Then she heard footsteps echoing in the corridor.

Were the arsonists expecting backup? If they were, her odds had just narrowed to at least three against one. If not, she'd been given her only chance. An unexpected arrival would distract the two men.

Jade grabbed the desk and boosted herself to her feet. She pushed away from the heavy wood and flung herself across the room. The man pouring gas dropped the jerry can and shouted as he saw her. His friend had his back turned, watching the door.

She skidded on the oily floor, the liquid soaking her shoes. The gunman swiveled back towards her and she saw deadly intent in his eyes.

"Don't shoot!" she screamed.

She ducked under the outstretched arm of the thug with the jerry can and smacked the butt of her gun into his face. It hit the pressure point under his nose and he reeled back, temporarily out of the fight.

The gunman had lined up his Beretta. For the second time, Jade found herself staring into its expressionless black eye. But this time she was closer. She had a chance.

She lashed out with her left hand in a swift chopping motion, knocking his gun arm away. The man's eyes blazed with hatred, his lips curled back from his ochre teeth. Jade cringed away from the thunderous blast as he pulled the trigger.

The shot lodged high in the wall, sending another shower of plaster tumbling downwards.

No fireball.

The gunman grabbed at her with his left hand. He caught her hair and his fingers ripped strands out of her scalp as she tugged her head free.

Then she grabbed the doorframe, elbowing him back as he lunged for her again. He stumbled over the shoes inside the doorway and skidded on the pooling gas, his arms wind-milling. Jade dived out of the room, closely followed by his accomplice.

As the gunman lost his balance and fell backwards onto the office floor, the Beretta discharged again.

The air seemed to gasp and shimmer as the fumes in the room ignited. Then, with a molten roar, the gas fireballed.

Flames boiled from the door as Jade sprinted down the passage, hearing glass shatter behind her as the windows exploded. She cannoned into the shopkeeper. He was standing in the corridor, rigid with shock and gripping a cell phone. Her savior. His footsteps had distracted the thugs. She knocked him flying, but tripped over his legs and fell down beside him on the dirty linoleum.

The jerry can man pushed past them and ran for the stairs, his pursuit forgotten. From inside the burning office, she heard a thudding noise and a high, keening wail. Blinded by smoke and flames, the gunman was trapped in the blaze. He was a murderous bastard, but even so, her stomach clenched in horror at his agonized cries.

But there was nothing she could do. She scrambled to her feet and helped the shopkeeper up.

"Downstairs!" she shouted, coughing as the thick smoke billowed towards them.

As Jade ran down the steps she realized she was following a trail of blood.

She burst out of the doorway and into the car park. It was as empty as it had been when she arrived. But now a set of tire tracks curved out of the exit and onto the road. Somebody had made a speedy getaway.

To her surprise, Jade saw the jerry can man heading down the street at a stumbling run. She saw a dark vehicle under the nearby trees, but as she looked, it pulled away. She ran out onto the road. The limping man had vanished.

The shopkeeper stood staring at the thick black smoke and leaping flames.

"Nkosi yami!" he cried before dialing a number on his cell. Moments later she heard him conversing excitedly with the emergency services.

She walked away on legs suddenly wobbly with shock and called David, hoping she could keep her voice steady while she spoke to him.

"Bloody hell," he shouted when she told him the news. "You okay, Jadey?"

She took a deep, trembling breath. "Fine, thanks."

"What do you make of this?"

Jade blinked, trying to erase the image of the gunman's eyes, cold and furious in his snarling face. Had his hatred been directed at her personally? She didn't think so. More likely at what she represented.

"It was brutal. Revenge or a cover-up, perhaps. They didn't expect to see me there." As she uttered the words, she wondered if they were true. Had the men known she was in the office? Why was one of them carrying an unholstered gun? She didn't know, so she continued. "They didn't hesitate to shoot. And they weren't working alone. I think there was a car waiting for them. When the office went up, the driver cleared out fast. I'll ask the shopkeeper if he saw anything. There's no sign of Grobbelaar. Just a pair of abandoned shoes inside his door."

She heard David tapping away on a keyboard. "You said the guy who ran away was injured. Burned, do you think?"

"No. Too much blood. My guess is he has a bullet in his leg, courtesy of his friend's second stray gunshot. Can you notify the hospitals if I give you a description? I'm sure those guys will have a record. Racially motivated violent crime would be my guess."

David sighed heavily. "Will do. But he won't risk going to a hospital, not with firearm injuries. He'll go to a sangoma, a witch-doctor. God knows what treatment he'll receive. Herbs, muti, purging. Maybe he'll survive, maybe he'll get an infection and die." His voice sounded flat, as if he didn't care either way. "That's the risk they run." He added something else but Jade couldn't hear him because his voice was drowned out by the blare of approaching sirens.

10

While they watched black smoke belching from the building, the shopkeeper told Jade that yes, he had seen another vehicle arrive shortly before he heard the gunshots. The car had driven past the shop and parked in the corner.

"A black Mercedes, with dark windows," he said. He couldn't tell her what model it was and he hadn't seen any number plates. He thought perhaps the car had no plates. When she told him the police were on their way, the shopkeeper closed his business for the day and left.

"I am from Zimbabwe," he told her, slightly shamefaced. "My identity document, it is not original. If the police find me here, they will arrest me and send me back home."

Jade couldn't argue with his logic. She wasn't about to hand the man over to the cops after his intervention had saved her life. She wished him well and watched him walk down the road, glancing back at the smoldering office as if he couldn't believe what had happened.

❀

In its tranquil country setting, Annette's house seemed a

world away from the fiery crime scene she had left behind. She'd had to stop on the way to buy some new shoes. The old ones stank of gas and gave her the uncomfortable feeling that a carelessly dropped cigarette butt would turn her into a human torch.

She was greeted by silence when she arrived at the gate. A brand-new white Lexus was parked next to the little Golf she remembered seeing there previously. Another car, towing a trailer, was turning to leave. The trailer had a logo painted on the side: Animal Anti-Cruelty League.

Piet was talking to the driver. When he saw her, he fumbled in his pockets for the gate key. Jade watched him pat each pocket with increasing alarm until he turned and saw he'd left the keys on the hood of the Golf. He hurried over and retrieved them. This time all he had to do was press a remote control and the motor whirred into action.

"I had it fixed today. The gate man came here earlier on," Piet said after she'd got out of her car. He looked calmer than when she had last seen him. "The lady from the *Star* newspaper was here yesterday. I feel I'm making real progress." He squeezed her arm. "Oh, and she passed my number on to a restaurant. I've just had a commission to do a wall painting for them."

Jade sighed. Piet's newly discovered celebrity status was an unwelcome development.

"And the dogs?"

"They're in the trailer. They're going to a woman who lives on a smallholding north of here. I couldn't keep them, Jade. They didn't respect me. I've been bitten twice. I was worried they would turn on me as a pack."

"Who else is here?" Jade glanced at the Lexus.

"Oh. A guy called Graham Hope just arrived. He's the person who originally sold this land to Annette's brother. He told me he read about her death in the papers." He nodded proudly. Jade could see how delighted he was by the power of the press coverage he had received.

Piet gestured to the door. "Go on inside. I'll be with you just now. I just have to sign some documents for the dogs."

Graham struggled to his feet when she entered, propping himself up on a pair of crutches. He was a little taller than her, brown-haired, with twinkling blue eyes. His handshake was warm, like his smile. He lowered himself back onto the couch and Jade sat down opposite him, in the same hard chair as last time.

Graham's right leg was in some kind of a medical cast, with metal struts and Velcro straps holding it in position.

"Good to meet you, Jade," he said. "Excuse my leg. I had an operation on my knee a while ago. I've only recently started driving again." He winked. "Automatic transmission only." He laid the crutches down on the floor. "Piet was telling me you're the investigator on the case. Are you a policewoman?"

She shook her head. "Private investigation."

He nodded. "I'm glad you're helping out. Poor Piet doesn't seem to be functioning well at all. Can't say I would be either, if my wife was murdered outside our home." He shifted position. The cast made it impossible for him to sit back on the cushions. He perched on the edge with his leg stretched out in front of him.

"Have you met Piet before?" Jade asked.

Graham shook his head. "This is the first time. I sold this property to Annette's brother Adrian. That was a good few years ago. One of my first sales. When he bought this place, it was nothing but empty veldt. Not so much as an outbuilding on it."

"He certainly improved it."

Graham nodded. "That's true. It's a beautiful piece of land. Have you seen what he did out back? There's a horse barn, acres of pole fencing, a dam. All well maintained. And this is an up-and-coming area. The new north, some people say. That's partly why I'm here now, but I'll explain more about that later."

He looked up as Piet walked back inside. "Hey there, Mr. Botha. Sorry about the obstacle in the middle of the floor."

Piet stepped over Graham's outstretched leg, sat down, and patted his pockets again. This time, his search was successful. He found his cigarettes and Graham stretched over and passed him a lighter.

Piet inhaled deeply. He held his breath for a long time before the smoke began to seep out of his nostrils. "So what can we do for you, Mr. Hope?" he asked.

Graham shifted his weight. Jade thought he looked uneasy.

"I wanted to pay my respects. Say how sorry I am this happened. I don't want to intrude on your grief. If I can help in any way, let me know." He paused. Jade was sure he was going to say more and, after a while, he did.

"I've been working in this area for a long time now," he said. "When something like this happens, a crime that makes newspaper headlines, people start to worry." He glanced at the folded paper on the table. "I'm out and about every day. I share the news and I hear people talking. At the moment, they're talking about what happened here, at Plot 4."

He sighed, and continued. "This sounds terrible. I'm not

a gossipmonger. I'm not one of those people who stop and stare at an accident scene. But I'd like to know if there's any further information available on what happened. My clients are anxious, and that makes me anxious too. Crime affects property prices. It causes panic sales. That affects me and the residents in the area." Graham stopped talking and produced a pack of cigarettes from his own pocket. "I'll light up too, if you don't mind."

Piet's cigarette already had a long section of ash on its end. He looked down at the table. No ashtray.

He tilted it upright, so the ash wouldn't fall off the end, and held it between thumb and finger. Then he hurried off in search of an ashtray, with his other hand cupped underneath for safety.

"He seems disturbed," Graham murmured, turning to Jade.

"Yes. Although I think he's always like this," she whispered. "Artistic."

"Ah." Graham nodded slowly. "That would explain it."

Piet returned carrying an ashtray and looking relieved. He put the ashtray on the pile of business cards. It tilted and his cigarette fell out. He grabbed it while Jade straightened the ashtray.

"The police are still looking into it," Piet said. "They haven't made any arrests yet. I'm still under investigation myself." He stubbed out his cigarette. "But they think it's a hijacking. Like the newspapers said." He sighed. "The criminals could be anywhere by now. That's why I'm angry the investigation is taking so long. The more time that passes, the more chance they have to disappear."

Graham nodded. His smile had vanished. "That's bad news

for you, my friend. Bad news for me, too. If an arrest was made, people would feel more secure." He reached into an inside pocket and took out a silver business card holder. He gave a card to Piet and another to Jade. Piet handed him one of his cards in turn.

"Please call me if you hear anything further," Graham said. "The sooner we can spread the good news that there's been progress, the better."

When Graham had left, Piet walked round to the back of the house. Jade could see that his spate of visitors had interrupted a gardening session. A trowel, fork, shears and a pair of gloves lay by one of the untidy flowerbeds. He pulled a water sprinkler across to another bed, put the gloves back on and squatted down on the dry grass. For a while, all she heard was the thunking sound of the trowel in the earth. Jade looked out over the garden fence, towards the dark shape of the horse barn and the fields that stretched away to the horizon like a golden eiderdown.

"I can't stand it that Annette's been taken from me, Jade." He looked up at her. "Living without her was torture. I don't know how I'm going to handle it when I go back to Cape Town. After we divorced, I used to spend hours wondering where she was going and what she was doing. Whether she was OK or not."

A weed landed at Jade's feet with a little thump, spraying soil over her new shoes.

"Is that why you had her followed?" she asked.

Piet dropped the trowel and swiveled round to stare up at her.

The frozen expression on his face told her all she needed to know.

"Followed? Who told you that?" Piet struggled to his feet, dusting soil off his jeans. He glanced at her, biting his lip, and then looked away.

"Never mind who told me. It's true, though, isn't it?"

"Well, I mean ..." He shook his head. "I didn't think it mattered."

"Piet." Jade stared down at the little man in exasperation. "You don't think anything matters. You didn't tell the police about Annette contacting a private detective, either."

"Yes, but that was different. I forgot about it."

"And you forgot about following her, too?"

"No, no." Piet's head swiveled from side to side, as if looking for the cavalry coming to rescue him. "I didn't forget about that. Like I said, I didn't think it was ..." He searched for the word and found it. "Relevant." He snapped his fingers. "That's it. I didn't think it was relevant."

"The police are going to think it's extremely relevant."

Piet looked at her, anguish in his eyes.

"That detective already said I was a suspect. I'm terrified of being falsely accused. Like the way it happens on TV. I don't want the police to arrest me, Jade. What if I get put in prison for something I didn't do? If you tell them this, they might think I'm guilty."

His voice had risen to a shout. He glared at her, breathing hard. "If I'd thought it was important, I'd have said so. I nearly told you about it when you were here the first time. Then I thought to myself it would confuse everyone if I started telling people about something that happened in—in January last year."

Now it was Jade's turn to look surprised.

"Last year?"

"Yes. In January."

"Not more recently?"

"No."

"Are you sure?"

"Of course I'm sure."

Jade watched him, waiting for him to explain further. But Piet turned away and stared at the sprinkler. It spattered on the leaves, the droplets sparkling in the sun. He walked over to it and dragged it sideways.

"Come inside," Jade said. "Let's have a cup of tea, and you can tell me all about it."

Without Graham Hope's cheerful presence and clumsy cast, Jade realized how quiet and empty the house had become. The wall unit was bare of everything except the photograph of Piet and Annette. The ticking clock had been packed away. Jade didn't think she would miss it, but she did. It had been a sound, something to intrude on the heavy blanket of silence. In Jade's experience there was always an oppressive stillness in a place where someone had recently died.

She made two cups of tea and sat down on the couch next to Piet.

"OK. Let's start at the beginning. I need you to tell me exactly what happened."

Piet took his cup and blew onto the surface before he sipped it. He put the cup down. The clinking sound it made when it touched the saucer seemed as loud as a drum roll.

"Well..." he started.

"Carry on."

"Oh hell. It's an embarrassing story, you know."

Jade wouldn't have thought it was possible for somebody so deeply tanned to blush, but he was doing a pretty good job of it. He looked up at the ceiling, glanced over at the photo, and then turned his attention back to her.

"Like I said, it was more than a year ago now. I asked my buddy here in Jo'burg if he'd keep an eye on Annette and find out if she was seeing anybody else." He cleared his throat. "It's stupid, I know. I wanted to try again with her. We'd been in contact but I had no idea—she could be so difficult to talk to. Especially about something like that."

"So you didn't want to ask her?"

He shook his head. "I—when I moved down to Cape Town I started seeing a lady there, for a couple of months. It didn't work out. But I never told Annette about it. Didn't want her to know that I'd failed, I suppose." He glanced at her again. "What could I do, Jade? I couldn't ask her. And I couldn't just fly up to Jo'burg. What if I found her living with another man? Then I'd be mad as hell.

"So I thought it would be better to find out for sure. My buddy knew what to do. He's an insurance assessor. He's followed people to see if they're faking claims."

Piet took out his cigarette packet again. With Graham gone, she didn't know how he was going to light up. She wasn't surprised when he placed the cigarette between his lips and promptly forgot about it again.

"Annette found him out, didn't she?"

Piet laughed. "She busted him after about two days. She marched right up to his car and banged on his window. Asked him what he thought he was doing. She must have thought he was a stalker. She gave him such a fright. He told me he nearly peed his pants. Then she phoned me and told me I was stupid, she said I should just have asked her, and she would have told me." He slapped his forehead in a frustrated gesture.

"Why didn't you mention it to the police?"

He shook his head.

"Why would I? I didn't think that my friend following her so long ago would mean anything to anybody now. It was just me being stupid. Like she said."

"Did you have her followed again, more recently?"

Now, Jade thought, Piet looked as uneasy as Graham had done earlier. He twined his gnarled fingers together and chewed the filter of his cigarette nervously.

"Annette phoned me last week. Just a couple of days before she died. She asked what was happening. She wanted to know if I'd got somebody else to bother her again. I said no. I said she must be imagining things."

Jade wasn't sure if she believed him. "You're telling me that you only had her followed once?"

"Just the once. And I found out what I needed to know. You can phone my friend now and ask him. I'll give you his number. He'll tell you I'm correct." He patted his pockets again, as if his cell phone or address book might have miraculously appeared there.

Jade scrutinized Piet closely. Was he lying?

"Annette was pretty sure she was being followed the first time it happened," she said gently. "And she was right. She was being followed."

"She was a sharp lady."

"Then why would you tell her that she was imagining things if she thought she was being followed again? Surely she'd proved she had an instinct for it."

Piet thought for a while. Then he shook his head in a small, defeated motion.

"Jade, I don't know. I thought maybe she was scared of

moving. Worried she was making the right decision. I'm like that when I get stressed. My mind plays tricks on me. I imagine the worst." He picked his cup up again. His hand was trembling. Tiny ripples scudded across the surface of his tea. "I just didn't want anything to get in the way of us. So I tried to reassure her." He sighed. "But I was wrong. I should have worried. I should have told her to be careful."

He put the cup down again without drinking.

Jade shook her head. "How could you have known? You weren't there."

"That's what I keep telling myself. What happened to her, Jade? Hiring detectives, being followed. What had she got herself into? Why didn't she tell me about it?"

"That's what we need to find out."

Piet didn't reply. He sat hunched over his tea. Jade was sure he was racked with guilt over his misguided advice to Annette. She couldn't give him any further comfort. Reason and logic were poor weapons against the assault of those terrible words, "If only."

"Did Annette have any staff?" Jade asked him, in a soft voice. "A domestic worker, a gardener, anyone who visited the house regularly?"

Piet shook his head.

"That was the first thing the police asked me. They said domestics always know what's going on. But she did her own housework. Her own gardening. She was house-proud. And she didn't like having strangers around her. She'd get the neighbors to help her with grass cutting and firebreaks out in the fields. Not often. A couple of times a year, I think."

"Any repairs to the house? Building? Recent deliveries or installations?"

"None that I know of."

"Where did she keep her accounts?"

Piet climbed slowly to his feet. "I'll show you."

Jade guessed that Annette's accounts system would be neat and tidy. Even so, she was unprepared for the rigorously ordered ranks of files that Piet unpacked from one of the boxes. The woman had covered every file in brown paper and plastic as if they were schoolbooks. She stared in awe.

She helped Piet carry the files back into the lounge. He put them on the coffee table and she paged through the most recent one. It was up to date. Annette must have done filing the day before she died. Each month was separated by a plastic divider. Bank statements, phone bills, water and lights accounts. Sundry expenses. If she ran a business, she would've liked Annette to control the accounts department, that was for sure.

The section for June wasn't complete. The bank statements were missing. She supposed they arrived at the end of the month. But some bills and sundry expenses were there. There was an invoice for a car service. Jade checked the details. It was for the vehicle parked outside the house. Other bills for groceries, dog food, gas, hardware. Annette lived modestly. No expensive purchases at hairdressers or clothing stores, even though she could have afforded them. Her bank balance was healthy. Much healthier than Jade could ever expect her own to be. Annette's current account stood at six figures, and Jade was sure there was more money stashed away in investment funds.

She flicked through the payments for May. Then she stopped. She noticed a plain sheet of paper, a printout from an Internet transaction. Neatly filed like all the others. It had been made to the personal account of D. Grobbelaar.

She was willing to bet that this was money Annette had paid Dean Grobbelaar for some form of investigation work.

Jade checked the amount. Seven hundred rand.

She frowned. Grobbelaar might be cheap, but that payment wasn't high enough to justify spending hours and days waiting around in a car, trying to spot somebody who was following her. Jade had done counter-surveillance herself, on occasion. It was difficult work. The hours were backbreaking and it was mindlessly boring. And at the same time, every long minute was potentially fraught with danger, because people who were following other people weren't too pleased if they noticed somebody was trying to catch them out.

Jade reckoned this amount would probably have bought Annette a half-day of investigation work, at best. What had she hired him to do?

She went through May again. Then she looked through the entire file to see if any other payments had been made. There were none. This was the only money Annette had paid to Grobbelaar. Seven hundred rand. A few hours of his time.

Jade looked more closely at the paper. She'd noticed something else. As a reference, Annette hadn't put her own name, she'd used "Ellie Myers."

"Do you know anyone called Ellie Myers?" she asked Piet. He was hovering anxiously over her shoulder, breathing smoke down her neck. He had found a way to light his cigarette. The strange burning smell wafting through from the kitchen made her think he must have used the toaster.

He looked at her blankly. "No. Why?"

"I've found a payment here. I'm pretty sure it was made to the detective her work colleague recommended. But the reference says Ellie Myers."

"I don't know an Ellie." Now Piet was frowning, too. Jade could see he was upset all over again, because he hadn't been able to share that piece of Annette's past with her either.

Annette wasn't very trusting. Could she have used a pseudonym? Then she looked at the paper again and answered her own silent question. No, no, of course not. Her account name appears here. He would have seen that. Pointless using a pseudonym as a reference on an Internet transfer. So who the hell is Ellie Myers?

Then she had another idea. She turned to Piet. "Did Annette have a computer at home?"

He shook his head. "No. I e-mailed her at her work address."

Jade remembered the desk opposite Yolandi's. Clean, shiny, and bare. Perhaps the company had reallocated Annette's computer.

Or perhaps not. Maybe it had simply been put away somewhere, or gone to the IT department for reformatting. In which case, there was a chance it might still have correspondence stored on it. If she used the Internet for the transfer to Grobbelaar, they might have communicated via e-mail. A naturally suspicious woman like Annette would probably keep a record of her dealings with a dodgy detective.

"I'll be back later," she told Piet. "Take care, without the dogs around."

"I will," he said. "I've booked into the City Lodge tonight. I don't feel safe here any more. I feel as if I'm being watched."

Jade checked over her shoulder as she drove out of the gate.

She saw only the empty road and the parched grass nodding in the wind. All the same, as she pulled away and left the lonely house behind her, she wondered with an uneasy chill whether somebody was watching her go.

II

Whiteboy sat behind the wheel of his car and laughed. Things were going well. So extremely well, they couldn't be going better if they tried.

The Botha job had gone exactly as planned. It had been as slick as the best he'd ever done. And he knew the rest of the job would go as planned, too, although the investigators were further ahead than he'd anticipated. It didn't worry him, though. He'd put a backup system in place immediately. From now on he'd be able to keep a closer eye on them. He wouldn't be surprised again. And, when the time was right, he'd set the score straight. In the end, justice would be done. His own unique form of justice.

He remembered one of the first times he had meted it out. Years ago, it had been. Back in the old apartheid days, when every white South African male was forced to report for military service. In a place whose name he didn't remember now. Somewhere near the Angola border. Where his unit was sent on some pointless mission.

He'd been running a scam with a colleague. It involved one of the kitchen staff, Farm Boy, a clueless white kid who was straight off the farm and as ignorant as pig shit. He was stupid enough to do whatever Whiteboy asked him, without realizing that if he was ever caught he'd been set up to take the fall, all on his own. He was also too stupid to realize that Whiteboy knew the exact quantities of the goods that were being sold off. He'd tried to keep some back for himself, even though they were both making money on it, even though Whiteboy was always fair. But this farm boy had tried to make too much money on it, had tried to screw Whiteboy. And that wasn't allowed.

They would meet late at night after roll-call, in a hollow near the dunes. Whiteboy drove a vehicle to their rendez-vous. One of the big armored trucks called Casspirs. Farm Boy walked. They met in the place where the supplies had been stashed earlier on, to share out the money and organize the distribution of another load. A ten-minute contact from beginning to end. Arranged whenever necessary, circum-stances permitting.

This time, it worked differently. The kid arrived as usual. He loaded the supplies into the Casspir. When he was fin-ished, Whiteboy jumped him from behind and got a rope around his neck. He couldn't do anything after that. He was immobilized. Whiteboy thought he would have been immo-bilized anyway from terror. Probably all he'd needed to do was shout and the kid would have dropped down dead of a heart attack.

But he didn't. That would have offended his own code. Instead, he clicked a pair of handcuffs onto each of the Farm Boy's wrists and ordered him to lie, face up and arms spread, splayed across the front of the vehicle. The boy resisted at first. He tried to scream, but a few tugs on the rope round his neck had sorted him out. Then he'd tied a rope to the handcuffs, running it through the APV's interior so that his victim's hands were tied apart.

Then he'd worked on his legs. First, he took off his boots and camo pants. Then he'd ripped off his underpants. By that stage, Whiteboy recalled, the little wimp had already wet himself. That was disgusting. His dick had looked pale and tiny, like a little white maggot. By way of punishment for having pissed himself, he had stuffed the warm and soaked underpants into Farm Boy's mouth and used another piece of rope to tie them firmly in place.

When he thought about it, his MO hadn't changed much since then. Clothing for gags always worked well.

After that, he'd knotted a rope to each of the boy's ankles and tugged the knots tight under the chassis of the big, heavy vehicle. Then he and Farm Boy, now splayed, naked and writhing, across the Casspir's angular grille, had gone for a good long ride in the bush.

This punishment wasn't his invention. It was a well-known method of torturing captured terrorists on the way back to camp, to soften them up for interrogation. He'd never done it before. But he liked to think that he'd improved on it, on his own, that night.

He drove through the thickest trees he could find. The Casspir was old. Its camouflage paintwork was already scratched in a thousand places and it was tough as old boots. Nothing much could happen to the vehicle. But the same could not be said for Farm Boy.

It was amazing, Whiteboy remembered, how a man could scream through a gag. Sitting behind the thick windshield, he had watched the strong thorny branches whip and rip into Farm Boy's white flesh, leaving hundreds of bloody lacerations behind them. He'd become increasingly bolder and more inventive. After all, it wasn't as if he would need to interrogate Farm Boy afterwards. He found a tree with a long, ragged stump of a branch jutting out. Long ago, an elephant or something must have broken it off. Whiteboy drove and reversed, drove and reversed. Each time, the branch ripped further up his victim's thighs. Closer and closer to where the little white maggot was cringing away.

It had been an anticlimax, in the end. Such pleasures often were. He had revved the engine before delivering the coup-de-grace and sent the vehicle hurtling forward in order to embed the branch in Farm Boy's groin. Whiteboy was looking forward to seeing what would happen. He remembered smiling as he put his foot on the accelerator, his armpits damp against his heavy body in the tropical night.

In his fear, Farm Boy found the strength to move himself further down the grille. God knows what he'd hoped to achieve by doing it. He was stupid until the end. The branch missed his groin. Instead, it ripped open a path higher up, through his stomach. It must have torn his diaphragm and ruptured his lungs, too, because he died quite quickly after that.

Whiteboy untied him and let his body slide to the ground. He undid the handcuffs and the ropes. Army property had to be accounted for, after all. Then he threw Farm Boy's trousers and shoes out on the ground after him. He was in the middle of nowhere, deep in the bush. He was confident that it would take a couple of days at least for anyone to find the body, and by then it would be well mauled by small predators, decayed and unrecognizable.

He'd stopped at a riverbed on the way back. For most of the year it was more or less dry, but the recent rains had swollen it to a torrent. He sluiced the front of the vehicle clean of blood. The next morning he overheard some talk that the boy might have deserted. Then it was discovered that supplies were missing, and everyone assumed that was linked to his disappearance. There was a half-hearted search for him a day or two after that. His remains were never found.

Shortly after that, Whiteboy was recalled from Angola and discharged from the army. But before he left, he heard through the grapevine that Farm Boy's parents were selling off their farm. They were broken by the disappearance of their only child. They'd been keeping the farm as his inheritance.

Just for fun, Whiteboy went along to see the setup. It was closer to civilization than he expected, northwest of Pretoria, on the way to the Magaliesberg mountains. The land bordered a little go-nowhere tar road, which in turn eventually led to a little go-nowhere town called Rustenburg. On the way, the road passed close to a nearby black homeland.

There were a few of those homelands dotted around back then. They were mini-states within South Africa, ones that the government had allowed the blacks to have in compensation for taking all their other, and better, land away. He'd heard that a rich Jewish bloke called Sol Kerzner was building some sort of gambling mecca in this particular homeland. He was going to call it Sun City.

Whiteboy thought it sounded like a fun place. Cards and slots, blue movies, naked dancing girls. All the stuff that you couldn't get in South Africa itself in the late 1970s because of the stupid outdated Calvinistic laws. He thought it might do quite well. And if it did, land along the Sun City road would become a sought-after commodity.

He bought the farm. It was extremely cheap and, because he arrived in his army camo and gave Farm Boy's parents some sad little story about how he was struggling to make a living and had been their son's best mate in the army, it was cheaper still. An extra special price for him.

It turned out to be an excellent investment. He'd subdivided it into ten smaller pieces and, over the years, sold off the sections. He'd sold the last one for ten times the original price of the entire farm.

The episode with Farm Boy had launched him into his future career.

❁

Whiteboy heaved his bloated body upright in the seat. Time to phone his contact for information. He believed in having contacts he could trust. He liked having a history with people, some water under the bridge. He liked to be able to rely on them. That was one thing he'd learned in the army. You watched your buddy's back, and he watched yours.

He snapped open the cell phone and made his call.

12

Following the route that Annette must have taken to work every day, Jade had an uneasy feeling that somebody was tailing her. In the last ten years and as many countries, her instinct had been sharpened, and she never ignored it. She glanced in her rearview mirror again. Three cars—a white van, a blue BMW and a cream-colored minibus taxi—were behind her. A few blocks ahead of her a black Mercedes with dark windows pulled onto the road. She couldn't see whether it had number plates.

She turned left at a T-junction. The van turned left, the BMW turned left, and the taxi stopped in the middle of the road to pick up a passenger.

Jade switched the radio on to listen to the local lunchtime news. A cash-in-transit heist. One robber dead, one guard critically injured. A police spokesperson said a surge of lawlessness was sweeping the country. The gas price was going up again, the rand had strengthened against the dollar, and Lindsay Lohan's personal stylist was telling the world about the star's addiction to shopping. That was it. Nothing about Annette. In radio terms, Jade hoped, her death was already old news.

She checked behind her again. The BMW was there. The van was there. The taxi had caught up and was trying to overtake all of them on a solid yellow line.

Jade turned down a side road, watching to see if anybody followed her. She saw no cars, although her uneasiness persisted. Either her instinct was wrong or the person tailing her was too experienced to be caught.

Rejoining the main road, Jade soon decided that if she were Annette, she would have moved to Cape Town too. Or found another job closer to home. Development was rife in the area, and traffic was at a standstill.

Stuck in an endless line of cars, she inched past a huge billboard announcing "A Place To Raise Your Brood" with a picture of an oversized duck swimming in a sapphire-blue lake. Below, bright red letters announced "Eagle's Eye Estate," "New Lifestyle Residential Properties!" "Secure Country Living! Homes Now Available!"

Further ahead on the left, all the trees had been cut down to make room for a paved maze of cluster homes surrounded by high walls topped with electric fencing that stretched as far as the eye could see.

On the right, more trees had been felled. A shopping mall that seemed to cover the same area as the Vatican City was being erected. Cement trucks and bulldozers crawled around the building site like industrious beetles.

"Eagle's Flight Shopping Center. Secure Commercial and Retail Properties" an equally large billboard screamed.

Jade forced her way into the next lane to pass a truck piled high with gravel. It labored up the hill, chuffing gray clouds of smoke from its exhaust. If the traffic was this bad now, she didn't want to think what it would be like when the residents of Eagle's Eye and Eagle's Flight moved in and started trying to get to and from work every day.

Further ahead, a row of traffic cones had been placed on the left side of the road, narrowing the two lanes into one. She watched the Jo'burg drivers struggle with the concept of giving way to fellow motorists. For every two cars that reached the single lane, one had to go first and one had to go second. But there were unwritten rules. Minibus taxis always went first. She watched a driver dispute this decision. He tried to pull ahead and cut a taxi off. The taxi driver leaned out of the window with a friendly grin and then waved a crowbar at him.

The driver let the taxi in ahead of him.

Jade laughed. It was a novelty to be back in a country where breaking the rules was practically a national hobby, where people who considered themselves honest citizens drove without licenses, dodged tax, and employed illegal immigrants. Where bribery was a way of life, whether it was to avoid a spot traffic fine or win a government contract.

The average South African's attitude to the law had given her father gray hairs, that was for sure.

She checked her mirror again. Close behind her was an angry-looking man in a big new car. He was weaving from side to side as if hoping to find a way past the traffic cones and crash barriers that now lined the road.

The taxi ahead of her stopped to let out a group of passengers, then pulled off again. They stood, flattening themselves against the yellow barriers, waiting for a chance to cross.

Jade stopped when she reached the little knot of people. Three men in threadbare overalls and a woman carrying a baby. They stared at her for a moment as if they couldn't believe a car was actually waiting for them. Then they hurried across the road.

The woman with the baby was slower. As she was crossing, the man in the car behind her blasted his horn. A long, impatient blast that caused the woman to jump in fright and stumble sideways. Jade looked in her rearview mirror. The man was waving his hands around his ears, shouting out words she was glad she couldn't hear. Then he lowered his hands and honked again.

Jade got out of her car. The wind was blowing strongly, kicking up dust from the bare soil and sending it scudding along in hazy brown clouds. She could hear the groaning of machinery and the sound of drills, and closer, the thrum of idling engines in the queue behind her. She glanced at the waiting cars and noticed a black Mercedes with tinted windows in the line. Was it the same one she'd seen earlier? Luxury vehicles were so common in this part of Johannesburg, she didn't know.

She walked towards the angry man. The taxi passengers, now safely across the road, stopped to watch her.

The man buzzed his window down. His face was red, his eyes concealed behind small round dark glasses.

"Is something wrong?" she asked, innocently.

"What the hell do you think you're doing?"

She looked him over. Luxury car, expensive suit. Gold watch around his wrist. And an air of supreme, aggressive confidence.

"I was letting people cross the road."

"They could have waited."

"For what? Christmas?"

"You were holding up traffic."

"The roadworks are holding up traffic. Look." Jade pointed to the cones and crash barriers. "Construction. See?"

Behind them, someone else honked.

"For God's sake, bitch," the man shouted. His mouth was open so wide she could see the gold fillings in his molars. "Get back in your car and drive. Because if you don't, I'm going to get out myself, and land you such a punch you'll be flat on your back in the road. Woman or not, I don't give a shit."

"All right, then." Jade walked back and climbed into her car. Behind her, she heard the man revving his engine in triumph. She pushed in the clutch. Then she popped her car into reverse and hit the accelerator.

Her car shot backwards. There was only room for it to travel a few feet before her rear bumper collided with the front bumper of the luxury car behind her. It was a small impact. She barely felt it. But for him, it was more serious. Because his airbag deployed.

Looking in the rearview mirror, she saw his body whip-lash backwards as the powerful bag shoved him out of the way, and then slump forwards again as the bag deflated. His expensive dark glasses fell out of the open window and shattered on the tarmac. His hands went up again, trying to push the half-empty airbag out of the way. He'd forgotten all about Jade. He was far too busy wrestling with the flapping nylon and, Jade knew, smearing the sticky white talcum powder from the deployed bag all over his dark suit.

She saw the taxi passengers at the side of the road shrieking with laughter and clapping their hands in glee. This was a sight none of them would ever forget.

Jade put her car into first gear and drove on. There was no need for her to check her mirrors now. For quite some time, there were no other cars behind her.

She examined her rear bumper carefully when she arrived at Yolandi's office. She couldn't see any marks on the solid black plastic. Good. She hadn't wanted to damage the car, or get David into trouble with the rental company.

"Control your temper, Jade," her father would have said, with that half-smile on his face that always left her wondering whether he was angry or amused by the headstrong behavior of his only child.

She wondered what he would say if he knew how far beyond the law she had gone, and how much further she planned to go.

13

While Jade waited for the receptionist to finish a phone call, the two managers she had seen last time walked down the corridor. They wore different ties this time. One solid red, one solid blue. She heard them discussing South Africa's recent cricket performance.

"All out in forty-three overs. Didn't even break the hundred and fifty mark. And Smith scored two runs. Two. What kind of a captain is that?"

"Unacceptable," the other man said.

As they passed by, one of the men stopped and stared at

her. He looked her up and down. Jade knew what he was thinking. In her jeans and jacket, she didn't look like a salesperson or a customer. So why was she waiting?

"Can I help you?" he asked.

"I'm here for Yolandi Storr," she said.

"Yolandi." He frowned. "And you are?"

"Jade de Jong. Investigator assisting the police."

The red-tied man sighed heavily. "I'd better help you, then. What is it you need to know?" He gestured to a row of silver metal chairs opposite the reception desk. Jade took one and the manager lowered himself onto the neighboring seat, shifting his weight uncomfortably in a way that made her wonder if he suffered from hemorrhoids.

"I need access to her colleague's computer. Annette Botha. I'm investigating her murder case on behalf of Superintendent Patel."

The manager stared blankly at her for a moment and then shook his head, as if murder, police investigation and South Africa's cricket defeat were too much for him to handle in one morning.

"You're here about the murder case?"

"Yes."

"OK. Sorry, I thought this was in connection with Yolandi."

"Why?" Jade stared at him with rising concern. "Are the police investigating her?"

"They'll want to talk to her, I'm sure. If she wakes up." He stared at Jade, his expression grim. "Yolandi was the victim of an armed robbery at her home last night."

"What happened to her?" Jade recalled Yolandi's frail body and timid demeanor. She would have been helpless against an intruder.

"Tied up and assaulted with a blunt weapon," the man replied. "She's in a coma now, with severe head injuries. The police say she was probably left for dead. Emergency services took her to Sandton Medi-Clinic."

Jade clasped her hands together. Her palms felt icy cold.

"Have they made any arrests?" she asked.

The manager shook his head. "Not yet. The guys got away, whoever they were. They were interrupted. A neighbor heard something, phoned to check, and when she didn't answer he pressed his panic button. When the robbers heard the alarm, they fled." He adjusted his tie, tugging it away from his fleshy neck.

"And the weapon?"

"Cops reckon they forced her door with a crowbar, then used it on her. I went round there this morning. The place is a mess. And the computer is gone, I'm afraid." He turned to her with an apologetic shrug. "Annette's machine, the one you asked about. Yolandi had it at her house, so she could finish off the year-end. After what happened to Annette, she didn't want to work late and drive home in the dark." He shook his head. "I'm sorry. The robbers took it, along with everything else."

14

Jade phoned David as soon as she was home. Moloi answered and told her he was in a meeting with Williams. She remembered Moloi as an enthusiastic rookie who'd joined her father's team shortly before she left, one of the first big intake of black recruits. Today he was a captain, David's right-hand man and, according to him, one of the few staff he could trust to do the best possible job.

She briefed him on the latest developments. A torched office, a missing detective, a stolen computer and one unconscious woman fighting for her life in intensive care. A black Mercedes with no number plates seen at Grobbelaar's offices.

Moloi said he would inform his boss immediately.

With David working late, Jade had no culinary obligations in the form of cop food. After she'd updated her case notes, she began to prepare some soup for dinner. Healthy, warming soup with lentils and chopped tomatoes. She wrapped a few giant garlic cloves in tinfoil and put them in the oven to roast.

When the soup had been bubbling for an hour, she switched off the stove, unwrapped the garlic and squeezed the soft insides out of the crispy cloves and into the pot.

She tasted it. Superb. A delicious, subtle combination of flavors. And yet she felt something was lacking.

Jade glanced over at the plastic container of chili powder. She pulled it closer and had a short mental battle with herself.

"You can't have chili with everything," she said.

Perhaps just a pinch would do. To liven it up a little.

Jade stirred in a heaped teaspoon and tried the soup again. Now it was perfect.

As she turned to the cupboard to find a bowl, she saw the fuzzy glare of headlights through the steamed-up kitchen window and then heard a honk outside her gate. She hurried to the door, expecting to see David.

It was Robbie, sat behind the wheel of a black BMW. He leaned out of the window when he saw her. His hair was gelled back on his head. The product had tamed the tight curls into uneven waves.

"Come here, Jade," he called. "I want to show you something."

Jade grabbed the keys and locked the security door behind her. She hurried over to the gate, bracing herself against the cold and wondering with an uneasy shiver how the hell Robbie had managed to find her. Was there a GPS tracker in the ammo bag?

He grinned at her and swung open the passenger door.

"I got connections who tell me things," he said.

Jade climbed into the car. The interior smelled of expensive leather.

"Your connections tell you there's a cop living next door?" she asked.

Robbie's grin widened. "They told me he's not home." He reversed out of the driveway and kicked up gravel as he pulled away.

"I thought you wanted to show me something in the car. Not take me somewhere in the car." Jade tugged her seat belt across and clicked it into place.

"We've got to go somewhere before I can show you." He sniffed the air. "What the hell have you been doing? It smells like an Italian just farted in here."

"I was squeezing garlic cloves. For soup."

Robbie made a face. "There's a bag in the back. Grab it, will you? I got us grilled chicken takeaways. Good food. Not this garlic crap. I got extra spicy for you. We can eat while we drive."

"Where are we going?"

"Wait and see."

Robbie turned onto the main road and flattened his foot on the accelerator while reaching for a piece of chicken. They flew past another car, overtaking on a solid line, Jade staring in horror at the headlights of the oncoming truck.

The driver blared his horn in warning. The BMW's engine roared as it surged forward. They nipped sideways just before the truck rattled past. It was carrying a full load of river sand. Water dripped from the tailgate.

"They must be doing night work," Robbie observed, licking his fingers. "Do you know there's actually a shortage of cement in the country? Too much construction. It's a great opportunity for black market product. I'm looking into it seriously."

"Robbie, that's interesting, but please drive slower."

"No worries, babe. This car has got airbags and stuff."

"Airbags are not designed to protect people from twenty tons of mass in motion."

"Chill. I'm a great driver, you know."

Jade trusted Robbie's driving skills about as much as she trusted Robbie himself. Fortunately, the traffic was on her side. When they turned onto the highway heading for Pretoria, a wall of red taillights ahead of them signaled a serious jam. Cursing, he hit the brakes. Jade loosened her grip on her seat. Now that they were moving at the same speed as an old ox-wagon she could relax.

"We're going the other side of the boerewors curtain," Robbie said.

"The boerewors curtain?"

"C'mon, Jade, you must have heard that expression before."

"Nope."

"It's a great description. You know what boerewors is—don't tell me you've forgotten just because you've been out of the country for so long. Well, northern Pretoria's all farmers and traditional Afrikaners now. Little suburbs full of poor whites. In the old days, they'd have worked on the farms.

Nowadays they still have that same mentality. I'm surprised we don't need passports to get there."

"Get where?"

"You'll see."

Robbie went through a tollgate and turned off the highway. A few minutes later, they were driving through suburbia. Small houses, narrow roads lined with trees. Jade remembered that Pretoria was also known as Jacaranda City. She wondered whether, in early summer, this street would be transformed into a purple-lined avenue as the trees produced their distinctive flowers. The branches were bare now, so she couldn't tell.

Robbie pulled up at an intersection and parked on the pavement.

"Come on. This way."

Pretoria's more northerly location meant it was usually a couple of degrees warmer than Jo'burg. It didn't feel warmer now. Outside on the street, Jade felt cold and exposed. Her footsteps seemed very loud on the tarmac. The small houses were situated close to the road. Close enough for people to watch them walking past in the yellow glare of the streetlights.

The air smelled of burning charcoal and crisping fat. Somewhere, someone was braaing meat outdoors. She supposed that people on the other side of the boerewors curtain were too tough to be driven indoors at night just because it happened to be winter.

"Here," Robbie whispered, pulling her arm. He pointed to one of the houses and crept forward.

Jade looked through the fence, across the narrow strip of garden. In the pool of light cast by the street lamp, the grass looked dry and untended. Behind the net curtains, Jade could see a shape moving slowly across the dimly lit front room. It looked odd—squat and square. It took her a moment to realize that it was the silhouette of an elderly woman in a wheelchair.

"What's this about?" she muttered, staring at the outline of the old lady.

Robbie's grip tightened on her arm. "Viljoen's mother," he hissed back at her. "This is where he'll be staying when he's out of jail. He's going to live with his old mum. I've heard it from a reliable source."

Jade continued to stare through the curtains. The old lady's head was bowed as she struggled to maneuver her wheelchair across the small room. When she came to a halt by the window, Jade saw that Mrs. Viljoen was ancient and shriveled, beaten down by age and ill health. Her two sons were murderers. One was completing his jail sentence. The other one was dead. She watched the old lady lean forward and switch off the light. Her arm trembled from the effort. Who would have thought that a frail woman like this could ever have given birth to two such monsters?

"Come on. You've seen the place now. Let's go."

Jade waited a moment more, contemplating the humble little house. Then she turned and hurried back to the car.

Robbie started the engine. The fan blew warm air into Jade's face.

"You brought me all the way just to see Viljoen's mother?" she asked.

He glanced at the dashboard clock, then back at her.

"Not exactly. Just killing time." His eyes flashed in the dim light. "I've got a job to do close by. Verna's busy tonight. I need your help, I need you to hold the wheel."

He climbed out of the car, opened the trunk and took out a set of number plates. Jade watched while he swapped the plates onto the front and rear of the car and threw the originals back into the trunk.

Her palms were suddenly slick with sweat. Her mind was racing. It had been ten years since Robbie had held the wheel for her. Ten years since she'd leaned out of the passenger window and stared, with cold and merciless accuracy, down the barrel of her gun.

She'd worked and traveled all over the world since then, always on the move, uneasy about spending time in any one place. She'd told herself she was running from Viljoen, that she wasn't prepared to return to South Africa until he was freed. Perhaps she had been wrong. Perhaps she was running from herself.

"Well?" Robbie drummed his fingers on the dashboard. "You up for it? We've got to get going. Deadline's in half an hour."

Jade didn't reply. She was remembering how she had lined up the gun on her target. How she'd squeezed the trigger, her hand steady, her finger caressing the cool metal, arms absorbing the recoil, sighting, firing again. How the shots had echoed off the buildings in the dark street.

The second time, the third time, both deliberately wide. Winging him, only because the first head shot had been deadly accurate, and criminals who could shoot straight were rare. Why narrow the field of suspects? Let the police think it had been a random hit. A lucky bullet.

How she'd been thrown forward as Robbie slammed on the brakes. She'd grabbed the dashboard, yelling at him. What was he doing? Why had he stopped? He'd jumped out and rifled through the dead guy's pockets, his shadow looming over the body in the glow of the headlights, darkening the blood that had splashed crimson onto the pavement. "Gotta make it look authentic," he'd told her, swinging into the driver's seat with a bulging wallet in his hand. "Let's get out before the cops arrive."

Jade shook her head to clear the memory. She'd done it once. She'd do it once more. But that was enough. Never again.

"Well?" Robbie asked again, his voice sharp.

Jade lifted her chin and stared him down. "No. I'm sorry, Robbie. I can't do this with you."

He looked straight at her, eyes narrow and predatory in the leather-scented gloom.

"Babe," he said, "I'm going to make you change your mind."

15

Before she could reply, Robbie pulled away from the curb and drove in silence, threading his way through the narrow winding roads, following a tortuous route that Jade couldn't memorize. She'd told him no. He hadn't accepted her answer. What was she going to do? Jump out of a moving car and try to find her way in late-night Pretoria with no phone and no money, and only an illegal gun for help?

She waited, watching the road, forcing herself to stay relaxed, stay cool, and not betray her rising anxiousness. After a while, Robbie began to talk.

"So this guy's got a daughter. Sixteen years old, pretty girl, good grades. No problems till she goes to a nightclub and some asshole pushes a few grams of coke up her nose and takes her to a motel for a night of fun."

Robbie glanced at a street sign and turned onto a main road.

"So now daddy's little princess is hooked. Instead of writing her Matric exams she's coke-whoring in Hillbrow, shacked up with a bunch of Nigerians. Then she climbs the ladder, meets a bigger supplier, moves in. He feeds her drugs, lets his friends play with her." He accelerated through a traffic light as it turned red. Jade didn't recognize any of the street signs, but she had a feeling they were heading south. Back towards the wealthy side of Pretoria.

"So all's well and good for her. Except one day," Robbie snapped his fingers, "something clicks in Princess's head and she runs away. Back home to Daddy, skinny as an Auschwitz prisoner and pregnant. So he gets her into rehab, sorts out the baby problem, and decides he's going after the main man. Princess agrees to testify, the police make an arrest, and everyone's looking forward to a day in court."

"Then what happened?" Jade asked, although with a sinking heart, she knew.

Robbie grinned, without warmth. "What do you think? Princess is home alone one afternoon, and there's a break-in. She gets five bullets in the chest. No key witness and, surprise, surprise, no case. There was a problem with it. Seems one of your friends in the police service didn't follow correct protocol so the file got trashed."

Jade watched the streetlights flicker over the windshield. Who'd been paid to quash the case? She swallowed, trying to keep a check on her mounting anger.

"So Daddy hired you?" she asked.

Robbie shook his head. "Daddy's dead."

Jade shivered. She'd been convinced that she wouldn't change her mind, regardless of threats or blackmail, although she'd been expecting both from Robbie. She was back for one reason, to take care of Viljoen. That was where it began and ended. Her burden of guilt weighed heavy enough already.

But the part of her that screamed with triumphant glee a decade ago, as she watched her victim slump onto the sidewalk, justice finally done, shouted in outrage now. What had happened to this girl was wrong and foul and vicious. And she could help avenge it.

Robbie's latest mission echoed Jade's own past. Was that why he'd known he could rely on her to help?

❀

"There's a problem with the Viljoen case," her father had told her when she arrived home one night during a February heatwave to find him hunched at his little desk surrounded by sheaves of papers and notes.

He rubbed his eyes and closed his notebook. Two beetles buzzed and banged around the lamp, casting crazed shadows onto the wall.

"Probably won't sleep tonight at all." When he looked at her, she saw the deep rings under his eyes. His lean face was lined with stress and his dull skin emphasized the grayness of his hair. At fifty-five, her father looked a decade older when he was worried or tired.

"Anything I can do?" she asked. She was familiar with the Viljoen case. She had flown to the little town of Redcliff, north of Warmbaths, in a mosquito-sized airplane along with her father, to help him with the initial investigation.

The Viljoen brothers were farmers and right-wing extremists, desperate to fly the Afrikaner flag and overthrow the incipient threat of black empowerment. They had a history of violent treatment and intimidation of their African staff. One day, finding equipment missing from the shed, they had accused two of the workers at random and summarily fired them on the spot.

Poor and shabbily dressed, the workers spoke very little Afrikaans. But they understood enough to know that their jobs were in jeopardy. Using the unfamiliar language of their employers, they attempted to defend themselves in halting and trembling speech. All they wanted to do was explain. But their defense became their sentence. The burly farmers were outraged that anyone would dare to question their judgment, especially two lowly black workers.

The older Viljoen was a giant of a man with massive shoulders, a square beard and a mane of silver hair. His temper was legendary. He grabbed the offenders and bludgeoned them to the ground in a frenzy of rage. At first, his brother tried to stop him, but the older man shouted at him and hit him in the face with his rifle butt. Bleeding from the injury, the younger brother buckled down and helped him tie the workers' legs together and fasten the ropes to the truck.

Viljoen senior then drove across the property to the fenced-off series of ponds where the brothers were experimenting with their latest money-making scheme, crocodile farming.

Behind the truck, the men shouted in anguish as their bodies were ripped raw and their heads and chests battered by the stony road.

Their wives and children ran behind. The women screamed and begged, holding out their hands as they tried to keep pace with the cloud of dust and the dreadful thudding of the bodies in its center.

At the crocodile enclosure, the Viljoens pushed open the

gate that led to the biggest pond, the one where the adult breeders were kept. The three bulls and five females were sunning themselves on the opposite bank. Alerted by the noise of the gate, the crocodiles moved to the water's edge and launched themselves into its fetid depths.

Barking out instructions to his brother, Viljoen senior slashed through the ropes, and the two men dragged the workers, semiconscious and bleeding, through the gate and dumped them on a heavily stained concrete ledge. As the ripples grew larger and small waves began lapping against the edge of the pond, the brothers headed back outside and waited to see what was going to happen, rifles ready, just in case.

The biggest of the crocodiles reached the ledge first. It gave one of the weakly struggling workers an experimental shove and then clamped its jaws around a leg.

The pond was a churning mass of crimson by the time the families arrived, panicked and breathless, a couple of minutes later. One man had already been torn apart by four of the thrashing beasts. The other worker was trying to pull himself forward along the concrete ledge, clutching at the fence and screaming for help. But as the families watched, another leviathan surged out of the pond, tore him away from the metal rails and dragged him down under the water.

One of the wives ran forward, shrieking in anguish, her skirt flapping, to try and fight her way into the enclosure. She never reached the gate. The elder brother raised his rifle and shot her in the chest. She was dead before her husband finally drowned.

Before any whispers about this atrocity could reach surrounding farms, the Viljoen brothers fired all their workers, threatening them with a brutal fate if any of them dared to speak about what had happened. All the same, over time, word filtered out. Tracing and interviewing the witnesses was a lengthy process, because many of them were too terrified to say anything at all.

❀

Commissioner de Jong had never been worried about race, gender or any other factors that differentiated one suspect or witness from another. He was only concerned with the dogged pursuit of the truth. Gradually, his dour patience and kind manner reaped results and the Viljoen brothers were taken into custody and formally charged with murder.

But now there were problems with the case. Standing in their little house on that hot February night, Jade was troubled by her father's words.

"What problems?" He might not be allowed to tell her, but if she never asked, she'd never know.

"Sabotage. Two important reports are missing. Other evidence has also disappeared."

"Any suspects?" Jade pulled her T-shirt outwards to let some air circulate around her body. The house was stiflingly hot.

For a while, she didn't know if he was going to answer. Other than the persistent trilling of the crickets outside, there was only silence.

Then he shook his head. "I can't tell you, Jadey. It's confidential. One way or another, it's my job on the line. This is a high-profile case. If anything goes wrong, I take the fall and then I'm out. I've got to get the investigation back on track and prosecute the person responsible for the sabotage."

"Do you know who it is?"

"I'm pretty sure."

"Will you be able to fix it in time?"

"I'm preparing everything tonight. Jacobs is driving me to John Vorster Square police station early tomorrow. We'll meet the prosecutor. Finalize details. Implement damage control."

Jade knew Jacobs, the Redcliff chief of police. He'd spent a couple of weeks in Jo'burg, working on the case with her father, and she'd been forced into his company more often than she'd have preferred. He was a pudgy man with bronze skin, a man whose racist attitude was at odds, she felt, with the history behind his shock of tight, black, curly hair. He made Jade feel uneasy. She didn't like the way he watched her. And she didn't like the way he touched her when her father wasn't around, his big hands cupping the flesh of her arm or waist, hot and greasy against her skin.

"Can I do anything to help?" Jade repeated.

Her father smiled. "You can bring me another coffee."

Coffee made, she turned back to look at him as she closed her bedroom door. He was bent over his work again, the mug steaming on his desk. His leather briefcase, soft and worn from years of use, rested against his chair.

It was the last time she would see her father alive.

❖

"What happened to Daddy?" Jade asked. The hoarseness of her voice surprised her. She coughed and swallowed.

Robbie's reply was slow and deliberate. His eyes didn't leave her face.

"The next day, Daddy died in a car accident."

Jade's breath stalled in her chest. She stared at him wordlessly. Her heart hammered as memories came flooding back. She barely heard his next words.

"Mummy hired me," he said. "She's gone to England and she's not coming back. But she wants him dead. She's paid good money for it. Doesn't know I'd do something like that for free, as a favor to society." Robbie rubbed his hands together as he waited for the traffic light to change. "So. I'm asking you one last time. You in?"

16

As they drove through the dark streets, Robbie outlined his plan.

"Guy's name is Hirsch. Lives in one of these high-security housing estates," he told her. "They're going up like weeds in this area. Rich folk want to feel safe. Safe from poor people." He laughed. "Except this guy, he's different. He wants to keep away from all the folk who'd like to kill him."

"So what do we do?"

"We've been keeping an eye on him. This evening he's meeting his squeeze for a bit of fun. He'll be home around nine p.m. Now Hirsch has an armed security guard who rides with him during the day. But on nookie nights he comes home alone. Drives straight into his garage. Bulletproof glass in his car windows. There's only one chance we'll have to take him down."

"What's that?"

"When he swipes his card to get into the estate. He's got to roll his window down to do it. We take him then." Robbie glanced at the dashboard clock. It read 20.45.

As plans went, Jade thought this one sounded suicidal. She'd never heard anything so crazy in her life.

"He lives in a security estate? The entrance will be guarded, Robbie. There'll be armed personnel watching us."

"Yeah, that's true, babe. Two guards on duty at night. But they won't be there."

"Where will they be?"

"Responding to a call from a resident. Mrs. Chalmers, who lives in number ninety-six. All the way on the other side of the estate."

Robbie pulled over to the side of the road and handed her a cell phone. He pulled a black beanie onto his head and adjusted the pair of mirrored sunglasses he'd put on. "We'll call the guardhouse as soon as his car passes us. I suggest you sound frightened. Say there's a strange vehicle parked outside your house and you've just seen a man run into your garden holding a gun."

A sleek silver vehicle swept past them.

"That's him." Robbie put the car into gear. "Make the call and let's get going. We're only going to get one shot at doing this, I'm telling you now. We mess up and he sees us, we're dead meat."

Jade spoke with a tremor in her voice that wasn't put on for the benefit of the guards. She felt out of her depth, shocked by the sudden turn the evening had taken. She hadn't done this kind of job for ten years. Was Robbie even telling the truth? Or was she about to become an accomplice in the murder of an innocent man?

As soon as she hung up Robbie floored the accelerator and they sped after the silver car.

"We'll stop behind him, but not too close," he said. "As soon as I jump out, move into the driver's seat and get ready to turn and go."

The road was lined with security estates that sported grandiose names and ostentatious entrances. Robbie slowed as he approached a construction site. "MOUNTAIN VIEW VILLAS. LUXURY DWELLINGS, SECURE ENVIRONMENT," the gigantic sign read. The place was being built by a company called White & Co.

"That's the second phase in progress. Hirsch lives next door. In Mountain View Phase One. Here we are." Robbie turned into the wide paved driveway, lined with palm trees and clay flowerpots. The headlights swept the spiky shadows of leaves across their path. He flicked a knob on the dashboard and switched the lights off so they could approach in darkness. He steered with one hand, tearing at the nails of the other, his lips pulled back from his teeth. Watching him, Jade took a deep breath. She wasn't the only one who was nervous.

Robbie eased to a stop a few meters behind the silver car at the security boom. He tensed as the mirrored window started moving slowly downwards. The area was quiet. No cars leaving, none arriving. It was just themselves and Hirsch. The perfect situation for an ambush.

Quietly opening the door, he strolled over, the gun materializing in his hand as if by magic. Jade scooted across the contoured leather to the driver's seat. Cold air rushed in through the open door. She drew out her Glock and held it by her side.

The window of the silver vehicle was now fully down. She saw a black-sleeved arm emerge. Hirsch hadn't seen Robbie.

Robbie reached the car, crouched and sighted. She jumped as she heard the whiplash crack of the shot. He didn't move. He must be checking his target was down. Her gaze snapped back and forth across the area. Nobody behind them. No movement from the guardhouse.

Then the back door of Hirsch's vehicle flew open and she gasped as a gray-suited man leapt out and sprinted round towards Robbie, a large black pistol in his hand.

Jade scrambled out of the car in a breathless instant. Their intelligence had been wrong. The armed guard was traveling with the drug lord. For whatever crazy reason, Robbie hadn't seen the man in the backseat. If she didn't react in time, his life expectancy would be measured in seconds.

"Crap," Jade hissed. Now she would be forced to shoot an innocent man to save Robbie's life—if a drug lord's security detail could be considered innocent. At any rate, he wasn't the one who dealt in illegal substances. He hadn't given orders for a sixteen-year-old to die. And he wasn't trying to kill her.

Worst of all, from her dimly lit vantage point, she would have to shoot him in the back to be certain of hitting him.

Tension thrumming through her body, and hating herself for the cowardly crime she was about to commit, Jade sighted down the barrel of the Glock, watching the man's blond hair blow back from his pale face as he rounded the car. She saw Robbie's horror as he stumbled backwards, trying to straighten up from his crouched position, attempting to raise his own weapon. But he was too late and too slow.

Jade squeezed the trigger. Once, twice, three times. The gun bucked in her hands, the shattering explosions ringing in her ears. The impact of the bullets sent the man reeling forward and down, like a drunk being forcefully evicted from a bar on the wrong side of town. His arms fell to his sides and he folded to the ground. His fingers scrabbled weakly on the tarmac as if attempting to clutch onto life. Recovering fast, Robbie leapt up and fired another two shots into the fallen man's head.

Then she was back in the car, feeling the powerful engine roar as she prepared for the getaway. Robbie dived into the passenger seat and slammed the door. Jade accelerated away in a tight, fast turn.

Glancing behind, she saw two men running to the silver car. The security guards, she was sure. Back from their fictitious call-out. She headed back onto the quiet road, past the construction signs, her legs quivering and a terrible coldness in her heart.

Robbie was slumped onto the seat, panting.

"Shit. Thought I was dead meat there for a second. You saved my ass, babe. Keep driving. Nice and slow, like a good citizen. Turn right here, then left to the main road. We can blend in with the traffic. God, my heart is racing. That's the problem with these drug lord fuckers. They have instincts we don't even know about. Something must have told him to keep the guard working overtime tonight." He drew a deep breath and looked more closely at Jade. "Hey. You OK?"

Jade shook her head, blinking tears away. She wasn't okay. She felt like turning the Glock on herself. She'd killed a man who had no part to play in Robbie's client's revenge, who was loyally protecting his employer. She had stepped too far over the line now. She was a murderer, no better than Robbie. No better than Viljoen.

"I'm fine." Snapping out the words, she joined the main road.

"No, you're not. I can see you're upset. I'm sorry you had to get involved. But how was I to know that stupid guard was driving him home?"

Jade's foot slipped off the clutch and the car choked to a stop. She turned to Robbie, eyes wide.

"The security guard was driving?"

He gave a shaky laugh.

"Couldn't believe it when I checked the corpse and saw I'd shot some dwarf in a tuxedo. I couldn't see into the back. It was partitioned off with more of that damn tinted glass. Next thing I know I'm looking down the barrel of a Little Eagle. Nice piece. Wish I'd had time to grab it. Anyway, point is, you shot Hirsch. He was your kill." He fixed her with a steady gaze as she restarted the car. "I owe you a big one, Jade."

She drove on, checking the mirrors for blue flashing lights, listening for the sirens she was expecting at any moment. And feeling relief slowly dilute her terrible guilt.

Robbie laughed again, louder and slightly hysterical. He elbowed her in the side.

"You're so cute sometimes, babe, you know that? You get all upset because you think you shot somebody innocent. As if that guard wasn't scum like the rest of them. He's probably the guy who did all Hirsch's dirty work on his behalf."

Jade ignored Robbie's humor attack.

"I'll tell you how you can pay me back," she said. "Find out who's getting paid to quash cases. You brag about your connections. Find me the bent cop."

He looked at her, eyes glinting, teeth bared in a grin.

"Consider it done."

17

Jade's cell phone woke her at five the next morning. It was dark outside and she could hear the chirps of the earliest birds above the insistent buzzing of her phone. She squinted at the screen, impossibly bright to her sleepy eyes, and recognized the number. It was David calling.

"Got a murder victim here, Jadey," he said.

Jade turned on the bedside light, blinking as her vision adjusted to its glare. The events of the previous night seemed a lifetime away. Relieved she could focus on the case again, she ran through the list of possibilities.

"Dean Grobbelaar?"

"Well, we've still got to ID the body. But it matches his description. No shoes. A friend of Grobbelaar's called in a missing person report yesterday. That poor bugger is standing by, waiting to take a look for us. It's not a pretty sight, I'm told."

"What happened? Where is he?"

"Out of town. In a wildlife sanctuary a couple of hours' drive north of Jo'burg. I'm on my way to the scene now. Apparently he was tied to a tree and chopped up. With a panga or an axe, I'm guessing."

Jade's skin contracted into gooseflesh that had nothing to do with the temperature of the room. "That's a terrible way to die. That's just plain unnecessary."

David gave the ghost of a laugh. "Why not shoot him and have done with it, you mean?"

"Well, yes."

"I don't know, Jadey. But chopping somebody to death is brutal. Unnecessary, as you say."

"What do you want me to do, David?"

"I've got a forensic team checking out Dean's office. I don't know if they'll find anything except ashes and soot, but why don't you head over there and see if you can fill in the blanks?"

Jade hung up. She walked across to the bathroom and showered. By the time she'd finished the frosted glass in the window was glowing in the light of the rising sun and the birdsong was a cacophony.

She was on her way back to the bedroom, wrapped in her

towel, when she heard a distinctive rattle. The security gate was being opened from the outside.

She froze, thinking of shootings and stabbings and people who used axes to chop people to death. She didn't have her gun with her. It was still under the pillow. There was no time to run to the bedroom. The front door swung open and the alarm started beeping.

To Jade's astonishment, a domestic servant in a pink uniform and frilly apron strolled into the kitchen, humming to herself. She pressed the keypad and turned off the alarm. She turned back again, and saw Jade standing in the corridor.

"Good morning," she said, smiling broadly.

"Morning," Jade said. She was sure it would take a few hours for her heart rate to return to normal.

The maid started clattering dishes in the sink. Still coasting on a wave of adrenaline, Jade returned to her bedroom. She pulled on jeans and a black jersey and holstered her gun. Secure, private, safe cottage? Hah. Wait till she got hold of David.

On the way to Grobbelaar's office, Jade called the hospital to check on Yolandi. A doctor told her that she was conscious and recovering from her ordeal. "She has no memory of the break-in, I'm afraid," he told her. "Very common after this type of head injury. Her daughter is here with her now. Just arrived from Canada."

Jade was glad that Yolandi would recover, but sorry that she couldn't identify her attacker. She wondered whether she had been assaulted by the same thugs who'd torched Dean's office. Did the thugs have a real motive for their actions, she wondered, or were they just hired help, paid to carry out jobs that the boss preferred not to do?

❋

The little shopping center was a hive of activity when she arrived. A police car was idling in the parking area. A cop stood in the sun outside the shop, notebook in hand. He was talking to a store assistant whom Jade didn't recognize. She supposed this man had a genuine identity book. He had ditched his shop-keeping activities in favor of the more high-profile occupation of being interviewed by the police.

The east wing of the office block was scorched and destroyed. Grobbelaar's office had been gutted. She didn't know what the forensic team could possibly hope to find beyond the obvious evidence of arson.

Jade walked up the stairs, coughing as the foul smell caught in her throat. On the landing, she looked out and saw Grobbelaar's car. Once again, the old Toyota was covered in a layer of frost. It seemed to be sagging on its worn tires.

Two forensic officers in protective gear were combing through the room, stepping carefully over fallen beams and piles of ash. The wooden filing cabinet was gone, reduced to a heap of charcoal. She'd never know what had been in the drawer marked "Pending."

She greeted the officers. They didn't need any help and Jade started to feel guilty all over again.

"Can I check out his car for you?" she asked. It might not be constructive, but at least it would give her something to do. Save them some valuable time, perhaps, and make up for adding to the workload of the South African police service through her actions the night before. They agreed. Armed with a pair of rubber gloves and a plastic evidence bag, she set off.

As she walked down the stairs, Jade tried to picture the

scene that had taken place when Grobbelaar was abducted. He'd worked in his office on his own. He must have been grabbed after the store closed, when it was fully dark outside.

If Jade had wanted to snatch him, she would have done exactly what she thought his killer did. Waited till he was about to leave and then shoved a gun into his face as he was stepping out of the office. She recalled the position of the shoes. Ready to go.

She was sure it would have taken two people to do this job. She didn't think Grobbelaar would have submitted to a lone attacker. He worked in a tough industry, probably had some kind of police or military background. Like the shaven-headed ex-cop friend of her father's who ran specialist courses in self-defense and bodyguarding and had given her an intensive month's tuition before she'd taken her first job.

"Never allow yourself to be forced into a vehicle," Jade remembered the hard-muscled man saying. "The best time to fight is before they take you away, so make the most of it. Fight dirty. Scream to draw attention to yourself. Whatever the hell you do, however poor the odds of success seem, they're almost always going to be better than when the bad guys drag you out again after the ride."

Physically, she imagined Grobbelaar had looked a lot like her self-defense instructor. So why had he given in to his kidnapper? Jade didn't know. She could only assume he'd been outnumbered and surprised. In which case, it was likely that his attackers also had a police or military background.

She remembered Annette's bullet wounds. Accurate, effective, placed to kill. Her shooter had skill and discipline. The same skill and discipline, perhaps, that had allowed someone to tie up, gag and disarm a big, tough private detective without a struggle.

So, one person to keep the gun trained on him. Another to remove his shoes. Or perhaps they'd told him to take them off himself. Then they'd secured his hands behind him. Forced the sock into his mouth to prevent Grobbelaar from drawing any unwanted attention.

Grabbed his laptop, leaving the power cable. Taken his cell phone. He would have been barefoot, so he couldn't do any damage with his feet. Not to them, or to whatever vehicle they took him away in. Then a quick march out of the door, down to the car. Into the back. Game over.

The private car park on the other side of the building was accessed through a metal door behind the stairwell. It was locked and Jade had to ask the shopkeeper for a key. The door clanged as she opened it. She walked in.

Here there was a security system of sorts in place. It was guarded by a fence and a gate, both topped with coils of razor wire. The gate was padlocked from the inside.

So, the people who'd taken Grobbelaar for a long ride in their car hadn't been able to access his vehicle. Or hadn't needed to.

She walked over to look at the Toyota. The frost on the windows had melted in places and she could make out the car's interior. A dusty dashboard. Cracked leather seats. She was sure it would have been about as comfortable as a broken armchair.

There were two beige folders on the passenger seat. They looked just like the others she had seen in the filing cabinet upstairs. Jade leaned forward, the icy glass pressing against her nose, and held her breath so it wouldn't steam up the window as she tried to get a closer look.

The top file had spidery writing scribbled on the edge. "Botha."

Bingo.

Jade felt her heart start to pound with the familiar excitement of the chase. She straightened up and tried the car door. To her surprise it opened, creaking on unwilling hinges. Grobbelaar had obviously felt his car was adequately secured behind the razor wire and metal gate. Inside the car smelled musty, of old dust and cigarette smoke. There wasn't even a radio. No wonder he didn't bother to lock it. She reached across to the passenger seat and removed the file.

It was a thin folder. Thinner than Annette's case file. There were only three pieces of paper inside.

The first was a printout of an e-mail written by Annette. It was short and to the point. "Dear Mr. Grobbelaar. Further to our phone call, I would like you to trace a woman called Ellie Myers. All I know is that in 1999, she lived in Bryanston and was married to a man called Mark. Please forward me your payment details and let me know when I can expect information. Many thanks, Annette Botha."

This page was clipped to one of Grobbelaar's ubiquitous client sheets. He had scribbled a couple of notes on it, but refrained from adding any lewd drawings.

The final page was a printout that looked as if it had been copied from an old voters' roll. It contained a list of names, identity numbers and addresses, sorted by surname. Near the top, a strip of pink highlighter wavered across an entry labelled Myers, Eleanor R. Her identity number and address followed. 48 Forest Road, Bryanston, Johannesburg. Just below her entry was another slash of pink. This one illuminated the name of Myers, Mark J. He was a few years older than Eleanor and his address was the same. It looked as if Grobbelaar hadn't closed this file yet. But at least Jade had something now. She had a place to start.

Grobbelaar's burnt-out office was a world away from the tree-lined streets of Bryanston. As she drove north of Jo'burg, the highway became more crowded, the cars bigger and more expensive and the drivers increasingly aggressive. It took her more than half an hour to reach the exact place she wanted. She had to make a few extra turns and retrace her steps because part of the suburb had been barriered off and turned into a security-controlled area. By the time she'd found the correct street, Jade was cursing the rich.

This part of Bryanston was where the old money lived. The houses were graceful—what she could see of them, because they were set back from the road behind high walls, in treed gardens, with ivy covering the gateposts. Most of the houses had triple-stranded electric fencing on the tops of their moss-covered walls, a new addition. Others went a step further, with security cameras placed at intervals, and a guardhouse at the entrance. She wondered who lived behind those walls and how much it cost them every month to maintain their security systems.

Forest Road was lined with old oak trees whose branches met overhead. Jade drove through the tunnel of dappled shade looking for number 48.

It wasn't there. She saw a number 46, and after it, a high Tuscan-style wall also topped with electric fencing. In contrast to the others along the road, this wall looked new.

A guardhouse separated two massive gates. Problem was, the gates led into a large cluster complex. It was called Oak

Grove, which was ironic seeing as the builders must have cut down the oak tree outside it in order to make room for the enormous gateposts that encroached onto the wide grassy verge. On the opposite side of the street, the last lonely oak stretched its branches across into naked sunshine.

Jade checked the piece of paper again. There hadn't been any mention of a cluster home.

She parked in the shade of the lone tree and walked over to the guardhouse. A tinted window slid open and a uniformed guard appeared.

"Can I help you?" he asked.

"I'm looking for an Eleanor Myers. She lives here." Jade looked at the expanse of tiled roofs that stretched into the distance, like an artificial mountain range, on the other side of the wall. "Somewhere," she added.

The guard consulted a clipboard, turned a page, and frowned. He moved across to the other side of the room and looked through a printed register. Jade watched him through the open window. Then, the entrance gates swung open and a white Jeep drove into the complex. She caught a glimpse of immaculate paving, low-fenced gardens and double-story houses. As the entrance gates closed, the exit gates swung open and a yellow Porsche drove out.

The guard returned to the window.

"I'm sorry, madam. We do not have an Ellie Myers on our list. Or an Eleanor. Do you know what number she's in?"

"No, I don't. Do you have a Mark Myers living there?"

He consulted the list again. "Nobody of that name either."

Jade looked up at him. She was beginning to feel out of place, standing there getting more negative responses than someone selling encyclopedias. Another car drove out of the gates. A Land Rover. The woman driving glanced suspiciously at Jade. What was she doing, distracting security like that?

"How many houses are in here?" she called up to the guard.

"Thirty-three."

Jade sighed. It would take her a week to ask thirty-three different people if they knew Ellie. "Is there an admin office I could phone?"

He passed down a business card to her.

"Thank you," she said.

"It's a pleasure." He slid the window closed and the sun flashed off the tinted glass.

She phoned the office while she was sitting in the car. It was warmer than her cottage. Perhaps she could rent a space under the oak tree and bring the case file along here every day.

A woman answered on the third ring. She sounded brisk and efficient, and Jade found herself wondering whether Annette would have had a similar telephone manner.

She introduced herself and explained that she was assisting the police with an investigation.

"I'm glad someone is," the woman said. "It seems to me they need all the help they can get."

"I'm trying to trace an Eleanor Myers. She lives at Oak Grove. Or did. Perhaps she sold up and moved away."

Jade heard the tapping of computer keys. She cranked her seat back and stretched her legs forward, jiggling the clutch pedal with her foot.

"No, dear. She's not on our current system, and we've had very few people move on. This estate is new, you see."

"And before that? Who did the land belong to?"

"It would have been a free-standing house, like all the others.

Let me see if I can make a phone call for you and find out. Can you hold on for me, dear, or would you like to call back?"

"I'll hold, thanks." Jade revised her ideas about the woman's similarity to Annette. From what she had heard of her, she couldn't imagine Annette calling anybody "dear."

She listened to the one-sided conversation. This was going to cost her in airtime. She hoped the results would be worth it.

Eventually the woman came back on the line. She sounded resigned.

"I'm sorry, dear. I've done my best, but we don't have anything that I can put my hands on right now for you. We only took over the administration of the estate when the units were fully sold, so we don't have access to previous records. But I'll keep my eyes open for you, and ask around," she said, as if Jade had all the time in the world.

For the sake of thoroughness, Jade walked down the road, ringing doorbells and shouting into crackly intercom systems. Perhaps a neighbor would know what had happened to Ellie Myers. But none of the residents were willing to come out from the safety of their secluded houses. At all of the homes whose bells she rang, the domestic servant claimed that the madam was not home. After the sixth attempt, she called it a day. She phoned David but he didn't answer, so she left a frustrated message for him.

On her way home, she stopped at a center called Country Lane. She'd passed it on the way out and thought it looked like a good spot for lunch. The shops had twee wrought iron signs and big green awnings. She walked along the pavement in their shade. She passed a travel shop and a saddlers, a gift shop and a place that sold tie-dyed hippie-style clothing. Across the way she could see a second-hand books and music store. Jade thought it would be a fun place to spend a relaxing couple of hours on a weekend. So far, since she'd been in South Africa, she hadn't had a relaxing couple of hours. Or a weekend, because she'd been working every day.

Viljoen would be released tomorrow. She might not have a weekend in the country at all, if things went wrong. If they went seriously wrong, she might never see a weekend again. Did Viljoen know she was back? Who were his contacts? Who had been watching her?

As she sat down at a restaurant called The Coffee Bean, she heard somebody call out a friendly hello. Graham Hope, the estate agent she'd met at Piet's house, was powering towards her on his crutches.

"Well, fancy meeting you here. I was going to grab a bite and then go and see my specialist for some therapy on this wretched knee." He looked hopefully at the empty chair opposite Jade.

"Have a seat," Jade said.

"You're sure you don't mind?"

"Not at all," she lied. She was preoccupied with finding Ellie Myers and annoyed with her lack of progress on the case. Her father had never been good company when he was bogged down in an investigation, and Jade realized she had inherited this trait. She wanted to eat in brooding silence and then go home and bang her head against the wall until a new theory fell out. She sighed. Perhaps the company would do her good.

Graham's crutches clattered to the ground as he carefully lowered himself into the chair opposite. "Dammit," he said.

"You can't believe how unwieldy these things are. I can't wait till this cast comes off."

Jade ordered a mug of house blend, and a tuna salad. Graham opted for a cappuccino and a bacon omelette.

"So what have you been up to?" he asked.

Jade gave him a brief, carefully edited summary of the last couple of days.

"The detective disappeared?" Graham's blue eyes widened. Jade wondered whether he was really concerned about property prices in northern Jo'burg, or whether he was a gossip who loved to hear bad news firsthand. If so, had his arrival here been a lucky coincidence? Or had he been following her, looking for a chance to hear more?

"That's right." She wasn't going to tell him that Grobbelaar had almost certainly been murdered. She didn't want to trigger a selling frenzy among his distressed clients.

"You deal with this kind of situation every day? Missing people, dead bodies, murder suspects?"

"Yes."

Graham bit his lip. "Don't you find it affects you at some level?"

Jade shrugged. "I'm sure it does. But I'm used to it. My father was a police detective. When I was little, there'd always be somebody on the phone when he was at home, discussing a case. I grew up hearing him ask where the body was, what evidence to look for."

"Now that's an unusual upbringing. And your mother? Where was she during all this?"

Jade looked away. "I never knew my mother."

Graham frowned. "Why?"

"She died when I was very young. When we lived in Richard's Bay."

"Yes, I know it. Beautiful place."

Jade didn't remember it. She'd been too young. She'd never been back and her father had never talked about it. He said the place had too many bad memories and it was best forgotten.

"It's on the edge of the malaria belt. There was a very wet summer the year I was born, and they had an outbreak in the town. She got cerebral malaria and fell into a coma. She died the same day, Dad said."

"Goodness. How dreadful." Graham stirred sugar into his coffee.

"She chose my name, though. It was the stone in her engagement ring. Dad couldn't afford anything more expensive. Diamonds have to be set in gold, and a ring like that was way beyond his pay grade. So he bought her a piece of jade set in silver."

"That's a lovely story. I thought you were named for the color of your eyes. I suppose that was just a lucky coincidence. Did you inherit the ring?"

She smiled. "It's still with my mother. Dad decided to leave it on her ring finger."

Graham put his cup down, reached across the table and squeezed her hand. Jade was conscious of the softness of his skin and the heat radiating from his palm. Was it a gesture of comfort? Or something else? He'd mentioned a wife last time they'd spoken and she'd seen the glint of gold on the third finger of his left hand. He was married. She hoped he was simply trying to be kind.

His touch didn't comfort her. It made her feel lonely, made her wonder how David's hand would feel if he did the same to her. Probably, his long fingers would be calloused and hard from years of handling a gun. And how would it make her feel if he touched her like that one day?

Graham withdrew his hand as the waitress arrived with their food.

She'd also brought a wire basket with four hot sauces in bottles ranging in color from pale green to deep fiery orange. Jade chose the orange bottle and poured a pool of the sauce on her plate. She speared a sliver of tuna with her fork and dunked it in the hot sauce. Graham watched her in amazement.

"You're not going to put that in your mouth, are you? That's Bandito's Habanero Sauce. It's the hottest one they make. You see that little white label on the side of the bottle? That's the heat strength indicator. Ten out of ten."

"Where else would I put it?" Jade chewed and swallowed.

Graham produced a handkerchief from his pocket and wiped his forehead. He laughed in disbelief.

"Just watching you do that makes me feel sweaty. How on earth can you stomach food that hot?"

She shrugged. "It's hereditary, I suppose. My dad used to eat fresh chilis with every meal. He'd hold them by the stem and bite into them as if they were fruit. He always maintained fiery food kept you healthy."

Jade cut a slice of tomato. Graham Hope was surprisingly easy to talk to. She'd have to watch herself. She didn't want to be charmed into accidentally giving away any unnecessary details of the case.

Graham stared at Jade as she swiped the tomato through the hot sauce.

"Each to their own, I suppose. Anyway, I was thinking about Annette." He forked a piece of bacon into his mouth.

"What were you thinking?"

"I had a client years ago. A wealthy woman. She would have been even richer, except her husband had a gambling problem. Her ex-husband to be more accurate, because she eventually divorced him."

"And what happened?"

"She was hijacked. The robbers took her along with them in the car and shot her later. The police found out, in due course, that the husband had taken out a one million rand life insurance policy in her name a year previously. Just before the divorce went through. The hijacking was arranged. He'd hired a gang to do it."

The waitress was hovering. Jade ordered a bottle of water.

"You're implying that Piet might have something to do with Annette's death."

"No, no. I'm not implying anything."

"Piet is under investigation, as he told you. Spouses, or ex-spouses, always are. They'll find out whether any policies were taken out in his wife's name. And check his bank records. Look for any suspicious transactions." Jade dotted more habanero sauce onto her lettuce. "Hired killers charge nice big, round numbers for their jobs. So people generally pay them in nice big, round amounts. That's what the police look for." She put the lid on the bottle and replaced it in the wire rack. "In any case, Annette didn't use the detective to investigate her husband. She was trying to trace a woman."

"Good heavens." Graham shook his head. "Well, if I ever hire a killer, I'll be sure to add on a few odd rands and cents to his price, to avoid suspicion." He glanced at her. "I'm joking, of course. But I am serious about Piet. I'm an excellent judge of character, Jade. Be careful of him. There's something about that man I don't trust."

18

David stared at the form slumped against the tree. The face was blackened with trapped blood, the puffy flesh swollen into a bloated mockery of human features that bulged over the brown packaging tape that covered his mouth. A brownish-red stain had discolored the inside of the tape. One lifeless eye stared sightlessly ahead. The other had been plucked out, leaving an empty red socket and a smear of blood on the swollen cheekbone below.

Around him, the team bustled back and forth. The pathologist had arrived and was unpacking his gear.

The game ranger stood next to David.

"Vultures," he said, pointing to the empty socket. "That's how we found him. Saw a whole bunch of them circling over the trees, so we came along to take a look."

He was a lean, bearded man with a rifle slung over his shoulder. He was looking at the body, whistling softly, with an expression on his face that David supposed was meant to convey that, out here in the bush, he'd seen it all before.

Normally such a display of unfeeling machismo would have irritated David. Right now, however, he was relieved that there was a local who could stand the sight without throwing up.

Grobbelaar was hanging from two cable ties buried in his neck. They had cut a groove into the tough bark of the tree trunk. Despite what must have been violent struggles, they hadn't snapped. Looking at his corpse, David hoped that his efforts to escape had caused him to lose consciousness, sparing him the worst of the torture inflicted on him.

His body was covered in a blue-black mantle of flies, some of them as big as David's thumbnail. Their hysterical buzzing drowned out the trill of the cicadas and the rustling of leaves in the wind. The air was tainted with a raw coppery tang. The smell of blood, with undertones of rot.

He couldn't tell where the first heavy blow had landed, or how many there had been. Grobbelaar's flesh was a mass of gaping wounds, encrusted with blood and surrounded by bloodied, tattered clothing. David could see splintered bone and torn muscle. Intestines spilled from the gashes in his stomach and ended in a half-chewed mass. Had vultures done this work, too? Or hyenas, or wild dogs?

Grobbelaar's knees had buckled over the set of cable ties fastening his ankles to the tree. Half-hidden in the leaves, his bare feet were swollen, the flesh mottled purple where it showed through the dried streaks of blood.

The ground was swarming with ants.

The ranger moved away from the body and stamped his boots on the dirt.

"It's what we always tell clients. Man is the most evil predator there is. Lions, leopards, crocs, even our wild dogs, none of them would kill like this. They kill to eat."

David nodded in agreement.

"When did you find him?"

"Just before we called you. Normally the sight of vultures wouldn't worry us. We'd have thought the wild dogs had made a kill, and left it at that. We breed them here, you see. But one of the workers' children on the farm next door wandered off into the bush a couple of days ago. We've been keeping an eye out for her. To be honest I was ninety-nine percent sure we were going to find the child's body here. I almost phoned the owner before we came out, to give him a heads-up."

"Is your reserve electric-fenced? How could this man have been brought in here without you noticing?"

The man shrugged. "We've got one section inside electric fencing. That's where the chalets are, where the guests stay. We don't want anything getting in there and making trouble. Guards at the gate, twenty-four hours." He spread his hands. "For the rest, we've just got normal fencing. Six-foot diamond mesh, with a couple of barbed strands on top. It's enough to keep the dogs in and the buck hardly ever jump out."

"I need to check the perimeter. Somewhere near here, I'm betting you've got a section of broken fence."

The game ranger squatted down and scanned the surrounding area. David waited and watched as he leaned forward, focusing on a point nearby. Then he straightened up again.

"If I'm right, I can take you straight to it. See between those two trees? Looks like the ground cover's been disturbed. Let's go check it out."

David couldn't see what the game ranger had noticed. But he followed him, leaves rustling around his feet, the yellow crime-scene tape surrounding the area flapping in the breeze as he lifted it and they stepped underneath.

They walked over a gentle rise in the ground. On the other side, David could see leaves crushed into the hard ground. A car had parked here.

The ranger whistled again. "So they drove in."

He turned to follow the tracks, walking alongside them and peering down at the dirt.

"Ground's so hard I can't see any tire treads."

David walked alongside him. The tracks curved round the contour of a hill. Grass sprouted in their center, but they were flattened, stony and dry.

"This looks like an old road," David observed.

The game ranger nodded apologetically. "I'm sure it doesn't help you, but it is a road. We recently bought this land from Sappi. You know, the paper manufacturers. That's why there's so little ground cover. No bushes, no shrubs. And tracks like this all over the place, where the logging trucks drove in and out."

"So they followed a logging track."

"Not difficult to do."

"Bloody hell."

They went down the hill. Now David could hear the noise of traffic and see the glint of the sun on wire. The fence was stretched between solid metal posts. The tracks ran under the wire and down to the road.

"Fence is still there," muttered the game ranger.

They walked closer. The fence had been cut, each section sliced through, and then neatly repaired. Shiny new loops connected the broken ends.

"They came in and they went out," David said. He looked at the earth by the side of the road where the car had driven away. Dry, hard, unforgiving. Winter terrain. The ranger was right. He doubted forensics would be able to get a tire imprint.

"Summertime, these woods can become a wetland," the ranger said, echoing his thoughts. "Deep with mud. They'd have left tracks everywhere. This time of year is bad luck for you."

Bad luck. That was one way of putting it.

Where was the weapon that had butchered the body? David stared around him. An axe, most likely. He didn't think a panga would have inflicted such deep, heavy blows. The weapon hadn't been left at the scene of the crime. It could be anywhere. It could have been thrown away, far out into the leafy forest. It could have been disposed of back in the city, in a dumpster. Or it could be wrapped in plastic, festering in the tire well of a car somewhere. He'd tell his team to comb the area anyway. It was a small chance, but their only one so far. If they could find the axe, it might lead them to the murderer.

19

Whiteboy ran his hand through his hair and considered his options. He was an excellent chess player. Given his other skills, his acquaintances often found this surprising. Incongruous. Like a street vendor who could quote Shakespeare, or a footballer who was also a gourmet chef.

He understood why. What he did, what he specialized in, were brash, bold acts of extreme violence. When people saw the results, they found it difficult to believe that there was any intelligence or premeditation behind them. They were wrong—the acts were always the result of meticulous planning. Like chess, which was all about planning and strategy and forward-thinking.

To be safe, Whiteboy believed in keeping at least three moves ahead.

He sat in his home office (a term which always amused him), thinking about his next move. His desk had a laptop computer on its polished surface and a plasma-screen TV was mounted on the wall nearby. Both of these were mere distractions from his work. Distraction always allowed him to focus better.

At present, he was flicking idly between his favorite porn sites, watching some real-time action. The play of flesh on flesh and the lure of hot, inviting orifices amused him. It showed what money could do. He didn't think for a moment that any of the girls who smiled for the camera while spreading their legs to accommodate outsized cocks actually did it for enjoyment. They did it for the cash.

He clicked on another site. Yes, money made the world go round. It smoothed the way forward. In his opinion, you could never have enough of it.

Whiteboy continued to ponder his next move. When his cell phone rang, interrupting his thoughts, he experienced a moment of irritation. Then he saw who it was. He took his finger off the mouse and stood up. Even though he checked his office frequently for listening devices and changed phone cards as often as he changed his underwear, he still wouldn't risk having a sensitive exchange in an enclosed area. Old habits died hard. He heaved himself out of his leather chair and strode out into the garden, where the rushing sound of the fountain cascading onto the marble stones below would shield his conversation from any eavesdroppers.

"Hey," said his contact.

"What's up?"

"I've spoken to 83 Rivonia Road."

"Great." Whiteboy had seen photos of the sprawling mansion situated on grounds that still managed to be spacious. A brilliant, unbeatable location. The plush hotels and tinted-glass office blocks of Sandton were five minutes away and development was spreading down Rivonia Road faster than floodwater down a culvert.

He had plans for that location. Big plans. Starting with demolishing the house. Those lovely stone blocks wouldn't be wasted. He could use them somewhere else. But that area was all about office space right now. People were begging for work premises on Rivonia Road at any price. He had plans for a mixed-use development. Four office parks with a central shopping area and a gym. All surrounded by security so tight and fierce it would make Alcatraz look open-plan.

"Who?"

"The husband."

"If he's out of the way it'll go through sweet?" Whiteboy trusted his contact's judgment. His information was always accurate and his skills were unique. Since he'd joined Whiteboy a few years back, every operation had been laughably smooth. Like checkmating your dumbfounded opponent in just two moves. Fool's mate, as it was called.

"Yup. He doesn't want to sell, but she'll sign. And she's not greedy."

"Any idea when?"

"He told me he works late fairly often. 'Specially near the end of the month."

"That'd do it."

"I'll keep an eye on him."

"I'll wait for your call." Whiteboy paused. "Any news on our other friends?" He was confident his contact would know what he was talking about. They'd always understood each other well. Back in the army days, they'd worked together a couple of times. And in the last few years they'd become a close team again.

His contact laughed. "I'm keeping them under surveillance. So far they're still a few steps behind on the wrong track."

"Keep watching. And stay awake. We can't afford our plan to fail. The detective's good, I hear. And the girl's father was good, too."

He knew about the girl's father. His contact did, too. They'd both been told.

"Don't worry. I won't get careless."

Whiteboy looked down into the bowl of the fountain. He could see his reflection. A pale, heavy face and dark phone, dancing in a hundred wavelets.

"You'd better not. I got involved with this operation as a favor to you, remember. And now I'm saving your butt. Again."

"I know."

"I don't want this to be the one that brings us down. I don't want to have to run yet."

"Nor do I." His contact sounded subdued.

"Good. Later, then."

Whiteboy disconnected and looked down at the splashing water.

"You'll be my brave boy, won't you? My brave little man," said a voice in his head.

He shivered at this, unexpectedly remembering the way the bath had smelled when he was a boy, a faint chemical soapy odor. The way hot water smelled stronger than cold water did and very hot water smelled the worst of all. He still thought he could tell its exact temperature by smell alone. Before his face touched the water in the basin, before his mother's relentless hand on the back of his infant neck had forced him into the steaming, suffocating depths, where he'd bitten his tongue and held his breath, feeling his face swelling and scalding and searing jets rush up his nose, doing his best not to struggle.

Because struggling made it worse. That was what he always told his victims, when he had a chance to tell them anything at all. Struggling makes it worse. Mommy knows.

He stared at the water, mesmerized by its dancing surfaces, almost unable to tear himself away. Then he realized he was clenching his jaws together so tightly his teeth hurt. For an unthinkable moment, he'd been a child again, carrying his schoolbag up the front steps of that claustrophobic little house where his mother waited.

❂

It was the uncertainty that was the worst. Sometimes she would be sitting in the wing-backed chair in the lounge, with the radio on and sandwiches waiting for him on a plastic plate, the brown bread topped with a thin scraping of Bovril or Anchovette. But other times, she'd be in an angry state. That was what she called it, "an angry state," although the words didn't come close to describing the destructive spectrum of his mother's uncontrollable fury. And when he walked through the door and saw her chair was empty, and heard the shatter of glass in the kitchen or the thudding of objects in the bedroom, or worse still, the splashing of water in the bathroom as she filled the steaming tub ready for his return, his schoolbag would fall to the ground and he'd be immobilized by terror.

When his mother was in an angry state, she had to take it out on somebody. That was what she always told him. And because there was nobody else, she took it out on him.

When he was about eleven years old, she made one of her infrequent appearances at a parent-teacher meeting. The next day, one of the boys from a class two years above him joined him for part of the walk home along a quiet stretch of road bordering a park. Whiteboy didn't speak to him. He never spoke to anybody if he could help it. But the boy said hello and greeted him by his universal nickname, which he'd been given on his very first day of school on account of his pale, pasty skin. "Hello, Whiteboy," he said, and introduced himself as Eddie, in a friendly tone that belied his next words.

"My dad knows your mom," he said.

Apprehensive, Whiteboy glanced up at the bigger boy but said nothing.

He continued. "She used to work at my dad's company a long time ago, but he fired her. He told me last night your mom is mad. She was put into an asylum because she went crazy one day and almost killed the lady she worked with."

Whiteboy turned away and increased his speed, hurrying along as fast as his chunky legs could carry him. But Eddie kept pace with him. He grabbed his shoulder and Whiteboy stifled a scream, because he'd clamped his fingers directly over the blistering welt that his mother had left there two nights ago when she'd pressed a hot iron against his skin and held the instrument there for an endless moment of agony, watching his flesh redden and burn, her teeth gritted and her eyes bulging with rage.

Grinning, Eddie released him. "You worried?"

Whiteboy shook his head, breathing hard.

The older boy looked puzzled at this lack of reaction.

"You should be," he said. "When the whole school knows about it, you will be. Because I'll tell everyone. You don't want that, do you? Nobody will ever speak to you again if they find out your mom's an insane bitch. You won't have any friends left."

Finally, Whiteboy spoke. "Don't," he said.

Eddie grinned again, triumphantly.

"I won't say anything if you go to Carlo's café now, and buy us two bottles of Coke. One for me, one for my little brother." He jerked his thumb at the small tow-haired boy lagging a short distance behind, smiling in exactly the same manner.

"Anything else?" Eddie asked his brother.

"Sweets," the younger boy replied. "Make him get some sweets."

Whiteboy looked up at him.

"I've got no money."

Eddie shrugged. "Then steal them. And bring them to my house later." He turned away and walked back to his brother, shepherding him protectively down the road where they lived.

That afternoon, Whiteboy stole the Cokes and the sweets, but because he was late home his sandwiches were hard and curling at the corners. And his mother was in a mild state and made him suffer for it. The next day, after another consultation with his brother, his tormentor demanded biltong, licorice and chewing gum for two delivered to their front door on his knees. He complied and sprinted home so he wouldn't be late, arriving sweaty, panting and distressed. Whiteboy knew he couldn't do this for much longer. For one thing, Carlo was starting to look at him suspiciously when he walked into the shop. For another, he was starting to feel an unfamiliar emotion—a white-hot, overriding compulsion that he'd never experienced before. The best way he could describe it was to think of his mother's words. "An angry state." That's what he was feeling. An angry state. Because he was being blackmailed, because he was getting screwed.

The older boy was too big and strong. He knew he couldn't overpower him, but, thinking things over, he realized Eddie's little brother was smaller, and weaker. And Eddie loved his little brother. That was clear.

The following day, Whiteboy discovered that Eddie had soccer practice after school and his younger brother was walking home on his own.

Whiteboy waited for him behind a wall opposite the park, and when the boy appeared he grabbed him by his fine blond hair and pulled him across the road, jamming a wad of toilet paper into his mouth so he couldn't scream. Behind a stand of bushes, he did his work. He was desperate and terrified and his actions lacked finesse—something that would come later, with practice. But, thanks to his mother, he knew how to inflict pain without leaving an obvious mark.

He kept the boy there for a while, because he didn't know how long it would take for him to learn his lesson well. After an hour, he stopped. He was getting bored. The little boy had thrown up twice, splattering wads of cheap bog-roll onto the short grass. He was crying and drooling and trembling all over, his skin was sickly gray, and he wouldn't meet Whiteboy's eyes.

"What will you say?" Whiteboy asked again. "Tell me."

The boy sniffed, and retched again. "I say he's been unfair to you and he must stop now and pay you back for all the things you stole or I'll never speak to him again and I'll tell Dad what he's done."

Whiteboy smiled, and another unfamiliar sensation swept over him. A warm, good, powerful one.

"And what do you do if he asks you whether I told you to say that?"

"I say no," the boy cried, choking on his snot, clawing at the grass with his hands. "I say no. Please don't hurt me any more. I say no."

❖

Whiteboy turned away from the fountain, grimacing. He didn't like it at all. He would have filled it in when he bought the place, except it was useful for camouflaging sound. The damn thing gave him the shivers the rest of the time.

❖

Jade took a winding route through the city and into the back streets of Turffontein to the area where she and her father had lived. She hadn't been back there since she arrived in South Africa. But tomorrow was Viljoen's release. Now was as good a time as any to revisit her past.

The neighborhood looked familiar. Small face-brick houses, tiny gardens, aging vehicles resting on withered grass or under makeshift corrugated iron carports. People in Turffontein couldn't afford security fences or high walls like the rich folk in northern Jo'burg. They had to make do with cheap burglar bars welded to their window frames and chains to hold their rickety gates closed.

David's old house looked more respectable than she remembered. It was neat and trim, freshly painted. As she cruised past, a car pulled into the driveway. A dark-haired woman in a crimson jacket climbed out and opened the gate.

A small boy jumped out of the car and raced through before she could stop him. Jade smiled as she heard the mother's loud admonishments. She continued to the end of the road, turned right and then right again into the road where she had lived.

Her house still looked the same, except the front wall had been repainted a hideous mustard yellow. The cracked tiles on the path were still there, and the red front porch hadn't faded. The garden was still a withered jungle. This house resisted all attempts to groom its surroundings. God knows, her father had tried hard enough during his rare free time.

An old woman cocooned in a long brown coat was sitting in a cane rocking chair on the porch. In the afternoons, Jade knew, the porch was a suntrap. It was the only place in the house where it was possible to be comfortable in winter.

The white-haired lady turned and stared at her car. She looked at least eighty, and, from her face, Jade thought she must have spent the last fifty years smelling something bad. Then she turned back towards the front door and called out. Jade saw the flicker of a television set through the front window. Somebody was inside, glued to whatever the local channels had to offer. When she was young, few people in her area had been able to afford a television. Although TV had become a household essential, she was sure that most Turffontein residents were still a step behind as she couldn't see any satellite dishes.

A blond teenager slouched outside. She sported a blank expression and headphones in her ears. Her short green jacket exposed a pale and flabby midriff.

The old lady had called for backup.

Jade climbed out of the car and walked to the gate.

"Hi there." She waved, trying to look friendly and unthreatening.

The old lady glowered. The teenager walked down the steps with a somnolent slowness and strolled down the broken path.

"My ouma says what do you want," she said. Her accent was thick with the inflections typical of southern Jo'burg.

"I used to live here. I just wanted to see the old place."

"She used to live here, Ouma," the girl yelled.

The lady shouted something back in Afrikaans, which had never been Jade's strong point. While she was still trying to work out what it meant, the teenager helpfully translated.

"My ouma says you don't live here any more and you must go away."

Jade bristled.

"Well, you can tell her thanks very much for her politeness."

The teenager looked embarrassed.

"Sorry," she said. "She's an old bat. I can't let you in. She calls the police for all the strangers she sees."

"Not a problem," said Jade. "Thanks for your help. I don't need to come in."

She crossed the road again and watched the house from a distance before she braved the traffic-clogged drive home. Her bedroom had been on the corner. She could see the sash window where she'd escaped on the night he came for her. Perhaps this teenager used it to sneak out at night and go and meet her boyfriends at the neighborhood pub. Did places hold memories? If they did, Jade wondered whether the teenager had ever felt a trace of residual fear, an unwelcome shiver down her spine as she swung her legs over the ledge and dropped down to the tangled flower bed below.

Jade had only been home a few minutes when she saw the flash of headlights and heard honking. She looked anxiously out of the window, wondering if it was Robbie, with another gig lined up. To her relief, the man outside the gate was David.

There wasn't time to take the gun off her holster, so she pushed it round to the back as far as she could. She didn't want David to know she was carrying. He'd have plenty of questions about where, and why, she had obtained her weapon. Questions she couldn't answer. She fastened her jacket and walked outside. He was speaking to somebody in the car.

"Jade," he called. "Come on over."

He turned back to the car, a silver Jeep Cherokee. Commissioner Williams was at the wheel.

Perched on the high leather seat, he didn't look as short as Jade remembered. But he was rounder than he had been ten years ago and he had given up the battle with concealing his hair loss—or perhaps the bald spot had spread to a size where he simply couldn't comb his hair over it any more. At any rate, his hair was now trimmed in a short horseshoe shape around his pate, which shone under the overhead light of the car.

"Jade." He smiled, stubby teeth peeking out through his mustache.

"Good to see you again, Commissioner."

The last time she'd seen him had been at her father's funeral. Robbie had told her not to go. It could be dangerous, he'd said. But she'd insisted and so he'd insisted on taking her there. She'd told him to wait in the car but he wouldn't. She'd hoped nobody was going to do anything to her at a funeral service with the bulk of the South African police force present. Apart from arrest her or Robbie, of course. That had been a real worry, but she'd risked it anyway.

At the funeral, Commissioner Williams hurried over to her, wearing a smart black suit with a white flower in the buttonhole. He had frowned at Robbie for a moment, as if half-recognizing him, then turned to her.

"Jade. So sorry for your loss," he said.

She nodded.

"You know Jacobs, the Redcliff cop who was up here helping us with the case? I don't know if you're aware that he was shot and killed last night."

Wordless, Jade shook her head. She looked him in the eyes, unblinking, palms cold, heart accelerating. How much did Williams know?

"I'm looking into the situation. There are some glaring irregularities. It appears that the Viljoen brothers were bribing an officer to sabotage the case." He leaned in closer. "My feeling is what happened last night might not have been a street mugging. I think Jacobs was their man, and for some reason the deal went sour and they paid someone to get rid of him."

She squeezed her hands together tightly, relief flooding through her. Her nails were digging into her palms. Williams was looking in the wrong place for Jacobs's killer. But he had given her some valuable information. The Viljoen brothers. Now she understood for sure.

"If my father was alive, he could have helped you."

Williams sniffed. "That's for sure. I'd have appreciated it

right now, more than you know." He squeezed her shoulder. "Sorry again, my girl. I tried to get hold of you for your input in organizing the funeral, but I couldn't track you down."

Jade looked around at the black-clad mourners, the flowers in the church, the plastic numbers slotted into the wooden holders indicating what hymns would be sung. She hadn't organized her father's funeral, but in the circumstances she knew he would have understood.

"I haven't been in touch with anyone recently." Not even David, because he was in Durban for a fortnight, attending a conference. For the first time ever, she'd been glad he wasn't around. She didn't want to put him in danger, too.

"I understand."

"I'm leaving tomorrow. Going overseas for a while. I need to be somewhere else right now."

He nodded. "Always good to have a change when something like this happens. Well, best of luck to you for the future."

He gave her shoulder another squeeze and walked away, leaving Jade to the awkward condolences and uneasy embraces of the other mourners.

20

Ten years later, Williams made no attempt to squeeze her shoulder. He simply leaned over and shook her hand, his tie slipping round the curve of his stomach.

"Circumstances could be better. But thanks for helping us out."

She noticed the cuffs of his shirt were fastened by gold cufflinks. That was something else she remembered. Williams had always been a sharp dresser. Her father had joked that he'd only become a detective so he could wear a suit and tie to work each day.

"It's my pleasure."

He squeezed her hand harder. "Your father's daughter. That's what you are, all right. De Jong was a fine man. Filling his shoes hasn't been easy. Especially with the problems we're experiencing now." His gaze was sharp and keen. "You should join the police service. We'd arrange you a special dispensation. Get you into a detective unit in no time at all. We need people like you. High-caliber individuals."

He hadn't referred to David. Jade wondered whether his compliment to her was a backhanded insult to him.

"I'll certainly give it some thought," she said. "Although my father and I agreed a long while ago that my personality was more suited to private investigation than to public service."

Williams laughed. "Either way, good to have you on board for this operation." He withdrew his hand. "Well, I'll be off. Good evening to you."

He buzzed up the window and pulled away, engine roaring.

David followed her inside. He tossed an armful of scatter cushions onto the floor and slumped onto the couch.

Jade fetched him a beer. "Long day?"

He took it without opening his eyes. "Longer than you can know. As you saw, Williams gave me a lift home. I thought it was a kind offer, but it was just an excuse for a major telling-off. I've been dumped on from a dizzy height. Non-performance, corruption in the department, low solve rate. All my fault. We've got performance reviews coming up in a week's time. I'll probably be the first-ever superintendent to get a decrease. If I'm lucky and I don't get a straight demotion. When he shook your hand I thought he was going to offer you my job." He drained the can and crumpled it in his fist.

Jade got him another. "Maybe that's his way of managing staff. Perhaps he doesn't have people skills. He's been in the department for ages, he's part of the old school."

"Let's hope so." David opened his eyes and sat up straighter. "God. This couch is like a bloody feather bed. So. Update on today's activities."

"Go ahead. I'm listening."

"The body's gone for analysis. It's definitely Grobbelaar. His buddy ID'd him."

"Any evidence?"

"Not so far. Apart from being butchered, apparently with an axe, there was no sign of a struggle. A couple of carpet fibers under his fingernails and a missing nail led forensics to believe he might have been transported in the trunk of a vehicle." David shook his head. "Rocket scientists, that's what I said. I told them they must be rocket scientists to figure out he was transported in the trunk and not sitting upright in the front seat waving at the traffic with all that tape wrapped round his head like the Bride of Frankenstein."

Jade suppressed a smile as she imagined the confrontation between David and the luckless forensic team. David was notoriously impatient and demanding when it came to getting professional opinions out of people involved in his cases.

"Whoever cut him up was tall and strong, probably six foot or more. And right-handed, according to the way the blows fell."

"And the axe?"

"It wasn't in the vicinity. We might never find it. I've put the word out in the surrounding area, got the local police on the lookout." He pushed himself straight again. "I'm so bloody tired I can't tell if it's me or the sofa that's the problem here. So, Jadey, that's it as far as the body in the woods goes."

He slid down onto his elbow. "That's better. So what's new on your side?"

Jade told him about her day. While she was talking, David pulled off his shoes and stretched his legs across the sofa. He didn't look comfortable, but she thought he was too tired to care.

She wondered who had deliberately chopped Dean Grobbelaar to pieces. What kind of a person could raise an axe and send it thudding into a human body, then work it loose, shift the grip on the handle and bring it down again, and again? Was he a psychopath? Was he mentally ill? She wondered why he had gone to such lengths to torture and kill Dean. Was it because the investigator had tried to discover more about Ellie Myers? Where was Ellie? When would they find her?

"Oh, I got your message," David said, eyes closed. "Since I'd only done twelve hours when I got back into town, I went round to check out 48 Forest Road. Couldn't have Williams thinking I was taking a half-day."

Jade curled her feet up on the chair opposite as David continued.

"Yup. Took me an hour in traffic just to get through Sandton. And why the hell did they fence off the whole of that bloody suburb? Took me another hour to find the entrance. It's like Fort Knox in there, and I'm damn sure it's illegal."

"You can go back tomorrow and arrest them."

David forced a smile. It looked out of place on his grim face and didn't survive long, but it seemed to put him in a more jovial mood. "I spoke to one of the neighbors. Met her coming home and flashed her. My ID, of course," he said, as Jade gave a snuffle of laughter. This had been an in-joke between them for as long as they had known each other.

"She didn't know where Ellie was. But she did gossip about the area. I don't know how accurate it was, but it was interesting. She was a chatty old bird. Especially when she saw my handsome face."

Jade corrected him. "She was probably babbling in terror."

"One fact's clear, Jadey. As long as I live, I'll never be able to afford property in Sandton."

"Unless you start taking bribes."

"Yeah. Well, they'd have to be big ones."

"Tell me what she said."

"Number 48 Forest Road was a triple-sized stand. Five hectares. They kept horses there. She told me she visited her sister in England for a couple of months and when she came back, she didn't recognize the place. The Myers had sold it to a developer after some sort of trouble."

"And then what?"

David peered up at her from his prone position. "Then the developer started going crazy. Now this lady knew the original house. She said it had some extraordinary number of bedrooms, an entertainment area, pool, the works. First of all, they put a garden fence around it and sold it off. Then the developer built thirty-two luxury cluster homes on the rest of the land. With five bedrooms each and their own pool and garden."

Jade tried to imagine living in a luxury five-bedroomed cluster home like that. What would it look like? She suspected it would be similar to the out-of-town residences of the rich people whose families she had guarded. She remembered automatic gates, endless driveways, imposing front doors imported from Indonesia or Italy. Gold taps and enormous baths. Marble finishes everywhere. Great echoing empty spaces filled with nothing but antique statues on pedestals. She'd never felt comfortable in those homes.

"And then what?"

"Then they built a whacking great wall round the whole estate and put in twenty-four-hour security. The houses inside sold for around six million each."

"As good as printing the money themselves." That was another favorite saying of her father's, when he spoke about people who had made an unseemly fortune.

"The lady reckoned the developer made around fifty million." David righted himself once more. "But there were hundreds of complaints from residents in the area, including them. Apparently the land hadn't been zoned for development and there were by-laws preventing subdivision into sizes that small."

"So the developer had greased a few palms?"

"Yeah. Might have channeled a few crumbs from all that profit in the right direction. The neighbors did get together to try and take him to court when they realized he wasn't just putting up a garden cottage, but the case got delayed and by the time anything could be done it was a fait accompli."

"What have the neighbors done since then?"

"They've been a busy bunch. The minute one development goes up, homeowners in the area start looking at the dollar signs and working out how much they can get for their own property. There've been a couple of other developments started in neighboring roads. A few more that they've managed to put the brakes on. But in the meantime they've forgotten about number 48. Number 48 is old news now."

Jade walked through to the kitchen and retrieved the heater. Then she went into the bedroom, unbuckled her gun belt and locked it into the bedside cupboard. She found two blankets in the wardrobe and brought them back for David. Then she sat down again on the chair opposite him.

"I wonder why Mark and Ellie Myers sold up."

David sat up on the couch. He shrugged off his jacket and loosened his tie. Jade wanted to walk over and wrap her arms around him. She didn't. She sat and watched as he lay down again and pulled the blankets tight around him. "Yeah, I wonder. Probably saw a chance to fund their retirement. Perhaps they were emigrating. Or wanted lots of money and didn't care about ruining the area."

"We need to find them."

"We'll follow up tomorrow. I'll get my team onto it first thing." He grimaced. "While they're still my team."

"David." Jade sighed. "If the other superintendent was so useless, it will probably be Williams in the firing line, not you. You'll be fine."

David didn't answer. A few seconds later, he started to snore.

Jade waited. "David," she said again, louder. There was no response. He was deeply asleep. His face looked peaceful. He looked innocent, younger, but somehow vulnerable, in a way he never did when he was awake.

She lifted her hand to her mouth and bit her nails, agonizing over what she should do. Having David sleep over on her couch wasn't a problem. Not at all, although if she had her way he wouldn't sleep over on her couch. They'd be pooling body warmth together in bed. But she really should wake him up and send him home. Tomorrow Viljoen was going to be released from prison. She had an early start ahead of her and she didn't want David around.

As she was considering her options, she heard honking outside.

"Shit," Jade muttered. She jumped to her feet. David mumbled something and pulled the covers tighter around him. He didn't wake up.

Grabbing her keys, Jade hurried over to the door and opened it as quietly as possible.

Robbie was at the wheel of his BMW. She got in and closed the car door. The heater was on full blast. He was gripping a can of cider in between his thighs—Robbie had never been one for cup holders. He lifted it to his lips, took a long pull, and offered it to her. She declined. He shoved it back between his legs and grinned at her, tapping out a rhythm on the top of the can with his fingernails.

"What's up, Robbie? Why are you here? This time the cop next door is home. Didn't your source tell you?"

"Big day tomorrow," he said. "Big, big day for you. Your friend gets out of chokie at last."

"Yes." Jade studied him. He looked wired, tense, hyperactive. Yesterday's adrenaline rush combined with large amounts of cider, she guessed. She'd never seen Robbie use drugs.

"So. We're going to follow him? Take him out, chop-chop, done and dusted?" He snapped his fingers.

"No."

"Why not? You crazy or something? He's going to come after you. I remember the last time you were as jumpy as a long-tailed cat in a room full of rocking chairs. Looking over your shoulder all the time. You want to be like that again?"

"He's already got people watching me. I want to wait and do it properly. I can't risk being caught."

They both looked round as headlights lit up the road. Robbie tensed. His hand slipped down and Jade knew it was on his gun. Anyone trying to hijack the Beemer would come off second-best if Robbie had his way. Before the car reached them it turned into a driveway further down. Just an honest citizen arriving home late. Robbie's hand moved back up to the wheel.

"In a couple of days you could be dead."

Jade felt uneasy. She didn't want to be parked in the road, arguing with a small-time gangster who, for some unfathomable reason, was going a few steps too far in helping with her problem. She didn't want to be parked in the road at all. What if David woke up and came looking for her? He must never know about Robbie. She'd be in trouble trying to explain why she had dealings with him. David would rightly feel that she had betrayed his trust. She didn't know what Robbie's history was with the police. But she knew he had a record.

"Not tomorrow, Robbie. There'll be people around. I'm not doing anything if he's got all his fanatical followers from the old days crowding round to congratulate him on his release. Let's follow him, see where he goes, get an idea of his routine. Wait a bit longer, till the fuss dies down."

Robbie drummed his fingers on the wheel. "OK. Fair enough." He opened the car door. "So. You going to invite me in for a coffee?"

Jade jumped out of the car. Robbie was already walking towards the front door.

"No." She hurried after him, trying to keep her voice down without seeming obvious. He stopped in his tracks.

"Why not?"

"Because I'm tired and I've had a long day and we've got an early start tomorrow. We both need to be alert."

"I can crash on the couch." He gave her a sidelong glance that confirmed the couch was the last place he intended to crash. His hand clamped round her waist and strayed upwards.

"What about Verna?" she asked.

Robbie looked smug. "Verna knows the deal."

This had happened before, the first time she met him. After they left the nightclub and he'd invited her back to his flat. She hadn't wanted to go, but she knew she'd be safer with him than without him.

He'd offered her his sofa and given her a T-shirt because her clothes were two days old and rancid with sweat and nightclub smoke. In the middle of the night, she'd woken to find Robbie next to her. His naked body was pressed against hers and his hands were groping around under the T-shirt.

"Yeah, babe," he'd said. "Ooh, babe."

At first, Jade had feigned sleep. When that didn't work, she'd tried to resist. He'd ignored her. His strong arms had thrust hers aside. He'd pushed her legs apart. Jade had listened to his harsh breathing and felt the rasp of his stubble against her face. She'd never felt so powerless. Perhaps this was part of the deal. Perhaps Robbie's help had to be earned through sexual barter. Terrified and exhausted, she'd been about to close her eyes and let him do what he wanted. Then she'd changed her mind.

She remembered that she'd reached down.

"Yeah, babe," Robbie had groaned. "Hold me. Yeah, like that."

Jade had gritted her teeth and then squeezed and twisted

her hand as hard as she could, digging her nails into his soft flesh. For one white-hot moment, she hadn't cared whether Robbie broke her arm, beat her up or kicked her out onto the street.

"Bayyyyb!" Robbie's voice had risen in a surprised and agonized screech. Then he'd flown off the sofa and collapsed on the floor, bent double with pain.

After that Jade had pulled the duvet tightly around her, hoping he couldn't see how violently her arms were trembling. "I said no," she'd told him, hoping she sounded calm and controlled. She was already regretting what she'd done. But to her relief, Robbie was completely cowed.

"No. You said no. I heard you." He'd raised his head and stared at her again in painful disbelief. "No it is. OK then. Fine. Be like that." Gathering the shreds of his dignity around him, he'd staggered back to his bedroom and slammed the door.

She wondered if he remembered this incident now, as she removed his hand from her waist and turned to face him.

"Robbie, sex is not part of our relationship. I've told you before. Go home and sleep in your bed. If you come in, there'll be complications. Then neither of us will sleep and tomorrow will go badly because we'll be pissed off with each other."

Robbie paused. Jade could almost see his brain working. His eyes lit up and he jumped to the wrong conclusion.

"Are you screwing that cop next door? Is he your new boyfriend?"

"No." It was the truth, but she was glad it was dark so Robbie couldn't see her blushing.

"I think you are."

"I'm not. And even if I was, it's nothing to do with you.

We're doing business, Robbie. You're my friend. Nothing more. OK?"

"You know, Jade, you're a fuckin' ice queen, that's what you are."

Robbie turned and stomped back to his car. Gravel sprayed from the sidewalk as he drove down the road. Jade watched him leave, relieved he was gone, but terrified that by rejecting him again she'd made a dangerous enemy.

21

Jade didn't sleep well that night. She didn't know if it was because David was in the other room or because she was going to see Viljoen at last. She stayed awake for what felt like hours, remembering what had happened on that fateful morning she left the little house in Turffontein.

Her father's coffee had stood half empty on his desk, a skin of cool milk wrinkling its surface. The lamp was off and his briefcase was gone. She climbed into her car and set off down the road to a surveillance appointment, taking the route that her father had when he'd left with Jacobs in the beige unmarked.

As she reached a bend in the road, she slowed down. There'd been an accident ahead, at the one traffic light that she'd always thought was a pointless waste of electricity. The road crossing it was a steep and narrow lane that, even when traffic was thick, never seemed to have any cars on it. This morning, there had been one.

A heavy truck must have been speeding down the lane and been unable to stop at the lights. The runaway vehicle had smashed into a car on the main road, crushing it under its wheels.

Jade could smell burning rubber and the choking fumes of scorched metal. She hurried across to the smoking body of the truck and the awful shape of the car underneath it. A small knot of people surrounded the accident.

As she walked closer, she felt her stomach clench. She recognized the crumpled car. It was Jacobs's unmarked. The driver's door was open but the passenger side was crushed under the chassis of the truck.

"Dad!" Jade screamed.

Jacobs grabbed her shoulders from behind. She turned and stared at him. He was wild-eyed, breathing hard, and his clothes looked rumpled.

"We've called an ambulance," he told her. "The ambulance is coming. Move away from the car, my girl. There's nothing you can do."

"We've got to get him out." She peered into the buckled mass of metal, the truck's grille mounted on top in a bizarre display of victory. She recoiled from the blood that was oozing out of the shadows.

Then, sirens wailing, the ambulance arrived. Paramedics leapt out and sprinted over to the car and started working through the narrow gap in the metal.

"Where's the truck driver?" someone asked.

"Must have run away," someone else said. "Probably didn't even have a bruise. The cab's hardly damaged."

"Probably drunk," the first person said with loathing.

Tears blurring her vision, Jade sat by the side of the road, staring blankly at the tarmac in front of her. Three cups of tea had been provided by the solicitous onlookers. She hadn't done more than sip at the first one because her hands were shaking too badly for her to get the cup to her mouth, and her chest was heaving in a series of dry sobs that she was sure would choke her.

She heard police sirens yipping and yapping followed by the screech of tires. An officer came and sat down beside her to ask some questions. She could hear the clank of heavy machinery and the hiss of hydraulics and the tearing scream of metal on metal. When she looked up again, the truck had been moved away and the paramedics were busy. She walked over, trying not to look too closely.

"Is he alive?"

The man shook his head. "He must have died on impact. Massive head injuries and internal trauma. Most probably he didn't even know what was happening."

They strapped her father's body to a stretcher and wheeled it away. Rubbing tears from her eyes as she watched, Jade recalled one of her father's sayings. "Even if things go wrong, even if tragedy strikes, it is essential to do your duty."

She took a deep breath. She would take the file and give it to David. He could finish the work her father had started.

"What are you doing?" asked Jacobs, stumbling to his feet as she walked towards the shell of the car. She steeled herself and looked in the passenger side. The seat and carpet were stained with her father's blood. She closed her eyes and swallowed hard, tasting bile in her throat. Then she looked again, forcing herself to get closer. The paramedics had cut through the seat belt to get him out. The canvas straps hung, frayed and useless, and she pushed them aside.

She looked in the back, under the seat, on the driver's side. Then she walked round the car while the tow-truck driver sat patiently, waiting for her to finish, and checked inside the trunk. And then, because she didn't trust herself to have searched properly the first time, she looked again, looked everywhere, her fingers sliding and scrabbling on the carpets, tears flooding her eyes again when she saw the dark red streaks on her fingertips and knuckles.

Then she straightened up and stared at the blue-white horizon and shivered in the heat of the glorious sunshine as she realized that things were perhaps not all that they seemed to be.

The briefcase was nowhere. It had disappeared.

The briefcase was gone.

The briefcase…

Jade felt hands clutch at her, and she screamed and struggled, fighting for her life, because Jacobs was there, waiting, and this time she couldn't escape.

Then she realized that she was in her bed, in the cottage. She must have fallen asleep and had her old nightmare. But there was someone holding her and it wasn't Jacobs. It was David.

"Jadey, are you OK? You almost gave me heart failure there. I heard you crying and screaming. I came to see what was wrong."

She held onto him tightly and he stroked her hair. Jade could feel her heart thudding, although now she didn't know whether it was from the nightmare or because David was sitting on her bed, gently holding her in his arms.

"No, it's nothing. Just a bad dream."

David carried on stroking her hair. His hands felt strong and sure as they cradled her head.

"Anything you want to talk about?"

"Not really. I dream about my dad's accident, sometimes."

She felt David's chest rise and fall as he sighed. "I wish I'd been in Jo'burg when it happened. I can't believe you had to go through something like that on your own. Finding your father dead in that horror crash. I'm not surprised you're still bothered about it. And then you disappeared and I didn't know where you were. We thought you'd had some kind of a breakdown. Post-traumatic stress. I was worried about you and so angry I hadn't been granted permission to leave that police conference in Durban, I nearly resigned."

She closed her eyes, aware of the warmth of David's body against hers. They had never been so close before. She squeezed her arms around him and felt him hold her tighter in response.

"Hey Jadey. I missed you."

"I missed you too."

"Are you okay now?"

"I'm fine. Thanks. Listen." She took a deep breath. "I've wanted to tell you this for ages. I've always thought—you know, with my dad around, you ended up being like family to me. Like an older brother. And that wasn't always the way I wanted to feel about you. Not at all." She took another breath. This was hard work. David's silence wasn't helping either. His hand had stopped stroking her hair. What could she say next? How could she explain her feelings to him?

"I think I'd like things to go further between us," she ended lamely. That was it. Her reserve of courage had run dry, her palms were icy and she'd rather face down a charging elephant than say another word to David about what was in her heart.

Then it all went wrong. She didn't know why. It was dark, they were close together on her bed, separated by a couple of layers of insubstantial clothing. She was sharing her thoughts, her secrets. Something could have happened. Should have. But it didn't. Instead, David pulled away from her and stood up.

"It's five-thirty in the morning. I've got to get going."

Jade struggled to her feet, rubbing her eyes. He hadn't answered her, hadn't shared his feelings in return. Why not? She'd have to wait until later to find out, because now he was pulling on his shoes and fastening his belt.

"I'll let you out," she mumbled.

"Thanks for letting me crash on your couch. Try and get some more sleep, and call me if you need anything."

She turned off the alarm and buzzed open the gate. He closed the door behind him, and she watched him leave, listening to the crunch of his footsteps on the road.

22

A single-lane main road, clogged with traffic, separated the grounds of Leeuwkop Prison from the large, semi-rural suburb where Jade passed a group of horses and riders as she took a shortcut through the back roads.

She drove slowly past the horses, listening to the clopping of their hooves on the tarmac. If she lived in this area, she could get a horse. There were plenty of places to keep it. She supposed that she'd need to learn how to look after it. There was feeding involved, grooming, the regular replacement of those metal shoes. It sounded like a lot of work, thinking about it. She supposed there were establishments where she could pay to have all that done for her. Livery yards or riding schools. She'd seen a few signs for stables along the way. They could teach her how to ride the horse too. That would be an advantage.

The leather of the horses' saddles and bridles gleamed. The riders were kitted out in tall leather boots and jodhpurs. Big padded helmets with air vents. They wore gloves and carried whips. There was a lot of equipment involved in riding, that was for sure. Even without the cost of the horse, it would be expensive to start up. Too much of an outlay for her. She moved back to the left-hand side of the road again. Perhaps owning a horse was too ambitious. But she could start with a cat, or a little dog.

She parked halfway down a side road, next to a security boom that was wide open and unmanned, and got out of the car. She was wearing tracksuit pants and trainers and a sporty-looking jacket that concealed her gun. She didn't think anybody would look twice at a woman out on a morning walk on the sandy track alongside the main road.

Jade had read that Leeuwkop Prison was built 40 years ago. The surrounding area must have looked very different then. She was sure that road had seldom seen cars back in those days and that the properties in the area must have been regarded as cheap farmland rather than sought-after semi-rural real estate.

❋

By the time the Viljoen brothers' trial started, Jade had already left the country. But she read about it, and she saw pictures of the two brothers in the newspapers. Older pictures of them at their farm and more recent pictures of the two standing in the dock. The elder brother looked like a Voortrekker leader, with his square silver beard and stern expression. The younger

Viljoen had a mustache and was shorter, more anxious, less sure of himself. He told the judge he had followed his elder brother's lead. That he always had since he was young.

The judge sentenced the elder brother to life imprisonment. As befitted a dangerous criminal, he was sent to the maximum security section at Leeuwkop. The younger brother was found guilty as an accomplice to murder and was sentenced to fifteen years, in the medium-security section of the same prison. After the day they were sentenced, the brothers never saw each other again.

Soon after the brothers were incarcerated, gang violence broke out in the maximum security section. The 28s had caused the trouble. They were a powerful gang, renowned for their tradition of taking "boyfriends" through force and coercion. They'd clashed with the relatively new Big Five gang, whose members were infamous for being prison informers.

Jade never knew whether Viljoen senior had been involved with the 28s or the Big Five, whether he was simply collateral damage, or whether somebody wanted him dead. After the violence had been brought under control by the prison authorities, it was reported that he was one of the four fatalities.

The younger brother had his term reduced to ten years for good behavior. Jade had read that he was a model prisoner. In the extensive grounds surrounding Leeuwkop inmates grew the bulk of the fresh produce used in prisons around the country. Viljoen junior had assisted enormously with the innovation of new farming methods and had been responsible for a substantial increase in productivity. In his own unlikely way, he would be leaving prison a hero.

❧

Jade watched the entrance to Leeuwkop. It was quiet. She took in the face-brick gateposts, the guardhouse with a security boom and the few cars driving in and out. She couldn't see a huge contingent of militant right-wingers gathered to welcome their idol out of prison. She couldn't see anyone at all. Except for Robbie, cruising through the traffic in a white Volkswagen Golf. He honked, and waved at her. Traffic was so slow she was walking faster than he could drive. She jogged over to the passenger side and climbed in.

"Undercover today," he said. "I don't want bullet holes in the Beemer's bodywork." He laughed. The interior smelled faintly of cigarette smoke and the fabric of the seats was worn. Jade wondered whose car he was driving. He didn't bring up what had happened between them the previous night.

Robbie parked the car by the side of the road opposite the prison. Traffic was still thick. Taxis stopped at the intersection, discharged passengers, and pulled away. Hawkers sold fruit and vegetables under fabric gazebos anchored into the dusty ground. Jade could see dented apples and blackening bananas and what looked like fruit salad in Tupperware containers, their lids damp with condensation.

Groups of people were waiting on the roadside, looking for gaps in the slow-moving traffic so that they could cross the road.

"We're not exactly going to stick out like a sore thumb in this chaos," Robbie remarked. "Want a piece of biltong?" He rummaged in a plastic bag on the dashboard. "This stuff's the real McCoy. Got it from a place in the Natal Midlands. Went down last week to get a couple of vehicles. Those cattle, they taste better than anywhere else in the country. Steak, biltong, it doesn't matter what the hell you do with those cows, you can't do it badly. Meat's in a class of its own."

Jade shook her head. She wasn't hungry, which was unusual for her. Partly because she lost her appetite whenever she wondered why David had pulled away from her, in silence, in the darkness of the early hours. And partly because she was apprehensive about seeing Viljoen again.

She wondered what cars Robbie had brought back. Stolen luxury vehicles, that was her guess. Robbie didn't go in for hijacking, or at least, he hadn't ten years ago. He'd once told her that his principles were too high. Robbie's principles, she had learned, were governed by standards that nobody else could hope to understand.

"He's out any minute now, hey?" He poked her in the ribs.

"Eight thirty, they said the bus arrives."

They watched the road. Jade saw an elderly white Mazda turn off the main road and drive up to the prison gates. The car stopped, reversed, and parked outside the boom.

"Bet that's his transport." Robbie shoved another handful of biltong into his mouth. "Fanatics obviously have less of a budget these days. Or it could be someone else looking to take him out, quicker than us." He laughed. "Don't think much of their getaway car, though."

Jade tensed. She could see the prison bus. It approached the gates slowly, as if the driver was reluctant to let his passenger reach them and walk out a free man. The guard raised the boom and the bus drove through and parked in the turning area outside the prison.

The driver strolled over to the guard at the gate. They had a brief discussion. Then the passengers stepped down onto the tarmac.

One black man, one white man. Business wasn't brisk in the departures area of Leeuwkop this morning. The black man looked confused, a teenager who was probably still flabbergasted that the system had landed him in jail. Jade wondered if he'd been a gang member. Or was now. She didn't think he could have committed a serious crime. Not if he was already being paroled.

Behind him was Viljoen.

She'd imagined he would be tall and strong, like his brother had been. Perhaps ten years ago he was. But prison had clearly aged him. He was a frail husk of a man. The wind tugged at his faded garments, threatening to pick him up and blow him away. His mustache was now gray and straggly and the hair on his head white and stringy.

"Hell's bells," Robbie said. "You didn't tell me he was a pensioner. We don't have to worry about putting a bullet into him. He'll probably keel over from old age before he reaches his mom's place."

Jade wondered if he could feel her rage like heat, radiating through the tinted glass of the back window. He had killed her father, as sure as if he'd fired the gun himself. The Viljoen brothers had paid Jacobs, and Jacobs had taken the money and engineered her father's death so that nobody would think it had been more than a tragic car accident. Except Jade. Because her father's briefcase was missing.

That had been her first warning. Investigating further, she discovered from the paramedics that the seat belt mechanism on the passenger's side of the car had been jammed closed, trapping her father in the car. Even if he'd seen the truck hurtling down the hill towards him, he would have been unable to escape.

The single witness to the accident said the beige car had stopped, for no discernible reason, in the middle of the crossroads. Engine failure, perhaps. The driver, Jacobs, had climbed out of the car and walked round to the hood. Then the approaching truck had blasted its horn and Jacobs had run for it, diving out of the way as it smashed into the stalled vehicle.

Jacobs confirmed this story, although Jade suspected he would have confirmed reports that aliens had beamed the truck down and landed it on the police unmarked, had a witness volunteered the information.

Afterwards, the police told her that the truck had been stolen from a nearby transport company. A fence was broken open in the night and the vehicle hotwired. She asked if they had found the driver. They said they hadn't. She asked if he'd left any evidence in the cab. They said they were working on it, but Jade knew from listening to her father that meant they didn't have any evidence at all.

The witness observed that Jacobs seemed distressed after the accident occurred. He'd run back to the car and half-climbed inside to try and rescue his colleague. Jade guessed he'd been making sure her father was dead, and collecting the briefcase. In the chaos that followed it would have been easy to dispose of. In all probability, the truck driver had taken it with him when he disappeared from the scene.

In her state of shock, her deductions had been hazy, her reactions slow. When Jacobs came for her that night, she realized almost too late that she was right. He was prepared to go to any lengths to complete his deadly contract.

Robbie glanced sideways. "Stop looking like that."

"I'm not looking at you."

"I know that. But your expression's making me shit myself. I've seen mercenaries gunning down the enemy in the Congo looking less pissed off than you do."

Jade tried to relax. "When were you in the Congo, Robbie?"

Robbie winked at her. "I've been a lot of places in the last while. Some you don't want to know about."

Viljoen and the black prisoner reached the car. The black man opened the door and helped Viljoen inside. He bent stiffly, fumbling his way forward into the passenger seat. The younger prisoner closed the passenger door and got into the back of the car. What was Viljoen, a committed racist, jailed for the brutal murder of three black farm employees, doing in a vehicle with a black ex-convict?

"What the hell?" Robbie frowned. "Was this the slowest kidnapping I've ever seen? Or did your friend just agree to share his car with a darkie?"

Jade shook her head. "I can't believe it either."

"Where's his welcome committee? Where's the gang of Voortrekkers with their rifles and swastikas and pointy white hats?"

"The hat-wearers were the Ku Klux Klan, Robbie."

"Whatever. You get my drift."

The Mazda pulled out into the traffic. Robbie waited for another few cars to go past and then followed.

Viljoen's lift drove at a steady pace. Jade could sense Robbie's frustration. He was itching to go faster—Robbie lived for speed. To compensate, he alternated between biting his nails and beating his fingers on the dashboard of his car in a manic rhythm that he kept up all the way to Pretoria. Jade knew there was no point in asking him to stop, but the sound was so irritating that she began to consider other alternatives.

Like knocking him on the head with the butt of her gun and taking the wheel herself.

They followed the same route that Robbie had used when he'd taken Jade to northern Pretoria. When they turned off the highway, the car in front of Robbie stopped at a red light, allowing the Mazda to gain a lead. With some catching up to do, Robbie finally left his dashboard alone.

They turned down the road where Viljoen's mother lived. Robbie's information had been correct. In the daylight, she saw the street name painted in faded black letters on the curb. Springbok Laan. They rounded the corner in time to see Viljoen being helped out of the car. Jade stared ahead, puzzled. The driver of the Mazda was also black.

Robbie was also surprised. "Holy shit. What's going on here? He got a lift from a darkie, too! The car was there to take the young guy home. They just dropped Viljoen off."

The driver took the old man's arm, steadying him as he stepped up onto the pavement. Jade stared. Viljoen's pallid skin drooped in bulldog folds. His faded shirt hung on his body. He nodded his thanks to the driver and shook his hand. His sagging face stretched into a smile as he shook the hand of the young prisoner. The two black men got back into the car and Viljoen walked down the short driveway to where the lady in the wheelchair was waiting at the front door. Jade looked back as Robbie drove past. She saw Viljoen lean forward and embrace his mother. She thought the old lady might have been crying, but then their car rounded the bend and she could no longer see the house.

Jade turned on her cell phone as soon as she got back home. She'd reluctantly agreed to let Robbie watch the old man's movements over the next couple of days. Not that Robbie's offer had been reluctant; he'd suggested it and practically twisted Jade's arm to make sure it happened.

Robbie's attitude made Jade deeply uneasy. Why was he so anxious to see Viljoen get what he deserved? She wondered whether he'd done a deal with somebody in order to profit from his death. She'd realized from bitter experience that Robbie was still taking money for hits. She remembered what he'd said in the car. "Guy like that, they're gonna be queuing up to shoot him when he's out. I heard that some of the government ministers had relations in those areas long ago. Poor relations. Black people. Working for sadists like him."

Had Robbie found somebody prepared to pay him a few thousand rand to see their own form of justice done? She wouldn't put it past him. But she didn't want other people involved, because then they might find out what she had done.

Viljoen didn't look like a dangerous man. Perhaps prison had changed him. Seeing him with his frail and helpless old mother, she'd felt pity for both of them. Perhaps his elder brother was the one who'd wanted to sabotage the case because he had more to lose. But then why was somebody watching her house, headlights off, the first night she'd come back?

The beeping of her phone interrupted her thoughts. She had a message from David. Listening to his voice made her remember his arms around her and his hands touching her hair. She smiled and called him back.

David didn't sound gentle or comforting. His voice was sharp and frustrated.

"Your friend Ellie Myers," he said.

"What's happening with her?"

"She's bloody deceased."

David's voice crackled. The connection made it sound like he was in outer Siberia.

"What? Deceased as of when?"

"Deceased as of five years ago. Just before her property was sold. I don't know what happened."

"And Mark Myers?"

"He's not deceased. That's all we know. He's not deceased and he clearly isn't living at his recorded residential address. So we can't find him."

"No other information on him?"

"Well, he hasn't emigrated. Officially, at least. But I'm beginning to wonder what the hell happened five years ago."

"Something did, that's for sure," Jade said.

"Yeah. Now we're coming along like the guys who missed the party. The trail's going to be stone-cold now." The line crackled again. She thought David was probably walking round his office, pacing from wall to wall like a caged tiger. She remembered he used to do that when things were going badly.

"Home Affairs couldn't find a record of Mark's parents, either," he continued. "Not that I think Home Affairs is capable of finding its backside with both hands at the best of times."

"How about Ellie's parents?"

"My team's looking for them now. But I'm not holding my breath."

"David. Do you sometimes feel like there's a dead end every direction you turn?"

"Yes, Jade. Surprisingly enough, that's exactly how I feel right now." He tried to say something else, but his voice broke up and the line went dead. Jade didn't call him back. David hadn't sounded in the mood for further conversation.

23

The next morning, when he called Jade before the sun was up, David sounded completely different. Excited. Like finally something was going his way.

"What's up?"

"The axe. They found the axe yesterday evening. The weapon used to kill Grobbelaar. They've driven it through to the Pretoria lab already and forensics are working on it now. They've got a two-week backlog, but the guy there owes me a favor, big-time. He said he'd have results by nine a.m. Come on over, Jade. I'm in my office. Second floor, Jo'burg Central."

The station housing the serious and violent crimes unit where David worked had been renamed Johannesburg Central after a thirty-year period under the name of John Vorster Square. John Vorster had been one of the most notorious propagators of the apartheid regime. Jade's father had explained the building's brutal history to her. As Minister of Justice in the 1960s, John Vorster, who went on to become prime minister, introduced new laws permitting prisoners to be tortured. Anti-apartheid activists were interrogated on the now infamous 10th floor and often died under suspicious circumstances. The elite Afrikaans police force never admitted the truth. The prisoner had slipped on a bar of soap in the shower, or fallen out of a window. People were clumsy. Accidents happened.

Jade looked up at the building which was nestled under a highway overpass. She wondered how many people had fallen screaming to their deaths from the high windows. Had their tormentors laughed as they watched them plummet to the ground?

As she approached the entrance she realized it looked different. The enormous bronze bust of John Vorster was missing. His giant head and shoulders had guarded this entrance for as long as she could remember. The brass plaque under the statue had been engraved with the hypocritical wording "Eendrag maak Mag—Unity is Strength." Jade was glad to see it was gone. She was sure that the citizens wandering in and out to report their stolen cell phones or get their documents stamped by a commissioner of oaths didn't want to walk in the shadow of a monument to a sadist.

David's office was neat and clean. His desk was bare, apart from the file on Annette and his computer. No photographs, no memorabilia, no personal touches at all. She'd once given him a brass paperweight in the shape of an eagle's head for his birthday. He'd thanked her for it and kissed her on the cheek, saying he'd put it on his desk. Jade couldn't see any sign of it now. She supposed a paperweight was useless if you didn't have any paper that needed weighing down. There was no sign of the knee-deep piles of old cases he had been complaining about.

"Grab a coffee." He gestured to a tray on the small round conference table. "We should have an answer any minute. They've been busy with it since this morning. I hoped we'd have something by the time you arrived."

Jade poured herself a coffee and sat down at the table. The coffee smelled strongly of burnt chicory. It tasted even worse.

"I see the standard of coffee's the same as ever."

"Unfortunately, yes. I usually have a private stash in my desk. Locked up. Otherwise people bloody steal it. In a police station! I mean, really."

"Where did they find the weapon?" she asked.

"It must've been thrown out of a car window. They found it in thick grass a few meters from the side of the road. On the highway back to Jo'burg, about twenty kilometers away from the crime scene."

"Who's 'they'?"

"Workers cutting firebreaks."

David stood up and walked over to the opposite wall. "We might have a lucky break this time. The guys who found it didn't touch it." He smiled, a mirthless grimace. "Too scared. Apparently the blade and a good part of the handle are encrusted in blood."

He returned to his desk and slid into his seat. "Forensics said they'd e-mail me photos as soon as they'd taken them." He frowned. "Yup. Here they are."

Jade got up and walked round the desk and leaned over David's shoulder. His deltoids and biceps bulged under the white cotton fabric of his shirt. His hair was clean and shiny. She wanted to touch it, put her face close and feel it tickling her cheeks. And she wanted to put her hand on his shoulder and feel those thick, ropy muscles under her fingers. He had used some sort of cologne earlier on. It was faint but spicy in the air. Had he been thinking of her when he applied it? Was he regretting yesterday's hasty departure? Or had she made a complete fool of herself by saying what she had? She moved away from him, her cheeks suddenly hot.

"Check this out," David said. His muscles bunched as he pulled his chair forward. With a click of the mouse, he enlarged the photo of the axe until it filled the screen.

Blood had congealed across its blade and splashed onto the handle, leaving behind dark brown trails and drips. It was a grisly murder weapon. She wasn't surprised the workers who'd discovered it had been afraid.

"They're checking it for prints," David said.

"You think they'll find any? Would Grobbelaar's killer have thrown away a fingerprinted weapon?"

He shrugged. "Maybe not. But people get careless. There's always a chance. When they've checked, they'll analyze the bloodstains. Would you like to make a million rand bet with me that the stains are a perfect match with Dean Grobbelaar's DNA?"

Jade shook her head. "I don't think there was that much axe-murdering activity going on in North West province yesterday. I'm not taking the bet with you."

David leaned forward. "Here we go. I've got more mail." He drummed his fingers on the desk. "Come on, come on. Open up. Tell us we've got a fingerprint here. And a match."

Jade craned over his shoulder, waiting to see what it said.

"They've got a print!" David shouted. "One crystal-clear, beautiful print on the base of the handle." He read further and his shoulders drooped. "Oh, shithouse."

"What?"

"They've run it through the system. No result. One print, no result. No bloody use, then."

"Why wouldn't he get a result?" Jade asked. "Would the guy be an illegal immigrant or something?"

"No." David sighed. He got up and poured himself a cup of coffee. He tipped in half the bowl of sugar, stirred, and took a gulp.

"God, you're right, it does taste like crap." Even so, he took another sip, more cautiously this time, and grimaced. "Yes, it could be the print of an illegal immigrant. But it could also belong to one of the millions of South Africans who don't have a damn criminal record. Our wonderful constitution still respects every citizen's right to privacy. The South African police cannot access Home Affairs data. Unless you're trying to ID a body, of course, then it's allowed. But the only fingerprints we have on our database belong to convicted criminals."

"Is there any way of getting round the system?" she asked.

David looked as if he was trying not to smile. "That's just the sort of question I'd expect from you."

"Well, is there?"

After a moment's thought his eyes lit up. Then he frowned. Jade thought he seemed nervous. He cleared his throat and adjusted his tie and hooked his pants up around his waist. Then he twisted his head from side to side as if he was trying to ease stiffness in his neck.

"I can call in a favor. I don't want to. I shouldn't. But I can."

"How?"

"I've got a contact in Home Affairs who can look up the print for us. Only problem is we can't use it as evidence in court. If it leads us to Annette's murderer, we'll have to find another way of proving he killed her."

"Well, then." Jade stood up. "Can you phone him?"

He nodded. "It's a woman. And yes, I can phone her."

Jade looked at the telephone. "Go ahead. Maybe she can check it now."

"This line's terrible. It's been bad all morning. I'll phone from the downstairs office." David pointed to the empty chair in front of his desk. "Wait here. I'll be back soon."

He hurried out. Jade stared after him. What was his problem? She picked up the phone on the desk and dialed zero to get an outside line. It sounded fine to her.

She went over to his filing cabinet and peeked inside. It was crammed with paperwork. So this was where his knee-deep pile of case files was now stored. At least they weren't such a fire hazard any more.

Exploring further, she opened his desk drawer. She wanted to find the damn paperweight. She'd had "To David from Jade" engraved on the base. It had cost her a fortune. What had he done with it?

Apart from the most basic stationery items the drawers were empty.

Jade only just managed to return to her chair before David hurried back into the office.

"I'm putting this on a CD. It's too sensitive to e-mail. She doesn't want to get into trouble. She'll put it on the system on her side, when she can."

"Are you hand-delivering it?"

"Yes. She's just down the road, in the Market Street office." David quickly copied the file. "There we go. Done." He glanced up at her. He didn't look happy. He looked tense and grim.

"Is everything OK?" Jade asked.

"Perfect. Fine. I'll chat to you later, then. Just push that button on the door latch when you leave. It'll lock from the inside."

With that, he disappeared round the corner.

Jade sniffed the air. Was it her imagination, or was the scent of cologne stronger? She took another sniff. Definitely stronger. David must have doused himself in the stuff when he went out to make his phone call.

She pressed the button on the latch and closed the door behind her. Then she followed the trail of cologne down the stairs and out of the police station.

Jade had tailed people on foot before. Some of them had been jumpy and suspicious, others had strolled along in blissful ignorance. She'd never been spotted, because regardless of the behavior of the target, she'd always been careful.

Following David down Commissioner Street, she suspected she could have let off flares and sung lewd songs at the top of her voice and he wouldn't have noticed. He was striding ahead, weaving through the slow-moving pedestrians on the pavement and dodging the roadside hawkers, swift and single-minded. Jade's only worry was that his speed would take him too far ahead of her.

He slowed abruptly and turned down a narrow side road. She expected him to continue along it until he came to Market Street, but he ducked into the entrance of a building instead. She couldn't follow him, because he would see her. She slowed to a dawdle, hoping that the woman he was due to meet was still on her way.

Jade had expected her to be unfamiliar, a stranger. She wasn't. To her dismay, she recognized her as soon as she saw her hurrying down the street from the opposite direction. The crimson jacket was unmistakable. She was the same dark-haired, coffee-skinned woman that Jade had seen climbing out of the car in the driveway of David's house in Turffontein.

Jade moved closer to the building's entrance and risked a glance through the dirty glass doors. In the lobby, the woman and David stood locked in a close embrace, heads together, arms entwined.

She whirled away and jogged back down the street. She felt sick to her stomach. What the hell was going on? Who was this woman? What did she mean to David, and why was she living in his house? More troubling still, who was the young boy she'd seen racing away from his mother to the gate? Could he be David's son?

Jade's legs suddenly went weak. It was as if a carpet had been yanked from under her. She'd spent ten years drifting round the world. Working, hiding, biding her time. But what had she expected David to do during those years? Sign up for the nearest monastery?

She crossed her arms and threaded her cold hands into her sleeves. She hadn't expected him to wait. But she hadn't imagined he would make such permanent life changes either.

She bit her lip and turned back, fighting to get some perspective on the situation. Any minute now they'd be out of the lobby, and then she could catch up with him and find out what was going on.

She waited, watching the throngs of passersby. Two men were strolling down the street holding greaseproof paper packets and the air filled with the vinegary smell of hot chips as they approached. As a rule, Jade couldn't resist chips, especially with lashings of chili sauce. Right then, the smell only made her feel sick all over again.

The woman left first. She marched out of the building, head turned aside, fumbling with the clasp of her handbag. She was wiping her hand across her eyes when she passed Jade.

David departed in a hurry, almost colliding with a passing pedestrian as he turned onto the street. He didn't apologize, but continued on his way, head bowed, arms crossed in front of him. Jade saw him shrug his shoulders as if he was ridding himself of unwelcome thoughts.

She ran after him and tapped him on the shoulder.

David swung round with a thunderous expression on his

face. Then he saw it was Jade. His anger dissolved. He stared at her for a moment, but she couldn't read what she saw in his eyes.

Jade felt a surge of furious disappointment. She knew if she looked at David for one second longer, she would give in to the powerful urge to punch him squarely in his stomach. Not that she expected to cause much damage. But she didn't want him to realize how strong her feelings for him were. If she hit him he would. She pushed past him and carried on walking. After a moment, she heard David's footsteps hurrying after her.

"Thanks for telling me," she said, looking ahead at the oncoming traffic and the clusters of people.

"Jadey." His voice was anguished.

"What's the situation?"

"She's my wife."

"Your wife. Right. What's her name?"

"Naisha."

"And the boy?"

David didn't ask how she knew. "My son. Kevin."

"Your wife and son. Why aren't you living with them?"

"We're separated."

"Not divorced?"

"Nope. Separated. Jade, do you have to walk so fast? Can't you stop for a minute?"

"No. Right now, I can't." She dodged to the left of an oncoming pedestrian and, with a stretch of empty pavement ahead of her, increased her speed. "Why are you separated?"

"It's a trial separation."

"How long?"

"We've been apart for a few months now."

"Do you still love her?"

"Jesus, what kind of a question is that? Yes. No. I don't know."

"Whose idea was the separation?"

"Her idea. Jade, please wait. Please stop."

She looked back at him. "What?"

"I'm sorry. I didn't mean to hurt you. I know I did, and I'm sorry." He met her eyes and she saw the pain in his face. "If it's any consolation to you, I'm living in hell at the moment. Please give me a break here. Help me out. I didn't want this to happen, any of it."

Jade didn't answer. Instead, she turned away from him and stalked off up the street. David didn't follow her and she didn't look back to see where he went.

24

Whiteboy was frustrated. His huge, airy house felt like a prison. Despite the bright windows and high ceilings and open-plan design, the interior was becoming claustrophobic. He was impatient. He wanted action. He needed the hot, brutal adrenaline-rush that was a perfect stress-reliever.

Whiteboy hadn't killed anything since the private detective, other than a couple of unseasonal mosquitos that he'd crushed after he'd caught them biting his arm. That was because of the damn fountain. Mosquitos weren't supposed to be able to breed in moving water, but somehow they were breeding there. He was certain of it.

When he felt this way, he was usually able to get rid of his tension by going out clubbing and picking up girls. The right type of girls. He liked them young and innocent, but susceptible to his own particular form of charm. He'd go back to their place, or book into a motel. Never to his place. He didn't want them knowing too much, in case there were repercussions down the line. Out of their minds on alcohol and cocaine, they were ready and willing to party the night away in the style that Whiteboy particularly enjoyed. He didn't care if they cried with shame and pain when they came down in the morning. He'd had his fun and would simply walk away.

Tonight, he didn't want to go clubbing because he was worried about the current situation. It was volatile, with too many variables. They needed to get it under control, and fast.

His contact had told him the girl was a looker. A spunky chick. Cheeky, with attitude. Whiteboy hadn't seen her up close, but he trusted his friend's opinion on her looks. And he knew she was daring. He'd seen her reverse into some guy's car and burst his airbag. The incident had amused him intensely.

A spunky chick sounded fun. He wondered if she'd struggle, scream, try to bite him when the time came. He hoped so. At the moment, he was so wound up the only way he was able to keep himself in check was by fantasizing about how he'd get his money's worth with her later on. He hoped he'd have the opportunity before he killed her. Just before would be his preference.

He was relieved when his other contact called back and gave him the go-ahead for a mission that he, Whiteboy, had suggested a while back.

"It's time for some misdirection," the contact said. "Let's do it."

"About bloody time," Whiteboy snapped. He didn't like to be ordered around by third parties. He operated best as an individual. He was a good leader, but nobody who knew him would call him a team player, that was for sure. In fact, most teams wouldn't dare to conduct the operations that Whiteboy handled on his own.

He got into his car, taking with him the Colt .45, carefully wiped, and the Z88, which fired 9mm rounds. The Z88 was a police-issue weapon, a local copy of the Beretta that had come onto the market at around the same time apartheid was ending. He'd chosen it for a reason. When the gun was first manufactured locally, they'd had endless problems with misfiring and other technical failures. Many of the faulty weapons found their way into criminal hands. They worked well enough most of the time, since their primary role was to scare people shitless. And if they fired once in a while, that was usually enough for your average dumb township criminal.

Whiteboy's Z88 had never failed him. But he always believed in creating a plausible scenario. He thought ahead. That was what separated him from the rest of the rabble. So in the townships, he would use a typical township gun.

He headed out onto the highway in time to ride the last wave of the evening rush hour. Where to go? Soweto would be easiest, but he was worried about the police presence there. The place had been awash with cops and private security vehicles the last time he'd driven through. It was as well policed as Sandton. Good news for the residents, bad news for him. Alexandra was also too civilized these days. The township had lost its violent edge. He would have to look further afield. An area where there was gang activity and recent unrest. Preferably a place where even the police were nervous and stayed away from the trouble spots.

He turned the car onto the highway heading north, decision made. The informal settlement of Diepsloot was the perfect location. There had been riots there recently. Taxi wars. Innocent commuters caught in the crossfire, leading to more violence and unrest.

Twenty minutes later, Whiteboy pulled off the highway and followed a stream of taxis up the main road. Past the neon sign for the Indaba hotel, which he was sure once had some sort of a reputation as a brothel. Pity he'd never had the chance to go there before it turned respectable. Past the turnoff for Dainfern, the swanky high-security golf estate. Whiteboy had no interest in that. The land was already developed. There was no opportunity there for him. And in any case, he hated golf. It was a pointless waste of time.

Whiteboy drove down a short, steep dip in the road and up the other side. He wondered if this was the *diep sloot*—the deep ditch the informal settlement had been named after. The road curved sharply and a taxi with a headlight missing veered into his path. He pounded his horn and the taxi driver corrected his steering, swerving the other way. Whiteboy seldom had a problem with taxis. He thought the drivers instinctively understood that they shouldn't try their luck with him.

He shifted his weight in the seat and turned the heater down. He slowed at a traffic light. This was Diepsloot. On his left. A dark, smoky labyrinth of tin shacks and cardboard walls and the shells of cars. From the smell of it, the residents weren't only burning wood to keep warm. They were burning anything they could lay their hands on, from garbage to car tires. A few houses had electric light, but their power was stolen, channeled down from the main lines via illegal cables. Every so often, he knew, some power thief would hit the headlines by getting fried when trying that trick.

Taxis bumped off the tarmac and stopped and started in an endless rhythm, floods of passengers emerging from the doors, hunched and hurried.

He saw two prostitutes standing at the traffic light. Their short, brightly colored skirts revealed brown chunky legs, and their arms were wrapped around their bodies for warmth.

"OK," Whiteboy said to himself. "Where does a white man go to find trouble in this place?"

He took a short drive through the township itself, bumping over the shocking roads that were more like dried-up river-beds than anything else. People stared at the tinted windows of his car with awe or resentment, depending on how they felt about the unusual sight of a brand-new Merc in their poverty-stricken world. Adrenaline hummed through his veins like electricity through a wire. He paused when he reached a shebeen, haphazardly built from concrete blocks and topped with a sloping tin roof. He could hear whoops and yells coming from the interior and the heavy bass thudding of some sort of music. Garage, hip-hop, R&B. It all sounded the same to him. The after-work party was well under way.

He shook his head. He didn't like these roads. A quick getaway would be impossible. He was positive he would find groups of tsotsis patrolling the surrounding roads, on the hunt for victims. He'd spent long enough in Diepsloot. He'd had his cultural experience for the day. It was time to get out.

Whiteboy found what he wanted at an intersection just beyond the township. A traffic light had been put up there; he didn't remember it being there the last time he'd been in the area. There was a good chance that someone would be waiting for an unwary driver as the roads grew darker and more lonely.

He drove for another ten minutes, choosing a wide circular route that took him around the area and back to the intersection. On the way he pulled over. He had two props in the cubbyhole of his car he was sure would be useful. One was a silky floral skirt. He'd found it at the house of one of the girls who'd provided him with a good night's entertainment and taken it away as a parting present.

Whiteboy opened the driver's door and let the skirt swing out into the road. Then he closed the door again. Now the section of trapped fabric would flap and flutter in the slipstream as he was driving along. Anybody who saw it would assume that a woman had slammed her long skirt in the car door as she'd climbed inside.

The second item was a fancy hairpiece: a pink band with long blond nylon "hair" stitched onto it. Put it on, and you had an instant hairstyle. He couldn't remember where he'd got that from.

He stretched it over his wide head. The nylon felt itchy and uncomfortable against his neck. Hopefully he wouldn't need to wear it for long.

Deception. His favorite strategy, one he had used many times in the past. Dupe the enemy into believing you are vulnerable.

He moved off again, going slowly, keeping his driver's window half open because he wanted them to see him, and because he didn't want to go home with a smashed window. He slipped an unlit cigarette between his lips and held his cell phone in his right hand, sandwiched against his ear.

Whiteboy steered with the heel of his other hand, which

also held the loaded Z88. He wasn't taking any chances. Some of these savages would shoot before they were even within shouting distance. But the kind of person he was hoping to target would want to get close enough to capture his victim alive.

Being a decoy was always a risk, but Whiteboy specialized in setting up situations where he—or his contact—played the role of a weak, harmless innocent. In spite of the danger, there was no better way to get the confidence of the people he wanted to trap.

He got lucky on his second circuit of the area. He approached the traffic light behind another car, an old Ford truck with a flickering taillight that had pulled in front of him a while back. From a distance, he saw the light was green. The Ford was in no hurry. It dawdled towards the light, and eased to a stop as it turned orange, and then red.

Whiteboy smiled. He felt intensely alive. He drew in a deep breath, inhaling the pervasive sooty stench of the township ahead, listening to the crickets in the roadside grasses and the sputtering engine of the car in front.

The Ford rolled back a slow half-meter. Now he was trapped. He couldn't pull out to the side of it and get away. Excellent. He clicked the safety off the Z88 and scanned the half-section of open window out of the corner of his eye. He dropped the cell phone under his seat.

Quicker than he could blink, they were there. Swift hands reached into the window, shoved his shoulder sideways, found the handle and yanked the door open.

Two guys. Young, black, vicious. A Beretta was jammed into his face as they snatched at him again, intending to drag him out of the car.

"You white bitch. Get out, you bitch," he heard one say.

Whiteboy raised his right hand as if in panic or surrender. His hand pushed the gun upwards, out of range. The move was easy, and it looked natural because they had the weapon far too close. Why didn't these fools go get some tactical training? They were hopeless amateurs.

There was no time to waste. The guy with the gun grabbed his shoulder again. His upper body filled Whiteboy's vision, blocking his escape from the vehicle.

Whiteboy swivelled the barrel of the Z88 towards him and fired, left-handed, across the bulk of his midriff.

The explosion was deafening in the confined space of the car. The guy sagged backwards and collapsed. Whiteboy heard the thud of his weapon hitting the tarmac. The sharp tang of gunpowder filled the car.

His friend froze for a second. Then realization kicked in. He ducked low, straightened up, and ran for it. The door of the Ford opened and he dived inside. The engine screamed in protest as the Ford careered away, backfiring, sparks shooting from the trailing exhaust pipe.

Whiteboy pushed the driver's door open wider. The man he'd shot had fallen face-up, hands outstretched. Blood was still welling from his chest. Without emergency medical help, he'd be dead in a couple of minutes. Whiteboy scanned the dark, empty road. It was unfortunate, but he didn't foresee emergency medical help arriving in such a tight timeframe.

His full lips curved in a small smile when he noticed the man's weapon was missing. His friend must have retrieved the Beretta when he ducked down before his desperate run for safety. That was good thinking under pressure. A gutsy move. He admired it. He'd like to have that guy work for him, doing the grunt jobs like burglary and arson. Not this asshole, though.

Whiteboy lit his cigarette with the car's lighter and took a deep, satisfied draw. Then he pulled on a pair of gloves. He took the Colt .45 from his car and picked up the man's right hand, which was already a dead weight. He arranged his fingers around the grip of the gun. For good measure, he picked up the man's left hand and planted a few more smudgy fingerprints on the barrel. Then he let the arms of his would-be hijacker fall to the ground. The gun thudded down next to him.

He scanned the road again. Far in the distance, he saw the twinkle of approaching headlights. He would have to move fast.

The man was wearing torn and dirty jeans and a cheap puffer jacket that he must have bought at a discount store. Whiteboy sympathized. It wasn't easy to make crime pay. Not everyone could do it. You needed a unique blend of ruthlessness and intelligence. He believed true criminals were born, not made.

The jeans and jacket both had pockets. He went to work. The inner pocket of the jacket was already soaked with blood, but that wasn't a problem. It would add authenticity to the evidence.

He whipped off the rubber gloves and flung them into the passenger well. He stubbed the cigarette out in his car's ashtray. He wasn't an idiot. He would never leave trace evidence at a scene. He was in his car and accelerating away by the time the approaching headlights rounded the bend.

✦

Jade knew she'd have to speak to David again at some stage. When she could face the idea. She'd come to terms with the fact that David wasn't her hero any more. He wasn't the older, more experienced idol he had been ten years ago. He was a man dealing with his own messy and complicated personal life, and it was bad luck for her that she'd become caught up in it. She had to accept that. After all, they were investigating a case together. Her father had always emphasized that the case must come first, whether she was working with people she liked, people she hated, or people who she felt had let her down.

So Jade put the case first.

She drove out to Annette's house. She wanted to see Piet again, find out if there were any other pieces of information he'd simply forgotten to share with her. Jade felt sorry for him. He had lost the woman who was close to him. More than that, he had lost his much-cherished dream of being able to make things right with her again.

Sometimes, Jade knew, losing your dreams could be worse than losing your reality.

"There's a lot I'd tell your mother, if she had her time over," her father had said on one of the rare occasions he had spoken about his wife. "Such a lot I wished I'd said. Don't be shy, Jade, when you need to tell somebody you love them, or you'll regret it one day."

She thought about those words as she was driving. She had tried to tell David how she felt, and it had backfired on her. David had other issues to deal with. He'd lost his heart to another woman. Or rather, as Jade saw it, to a conniving bitch who'd probably only fallen pregnant in the first place in order to entrap him.

❧

Piet wandered out of the house wearing a paint-spattered tracksuit and his ancient sandals. He buzzed her inside, keys in one hand, brush in the other. The circles under his eyes looked darker than ever and his hair stood on end in a wild, tangled bush.

"Jade. It's good to see you. Is there any news?"

"Nothing concrete yet." She climbed out of the car. "But we've been working non-stop. We're pursuing a few promising leads."

Piet was too naïve to realize this meant no progress had been made.

"That's great. Come in."

Jade followed him into the master bedroom, where sheets of newspaper covered the carpet. A stepladder stood on the newspaper and a tray of paint and an artist's palette were balanced on what looked like a clotheshorse. Piet had outlined an intricate pattern of leaves and flowers on the wardrobe door and now he was filling it in.

"I have to do something to distract myself from this business." He took a heavy step onto the bottom rung of the ladder. "My wife has been murdered. And now the police are prying into everything. My bank statements. My insurance policies. Nothing is private any more. They're still making out like I'm guilty." He set the brush down and twisted round on the ladder. His eyebrows spiked in all directions and he had a smudge of green on his nose. "I don't want Annette's money. I've already decided I'm going to donate it to charity. To the Animal Anti-Cruelty League, because I feel guilty about giving away her dogs.

"So I don't know why they're doing this." He turned back to his work. "I mean, I've been cooperating with them for more than a week. Are they getting impatient because they haven't found a suspect yet?"

The bed had been stripped of linen. Jade perched on the edge of bare mattress, patterned in blue and white. "Not at all. But they can't clear you immediately, either. Bank statements and insurance policies take a while to obtain. It's all routine, Piet. You needn't worry."

She watched as he swept his brush across the palette. He dabbed paint onto a leaf, adding more green to an area already dark green. He withdrew the brush and leaned backwards, evaluating the result with his head on one side. Jade could see no discernible difference. But then, she wasn't the artist.

"Tell me about Annette," Jade said.

Piet looked over his shoulder at her. "But I told you already what she was like."

"Tell me again. Why was she so private?"

He dabbed the brush in the paint again, his movements practiced and confident. He looked contented and sure of himself when he was painting. As if this was a world he understood, one where nobody killed or threatened or lied.

"She had to rely on herself from an early age." Piet dabbed, inspected, and dabbed again. "Her parents died before I met her. Cancer. They were chain smokers, both of them. Annette never touched cigarettes. She hated that I smoked. That was another problem between us."

"So she had no family except her brother?"

"No family apart from him. Family was important to her because she had so little. She loved her brother. And even when we divorced, she kept in touch with me."

"You two never had children?" Since seeing Naisha and the boy she now realized was Kevin, Jade had decided she needed to ask these questions upfront, so the answers couldn't come back to bite her later.

Piet shook his head. "Annette couldn't. She had women's problems. Endometriosis, I think they called it."

"And her brother?" Jade was thinking about the two golf trophies on the wall unit. Now they were packed away with everything else.

Piet shrugged. "Adrian was married and divorced. Many years ago. No kids." His face pulled down into mournful lines. Jade wondered whether Piet had wanted children.

"What was his wife's name?"

"Tracy. I don't remember her maiden name. She lives in Ireland now." He looked over his shoulder again, apologetically. "Not Ellie. I don't know who Ellie was. Annette never said anything about an Ellie."

Jade's cell phone rang. She jumped. She couldn't help it. She scanned the incoming number and her stomach knotted. It was David calling. She didn't want to speak to him, but the case came first.

"Hi," she said.

"Jade. Where are you?" David's voice thrummed with tension.

"I'm with Piet, discussing a couple of things."

"Shit," he muttered.

"What?"

"Just move away from him, OK? Get somewhere private. I need an urgent word."

Jade stood up. "Sorry, Piet. Emergency call."

He nodded without turning away from his painting.

She went into the garden and looked at the view again. Yellow grass, blue sky, wooden fences, red brick barn.

"Are you there?" David asked.

"Of course I'm here." Control yourself, she thought. Be nice. Don't snap.

"Officer Moloi has just come into my office with evidence relating to Annette Botha's case."

"Go on." Jade walked down the hill towards the horse barn, feeling the long grass brush against her knees.

"The Diepsloot patrol unit found a body just outside the informal settlement last night. A gangster, shot dead in the road. He had a thousand rand in his pocket, which, amazingly, didn't disappear before we came along, a Colt .45 firearm, and a business card belonging to one Piet Botha. The weapon's already at ballistics for test-firing, to see if it's the same .45 used to murder Annette." He paused. "I've got a car on the way. We're arresting Piet and bringing him in for questioning."

Jade walked through the wood-framed doorway into the horse barn. The roof was high and large windows flooded the place with light. The barn was divided into roomy stalls. Down its center was a wide corridor paved with a rubberized material. It was springy underfoot. She stepped along it, her footsteps soundless.

"Jade? Are you there?"

"That can't be right. I just don't think Piet could have arranged that. He can hardly organize for the gate to be opened when somebody arrives."

"The evidence contradicts that. We have to bring him in."

"David, he's not acting guilty. I don't believe he's a liar. He's just a sad little man who's missing his wife. And he's terrified of going to jail. I'm going to feel like Judas if I know you're coming for him and I don't say anything."

"Please stay there, Jade. You can tell him, if you like. Maybe he has an explanation." David sounded unconvinced.

Jade turned and walked back along the rubber matting. It was smooth and still looked brand-new. Then it dawned on her that the barn didn't smell of horse. There was no manure. No flies. The concrete floors were clean and unstained. No traces of straw, or whatever horses ate. Horses had never lived here. The barn was an empty shell.

"I'll tell him," she agreed reluctantly. "Maybe there's a reason for it. Personally, I think someone's setting him up."

She went back up to the house with leaden feet.

Piet stumbled off his ladder when she told him the news. He collapsed on the bed, buried his face in his hands and started to sob.

"Jade, I don't believe this. How can it be? This is a bad dream. I'm living in a nightmare." He looked up at her, his furrowed face streaked with tears and paint. "How can a gangster have my business card?"

"Piet, we have to try and think clearly here. The sooner the police have an explanation, the sooner you'll be out of custody. Did you have your wallet snatched at any stage? Was there a burglary at your house?"

Jade looked at him, hoping against hope that something plausible had happened. How had his card ended up in the clutches of a township tsotsi? She needed to think for him, because she could see Piet wasn't capable of coherent thought at the moment.

He shook his head. "No burglary."

"You've been giving your business cards out to all the press who've been round to get your story. Perhaps the guy got hold of your card that way."

"Perhaps." Piet blew his nose. Jade saw that his hands were shaking. "How can we tell?"

"The detectives will have to follow up. In the meantime, you need to get ready to go. The patrol vehicle is on its way."

Piet looked at her, wild hope in his eyes. "Jade, I've had an idea. I'm going to make a run for it. Now, in the Golf. I'm going to escape them. Will you cover for me?"

"No, Piet, please don't do that. Or you'll be in worse trouble." Jade grasped his shoulders. "We'll sort this out as quickly as we can. In the meantime, put the lids on your paints and get yourself a warm jacket. Not an expensive one. Something old. It might be chilly in those cells."

"Will I be locked up with other people?"

She nodded. "There's usually three or four in each holding cell."

Piet's knees quivered and he slumped back onto the bed. "I'm going to be anally raped, I know it. They're going to beat me up. Please don't let them take me, Jade."

She walked over to the mural and carefully moved the clotheshorse aside. Piet had a few clothes in the cupboard. She chose a thick hooded jacket with old paint stains on its front. Nobody would fight him for that, she hoped. She found a pair of socks on a shelf and took those as well. She pushed Piet's arms through the sleeves, feeling as if she was dressing a child for school. He put his socks on and tightened the Velcro on his rafters.

"I need to go to the bathroom." He shuffled away, arms wrapped round his body.

When he returned, the car was honking at the gate.

"Will you lock up, Jade?" he asked. "Will you take care of everything till I get back?"

"Of course," she reassured him. "Call me as soon as you're out, too, and I'll pick you up."

"They're not going to handcuff me, are they?"

"Shouldn't think so," she said. But she was wrong. The arresting officers were new and keen and weren't prepared to bend the rules. Suspects under arrest had to be cuffed. Piet stared in horror, tears welling in his eyes as the officer fastened the metal bracelets around his wrists. He looked small and alone in the back of the police car as it turned out of the driveway and disappeared down the road.

25

Jade put the lids back onto the tins of paint and put them back in the tray with the others. She found some paint thinner and an old jar in the scullery. She left the brush to soak and took the stepladder out to the yard.

There wasn't much else to straighten up. The kitchen was filled with cardboard boxes ready for transport and storage. She could see which ones had been labeled by Piet. His writing was large and bold, the capital letters written with a flourish. There were more boxes in the corner that Annette must have packed before she died. They were carefully sealed and had small neat lettering on their sides. "Books," "Bathroom" and five or six large boxes labeled "Adrian—Sport" and "Adrian—Personal."

Jade heard honking outside. For a crazy moment, she thought the police vehicle was back, bringing Piet home again. She ran outside with the remote in her hand.

David was at the gate.

"Open up, Jade. We need to get moving."

She locked up the house and hurried over. "What's happened?"

He waved a sheet of paper. "We've got a match for the fingerprint on the axe."

David looked relaxed, almost unconcerned, but Jade could tell from the set of his jaw that he was already on the chase. She took the paper, trying not to think about the fact that it had been procured for him as a favor by his wife. She was going to focus on the task ahead and try to forget what had happened the day before.

Her eyebrows rose as she read through the printout. "This thumbprint belongs to a woman."

"Yup. We're on our way to find her."

Thandi Khumalo lived in a rented flat in an apartment block opposite a park. It looked like tranquil suburbia, but the steel access gate and the perimeter fence topped with razor wire told a different story.

They found the caretaker in the garden fixing a security light.

"Thandi? I'd be surprised if she could even lift an axe." He laughed. "But she works at a hardware store, so she might have sold it." He gave them the address; she worked near Sandton.

They got back into the police car.

"We can take a short cut through Alex township. If you're not scared."

"I'm more scared driving through Alexandra with a cop than I would be on my own."

David grinned. "Me too."

Looking through the car window, Jade was surprised at how the sprawling settlement had been improved. Rows of modest houses were set out in geometric formation, forcing the corrugated-iron shacks into retreat. Jade could see power lines and streetlights. The air was clear. People had planted flowers and trees in the spaces outside their homes.

"It's a lot better now," David declared. "The houses on this side of the road were built for athletes competing in the All Africa Games. When the games were over, they were passed on to residents, and they've carried on building houses from there. Most of the townships are the same, now. Low-cost housing is starting to take over." He nodded approvingly. "In a hundred years or so, there probably won't be any crime at all. Everyone will be happy, in their own little homes with electricity and television."

"Pity you won't be alive to see it."

"Speak for yourself. I plan on living till at least a hundred and eighty."

The hardware store where Thandi worked was in a newish shopping center. Thandi herself was sturdy and short, with a bright smile and straightened hair gelled back and held in place by a butterfly clip. She wore blue jeans and a black golf shirt with the hardware store's logo on the pocket.

David explained the situation. The store manager hovered in the background, keen to hear the latest news from the world of crime fighting. Thandi listened, leaning forward, eyes wide and attentive. When he told her that a murder had been committed with the axe, her hands flew to her mouth in horror.

"Eish!" she said.

"Do you know anything about it?" asked David. He opened his file and passed her a photocopied sheet with the axe's measurements and a 10x8 color photograph.

Thandi and the manager looked at the photo as if it was

going to leap off the page and attack them. They glanced at each other and nodded.

"This is the type of stock we sell," the manager confirmed.

"Thandi. Did you sell an axe recently? Or pack one onto the shelves? Handle one at all?"

Thandi thought for a while. Then she nodded.

"On Monday morning I sold such an item to a customer."

"And before that?" David asked. "Any other sales?"

She shook her head. "That was the only axe I have sold for a while. People like to buy them at the start of winter, in May. Now it is nearly July."

David leaned forward, his expression intent. "Tell us about the customer."

She thought some more, pursing her lips and rubbing her fingers together.

"He asked me for equipment. Axe, hedge-clippers, a crowbar. And gloves. I fetched everything for him. He made me walk all around the shop."

Jade and David exchanged glances. Yolandi had been assaulted with a crowbar on Wednesday night. Had this man purchased the weapon used to attack her as well?

"How did he pay?"

"Cash, I think. Yes, because he counted his change as if I was stealing from him. Then he told me to pack the shopping for him. He took the bags and left the shop."

The manager cleared his throat. "Monday morning. Would a security video help you? We've got one in place here. I'll get it for you and then you can play it back and see him." He rushed off to the back of the store.

Thandi continued. "He was a white man. Tall."

Jade looked at Thandi, who, if she wore platform shoes,

might have reached five feet in height. To her, the word "tall" probably covered a broad range of possibilities.

"Taller than him?" She pointed to David, who drew himself up to his full six foot five. Thandi's head came to the middle of his chest.

"Maybe." She had to crane her neck in order to see David's face. "Maybe as tall as him."

"We'll see more from the video," David said. "Tell us anything else you noticed about him."

"He had short hair. Brown, I think. Or red. He did not smile. He had something on his face." She smoothed her fingers along her cheekbone in demonstration. "Here on his face. Like scars."

"His age?"

She shrugged. "Not young. Not old."

"What about his voice? Did you notice any accent?"

Thandi thought about it. "He sounded ordinary. Like any white South African guy."

David scribbled notes. "Anything else? Did you see where he went afterwards? His car?"

Thandi shook her head. "Perhaps if you ask the car guard. He is good with remembering people."

They thanked her, and she headed over to the till, head held high, proud at having been able to help.

The manager brought back the security tapes for Monday that covered the hours from nine a.m. to one p.m. "Shout if you need any others. But we checked on the computer. The purchase was made at ten past eleven."

Before they left the shop, David took a couple of digital photos of the till area using his cell phone. He asked the manager for a Stanley tape measure to record the height of the counter. To Thandi's amusement, he measured her too. "These photos will help the techie with color analysis from the black and white footage," he said. "Should be able to get the guy's approximate height as well, with these references."

Jade went out to talk to the car guard, but their conversation was not as fruitful. The man said he knew all the regulars, but he did not remember a man with a scarred face.

"So he's not a regular." David looked disappointed. "Suppose it would be too good to be true if he was."

"Makes sense," Jade said. "You wouldn't go and buy a murder weapon from your local hardware store. We were lucky that Thandi remembered him. Otherwise we'd be as deep in the dark as we were when we started."

Jo'burg Central's media center sounded grander than it looked. It was in fact an old meeting room equipped with a TV, a video and DVD machine, some basic computer equipment and a variety of uncomfortable chairs. After the technician had copied the tapes onto DVD, he, David and Jade went in and settled down to watch the footage.

"They've got the time running at the bottom of the screen on digital display," the techie said. "Where do you want to start?"

David turned to Jade. "How about ten past eleven, when the man made the purchase? Then we'll see what he looks like, and we can go back and see when he came in."

"Sounds good," she said.

Jade watched as the day in the life of a hardware store flickered past at high speed in grainy black and white. The security camera had been set up to show the shop doors and the two tills. The till staff had their backs to the camera, the customers faced it. She wondered whether its primary purpose was to keep the clients or the staff honest. As the technician fast-forwarded, people raced in and whirled past and scuttled out. Money and goods whipped from hand to hand. The security guard near the tills zigzagged to and fro like a goalkeeper.

"Right. Let's slow it down here." The time was 11.05. He pressed a button and the scene shifted to normal speed. They watched an old lady hobble past. Her progress seemed infinitely slow. She left the screen and the two tills stood empty. The technician's finger hovered over the fast-forward button.

"No," David said. "Wait."

A minute later two more customers appeared. Then Thandi came into view, pushing a trolley. She was easy to spot, being a head shorter than everyone else and two heads shorter than the bulky man who was following her. His head was turned towards her and his back was to the camera. Jade watched her push the trolley over to the till and unload the goods.

The technician pushed another button and the scene went into slow motion. The man had his hands in the pockets of his jacket and was keeping his head down.

"Shit. The bugger knows there's a bloody camera there." David shifted in his chair.

Thandi hefted the axe and the other items onto the counter, scanned the purchases and looked up at the man.

"She's touched that axe all over its handle," Jade said.

David nodded. "He must have wiped it. He was careful. Just forgot about the base."

The man produced a wallet from his pocket and counted out seven one hundred rand notes. Thandi gave him his change. Then he pointed at the plastic bags on the counter.

She started packing his goods. The axe was long and heavy and Jade saw that she'd had to support the base of the handle with her thumb in order to get it in a bag.

The man picked up his purchases and strolled out of the shop.

"Crap," David said. "Couldn't he have looked up?"

"Don't worry," the technician said. "That footage told us something."

"OK. Before we go any further, let's backtrack and see what he did when he came in."

"How far shall I go back?"

"How long does it take someone to decide what bloody axe to buy? They're all the same. Go back fifteen minutes and let's see if he's there."

Ten minutes before he left the shop, the man strode in, hands in his pockets. He went straight past the tills and headed for the gardening section.

"There you have it." David banged his fist down on the table. "Guy couldn't even smile for the bloody camera."

"Doesn't matter," the tech said. "We'll run it again. I'm seeing enough of his face to get a few good stills. Can't ask for more. A camera like this, it's put in for the staff more than the customers. You see how you can watch everything they're doing when they turn to the cash drawer?"

He zoomed in on a frame. "This is the best one I see, but there's a few other good ones. We should be able to get his approximate height and weight, too."

"How long will it take?"

The techie sighed. "You don't want to know what my backlog's like." Then he saw David's face. "For you, Superintendent, we'll prioritize it. I'll call you in a couple of hours."

26

Jade sat with David in his office. Now that the excitement of tracing the axe was over, the silence between them felt uneasy. She didn't know what to say to him. She was worried that if she spoke, she would end up saying something she would regret. Or he would misinterpret her words. Instead, she stared at the wall opposite her and said nothing. She was relieved when the phone rang. The sergeant at the front desk was on the line. David put the call on speakerphone. Jade wondered if he did this in the interests of transparency, so she wouldn't think it was his wife calling.

"We've got a man here to see you," the sergeant said.

"Well, go on then. Why are you phoning? Just send him up."

"Superintendent, I think in this case it would be easier for you to come down."

Graham Hope was waiting downstairs in the foyer. The sergeant had thoughtfully found him a chair. He sat perched on its edge, his bad leg stretched in front of him, his crutches on the floor beside him.

"Ah, Jade. Good to see you again." He fumbled for his crutches and used them to haul himself into a standing position. He held out his hand to David. As he did, one of the metal sticks tumbled to the floor again. The loud clatter caused people in the queue for the front desk to turn and stare.

David bent and picked up the crutch and handed it to the man.

"Thank you, thank you. As I've said to Jade, I'm counting the days till this damn leg is mended. I'm Graham Hope."

"Superintendent Patel." David shook his hand.

"I was passing by. The deeds office is down the road and I had to pick up some documents for a house sale."

David said nothing. Just nodded and waited for the man to continue.

"Actually, I'm here on behalf of one of my clients." He stopped and looked abashed. "Jade is going to think I'm a fearful gossip, and I'm sorry about that." He winked at her. "But I had to make a personal visit and confirm this with you." Hope paused again, propped his elbow on a crutch, and scratched his chin. "This is rather embarrassing. I don't know why I have to be the one to ask these questions. I'm the front man, I suppose. Speaking on behalf of the community. I heard Piet Botha was arrested earlier today, so I've just popped in to confirm whether it's true."

David groaned. Then he turned to Jade with an incredulous frown. "Did you tell him this?"

Jade glared at him. "No, I did not. What do you think, I go around leaking information on the case as soon as your back is turned?"

Graham reached out and took her arm. Was it her imagination, or did she see David glance at his wedding band and then at her, an unreadable expression on his face?

"I'm sorry. Now I've put the cat among the pigeons." Graham blinked, and smiled disarmingly. His expression looked innocent, but Jade realized he had picked up the tension between them immediately. Graham's amiable manner concealed lightning-sharp instincts that would have made a top investigator proud. Now, she guessed, he would use the situation to his advantage.

"I didn't mean to do that." He continued speaking, proving her right. "And, Superintendent, I'd like to confirm that Jade has never discussed any aspect of your case with me that she shouldn't have, not even during our pleasant chat over lunch the other day."

Jade glanced down. David's arms were by his sides. His hands had balled into fists. Was he jealous? Or did he disapprove of her having lunch with a married man? She lifted her chin. How dare he be jealous. And if he disapproved, then why was he round at her cottage like a hungry dog wagging its tail every time he thought there was a chance of getting some cop food? How hypocritical could a man be?

"No," Graham shook his head, eyes twinkling. "I'm here because of a random and unconfirmed sighting. A neighbor saw him being driven away in a police vehicle, and thought she recognized him."

David looked at the man with dislike. "Yes, Piet Botha is in police custody at present," he snapped.

Graham beamed. "Well, that is excellent news. You don't know it, Superintendent, but you've made our day. I've always thought that part of the northwestern suburbs is one of the safest in Johannesburg. That's what I tell my clients, at least. If this had been a random hijacking, I would have been proved a liar. As it is, I think we can all stop holding our breath and looking over our shoulders." He gave Jade's arm a final squeeze.

"I'll be off. Many thanks. And congratulations, Superintendent. We can all sleep easier knowing the South African police service is working so tirelessly."

He fumbled with his crutches, threaded his arms through them, and swung away towards the door.

"What the hell?" David asked. "Is he legal to drive with a leg like that?"

"His car's an automatic." Jade turned and walked back up the stairs.

"Oh, so you've been in his car?"

"David." Jade stopped on the step above him and turned towards him, infuriated. With the extra height it provided, she was almost eye to eye with him. "I have not been in his car. He told us the first time we met him at Piet's place that he drives an automatic. What on earth is your problem with him?"

David shook his head. He pushed past her and continued up to the second floor, his heavy footsteps echoing in the stairwell. By the time they'd reached his office, he'd brought his temper under control again.

"Nothing. This case is getting to me, that's all." He pushed open the door. "Bad enough without having a human broadcasting system conveying information to the general public before my goddamn team even knows about it."

David had a fan heater in his office. Its gentle rattling and buzzing was the only noise Jade could hear as she followed him into the room and sat down again. She began staring at the wall again, and saw David staring at the one opposite. They didn't speak. David's stomach rumbled. In the tense silence, the noise sounded like Vesuvius erupting.

They both jumped when the phone rang. David grabbed the receiver on the first ring.

"Yes. Yes! Fantastic. Bring them along."

He slammed the phone down and turned to Jade, his ill humor forgotten. "That guy's the best in the business. He's on his way now."

The tech brought five A5 photo prints with him. He spread them out on the desk.

"He's very pale-skinned," he said. "At first I thought I was messing up the color balance, but when I tried a normal skin tone, it looked like the shop had had a power failure, it's so dark."

They looked down at the prints.

The man's jaw was massive and heavy. His lips were full and his nose looked twisted, as if it had been broken. His pale skin was blotchy, with reddish-brown scars on his cheeks and nose.

"He's no oil painting, that's for sure," David muttered. "What's with the skin? Thandi said he had something on his cheeks. You can see it in that pic. On his nose, too."

"It's some sort of pigmentation. Freckles, perhaps, or scarring from sunburn. I've sent the pics to a professor at Wits University to see if he has any other ideas."

"Looks bloody unhealthy."

"His hair is red, we think. With black and white footage, we can't be sure. But red hair would match his skin coloring."

"His age? His height?"

"At least six feet two. Between thirty-five and fifty years old. And weight probably around a hundred and twenty kilograms. He's overweight for his size. Heavy but not obese."

"Thanks." David clapped the man on the back. "Let us know more as soon as you know."

The technician must have called in some favors of his own, because he phoned back again later with more news. David put the call on speakerphone so Jade could hear the report first-hand.

"About the scarring on his cheekbones and nose. The professor at Wits says it might be from burns. Scalding, perhaps. Probably also the result of long-term exposure to the sun."

David replaced the handset.

"Sun exposure and a local accent. So our friend's probably been in South Africa most of his life."

Jade realized what he was thinking.

"He would have done national service."

"Yup. A compulsory stint in the Army, same as any other white guy. Army service was two years, right up until the late eighties. It was only dropped after the 1994 elections. So, if he wasn't a draft dodger, and he grew up in South Africa, there's a ninety-nine percent chance that he would have spent at least one year, probably two, in the Army." His face broke into a triumphant grin. "Private Jade de Jong, since you enjoy spending long hours with strange men, I hereby volunteer you for the research task force."

27

Defense Force headquarters had undergone one of the many name changes that had swept South Africa during the last decade. Sometimes Jade felt she had returned to an entirely different country.

Headquarters, originally called Roberts Heights, was nestled at the foot of the hill where the Voortrekker Monument had been built. In a fit of nationalism, the old regime had renamed the base Voortrekkerhoogte, or Voortrekker Heights. When the ANC came into power, that name had been discarded. The new name was Thaba Tshwane, which Jade personally thought sounded like somebody sneezing.

Apart from the change in signage, the Army base looked the same as Jade remembered it from her few brief visits long ago. When she drove through the gates early the following morning, she was shown through to the office of the Chief Directorate of Human Resources. The director was a tall man with close-cropped hair and a ramrod-straight carriage. His voice was clipped and brisk with a surprisingly English accent that Jade had noticed when she had phoned him the previous afternoon.

Once he'd heard her story in person, the director picked up the phone.

"I need to access all staff records from 1974 to 1989. We'll need two of you to help us search through the files. I'll see you at the records office in five minutes."

He gestured to Jade.

"Come on. Let's go."

The lawns outside the admin center were the only place in the South African winter highveld that were emerald green and lush. Jade saw two soldiers weeding and trimming and another one moving a sprinkler around. In the Army, anything was possible, she supposed.

The director gave two corporals the job of locating the paper files and carrying them from the vaults. He sat with Jade and got ready to search the computerized files.

"We should start with height," he decided. "What are our parameters?"

"Let's take everyone over six foot."

"Fair enough. That'll weed out three quarters of them."

Jade was glad she'd come early, because the task in hand seemed endless, with record after record flashing up on the screen, and the two helpers running backwards and forwards with armfuls of files. She was pleased that they were also diligent about keeping her coffee cup refilled.

They went through the first five years' worth of files before lunch. The following ten after lunch went more quickly.

"Were you already experiencing reduction in numbers?" Jade asked.

The director nodded. "Every year you could see a difference."

By half past three the computer work was over. Jade looked at the massive stacks of paper files she would need to go through one by one and sighed.

With the color photo provided by the tech as reference, she started searching through the records. Each file contained an identity photograph and a full description. She looked at the photos of the young men who had been forced to sign up for military service in the old South Africa.

The men looked so young, so innocent. Wide smiles, guileless eyes, skin scarred with acne but otherwise smooth. She was sure that when the photos had been taken, the men had no idea what their future held, or the part they would play in enforcing the apartheid regime, like pawns in a flawed game of chess.

At half past five she found the file she needed, although she didn't realize it at first. The repetitive mechanical processing of paper had lulled her into a stupor. She flicked through its pages automatically. Then she stopped, went back, and looked again.

The man was called Garth Whiteley and was from the 1976 intake. The records stated that his hair was red, his eyes blue. He'd squinted at the camera, unsmiling. In the black and white photograph his skin looked doughy and pale, blotched with grayish streaks of scarring over his cheeks and nose. He had a bulky jaw and a nose that looked identical to the one of the man in the hardware store photograph.

"I think we've found him," she called.

The director came over and took a look.

"Seems like a match to me. Whiteley. Let's see what happened to him."

He turned to the computer and typed in a couple of commands.

"He spent three months in basics. Then he went through to intelligence. Obviously a clever boy." He frowned down at the yellowed pages. "Looks like he spent three years in the army, and most of it under the command of my friend General Nel. I can call Nel if you like. He's still around. Find out more about Whiteley."

"Thank you," Jade said.

The director got on the phone. He talked and listened, scribbling notes on his pad. Jade waited, looking at the pages that were completed thirty years ago. His identity number was there. His home address too, although she doubted he would still be living there. It was for a house in Townview, Germiston. Back then, it had been a place where working-class whites had lived. Now, Jade was sure it was close to being a no-go area. She wondered if Whiteley had wanted to do his national service. Being poor, he wouldn't have had a choice. Rich boys who didn't want to do national service had emigrated or pleaded that they were medically unfit. With the help of an obliging family doctor, any excuse could be fabricated.

"Right. I've got some interesting information for you." The director put the phone down. "Nel remembers him well."

"Fantastic. What was he like?"

"From the Army's point of view, he was a contradiction." He glanced down at the paper. "Nel says he was orphaned just before he was called up. His mother, a single parent, committed suicide by drowning herself in the bath, apparently. Whiteley qualified for exemption because of that, but he chose to join up anyway. He was overweight and unfit. Barely made it through basic training. But he had a brilliant strategic mind."

"Hence the move to intelligence?"

"Exactly. He performed well for a year, worked his way into

a leadership position. They sent him to the border, then to Angola, where he ended up in charge of a unit after the commander was killed in a training accident. That was when the trouble started."

"What trouble?"

"Theft of supplies. Theft of equipment. It happens from time to time, but this was on a serious scale. Looting of the surrounding villages. A couple of the troops in his unit must have been intimidated, because when we investigated they wouldn't say a thing. Another couple of troops went missing. Suspected of desertion, but you never know."

"What did General Nel think at the time?"

"At the time, he thought Whiteley was a poor leader, that he was letting his troops run riot. It was only later that he realized Whiteley was behind it all. Nel reckons he was selling equipment and supplies to the enemy, the SWAPO terrorists. Getting cash or diamonds in exchange. He didn't have a shred of proof, so he couldn't arrest him, but he got him recalled to Pretoria and discharged from the Army."

"Did he ever see him again?"

"Never. But he wasn't surprised when I said he was a suspect in a criminal case. He said Whiteley was a violent man. And a dangerous one." The director paused and paged back through his notes. "But he didn't call him Whiteley while we were talking. He referred to him as Whiteboy. A nickname, I suppose."

28

David's team was waiting for him outside the station at six the following morning. After checking Whiteley's current details he discovered he still lived at the same house in Townview that had appeared on his Army records. He thought that was odd, since, according to Jade's research, the man had spent most of his Army years enriching himself at his country's expense. Perhaps he'd gambled his fortune away.

They were all wearing Kevlar vests. Whiteley was a violent and potentially dangerous criminal. The tension in the car was tangible and David found himself driving in an uncharacteristically conservative fashion, watching the road ahead with both hands tight on the wheel. He wished Jade was there to make a cheeky comment and ease his nerves. He knew how she felt about his usual driving style.

Townview was an area of narrow streets and steep hills. Seeing the littered gutters, smashed windows and cracked paving, David thought that compared to here, almost anywhere could be classified as a good neighborhood.

They passed a couple of people hurrying along the pavement, looking cold. A young couple, dressed in the generic uniform of whatever chain store they were headed for to do their day's work. A single girl with a pasty face and a grubby cream jacket, wearing a very short skirt. She stumbled on the paving in her high heels.

David was sure she was on her way home, rather than on her way out. She had probably been dropped off at the main road by a client who, in contrast to his behavior the night before, wasn't prepared to go all the way with her the morning after.

He pulled over, parked on the pavement outside Whiteley's house, and climbed out as the backup vehicle stopped behind him.

The tiny house had peeling paint and a yellowing picket

fence. He saw overgrown grass in the square of garden, dead branches hanging low over the fence, and a garage with a closed door. A dog kennel and a shed were crammed between the house and the fence. The dog kennel didn't seem to be occupied, and the door of the shed hung half open.

"You stay behind us," he told the junior members of his team. "You come with me," he told Moloi. The solidly built black officer walked by his side. Weapons ready, the other men took up positions to the left and right, where they could cover the front door.

David walked the short distance from the car to the door, shoulder to shoulder with the other officer. He raised his fist and hammered on the door. The sound was as loud and heavy as a drum.

There was silence for a minute. Then David heard footsteps inside the house. At the same moment he felt Moloi tense.

The door opened. The man they'd seen in the hardware store stood before them, hands on hips. His head was inclined to one side, brows raised and full lips in a half-smile as if he was curious, but unworried, about the presence of four policemen outside his front door in the early morning.

He wore faded blue jeans and a black T-shirt that stretched taut over the curve of his stomach and emphasized the pallor of his scarred face.

"Mr. Whiteley." David stepped forward. Whiteley was a couple of inches shorter than him, but the man carried himself tall. His bulk was intimidating. David straightened his back and squared his shoulders, and looked straight into the man's eyes. "I'm Superintendent Patel from Johannesburg Central's Serious and Violent Crimes Unit."

Whiteley met David's stare. "Yes. Can I help you?" His voice was slow and toneless. His pale eyes were as emotionless as his voice.

"We're here because we have reason to suspect that you are involved in the murder of a Mr. Dean Grobbelaar."

Whiteley snickered.

"What proof do you have, if I might ask, gentlemen?"

"Sir, we have proof linking you to the purchase of an axe. A weapon which was subsequently used to murder Mr. Grobbelaar. We have warrants to search your premises and to arrest you."

Whiteley shrugged. "I bought an axe a week or so ago. I bought a lot of equipment." He looked out at his dismal garden. "I was going to tidy the place up. I put the stuff in the shed." He pointed to the wooden door that swung open in the breeze. "It was broken into, unfortunately. The night after I bought it. I reported it to the local police station in the morning."

He looked David in the eye and his puffy lips widened into a smile that didn't reach his eyes. "Aren't the police shocking? Haven't even had one cop round yet to take a look."

"Check that out," David said to Moloi. He turned back to Whiteley. "Where did you report it?"

"My local cop shop. Townview. Feel free to check. Assuming they haven't lost the records. I dialed the emergency number first. That 10111 number everyone's always talking about. Do you know, it didn't even get answered? I was glad I wasn't being raped or killed or anything."

Whiteley's smile stretched into a broad grin. From where David was standing, in the pale morning light, his face looked like a death mask.

"Sir, I'm sorry nobody investigated your break-in further.

We'll follow that up. In the meantime I must ask you to accompany us to the station."

"Am I under arrest?"

"Yes, you are."

Whiteley raised his eyebrows. "Well, this is a first. My lawyer will have fun with it. Human rights and all. Am I allowed a phone call?"

"At the police station. Not here and not now. Please get into the vehicle over there."

"Can I lock up my house?"

"We'll do that, after we've searched it."

"And if there are items missing when I come back? This is a dangerous area, you know."

Only when you're in it, David thought. He kept his tone polite. "When our officers have searched the house, they will secure it properly. The keys will be kept until you are released."

"Kept by the police. Now that fills me with confidence." Whiteley yawned and stretched. "Can I get my jacket?"

"We'll come with you."

They didn't have far to go. The jacket was lying on top of a chair in the lounge. An old chair with a tattered corduroy cover and stuffing poking out of a hole in the cushion. It stood opposite an entry-level television set. Its scratched frame and old-fashioned buttons gave away its age.

Whiteley slung the jacket over his shoulders. David stood alert while Moloi patted him down, checking the man's body and jacket pockets for weapons. He found none.

"Let's go." They walked across to the car. Whiteley tossed the house keys over to Moloi. It was a poor throw, and the officer fumbled the catch. Whiteley sniggered again as Moloi bent over and scrabbled for the keys in the ragged grass.

David clenched his teeth. He didn't like this at all. Not the man's disrespect, he was used to that. What he didn't like was the fact that he felt he was being set up. His gut told him that Mr. Whiteley was two steps ahead of the game. That he had in fact been waiting for them.

He indicated the back door.

"Get in please."

"No handcuffs?" Whiteley yanked open the back door and heaved himself inside.

David climbed in the driver's seat. The younger officer got into the back with Whiteley.

"We'll risk the trip without handcuffs, sir. After all, we don't want to offend your human rights unnecessarily."

David started the ignition and drove to the station.

An hour later, he was on the phone to Jade.

"We've got Whiteley in custody."

"What's he saying?"

"Not a bloody lot. He claims he's an unemployed construction worker."

"Right. Do you believe him?"

David sighed. "At this stage, I wouldn't believe him if he told me what time it was. He's a liar. And he doesn't respect the police either. He's playing with us."

"What about the axe?"

"Claims he had a break-in the night he bought it, and it was stolen. Also claims he reported the crime."

"And did he?"

"I'm following it up. As fast as I can. His lawyer's arrived, and he's a complete asshole. He's ordering us to release Whiteley. And he's starting to ask difficult questions about how we traced him through the axe. He wants to take the matter higher. If Commissioner Williams finds out what we did, I'll be in deep shit. I'm hoping Whiteley lied about the burglary. Then I'll have some leverage."

Jade made a sympathetic noise. "Unemployed construction workers can obviously afford the best legal advice in the business. Does he have an alibi for the time of the murder?"

"He says he was at home alone."

"Fancy that. What's in his home, anyway?"

"Jadey, not a lot. Not a lot at all. My guys have just rung; they've finished searching. Won't you drive over and take a look before they go? I want you to tell me what you think."

David slammed down the phone, then picked it up again and dialed the Townview station.

After two phone calls to Townview had got him nowhere, David lost his temper. He was sick of hearing that the officer in charge was busy or on another call. He grabbed his car keys, marched out of the building and started his engine with a roar. If they wouldn't talk to him on the phone, wait till he pitched up on their doorstep. They would talk then, all right.

The Townview police station was dusty and dirty, with yellowing notices on the wall informing the public about things nobody bothered to read. He shook his head as he thought what Jade's father would do if he saw the average police station today and how it compared to the ones he commanded.

Commissioner de Jong would have exploded in a bout of furious energy, a trait that Jade had inherited and, because of that, always amused him. He would have scrubbed the place down, put in a request for new chairs, ripped the old posters off the walls. He would have repaired and patched and given the place a fresh coat of paint. Removed those dusty old blinds and brightened the place up. And knowing Jade's father, if it still wasn't bright enough, he would have knocked another couple of windows into the wall himself without bothering to ask permission first.

David's greeting was not returned by the large lady constable at the front desk. She looked up at him with dull eyes.

"Yes?"

"I'd like to see your station commander."

"In connection with?"

"Private matter. And urgent," he added, as she heaved herself to her feet and lumbered across the room. She was unfit and unkempt and her uniform was stretched to its limit in every direction.

David was kept waiting another half hour, which did not improve his mood. He watched a long line of people form and edge forward with excruciating slowness. He listened to the list of crimes. Cell phone theft. Handbag theft. Car hijacking. House break-ins. The police station was evidently understaffed, the officers demoralized. If de Jong were there, redecorating wouldn't have ended with the paint on the walls. He would have put in a few new faces and shoved fireworks up the backsides of the existing staff. Or maybe not. Maybe the system was crippled to the extent that even the most dynamic individuals couldn't change it.

The Townview Station Commander was a sorry specimen. Overweight, wheezing and with a deliberately sluggish manner that had doubtless filtered down to the other officers. He looked about fifty, although he was so fat it was difficult to tell.

"What case are you talking about? Couldn't the constable at the front desk have helped you?"

"I don't have the time to spend an hour explaining it to her and then have her refer me to you. I've got a man in custody with a lawyer who's got his stopwatch on, counting the minutes we're detaining him without 'adequate' proof."

"You say it's a burglary?"

"It was reported to your station nearly a week ago, but you never followed it up."

The commander shrugged. "A burglary is a low priority case."

David felt his jaw clench. "A burglary is a crime. That's what the South African police service is for. We fight crime."

A mound of case dockets lay on the desk, papers spilling everywhere. The chief pushed a couple to one side and then gave up the search. His eyes were red-rimmed, and he wouldn't meet David's accusing stare. David would have bet a million rand that in the bottom drawer of his desk there was a bottle of alcohol.

"It obviously didn't come through to me. It must still be waiting at the front desk."

"What the hell are you doing leaving dockets in your front office?"

"It's our policy here." He raised a hand and fiddled with his nose.

"You don't really give a shit, do you? You're just marking time till your retirement."

"I will not be spoken to like that." The chief pushed his chair back and it toppled over, landing on the tiles with a crash.

"Then do your job. Find me the bloody report."

"Get out."

"Not until I've got what I need." David towered over the

man, looking down in disgust at his greasy scalp. The commander looked up at him and then he shuffled through to the front desk and barked out an order. The lady constable with the ill-fitting uniform stopped pretending to help the long line of customers. She let out an impatient sigh and, dragging a chair behind her, plonked herself down next to a pile of dockets on the dirty floor.

David stood and watched her. He was fuming, but he knew that the people stranded in the queue were probably even angrier. If he hadn't been in such a bloody hurry to get back to his office, he would have dragged the fat officer's sorry ass over to the counter and told him to deal with the public himself.

It took the constable twenty minutes to sort through the folders. Eventually she unearthed a single sheet of paper. She handed it to her boss.

"Here you are," he said, passing it to David.

It contained words written in an indecipherable scrawl. He squinted down at the uneven letters. A phone call had been made to Townview Police Station on the date that Whiteley had stated. The sergeant who had taken the call had recorded his name, ID number, address and landline number. A semi-literate sentence beneath stated that "tools for cutting the garden" had been stolen.

"So. This report was made, but never followed up?" David asked.

The two officers stared at him in silence.

David made a copy of the report, strode out of the station, climbed into his vehicle and roared away.

The Townview commander was a fool and his paralyzing incompetence had turned an already struggling station into an incapable one. It had also made David's situation impossible. What with this inefficiency, his lawyer's threats, and no legally obtained evidence to tie Whiteley to the crime scene, they wouldn't be able to keep him in custody any longer.

29

Jade pulled up outside Whiteboy's house. Before she walked in, she went over to the shed. The broken door was hanging open. Streaks of silvery dust showed that the team had fingerprinted it already. She peered inside. It was empty. Next to it was a dog kennel. She squatted down and looked through the wooden entrance at the bare floor. It had been a long time since any dog had slept in there.

Then she went into the house and had a look around. Some of the old houses in the less fashionable parts of Johannesburg had been beautifully finished. She'd seen homes in Kensington with intricately crafted pressed ceilings and smooth, golden-hued wooden floors. Their owners took pride in restoring them to their original glory, displaying the workmanship and attention to detail that the new rich in their Sandton mansions didn't understand or appreciate.

This house was not one of them. Instead, she found herself standing on a frayed gray carpet. The paint on the walls looked yellowish and old. The hallway was dark; the naked bulb suspended from the ceiling by a duo of electrical wires had blown.

She stepped into the lounge, where the light was only brighter because the morning sun was shining through the window. The sun's rays picked out the motes of dust whirling in the air. The wooden arms of the chair and the top of the television were dulled by grime.

The bedroom and bathroom were basic. The double bed sagged in the middle. A duvet lay crumpled on top. In the cupboard were a few garments similar to the ones Whiteboy had been wearing when he was taken away. Faded jeans, T-shirts with stretched necklines and sweat stains under the arms. Jade saw a toothbrush and a razor on the bathroom windowsill.

After she'd completed her tour of the house she phoned David.

"What do you think?" he asked.

"I think he lives somewhere else."

"I think so too."

"This place looks empty. It's as if he's moved in for a day or two. There's no food in the kitchen. Just a tin of coffee."

"Canvass the neighbors. See if they know anything."

"Will do."

Jade left the lonely house. On her way out of the gate she looked at the garage where the officers were now busy. Inside was an ancient-looking truck with a splintered headlight. The grille looked uneven, as if the car was sneering at her. She wondered if it contained any useful evidence. She doubted it. Where was the black Mercedes that the shopkeeper had seen pulling up outside Grobbelaar's office? That car would be a treasure trove of damning evidence.

Jade didn't have any luck with the neighbors. The lady next door to Whiteboy was stone deaf and short-sighted. The house opposite was locked up and empty. For sale, if the sign that had fallen flat on its face outside could be believed. She went back to her car feeling discouraged. Like her father used to say, "Sometimes you get a break in a case and sometimes you just don't."

David was on the phone when she walked into his office. From the cagey way he started talking when he saw her, and the fact he wouldn't look her in the eye, she deduced he must be speaking to his wife. She left and went to wait in the corridor. Why did life have to be so damn complicated? She drew her fist back and punched the wall, imagining it was Naisha's irritatingly pretty face.

Williams rounded the corner. He looked alarmed to see Jade assaulting government property. She lowered her hand in a hurry, and said good morning. He returned the greeting but didn't stop to chat. He bustled past towards his own office. She hoped her actions hadn't further prejudiced him against David. Although she was sure she wasn't the first person who had stood outside an investigator's room and taken out their frustration on a wall.

"Jade," David called.

She walked back into his office rubbing her knuckles.

"How's Piet?" she asked.

David shook his head. "Not coping well."

"Is he safe, at least?"

"Safe enough. He's with two other guys as badly scared as he is. Neither of them looks violent. I've just bought them a pack of cigarettes."

"When's he getting out?"

"When we've cleared him. Although, if we can't link him to the crime, we are obliged to release him on Tuesday." He sighed. "Williams wants us to confirm that he didn't arrange the murder of the gangster as well as the hit on his wife."

"Williams is seriously overestimating Piet's abilities."

David rolled his eyes. "I know. But in the meantime, I've got us another lead."

"What's that?"

"Ellie Myers' father. Name of Bill Scott. He lives in Hermanus, in the Cape. I've booked flights for us tomorrow morning." He smiled. "Pack your bags, Jadey. We're going to the seaside."

The 8.30 a.m. flight took off in the chill of a Johannesburg winter morning.

"Weather in Cape Town will probably be crap," David predicted with gloomy satisfaction. "Bound to be as cold as this, and pissing with rain."

He was wrong. The plane descended from a bright, cloudless sky, and they walked across to the airport in mild sunshine. A few minutes later, they were in a hired car heading out of town on the N2. Jade was at the wheel. She'd told David it was her turn to drive. He could navigate.

"Ever been to Hermanus before?" she asked him.

"Never."

"Me neither. When you mentioned the name, I had this image of a sleepy little town filled with retirement homes."

"Probably is." David studied the map. "But it's also a tourist attraction. Famous for the Southern Right whales, according to this brochure. They come into the bay to mate. Walker Bay, it's called." He squinted at the printed information. "Hey, check this out, Jadey. We've arrived bang at the start of their breeding season. It begins in June and carries on till October. We can sit on the cliffs and watch whales shagging."

Jade smiled. "With such a poetic description, how could I resist?"

"I'm a born tour guide." David cranked his seat back and gazed out of the window. "Welcome to the fairest Cape. Great weather, nice mountains. Are those vineyards I can see in the distance over there?"

Ever since Jade had seen David with Naisha, she'd felt uneasy in his company. Awkward in a way she never had before. Whenever she thought about what she had said, she felt herself start to blush with embarrassment. She wished she could turn back the clock, so she could have known what the situation was before she'd behaved like a lovelorn idiot, not afterwards. Why hadn't David told her, for heaven's sake? Hey Jade, he could have said. About this spark that you've always felt between us—well, it's not going to happen, because I'm married and still in love with my wife. There. Easy. She would have told him had the roles been reversed.

Or would she, Jade wondered. She hadn't actually told David much. He didn't know about her dark past. What would he think if he knew he was sharing a car with a woman who had killed in cold blood?

Jade shivered. He must never know.

The drive to Hermanus took just over an hour. By the time they were driving into the middle of the tourist town, her tension had abated and she felt more relaxed in his company once again.

"Marine Drive is on the seafront. Or rather, the cliff front. Turn right here."

The coastal road was lined with holiday cottages and B&Bs. Jade drove along slowly while David peered at the house names.

"Villa Tranquilla. Who the hell thought that one up? Whale View Cottage. Whale Watchers' Retreat. Southern Right Manor. You'd never think there were whales around here, would you? Keep going. We're nearly there. See? Here we are. Number thirty-three. Looks like old Mr. Scott doesn't have a name for his house." David exhaled and folded the map. "That's a welcome relief, isn't it?"

Jade climbed out of the car and stretched her arms. The air smelt and tasted salty. She walked over to the side of the road and looked down the short, steep slope at the waves breaking on the rocks below. Seagulls wheeled overhead. She could see a couple of ships far out on the horizon. Closer by, a couple were strolling along a path that overlooked the cliff-side view. They looked content together, fingers entwined. As she watched them, the woman said something to the man and they both laughed. He leaned over and planted a kiss on her neck. Watching this display of casual affection, Jade felt a stab of unreasonable jealousy and looked away.

"Beautiful location," she said.

David nodded, and straightened up from adjusting his shoelace. "Might put in a request for a transfer down here when I get fired from the unit. Become part of the local constabulary."

"Don't know if there's enough crime for you to have a job here. Look at all these houses. They don't have electric fencing. Some of them don't even have walls. This is like Jo'burg was when I was a little kid."

"There's always crime, Jade. Stay here for a month and you'll hear the stories. Same as anywhere in the world. It always looks like paradise till you buy a house."

Mr. Scott's property was large and white-walled, with a low

iron gate. There was no bell or intercom visible. No security system at all that she could see.

"Guess we just walk up and knock. What an unusual experience." The gate opened smoothly. She walked up the path and knocked on the white-painted front door, David close behind her.

After a long pause she heard deliberate footsteps. The door swung open.

An elderly man stood under the high arch of the doorway. His gray hair was neatly combed over a bald patch on the top of his head and bushy white eyebrows veiled his piercing blue eyes. In spite of his age, his bearing was authoritative. He glowered at the two strangers on his doorstep as if they were collecting for a charity he didn't approve of.

"Can I help you?" His voice was surprisingly deep. It rasped in his throat.

"Mr. Bill Scott? My name is Jade. This is Superintendent Patel of the Johannesburg Police Service. We've come down here to try and obtain some information regarding a case."

The old man's mouth tightened. "What case would that be?"

"The murder of a Mrs. Annette Botha. We have reason to believe that somewhere along the line, a Mrs. Ellie Myers might be linked to it. Would that be your daughter, sir?"

He nodded wordlessly, but volunteered no further information.

"Would it be possible to speak to you for a few minutes?" Jade asked. "Whatever you can tell us will be most valuable."

Bill shook his head. "It's not a subject I choose to speak about. It's very painful to me and I can't see how it's relevant. My daughter was unlucky. She was a victim of crime and her hijackers were never found. I suppose I'll have to answer your questions. But please be brief."

Jade took out her notebook. She wondered whether, for the sake of brevity, the old man would conduct the conversation in the doorway, forcing her to prop her notebook against the doorframe and David to stand behind her like some kind of guard.

He looked at the notebook. "You'd better come in." He turned and led the way down the passage.

They followed him inside, David closing the front door behind them. Then they entered a little paradise.

The tiled corridor opened into a spacious living room. The entire front wall was a giant window that looked out onto a sloping green garden and had an endless view of the sea.

A plush-looking white leather lounge suite faced the window. A dark wood coffee table topped with glass stood on a blue and white carpet. A blue vase studded with what looked like lapis lazuli contained a bunch of white lilies. It stood on a polished cabinet next to the window.

Two framed photos flanked the vase. Both frames were engraved. One was a formal portrait of an older woman with jet-black hair and a string of pearls around her neck. The other was of a younger woman. Also a studio shot. She was smiling at the camera. Her skin was tanned and her dark hair hung loose on her shoulders. Jade moved closer in order to read the scripts. The engraving under the older lady read, "Mary Scott. 12 May 1935–14 June 1997." The younger girl's script read, "Ellie Scott. 20 June 1966–22 February 2001."

Bill Scott's loved ones. Both dead.

Looking closer, Jade realized that the flowers in the vase were made of silk. Very life-like, but silk.

Bill saw her standing by the cabinet. "My wife passed away after a stroke," he explained. "Take a seat." He gestured to the sofa as he lowered himself into the chair nearest the door.

The sofa felt as plush as it looked. It was so blindingly white she was worried she would dirty it. David waited for a minute and then sat down next to her, in such a way that she thought he was also worried about leaving a mark. Jade leaned back into the cushions and looked out of the window, watching the waves roll into shore and wondering whether she would see a whale.

"So. You want to know what happened?"

Jade unclipped her pen. "Yes, please."

"She arrived home late one evening. The twenty-second of February. Five years ago. She stopped outside the gate while she waited for it to open." The man sighed; a ragged, hopeless sound. "Ellie was pulled from the car and shot. She died before the paramedics arrived. They took the car, an Audi if you need to know. The vehicle tracking company found it twelve hours later in Linbro Park. Abandoned, undamaged and locked." He raised his head and stared out over the ocean, where clouds were scudding on the horizon.

David broke the silence. "Did the police find any evidence? Fingerprints? Any witnesses to the crime?"

Bill shook his head. "The police found nothing."

"The car might have been abandoned if the hijackers suspected it had a tracking device. They'll often hide a vehicle in a secluded spot and watch it for a day to see if anyone comes along," David said.

Jade glanced out of the window. The sky had turned gray and white-crested waves were forming. Ellie Myers and Annette Botha. Both hijacked in their driveways. Both shot dead. What was the connection between them? How had Annette known about Ellie? Why had she decided to trace her so long after her death, only to suffer the same fate herself?

"Annette was murdered in similar circumstances," David said. "We need to know if there was a link between the two women. We need to find a person who knew Ellie well. Do you know where her husband is?"

He shook his head. "I don't know where Mark is, and I don't care much, either." His voice became stronger. "I never approved of him. Ellie married him against my wishes." He lifted his chin and Jade caught a glimpse of what he must have been like in his prime. An arrogant man. A dominating father. Somebody accustomed to getting his own way, no questions asked.

"Why?" Jade asked. "Why did you dislike him?"

The old man got to his feet and walked across the room. He lifted the vase and straightened the cork mat underneath. Then he adjusted the position of the two photographs. Jade hadn't noticed anything wrong with them. She thought Bill was probably giving himself a moment to consider.

He returned to his chair and looked straight at them.

"I wanted my daughter to do better. Mark was a likeable man, don't get me wrong. Good-looking, charming, pleasant company. But he was a freeloader. He lived off my daughter. I owned a highly successful law firm, and I made sure my family never wanted for anything. I would have liked Ellie to marry a man with similar principles. Mark dabbled in business. This and that. He was a good salesperson. He sold insurance at one stage. Then he lost interest, and it was something else. Next thing, he was selling houses. She bankrolled all his projects. None of them succeeded."

Jade glanced at David, remembering what he had told her about the development at 48 Forest Road. "If Mark sold houses, did he sell Ellie's place after she died?"

Bill shook his head.

"Mark inherited the house. But he didn't want anything to do with it after what happened there," he said. "He spoke to me at her funeral. Said he was selling it at a giveaway price. He asked me for my banking details. He told me he didn't want to benefit from it. He wanted the money to go to me."

"Did he ever pay you the money?" David asked.

Bill straightened in his chair again. "I didn't give him my banking details. I didn't want the money. He knew my opinion of him. Giving me the proceeds from the sale of my daughter's house wasn't going to change that opinion." He pursed his lips. "A banker's check for one million rand arrived in the post a month or so later. I tore it up."

Now Jade understood why the frame on the cabinet had been engraved with Ellie's maiden name rather than her married name. Jade was beginning to feel sorry for his daughter. She'd drawn the short straw in the father department, that was for sure. Having family money wasn't everything in life. And why couldn't he have swallowed his pride for long enough to cash the check and donate the money to a deserving charity?

"Could we get a list of her friends from you? University friends, work contacts, anyone else we could talk to?" David stood up, letting Mr. Scott know that they'd asked all their questions.

"She didn't have a job. With the trust fund I set up for her, she didn't need one. But she kept busy. She played a lot of sports. I'll send you the names of her friends, her sporting contacts. People who knew her."

"That would be great." Jade got up too. She looked out at the changing weather. Rain was lashing against the window and the sea was dark and angry. David was already walking down the passage to the front door. As she turned to go, Bill grasped her arm.

"Please find her killers. Find them for me. I want to see them brought to justice."

"We'll try." Jade covered his hand with her own and gave a gentle squeeze.

"When Ellie died," Bill paused, and his expression softened. "When she died, she was three months pregnant. She never told me. We didn't communicate much after my wife died. That was my fault. I still blame myself today." Quite unexpectedly, his eyes filled with tears.

Jade put her arm around the old man and hugged him. She felt his shoulders shake. She knew how he must feel, with paradise all around him but inside him, a living hell that wouldn't end.

While she tried to comfort him, Jade watched the rain pelting down and the swells building. Then she saw it. A huge dark shape leapt out of the water and flicked its enormous tail just before its massive body crashed back down into the churning water. A Southern Right whale, cavorting in the sea.

30

They sat in a coffee shop looking out at the worsening weather. Jade ran her fingers through her hair and shook it out. After the short sprint from the house to the car, and the equally short sprint from the car to the shopping center, she was soaked.

"That's Cape Town weather for you," she said. "Four seasons in one day."

David shrugged his jacket off his shoulders, brushed off the raindrops, and hung it on the back of his chair.

"At least you saw a whale," he grumbled. "If I'd known you were going to spend half an hour hugging the old guy, I'd have stayed and looked out of the window, too."

They ordered some food. David chose a hamburger from the lunch menu. Jade opted for chicken and chips.

"And bring the Tabasco," David told the waitress.

"Thanks," Jade said.

Rain pelted down outside.

"It's going to be a fun drive back to the airport," David said. "For you, that is. I'm going to wind my seat back and have a nap. I always sleep well in the rain."

"Why did they both get shot?" Jade asked. "Why did Annette hire a detective to trace Ellie?"

David nodded. "Were they really hijackings?"

"According to your evidence, Annette's murder was a hit arranged by Piet." Jade stared accusingly across the table at him.

"Don't look at me that way, Jade. I have my doubts about Piet as a suspect in spite of evidence that could be good enough to send him to jail. That's why I'm down here following leads with you, instead of up in Jo'burg pursuing the case against him. But still, how did a Diepsloot gangster with a criminal record end up in possession of his business card?"

Jade frowned. She couldn't answer him. They sat and ate, watching the sea, hoping to see another whale.

The drive back to the airport was a two-hour slog. Traffic crawled along, and the gray sheets of rain limited visibility to a car's length in front of them. They passed two accidents along the way.

The congestion was no better inside the airport. The queues for checking in snaked round and round Cape Town Domestic. Jade heard tourists complaining in Dutch, German, French and Italian. When they finally reached the check-in desk, they were told that the airport had just been closed due to bad weather.

"Your plane was grounded at Johannesburg airport an hour ago," the stewardess explained to them in doleful tones. "It's difficult for the smaller planes to land in this weather. If the airplane can't land here, it can't fly back again, you see."

Her logic was inarguable. Jade tried a different angle. "Any other flights? Could we go on standby anywhere else?"

"There are a couple of planes that could take off tonight if the weather improves." The stewardess indicated the crowded airport. "Unfortunately, I think that there will be lots of people wanting seats on those planes. I still have a few vouchers left for the Road Lodge, here at the airport. You can stay there overnight and I can check you in now for the first flight tomorrow morning."

Jade looked at David. He shrugged. "Unless you want to rehire the car and spend the next eighteen hours on the road driving back to Johannesburg, we don't have a choice, do we?"

The room at the Road Lodge was small, neat and clean, decorated in cheerful blue and red. It had one double bed. She remembered the times she'd shared a bed with David in the distant past. Three or four occasions, perhaps. In cheap motels and strange cities, where she'd accompanied him on investigations and accommodation was scarce. Sleeping companionably, back-to-back and fully clothed. Even if she'd always dreamt about what would happen if he rolled over in the deep of the night and kissed her the way she'd always wanted him to.

Now, looking at the double bed, she felt awkward and embarrassed all over again.

"Sorry, Jadey," David said. "Do you want to see if there's another room available?"

The porter caught his attention. "All the twin rooms are taken, sir. Only the double rooms are open."

"That's OK. We'll live with it."

While David showered, Jade went downstairs and bought a selection of chips, chocolate and soft drinks from the vending machines. They could have a junk-food supper and fall asleep to the sound of their teeth rotting.

After her shower, she put on the spare T-shirt she'd brought with her and folded her clothes ready for the morning. Then she climbed into bed as quickly as possible, keeping so far over to her side that she was worried she'd tumble out onto the floor.

"So Mark Myers was a freeloader," David said. He was sitting up, propped against his pillows, programming the alarm clock on his cell phone.

"Sounds like it," Jade agreed. "But you can never tell. We've only heard Mr. Scott's side of the story. Mark might have been an honest, hardworking man who just wasn't quite as rich as his wife."

David put his cell phone down and turned off the bedside light. "You're right, Jadey. Two sides to every story."

Jade edged her feet down into the chilly depths of the sheets. David was so far away from her she'd have more chance of sharing body warmth with the person in the room next door. The discomfort of the cold bed prompted her to ask him an uncomfortable question. "What's the other side to your story? Why did your wife leave you?"

There was a tense silence on the other side of the bed.

Just as Jade started to say "Sorry I asked," David spoke.

"She had an affair."

Jade's head whipped round, facing the darkness where he lay. "What?"

"She had an affair," he said again. His voice wasn't angry or sad. He sounded empty and emotionless. "With a neighbor. I knew him. He was a nice guy. They managed to keep it secret until I came home early one day and caught them."

"Oh, Jesus, how awful." Jade's heart was pounding so hard she wondered if he could hear it.

David gave the ghost of a laugh. "I wanted to kill him when I saw them together. I threatened him with my service pistol. I actually had it against his head. I could have pulled the trigger so easily. I don't know why I didn't. He ran outside as soon as he had a chance."

"Wasn't only his fault," Jade said, and immediately wished she hadn't.

She heard the bedsprings creak as David turned over. Now he was facing her, she thought, but she couldn't see him in the dark. The expanse of cold starched sheets between them seemed like an insurmountable barrier.

"I know, I know. I told myself I'd caused it, that my working hours were crap and my job stress was through the roof, but yes, Naisha knew what she was doing. Although I never wanted to kill her. Only him."

"Where's he now?"

"They broke it off. He took a job in Pietermaritzburg and moved down there within a month. I don't know if they're still in touch. Then Naisha wanted some time apart from me, to sort her head out. She was devastated by what had happened. So I found the place in Kyalami."

Jade didn't say anything. She didn't know what to say. She wanted to reach out to him and hold his hand, put her arms around him, offer him some comfort just as she had done earlier for Ellie's father in the beautiful, lonely room by the sea. But she couldn't. David cleared his throat. After another pause, he continued.

"When we met in town, when I gave her the fingerprint disk, she told me she'd thought about it. She wanted us to try again. That's what she said to me."

Jade suddenly wished she was somewhere else. She didn't want to hear what David said next. Not while she was lying beside him in a hotel bed that felt as wide as the distance between two stars. She didn't dare to breathe, as if by not breathing she could somehow influence a decision that had already been made.

"What did you say to her?" she asked.

"I told her no."

Now she really couldn't breathe. "Why?"

"Don't know. Just felt like the right decision."

"Oh." Jade stared up into the dark. She wished she could see his face.

"If I had my time over," David said. He never finished the sentence. The next moment Jade heard the bedsprings twang and felt his arm coil around her and pull her towards him. Then her face was bumping against his and his mouth was on her cheek, and then suddenly, urgently, on her lips.

Jade found herself wrapping her arms and legs around him as he pulled her even closer.

His breathing was rough as he touched her with trembling hands, stroking and caressing with a hunger that echoed her own. She heard him say sorry, and whisper her name over and over before he kissed her again. She knew there was no going back. Whatever the consequences, good or bad, right or wrong, she would always have this night.

31

When Jade switched on her phone again, she had three urgent messages from Robbie.

She had spent the flight in a sleepy trance, reliving the memories of the night. The car journey back from the airport passed in much the same way. Back home, she climbed out as quickly as she could, before she could follow through on any inappropriate ideas like kissing David goodbye. He had to make his own choices now. There was nothing she could do.

She phoned Robbie back. He sounded as if he was driving.

"Where were you? I've been hunting for you."

"On the early flight from Cape Town."

"I'm coming to fetch you now. We need to get going with your friend Viljoen. Chop-chop. This morning."

Jade rubbed her eyes. She needed a shower. More than that, she needed eight uninterrupted hours of sleep. But time was limited. Piet was languishing in a holding cell. She had a busy Monday lined up.

"Why today?"

"What, you want to wait till your next birthday or something? We've been following this guy nonstop since he came out of prison. Verna and me. We know his moves. He'll walk to the shop later on. Before lunch. Like he does every day. C'mon. Let's get it done. Today's a good day, I'm telling you. I know these things. So I'm on my way. If you don't want to go, I'll do it for you."

Jade sighed. "Give me twenty minutes. I need to shower."

She showered, changed into fresh clothing and strapped on her gun belt. She walked into the kitchen in time to see David's unmarked driving past her house. He was off to work. She wondered if he had thought of her when he stood in the shower, with the rising steam carrying the scent of her as the hot water hissed down and washed it off his body.

Robbie pulled up outside her house one minute later. He was driving his BMW, but Jade noticed it had different plates.

His timing was uncanny. How had he known exactly when the cop left home? If he'd cut it any finer, she thought he would have probably ended up in a head-on collision with David on the narrow road.

"Let's get going." He reversed out of the driveway and Jade steeled herself for a wild ride. In the end, it wasn't as bad as she expected. Robbie turned onto the main road and drove sensibly towards the highway.

"What's up with you? Did you take an advanced driving course?"

"Speed traps and roadblocks. Someone called in and warned me." Robbie indicated his cell phone. He turned to her and grinned. "D-day at last. You know, Jade, you're a gutsy chick. You've got bigger balls than that Muffin the Wonder Horse. You follow through. I never thought you'd do it the first time. I swear to God, right up until the moment you pulled the trigger I thought you were going to back out and I'd have to do some damage control." He shook his head, eyeing her with admiration. "You haven't changed, have you? Tough as ever. I haven't forgotten how you saved my ass the other night."

Jade had had no intention of backing out. Not since the first night after her father's death, when she had been alone in the little house in Turffontein and Jacobs had come for her. She remembered waking from a troubled sleep to what was then the most terrifying sound imaginable. The creak of a floorboard in a house she knew was empty apart from herself. The rattling of her locked bedroom door. She was scrambling out of the window when she heard the lock splinter and the door give way. Crouching outside the gate behind his new unmarked, she saw Jacobs turn on the light. She saw the steely gleam of the long knife he was carrying. Then she'd turned and fled, running down the dark street, breath sobbing in her chest. She had escaped. And she had come back later, with Robbie, to even the score.

Robbie's voice dragged her back to reality.

"What're you thinking?" he asked.

"Nothing."

"Well. Better start thinking if we're going to get this done right." His tone was unusually sharp. She saw him take one hand off the wheel. He lifted it to his mouth and tore at his cuticles. Jade realized he was nervous.

❀

David arrived at work exhausted but content in a way he hadn't been for a long while. Naisha was a beautiful woman, a charming companion, a true professional at work, an excellent mother at home. But he was now acutely aware of their differences. She didn't understand police work. The inherent danger and violence in his job disturbed her. When he spoke about his day, she didn't want to hear. Over the years, their communication had fizzled into uneasy silence. And then she had looked elsewhere for the companionship she lacked.

Jade had always been like a sister, a best friend, someone who instantly understood every thought in his head. And last night had felt so right. Amazingly, heart-stoppingly right. When he thought about it, he found it difficult not to let a silly grin take over his face. He couldn't control the heart-pounding excitement that flooded his body, making almost everything seem trivial except the thought of seeing her again.

But he had Kevin to think about. The boy had lived without his father for too long already. David's occasional weekend and evening visits always ended with tears, Kevin begging him to stay. When he married Naisha, David had promised himself he would make the relationship work, that they wouldn't become one of the depressingly high police divorce statistics. He was resolute that if he had children they would grow up with both parents in a secure home environment.

David pushed the troubling thoughts aside. Despite his tiredness, he had a feeling it was going to be a good day.

He was wrong.

He walked over to his filing cabinet and took out the files he needed to work on most urgently. Before he could open them, he heard a tap at his door. He looked up.

Williams stood in the doorway with two senior investigators from the Scorpions, the elite high-profile investigation unit that specialized in serious political and organized crime. He recognized one of them as a sniper. All three of them wore Kevlar. The sniper was in camouflage.

"What's up?" David asked, walking round his desk to shake hands with the trio.

Williams didn't offer his hand. His face was grim.

"Superintendent Patel, you've been working with Jade de Jong on the Botha case."

David frowned, puzzled. "Yes, I have. I cleared it with you before I asked her. We've got a suspect in custody, and we're making good progress. Why? Is there a problem?"

"Yes, there is." One of the investigators stepped forward. "We're about to arrest a second suspect related to your case."

David felt a shiver of unease. Something was wrong here. "Who are you arresting?"

The thickset officer regarded him with a faint smile. "Jade de Jong," he said, his voice neutral.

"What the hell are you talking about? She's done nothing wrong." David glared at the man, his hands bunching into fists.

"It's not what she's done. It's what she's about to do."

"How do you mean?"

The man checked his watch, a waterproof Rolex copy. David had seen street hawkers selling them outside the station. "We've got confirmed intelligence that in approximately an hour and a half she's going to make an attempt on the life of a paroled prisoner, namely a Mr. Viljoen."

"What?"

The man nodded. "Her father was instrumental in his conviction. It was a high-profile case. Attracted a lot of publicity. Both brothers received death threats while they were on trial. One died in prison, and we've just been informed that she's going to shoot the other one. Today."

David stood stock still, feeling like the world had turned upside down.

"Jade wouldn't do that. Who told you? They must have their facts screwed up."

"An informer."

"Well, your informer's given you the wrong information." David turned back to his desk and reached for the phone. He dialed a number.

"What are you doing?"

"I'm calling her. She'll confirm it's bullshit."

The officer grabbed David's shoulder and pulled him away from the phone. The receiver fell to the floor. The man placed his finger on the cradle of the instrument, disconnecting the line. "Superintendent, you don't understand. Our information is accurate. Our facts are confirmed. If you try to make contact with this woman now, you'll be perverting the course of justice and we'll arrest you along with her."

David stared at the man in frustration.

"I can't believe this."

The officer shrugged. "Please come with us."

"Come with you? Why? I've got a week's worth of paperwork to finish off this morning. I've got a suspect in the holding cells who'll be released in twenty-four hours unless I can prove the case against him."

"Scorpion cases take priority."

"If you're so good at your job, why do you need me?"

"Patel, if we leave you here the first thing you're going to do is to warn the suspect. Come with us, please."

David looked at the receiver swinging on the end of its line, scraping against the tiled floor. Then he looked back at the men. He saw Williams shaking his head, pale with fury. David clenched his hands again. How could they accuse Jade of planning such an unlikely crime? He wanted to punch the investigator, but his words had planted a tiny seed of doubt. The Scorpions only made arrests when they were sure of their facts. Did he really know Jade as well as he thought? Or was there a darker side to her, one that he'd never seen? His fingers were bruising the flesh of his palms. With an effort, he relaxed his hands. "OK," he said. "Let's get this over with."

He walked with the men to an unmarked car outside the building and got inside.

32

Jade stared blankly at the rows of cars on the highway. She felt oddly out of control, as if she were being dragged into an unwanted future against her will.

"Why are you helping me with this, Robbie?" she asked.

His yellowed teeth tore another strip of skin from his index finger.

"Believe me, it's not for my health," he said.

"Why, then?"

He shrugged. "I said I would. When you left, ten years ago. We had an agreement. Jacobs then, Viljoen now. Two fewer racist pigs in the world. No problem for me." He turned to her, sucking his finger. "You see, Jade, you think I'm just a gangster, some crazy guy who likes killing. That's not how things are. You don't understand me. Why do you think I never deal in hijacked cars? I don't kill for fun. I only kill the guys who deserve it, and that guy deserved it long ago. I saw what he did to you." He drummed his fingers on the dashboard.

"A leopard doesn't change his spots. I know that better than anyone, Jade. I grew up on the streets in Westbury, you know. Slap bang in the middle of the ganglands. Then, when I was twelve, my mum landed a better job. She sent me to a good school in the north of Jo'burg. I didn't want to go. She didn't want me to end up a criminal. I could have changed, could have ended up being the CEO of some bloody company for all I know. But I didn't want to. So what am I now? A better-educated criminal, that's all. I'm a goddamn chameleon. I can speak English like a white man, but put me back on the street with my friends and you wouldn't ever know I even went to school, the way I talk. Same with Viljoen, I'm telling you. Man knows how to play the game. Two weeks out of prison? He'll be back to his old ways."

He turned off the highway and followed the route to Viljoen's suburb. The superette was a few blocks away. The corner building was low and modest, with a small sign outside. Perhaps it had been a house before it was converted into a shop. Robbie braked and stopped a few meters away.

"Why did you ask why I was helping you?" he said.

"Just wondering." Jade looked ahead and then behind her. The road was empty. She couldn't work out what was making her feel uneasy.

"What are you looking at?" Robbie's teeth had drawn a bright bead of blood on his finger. He stared at it, wiped it on his jacket, and then gnawed the skin again.

"Checking the road, that's all."

"It's clear. I told you. I've been here a few mornings now. I know what goes on here. Which is nothing much, as you see."

Jade nodded. "I see."

The shop wasn't exactly a hub of commerce. The entrance opened onto the four-way stop which meant that Viljoen would have to walk round the corner to go in. That was good. It meant it was less likely that any customers would be watching when he walked out and turned the corner to go home. And if they were there, what would they do? Their car would cruise past. Shots would be fired and it would pull away and disappear.

"Here he comes. Out for his daily constitutional. On his way to get the last bread and milk of his life." Robbie sat straighter in his seat. "He's alone. Couldn't be better."

Jade watched the entrance. A black lady strolled inside. She was wearing a domestic worker's uniform. Perhaps she had been sent to get some emergency groceries. Or perhaps she was on her mid-morning break. Jade realized she hadn't seen many domestic workers in this area. People here were mostly too poor to afford help. The lady didn't seem to be in a hurry.

She saw Viljoen approaching, tottering forward on frail legs. He looked anxiously to the right and the left, nervous about his own vulnerability. The blue collar of his shirt peeped out from under a gray jersey which hung off him, as if it had been bought for a larger, stronger man many years ago.

They waited and watched. Viljoen rounded the corner and walked inside the shop.

"He's usually about five minutes," Robbie said.

Behind them, a car was coming down the road. A cheap generic model with mirrored windows. As it passed, it slowed down. Jade glanced at the windows, but all she saw were the reflections of the blue sky and the dark shape of Robbie's car. It turned left at the four-way stop.

Jade saw another man walking towards them on the other side of the street, wearing a bulky jacket. He was marching briskly down the road. He didn't seem to be paying attention to his surroundings, but all the same he was another witness. She didn't want witnesses.

She looked at the digital clock on the dashboard. When Viljoen had gone into the shop it had been 10.48. The numbers flicked forward. She undid her seat belt, curled her hand around the butt of her Glock and drew it out of her holster. Her finger brushed the trigger. She swallowed. There was no time to think about anything else. She needed to focus on the gun and on her target.

At 10.54 Viljoen hurried out again, carrying a white plastic carrier bag.

"You know they make you pay for your grocery bags now in this country?" Robbie said, inching the car forward with an impatient rev of the accelerator. "It's a shame, really it is. Supposed to help reduce littering but all it does is make the supermarkets richer. Still, he can obviously afford the thirty cents or whatever it is."

Looking at the bag's slim outline, Jade thought he probably couldn't afford much else.

Robbie clapped his hand onto her leg. "Right, babe. Let's go do this."

He eased the clutch in and the car moved off smoothly down the road.

Jade watched the shape of the old man become clearer as they drove closer to him. He didn't look like a dangerous political criminal as he stumbled along, heading back towards his home, shadow wavering on the uneven paving.

They passed an empty plot, rubbish lining the long grass growing there. Deep inside a clump of bushes in the center, Jade saw light glinting off a metal surface. She turned her head to look closer. The flicker had come and gone as they passed, but it reminded her of the sun's reflection off the barrel of a gun.

She twisted in her seat and looked out of the rear window. The pedestrian on the side of the road had stopped walking. He turned towards them, watching. Her head whipped round. The domestic worker had come out of the corner shop. She was hurrying along the sidewalk in their direction, her stride suddenly urgent and purposeful.

"Robbie, wait." They were a few meters away from Viljoen. "Something's not right here."

"Couple of seconds more and it'll all be fine." He buzzed the passenger window open. "Point and click, Jade. Just like you did last time. Don't lose your nerve now. Don't let me down."

Jade struggled with him, trying to buzz the window up again.

"Jade, what the hell? Look, do you want me to do it?" Robbie's hand closed over hers. "I'll help you. Here, give me the gun. Grab the wheel."

"It's a setup. There's a sniper in the bushes. Those are plain-clothes detectives on the street," Jade screamed at him, so loud that the elderly man looked round in alarm.

"They can't be." Robbie wrestled the gun out of her hand. He sounded confident. "My contact said today was the day. The cops don't know a thing."

"They do."

With a loud crack, the glass of Robbie's back window shattered.

He dropped the gun and grabbed the wheel.

"Shit! We're being shot at." He smashed his foot onto the accelerator. The engine roared and the tires shrieked. Jade heard more shots ring out behind them.

"They go for the tires, we've had it." Robbie swung the vehicle sharply, slewing it from side to side, dodging the bullets. Jade braced herself against the dashboard. With a cold flood of realization, she knew she'd been wrong. She'd been wrong about almost everything. She didn't know if she could make things right. Perhaps the truth would be as elusive as it had been ten years ago. But she had to try. She had one chance, and she knew one chance was all she would get.

Her body slammed against the passenger door and rebounded into Robbie. She felt his arm, as tense as a steel cable, controlling the wheel.

"Did you sell me out to the cops, Robbie?" she yelled above the wailing of the tires.

"Jesus Christ, I swear I didn't, Jade. I don't know what's going on here. I never sold you out. I wouldn't do that."

"Stop the car," Jade screamed.

"You crazy, babe? I stop this car now, we're on a one-way trip to hell. Via the holding cells, if we're lucky."

"Stop the car. Just for a second. I'm getting out. I'm going to go, whether you slow down or not." Jade wrenched the door open, fighting the slipstream, icy air stinging her eyes. She saw the tarmac rushing past, and readied herself to jump.

"For Christ's sake." Robbie braced himself against the wheel and stamped on the brakes. The car skidded to a stop, flinging Jade forward. Her head struck the windshield and her vision exploded into a thousand stars.

Then Robbie's hand was on her back. He shoved her out of the car.

"Go," he yelled.

He'd pulled away before she'd even stopped rolling. Rubber tore from the tires and smoked on the tarmac. He took the corner on two wheels, just as the vehicle with the mirrored windows appeared at the top of the road again, engine racing as it accelerated towards them. The car screeched to a halt and two figures jumped out. Then it roared off again in pursuit of Robbie.

Jade took no notice of the car, she just followed the black trail and the smell of burning rubber back down the road. Her shoes crunched over the broken glass from the BMW's rear window. She walked into the sights of the sniper she knew was waiting for her.

She swung her arms by her sides. She had no weapon on her.

Viljoen was crouching on the grass, his hands over his head. The shopping bag lay beside him. The contents had spilled out. A loaf of bread, a half-liter of milk, a pack of vegetables for soup.

When she reached him she held out her hand.

If she was wrong, the person in the bushes wasn't a police sniper. Then she would die. If she was right, but the sniper was jumpy, he might still shoot her. Hopefully he would be experienced. Then she wouldn't know about it. She wouldn't know anything at all.

Jade waited. A bird fluttered down and hopped along the pavement in front of them. It pecked at a piece of orange peel and then flew away. The old man looked up at her, his eyes full of anxiety. He took her hand and she helped him to his feet. He moved stiffly.

She bent down, packed his groceries back into the bag and handed it to him.

"Wat gaan aan?" he asked her, in Afrikaans. What's happening?

Jade replied in English. "I don't know what the shooting is all about. My name's Jade de Jong. I want to ask you a couple of questions, Mr Viljoen. Can I walk with you?"

"Jade de Jong?" He squinted at her, hobbling forward on legs still jerky with fright.

"My father was Commissioner de Jong. He handled your case. Back in 1995, when you were arrested."

The man nodded sadly. To Jade's relief, he switched to thickly accented English. "Ja. We were arrested in December '95. I remember de Jong."

Jade could see the people from the car approaching. She felt a chill of despair. Williams and David were walking towards her, side by side. The other plainclothes detectives—the man in the jacket and the woman dressed as a domestic worker—watched from a distance.

Viljoen glanced nervously at the approaching men and then back at Jade.

"I need to know something, Mr. Viljoen."

"Ja. You can ask me."

"Did you or your brother have anything to do with the murder of my father? Did you know about it? Were you involved?"

Viljoen looked at her in total bewilderment. "Your dad was murdered? De Jong? No, I didn't know that. I'm sorry. How did it happen?"

Jade stared into his eyes. She couldn't see a lie there. She didn't answer his question.

"Did you or your brother bribe a cop to sabotage your case?"

Viljoen gave a half-smile. "No. You don't understand my brother, Ms. de Jong. He was a madman. He thought there was no case against us, that we would be found innocent. Until the day they sentenced him, he believed that he was right and they were wrong."

Williams strode up to them, mustache bristling. "What the hell's going on here?" he shouted. "That was an attempted assassination, my girl. We're going to arrest your accomplice in that getaway car. And we'll have handcuffs on you faster than you can say 'Guilty.'"

"He wasn't an accomplice," Jade said.

"We have it on good authority he was."

She shook her head. "He helped me locate Mr. Viljoen. That's all."

"You located Viljoen in order to kill him."

The old man recoiled from Williams. He moved closer to Jade, despite the commissioner's accusations, as if she could protect him from the frightening words as easily as she had picked up his shopping bag.

Jade spread her arms. "I don't even have a weapon. Was I going to break his neck with my bare hands?" She stood her ground and stared down at Williams, who glared back up at her. "I wanted to ask him some questions relating to the death of my father. I got answers from him. The only shots fired were from your police sniper." She indicated the camouflaged man in Kevlar emerging from the bushes.

"Did the occupants of the car have a weapon?" Williams asked the sniper.

The man brushed dry leaves out of his hair.

"They were struggling with a weapon," he said. "I fired a warning shot and then attempted to disable the vehicle by shooting out a tire."

"You didn't shoot very accurately," Williams snapped.

"The car was all over the road, Commissioner. And there was a civilian directly in my line of fire." The man sounded defensive.

Williams shrugged. "It doesn't matter now." He turned back to Jade. "You were struggling for possession of a weapon, with intent to commit murder." Jade glanced at David. He stood statue-still and silent. She wondered what he was thinking, and if he knew that what she was saying was a lie.

She shook her head. "My driver was nervous. We saw a man with a gun in the bushes as we passed. He thought we might be hijacked if we stopped the car to talk to Mr. Viljoen. He wanted to have his gun ready for self-defense. I was trying to persuade him to put it down. I didn't want Mr. Viljoen to be frightened. Then our back window was shot out and my driver panicked." Jade put her hands on her hips and waited. Williams was still glowering at her, but she could see some uncertainty in his eyes. He didn't have grounds for her arrest. She had been insanely lucky. The police sniper had fired the first and only shots. Hopefully, that meant David would be out of trouble too.

Williams's walkie-talkie crackled.

"We lost the suspect, Commissioner," a voice said. "He got away from us on the back roads."

Jade felt a surge of relief.

"Roger. Return to the scene, then." Williams sounded disappointed. He turned to Jade. "You're off the case, as of this moment." Then he turned to David, jabbing a finger into his chest. "And Superintendent, you're suspended with immediate effect, pending a disciplinary inquiry."

33

Jade couldn't get hold of David on his cell. She couldn't get hold of him on his landline either. And he wasn't home. Not at his upstairs room next to her cottage, at any rate. Not by eight in the evening. Not by midnight, when she walked outside huddled in a jacket to check. The carport was empty and the window above the garage was dark. Which left only one logical place for him to be. And she didn't want to think about that unpleasant possibility.

She was off the case. David was off the case. The investigation was stalled. The evidence against Whiteboy had proved insubstantial and he'd been released. Jade was sure that by now he had vanished. She was willing to bet that the dilapidated house in Townview was as deserted tonight as David's rented room.

A few minutes after one a.m. her phone beeped. She had a message.

"Jade." Robbie's voice was loud, and it hummed with stress. "I'm still hiding out. How could it all have gone sour like that? Call me when you can."

She pressed the key to return the call. He answered immediately. From the background noise, Jade guessed he was drowning his sorrows in a bar somewhere.

"Where are you?" she asked.

"I'm lying low."

"The cops raid late-night drinking establishments, you know."

"Oh shut up, Jade. Stop jumping to conclusions about me. I'm in the Cat's Pajamas. A twenty-four-hour restaurant." He said the last word slowly as if to emphasize his respectability. "In Melville. West of the city. Come join me."

Robbie sat at a corner table, his back to the wall. Jade looked around. At two in the morning, a twenty-four-hour restaurant attracted an interesting variety of clientele. Some of the customers hunched over their whiskies and nachos looked like gangsters. Others reminded her of vampires risen from their coffins. Robbie had chosen his hideout well. He blended right in.

Jade sat down next to him. She wanted her back to the wall, too.

He pushed a glass over to her. Amber liquid sloshed around two ice cubes. "Whisky. For you."

Jade cradled the glass in her hand and took a large gulp.

"I need my gun," she said.

Robbie's face twitched and his eyes darted from side to side. He looked shaken. Jade had trusted him. Had she been wrong?

"I'll get it for you. I don't have it on me now. Too risky. If they bust me and link the ballistics to that other shooting in Pretoria, I'm in deep shit."

"Where's Verna?"

"Home alone. The cops have been round twice. Once to the shop, once to our house. She's telling them I'm out of town, that I left on a business trip yesterday morning."

"What happened?" Jade put her glass down and leaned towards him.

Robbie leaned away. "I'll tell you. I'll tell you everything. But don't get mad at me, all right? I'm warning you right now, you wouldn't have done any different."

Jade preempted his explanation. "Were you dumb enough to carry out a hit on him?"

Robbie looked at her, hurt. "It was money for jam, OK? I didn't tell you because I knew you wouldn't have liked it. But I was going to share the bucks with you when I was paid."

Jade was absolutely certain he was lying. About sharing the payout with her, at any rate. "Really? Have you been paid?"

"Well, no. I mean, it's all null and void now, isn't it? The target's still alive."

They paused. A waitress was hovering at their table. She had a piercing in her lower lip and a huge metal crucifix around her neck. Jade thought she probably wore it to ward off vampires.

Robbie ordered nachos. After a brief scan of the menu, so did Jade.

"Did you know the cops would be there?" she asked when the waitress had gone.

"Honest to God, I had no idea it was a police setup." Robbie stared at her, eyes steady and unblinking. Not that that meant anything. Once, on a nighttime game drive in the Kruger National Park, Jade had seen a caracal on the hunt look at a baby gemsbok much the same way. A moment later, it had sprung forward, claws bared, and seized the unsuspecting fawn.

"My contact told me the opposite," Robbie continued. "He said Monday was the day to do it, no question."

"Who approached you for the hit? Who was this trusty contact?"

"I don't know."

Jade buried her face in her hands. When she'd raised her head again, she took another large gulp of her drink. "Robbie. How can you not know?"

"We spoke on the phone. He told me government people wanted Viljoen out of the way because of political sensitivity. It made sense, seeing as how the new government are all blacks, and those workers were friends of their friends. Look, Jade, it sounded genuine as hell. I trusted him. And I'm a suspicious guy."

"You're stupid."

"I am not."

"You were sold out. Your contact was an informer."

"Well, maybe the guy got arrested for something else and had to make a deal."

Robbie's eyes widened as a large man wearing a collared shirt pushed through the crowds towards their table. The man lifted his head and regarded them for a long, slow moment. Then he pulled up a chair at the neighboring table and sat down. Robbie exhaled, a long, shaky breath.

"I can't take this stress, Jade."

"Then don't take on dodgy jobs from people who tell you they have government contacts."

Robbie slapped a hand against his chest. "I'm patriotic. I love the new government. I'd do anything to help them. They look after entrepreneurs like me. In the old days, it was so difficult to do business. Now it's a pleasure. Pay off a few people, and there's no more worries."

The waitress returned with the nachos. Jade asked for a dish of chopped chili. She wondered who had sold Robbie out, and why. Was it somebody he'd screwed over in the past? She was sure there were more than a few of those. If you lined them up, the queue of people who'd got the short end of a deal with Robbie would probably stretch around the block. But that wasn't her problem. He had got her into trouble.

That was her problem. Right now, she couldn't do anything about it.

"Viljoen didn't kill my dad."

"Huh?" Robbie pushed a nacho into his mouth with his fingers.

"He didn't arrange the hit."

"Who did, then?"

"I don't know. But the Viljoen brothers weren't sabotaging the case. The elder brother thought he had a God-given right to do what he wanted and stay out of jail."

"So who was paying Jacobs, then? Who was sabotaging the case?"

Jade shook her head. The food was excellent. She hadn't realized how hungry she was. She ladled chili onto another mouthful. "Perhaps we're looking at it the wrong way round. Whoever sabotaged the case might have wanted to keep the brothers out of jail, so they could take their own revenge."

Robbie frowned, considering her theory. "Could be."

They ate in silence, listening to Led Zeppelin playing in the background.

"I was wrong," Jade said, scraping the last piece of chili out of the bowl.

"No, I was wrong. I screwed things up for you. Sorry." Robbie took a wad of fifties out of his wallet and counted out four of them. Jade watched him with suspicion. Robbie didn't do apologies. Why was he saying sorry now?

He sounded determined. "I'm going to do some scouting around, babe. I'll find out who sold us out. Then I'll put a few bullets into him. To say thank you very much, from both of us.

"Dinner's on me, to make up for it." He slid the notes under his empty glass. "You're lucky. You can go home and sleep now. I've got to keep on ducking and diving till the heat's off."

Jade didn't go straight home. She skirted Johannesburg city and drove through Turffontein, along the empty roads. She didn't want to go there, but she had to know.

She stopped when she reached David's house. The lights were off and the place was quiet. David's unmarked was parked in the driveway behind Naisha's car. Jade pulled over and watched the silent house for a long while before she drove away.

Now beyond the point of exhaustion, Jade found sleep was impossible. She gave up trying just before dawn. She moved her heater into the kitchen and put the kettle on. There were no books in the cottage. None she wanted to read, anyway. And no satellite TV. There was nothing for her to do except the one activity she wasn't supposed to pursue any more. Working on the case.

She was so accustomed to doing it, she found it difficult not to. Out of habit she took her coffee to the table and turned the pages over, reviewing her notes, searching the evidence for anything they had missed.

She'd even drawn a timeline.

On the twenty-seventh of May, Annette had called Dean Grobbelaar, private investigator, to trace Ellie Myers. She had transferred an advance payment to him for his efforts. A week later, she'd mentioned to Piet that she thought she was being followed. On the seventh of June, she'd been murdered. And on the fourteenth, Dean Grobbelaar had been hacked to death with an axe.

Jade added two more dates to the timeline, right at the

beginning. 22 February 2001. The date of Ellie's murder. And a month or so later, Mark Myers had sent a check for the sale of his property to his father-in-law, and disappeared out of his life forever.

She frowned as she wrote the final entry. The sale of the property. They'd tried to trace Ellie Myers. But they hadn't looked at the other side of the equation.

Who benefits? That was a question her father had always advised her to ask. Sometimes, he told her, it would be the only question she'd need to ask.

Mark Myers had sold the property for one million rand. A giveaway price. He was traumatized by the death of his wife, his pride wounded by the uncompromising attitude of his father-in-law. Perhaps he thought he had nothing to lose. That didn't alter the fact that somebody had gained from the transaction.

Jade remembered David sitting at the table opposite her, telling her about the prices of the luxury homes at 48 Forest Road. How much had the developer made on that project? She knew David had said it was a mind-boggling sum.

So. Who did benefit from Ellie's murder?

The person who bought the property from Mark.

At eight a.m. precisely, she phoned the cheerful lady in charge of the Oak Grove cluster development.

"The name and contact details of the developer? I'm sure we can give you that, dear." The lady sounded bright and breezy, as if she had walked into the office after a healthy breakfast, a good coffee and a pleasant drive through easy traffic. Jade envied her.

"It was done by a company called White & Co." She gave

Jade the details. Phone number, fax number, postal and e-mail addresses.

When the woman said the name, Jade jumped. For a moment she thought the lady was going to say Whiteboy. Then she remembered the job they'd done in Pretoria. White & Co had been developing phase two of the luxury villas where Hirsch stayed. But now the two names seemed eerily similar. Could there be a connection? Was this Whiteboy's venture?

"Who's in charge there? Do you know?"

"I couldn't say, dear. We dealt with the contractors, mostly. The company outsourced most of the work. Architecture, design, and of course we took over afterwards to do maintenance and upkeep. The only job White & Co did themselves was the subdivision and the property sales."

Jade rang off and tried David again. His cell went straight through to voicemail. She didn't leave a message. He could see her number on the screen. He'd answer if he wanted to.

Next, she tried the phone and fax numbers of White & Co. On both calls, she listened to a recorded message from Telkom telling her the number she had dialed did not exist.

The number might not exist. But perhaps the company still did. She paged through the file until she found Graham Hope's business card. She hoped the friendly estate agent could advise her on how to find it.

Graham answered on the second ring. Jade explained what she needed.

"That's a difficult question for so early in the day." He also sounded keen and perky, full of energy in spite of having a dodgy knee. Perhaps everyone felt the same way this morning. Except her.

"I was hoping it would be easy."

"You see, what some developers do is set up shell companies."

"And outsource all the labor?" Thanks to the cheerful lady she had spoken to earlier, Jade was well-informed about the industry's usual business practices. At least, she hoped she sounded that way.

"Exactly. Then when the project is finished, they close the shell. That makes it more difficult for anybody to sue them afterwards, if problems crop up. Which they invariably do."

"Oh," Jade said, disappointed.

"I'll have a look for you, ask around. Perhaps they're still going." He laughed. "Perhaps their phone lines have been stolen. Lines get stolen all the time these days, for the copper wire."

While Jade was wondering who to call next, she heard a car on the road outside. Looking out of the window, she saw David's unmarked rattling down the road. He skidded to a stop outside his automatic gate and waited for it to open.

Jade grabbed her keys and fumbled with the alarm code and the security door. Number pads and double locks were all very well for keeping the criminals at bay, but they weren't designed for letting you out of your house in a hurry.

Finally, she yanked the door open, pressed the button for her gate and sprinted down the road after him. She slipped through his gate just before it closed.

David was already out of his car and up the stairs. He hadn't seen her. He was probably rushing so he wouldn't have to. She ran up after him. The wooden door at the top of the stairs was shut but unlocked. She opened it and stepped inside.

The room was empty. She could hear the sound of a shower behind an adjoining door. She sat down on the bed to wait, the duvet cold and smooth underneath her. There was a bricked-off annex on the other side of the room. She could just see the corner of a stove behind it. Opposite the bed was a desk. The wooden surface was bare apart from two objects: a framed photo of a young dark-haired boy and the brass paperweight in the shape of an eagle's head that Jade had given David years ago.

The noise of the shower stopped. A minute later, he came out of the bathroom. He was stark naked. For some reason, Jade hadn't expected that.

He stopped dead when he saw her and treated her to an icy scowl.

"What are you doing here?" he asked. His expression changed when he realized his state of vulnerability. He looked around for something to cover himself up. Nothing was immediately available in the tidy room. He started to turn back towards the bathroom for his towel. Then he shrugged and gave up on the idea. He walked over to the wardrobe and sorted through it, just as he might have done if she wasn't there.

"You haven't been returning my calls."

"I haven't got anything to say to you." He tossed a pair of black trousers onto the bed.

"Well, thanks for hearing my side of the story."

"Jade." A white shirt landed on top of the trousers. "I don't want to hear your side of the story. We're both better off if I don't know what you were doing there with a guy that Williams tells me is a well-known gangster. Apparently a vehicle matching that description was seen at the scene of a double murder in Pretoria recently. And you lied to Williams, Jade. You lied to me too. You covered your ass. Don't deny it. I know you too well for that." He opened a wooden drawer inside the wardrobe and rummaged for underwear. "I'm in deep shit at the moment. My career's as good as over. In a couple of days I'll be officially out. I'm actually going for an interview this morning with Home Affairs. Naisha organized it for me yesterday."

He threaded a leg into a pair of red underpants, lost his balance and hopped around frantically as he tried to get his other leg in. Jade could see he was cross that she had witnessed this undignified maneuver. If she hadn't been on the point of tears, she would have laughed.

"Is there anything else you need?" he snapped.

She shook her head. "Not really. I'll leave now, I think. Buzz the gate open for me, will you?"

"I can't from up here. You'll have to wait a minute." He pulled on his shirt and trousers and knotted his tie. The bed creaked as he sat down to put on socks and shoes and creaked again as he stood up. He slung his jacket over his shoulder. A piece of paper fluttered to the ground from the inside pocket.

"You dropped something," Jade said. She picked it up and looked at it. It was a photocopy of a list of handwritten names.

David's mouth twisted. "That's a copy of the fax that Bill Scott sent through yesterday. I was going to give it to you. Throw it away, will you? Together with the rest of your documentation."

He pulled open the door. She put the folded paper in her pocket and walked down the stairs while he locked up. She heard his heavy tread behind her and then the gate rattled open.

Jade trudged back to her cottage. David passed her on the

road, accelerating furiously. The way he was driving, she hoped he didn't crash the unmarked before he had to return it to the station's car pool.

Jade wasn't on the case any more. But she couldn't walk away from it. Not while Whiteboy was at large and Piet was in jail. And not while she didn't have a clue why Annette Botha had wanted to trace Ellie Myers before she, too, was murdered outside her gate.

She felt naked without her gun, but for now there was no way of obtaining another weapon. She'd have to pressure Robbie to return her piece as soon as he could.

If he was intending to return it at all. If he didn't have other plans for it, plans he wasn't telling her. Who had offered money for Robbie to murder Viljoen? Or had he been hired by somebody else to misdirect her and lead her into the jaws of a police trap?

She grabbed her car keys and drove down the road at a speed rivaling David's.

34

Annette's house looked quiet and undisturbed. Jade stopped outside the gate. Although the morning was bright and sunny and the road was deserted, she couldn't help glancing nervously behind her. What if a gunman jumped out of the long grass and overpowered her, as swiftly as the caracal that had leapt on the little buck?

She didn't get out of her car. She read the phone number on the estate agent's sign and dialed it using her cell phone. First time around, the likeable Graham had sold this piece of land to Annette's brother. Who had sold it the second time around? And who had bought it?

"I need to get some information," she told the man, when he answered.

"Right. Right." He cleared his throat with a dry, "ah" sound. "I'll be happy to help you. If you'd like to pop round, I'm, ah, in the office for another hour. Then I'm out, selling houses."

Her willing helper was a balding man wearing a suit and tie. A Range Rover was parked outside his office. Literature from the Freemasons lay on his desk. His handshake was warm and friendly and Jade soon discovered the throat-clearing was some kind of nervous habit. He couldn't get through a sentence without doing it.

He didn't know Annette Botha had died. His eyebrows rose in concern and he offered his condolences. Then Jade asked him about the property.

"Yes. Mrs. Botha's land. I sold that for her. She was, ah, pleasantly surprised by how quickly it sold."

"Who bought it?"

"A consortium. They bought some land nearby for development a while ago. When this came on the market they snapped it up. They were keen to, ah, start a second phase. An equestrian development, I believe."

"What's the name of the consortium?"

"Well, I suppose you'd call it Life Direct. An, ah, insurance company. They are the major investors. Although they've also got a black economic empowerment group on board with them, as all the large companies are obliged to do these days."

A consortium. Not a renegade developer. Jade watched the man take the Freemason papers and throw them into the dustbin. His fingers were dotted with short white hairs and he was wearing a gold wedding band.

"Did Mrs. Botha sell it for a good price?" She was stabbing in the dark. She didn't know what the right question would be. If there was a right question.

"Oh yes. Fair market value. Which is quite high. It's a beautiful property. Idyllic location in a fast-growing area. Amazing, ah, potential."

No point in pursuing that avenue, then. Annette's death hadn't had anything to do with the sale of her land. She couldn't investigate a scenario that didn't exist. But perhaps, while she was here, this man could help her get closer to locating White & Co.

The agent turned to his laser fax machine and removed a document from the out-tray. The wheels of his chair slid smoothly over the seamless wooden floor.

"Tell me more about property development in Johannesburg," she said.

He slid his chair back over to the desk. He looked amused.

"Property development? I always think that's like the winter flu. At the moment there's, ah, a lot of it going around. Such a demand for houses, you see, with the emerging black middle-class. The, ah, black diamonds, they call them. They all have to live somewhere." He beamed at her. "And therefore many of the white people, in turn, have to live somewhere else. Hence the, ah, housing boom. And the economy is favorable at present. Extremely favorable."

"What's the market like?"

"South Africa is a developer's dream. Especially since the end of apartheid. For most people with the, ah, capital to start up, it's like winning the jackpot at Sun City."

"Why?"

The agent's cell phone rang and he glanced at the screen. If it had been a client, Jade was sure he would have taken the call. But he pressed the button to silence it. Probably his wife, she thought. Or the Freemasons.

"Compared to almost every other country, our market is wide open. Not controlled by the large international companies although of course, they're doing their damnedest to, ah, take over again. You see, they all pulled out of the country during apartheid. When sanctions were imposed, and the going got tough." He chuckled. "South Africa moved a lot faster than they did. Apartheid ended, Mandela came into power and the economy did a turnaround while all the building giants were still scratching their heads and wondering if it was safe to go back in. So there was a lot of money to be made. Anyone with a truck and a building crew had a chance, really." He folded his hands.

Jade thought of the pseudo-Tuscan gateways and high walls and guard-houses. She'd seen a lot of them around. 48 Forest Road, and many others. Every time she stopped at a traffic light, there seemed to be people handing out glossy brochures for developments with imposing names and detailed architect's drawings and glowing descriptions.

"If you were a developer, how could you make the most money?" she asked.

He nodded, the flesh underneath his chin bobbing slowly up and down. "A very good question. Apart from building cheaply and taking shortcuts, which of course has legal ramifications at a later stage, I'd say the key is getting hold of the right property, the right piece of land. Geographically sound, no legal issues. And in, ah, the right area. The developers I know tell me the same sad story every time. The properties they really want aren't for sale. And unfortunately, when a developer comes knocking at the door, the owners usually add an extra zero to their asking price, which eats up a large portion of the, ah, profits. Sometimes properties become so expensive to obtain, the developer ends up suffering a loss."

Jade braced herself for the dry throat-clearing she knew would follow. She wasn't disappointed.

On impulse, she asked him, "Have you heard of a developer called White & Co?"

He thought for a while. "I can't say I have. As I told you, there are many, ah, fish in this particular sea."

"How would I find them?"

"I couldn't advise you on how to trace them." He cleared his throat again. "Of course when they sell, or let their development out, they would have to use a registered estate agent. Like myself." He opened his desk drawer and brought out a sheaf of papers. He sorted through them and then handed one to her. "Here're the contact details for the, ah, estate agents board. They might be able to help you further."

Jade got on the phone as soon as she was back in her car. She didn't have a hands-free kit. If the traffic cops saw her, they could saddle her with a hefty fine. Right now, that was the least of her worries. She held the phone with her right hand and steered with her left. When she needed to change gear, she jammed her knee against the wheel. David would be so proud, she thought, if he could see her now.

She asked the woman at the estate agents board for the contact details of registered agent Garth Whiteley. After a short pause, the woman replied.

"We don't have a registered agent of that name."

Jade changed gear again, and checked her mirrors for any signs of blue and white Metro Traffic Police vehicles.

"You must have. There must be one of that name. Can you check again?"

"I'm looking at the list of agents right now," the woman said. She didn't sound too pleased about being doubted. "There's no Mr. Whiteley on this list. I can assure you of that."

Half an hour later, Jade parked under the lonely oak tree and walked across the road to the Tuscan housing complex built by the elusive White & Co. The security guard leaned out of his window. Jade asked if he would mind her questioning some of the residents while they were driving through the gate. Police work, she told him, fingers crossed behind her back.

He agreed, but said she mustn't take too long. That was fine with her. She didn't want to take too long, either. She was burning with impatience.

The first resident out of the gate was a red-haired woman driving a white Audi.

"Can I ask you a quick question, please?" Jade approached the car.

"No," the woman replied rudely, before she sped off.

Jade raised her eyebrows. The rich were friendly folk, all right. She saw the security guard watching from the guard-house. He gave her a sympathetic shake of the head. Presumably, he dealt with people like this all day.

The next lady out of the gates didn't know. Her husband handled those affairs and he was at work.

She got lucky with the third resident she asked. The

woman pulled into the driveway and opened her window when Jade approached.

"Yes, I'm sure I can find that for you." She nodded at the passenger door of her Jeep. "Hop inside. I'll check in the house." She tossed a towel onto the back seat to make room for Jade.

This lady had been to the gym. She was wearing a designer tracksuit top and shiny leggings. "Let's go," she said, turning the wheel with manicured fingers. Dark-haired, tanned and sporty-looking, she could have been Ellie's sister.

Jade waited in her tiled living room. She put her hand down and touched the polished granite. It was warm. Underfloor heating, as she'd suspected.

"Here you go." The woman hurried back with a document in her hand. Jade scanned the page expectantly, looking for the agent's name. When she found it, she nearly fell over backwards onto the expensive floor. She blinked, and looked again. She hadn't been expecting this.

The home had been sold by Mark Myers.

"Let me double-check this with you," Jade said, when she could speak again. "You bought this home after it had been developed by White & Co?"

"Yes, that's right. Mark showed it to us a couple of years ago. It was brand-new. Recently finished."

"What was Mark like?"

"He was a lovely guy. A good salesman. Asked us lots of questions, made sure we were happy, the usual shebang."

"What did he look like?"

She laughed. "Oh, I don't know. Average height, not fat, not thin. Brown hair. Not bad looking. He had a nice smile." She pulled a card out of a paper clip. "Here's his card, if you want it."

Jade thanked her and set off back to the estate's imposing gatehouse. The cheap sale Mark had made to White & Co. had camouflaged the real deal. The money he'd sent to Bill Scott had been a smokescreen. Mark had been back again, cheerfully reselling houses on his wife Ellie's estate for vast sums of money after her death. Was he one of the enemy?

The woman at the estate agents board didn't sound too thrilled to hear from Jade again. Jade had to use all her charm to get what she wanted. When charm didn't produce the results fast enough, she brought out the big guns.

"I think it would be easier if I came round to see you in person," she said, firmly.

"No, no, that won't be necessary." The woman was galvanized into action by the unpleasant prospect of having Jade leaning over her desk and breathing down her neck. "I'll call you back in an hour with the information."

Jade waited in her car, parked outside Oak Grove. She was safe enough there. The security guard was keeping an eye on her. She examined Mark's business card and dialed the cell number printed there. It rang through to an automatically generated voicemail message. Mark wasn't answering her call.

She tried David's phone again. No reply. She didn't know whether he was ignoring her or whether he was signing his letter of appointment at Home Affairs. She left him an urgent message. Then she started her car and headed for home.

Jade didn't know whether luck or instinct made her decide to change her route on the way back. She was starting to feel exposed, arriving back at the cottage from the same direction every time. Whiteboy was on the loose in Jo'burg. She needed to be more careful.

Approaching from the other direction was difficult. She had to take a complicated route over deeply rutted sand roads fissured with erosion channels and drainage ditches. When she finally jolted round the last corner, she was glad she had taken the trouble.

A black Mercedes was parked outside her house, off the road, concealed in the deep shadows of a tree. The shiny, low-slung vehicle looked out of place on the country lane. It was parked facing away from her, its sleek hood pointing towards the road she usually approached from.

Jade couldn't see a number-plate on the back of the car. She didn't have her weapon with her. She would have to run.

She forced her small car to a stop and twisted the wheel as she threw it into reverse. She pulled out of the three-point turn and headed back the way she had come. Checking her mirror, she saw the Mercedes swing sideways, dust kicking out from under its heavy tires. The driver had seen her and he was coming after her.

35

Jade skidded round the corner, feeling her tires slip on the dirt as she sped down the road. Flying over the rutted surface faster than she'd ever been down a dirt road before, she felt the car become airborne over the bigger bumps. She held the wheel tightly, keeping it straight, trying not to panic. Trying not to overcorrect or to brake too suddenly.

A black shape appeared in her rearview mirror. The Mercedes was in pursuit.

"Great," Jade said through gritted teeth, gearing down to take another corner. The car slid sideways and kicked up a coarse shower of sand. For a heart-stopping moment she thought she was going to lose control. Then the car righted itself and she flattened her foot on the accelerator as she hurtled down a long straight stretch.

Looking behind, she could see the Mercedes was gaining. Hardly surprising. When two tons of finest German technology was pitted against a generic, entry-level machine with an underpowered engine, what the hell else did she think was going to happen?

She needed her gun. She'd rather turn and fight than write herself off when her pursuer finally forced her into misjudging a bend. And this surface was treacherous. Sharp stones, areas as dry as the desert and sand in drifts and hollows. Rattling over the road at a suicidal speed, she'd roll in an instant if one of her wheels hit a deep enough patch of the soft stuff.

It was easy enough for the heavier, stronger Mercedes. All the driver had to do to avoid losing control of his car was follow her exact path. She was sure her tracks were visible, even in the tan-colored clouds of dust that plumed out behind her wheels.

"Dammit, Robbie, why couldn't you have brought the bloody gun with you to the restaurant?"

As if he had heard her words, the driver of the Mercedes started shooting. Jade heard the crack of the gun and ducked reflexively. She felt the car veer terrifyingly to the left as its wheels caught the edge of the sandbank on the side of the road.

"Shit. Bad idea." Jade straightened up, her hands tight on the wheel as she fought to steer the car out of the skid. Inch by inch, the tires regained their grip on the road and she guided it back to the center. Glancing in her rearview mirror, she saw the driver was shooting from out of his open window. She could see his hand, pale-skinned, gripping the gun.

"Good. Go on, slow yourself down. Think you can shoot and drive and still keep up with me?" Jade forced herself to stay upright, although all her instincts screamed at her to get down when she heard another shot. On these rough roads, it would be a miracle if he put a bullet through her head or her tire. Especially if he was trying to steer while he aimed. She was putting herself at greater risk by ducking down and trying to avoid the bullets. Which, she thought, was probably what the driver behind her was hoping she would do.

Jade saw his arm disappear back into the car. He'd obviously realized shooting was a waste of time. She still had all her tires and her window glass and she had gained a precious few meters of additional ground.

In another couple of seconds, the car behind her had made up the distance. Jade knew she didn't have much time. Before she reached the next crossroads, she'd have to abandon the car and head for an open field. There, she would see if she could outrun a man with a gun.

The road curved to the left. This was the worst part of the route. Jade had nearly turned back when she'd been coming the other way a few minutes earlier. It was the section where steep speed bumps alternated with deep concrete drainage ditches. She remembered thinking that if she lived down this road, a four-wheel drive wouldn't just have been optional. It would have been essential.

Now here she was, approaching the ditches at a speed that she was sure no four-wheel drive vehicle had ever attempted.

The little engine screamed in protest as Jade slammed the

car into first gear. Sand shot from under the tires. The car dipped and twisted violently and Jade heard a metallic scrape as the transmission caught on the concrete rim of the first ditch. The car bounced upright again. She was through and still good to go.

As she ramped over the speed bump, hearing the transmission take another round of battering, she glanced behind her. The Mercedes was having more trouble with the ditch than she expected. It was heavy and low-slung, unlike her high-riding vehicle. She heard a banging, scraping noise as the underside of the big vehicle caught the edge of the concrete.

"Ouch," Jade said, wondering if a piece of the car's expensive bodywork had been left behind on the road. She hoped so.

She thumped through the next ditch. The impact sent her flying skywards and her head collided painfully with the roof of the car.

When Jade opened her eyes, she thought she was hallucinating. Two red security vans had pulled into the road ahead, blocking the junction. The drivers got out and stood behind the vehicles, facing the oncoming cars. Jade thought the men looked nervous.

She breathed out in relief as she scaled the final speed bump and skidded to a halt before she crashed into the impromptu security barrier. Behind her, the Mercedes swung sideways again, its hood buried in the roadside grass. The car reversed, turned, and sped off back the way it had come, engine howling. Again, Jade heard the sound of the car colliding with the edge of the steep ditch.

"Eina," she said. "That must have done some damage."

She staggered out of her car, knees weak and arms trembling. She felt as if she was floating towards the two guards.

They had sturdy bulletproof vests strapped outside their shirts. One man was armed. The other carried a truncheon. The words "Tactical Security" were emblazoned in yellow on the sides of both vans.

The guards had a quick conversation. Then the man with the pistol climbed back into his van and set off in pursuit of the Mercedes.

The other guard hurried over to her.

"You OK?" he asked.

"Fine. Now that you're here." Jade shook his hand. "Thank you."

"Was it an attempted hijacking?"

She nodded, settling for the easier explanation. "Yes."

"A resident reported reckless driving and gunshots. We were patrolling in a neighboring area." The man looked pleased with himself to have arrived in time to prevent crime.

Private security. Jade took a deep, trembling breath. Every South African resident who could afford the monthly costs signed up for it. In return, the security firms patrolled their clients' neighborhoods, looking out for suspicious vehicles and responding to calls from residents. In her headlong flight down the road, she hadn't had time to notice the grassy plots and farm-style houses that lined the road. But somebody had seen her and called for help.

Jade decided against going back to her cottage. She thought of asking the security guard to accompany her, but the guard wouldn't be able to wait around indefinitely. And the man in the Mercedes would know she was there, because he would see her car.

Where could she go? The lady from the estate agents board

was calling back in half an hour. She needed to be somewhere safe, where she could speak to her calmly, and then get on the phone again to find out what the hell was going on.

Jade mulled it over. Then she nodded. She knew where she could go. She got back into her poor little car and headed west, checking her mirrors for any sign of the dark vehicle.

Annette's house looked secure. From outside, she could see that the front door and gate were closed, just as she had left them. She couldn't see any other vehicles on the road. The gate rattled open and rattled shut again behind her. Jade drove round the house, off the brick driveway and onto the grass that Piet had recently watered. He had wasted his time. The frost had turned the lawn a depressing shade of beige.

She parked the car and walked back round the house. Her car was invisible from the road. Nobody would know she was here.

She unlocked the front door and stepped inside, then turned and locked it again. The house was quiet. Jade breathed in and waited. It felt peaceful. Empty. She couldn't sense the presence of another human being. Everything was in its place.

All the same, she walked round the house checking every cupboard, looking behind every door. The paint had dried on the wardrobe door in Annette's bedroom. The design looked beautiful, even though she was sure Piet still had hours of work to do on it.

While she was checking the final room she heard her cell phone ring. She sprinted back to the lounge and pulled it out of her bag.

The woman's crisp voice was loud in her ear. "Ms. de Jong? I have the information you're looking for."

Jade scrabbled in her bag for a pen. Paper was more of a problem. Her notebook was on top of the case file in her cottage. She dug in her pocket and pulled out the photocopy that David had given her. She could use the blank side of the page and write small.

"Mr. Mark Myers seems to be the official agent for a company called White & Co. All his sales were done through them. White & Co is owned by a Mr. Whiteley."

"Yes?" Jade's pen hovered over the page.

"I'm going to give you some names of their recent developments in Johannesburg. To list the individual homes would be a waste of my time," she said firmly.

"Thank you. I really appreciate your effort," Jade said. She knew when to be humble.

The woman gave her a list of names and Jade wrote them down. Lake View Manor, Sandton Ridge, Fairway Lodge, Sun Valley Estate. Names that inspired the imagination. Names that would appeal to buyers seeking luxury and status.

Of course, she reminded herself, that didn't mean the places weren't horrid little houses with crumbling finishes and no room to swing a kitten. After all, you could call a place whatever you wanted. She'd have to wait and see for herself.

"Do you have contact numbers or any information about the sellers?" she asked.

"No, I do not. I suggest you contact the estates themselves. Or better still, deal with Mr. Myers directly. I don't know why you didn't think to do that in the first place."

Jade heard a click in her ear as the woman replaced her receiver. She sincerely hoped she wouldn't have to phone her again.

An hour later she'd obtained contact numbers for three of the estates. They were all located in Jo'burg's northern suburbs. She decided to take a drive and speak to the management in person. She would use Annette's house as a base and return later in the evening. She felt safe there.

❀

Whiteboy loved the thrill of the pursuit. He loved knowing that he was half a step behind the enemy, and gaining. In Angola, tracking down rebel forces, he recalled the exhilaration he'd felt as he'd got closer, and the hot, delicious triumph that had washed over him when the terrified men had realized that they were surrounded and outmaneuvered, that there was nowhere left to run.

His ultimate strategic success was when he duped his pursuers into believing that they were doing the chasing. When they believed that they were gaining on him, while every step that they fought so hard for was taking them further into the trap that he had set.

He believed it was time to put a similar plan into operation now.

The call that he had been waiting for finally came through. Cell phone reception in this area was up to shit, one of its few drawbacks.

"How are we doing?" he asked his trusted contact.

"Everything's ready."

"Plan A and plan B."

"Exactly."

"Plan A, we stay." He looked out of the window. The house he was currently occupying was pleasant enough. It should be. After all, he had built it. They'd agreed it would be a smart idea to keep a couple of homes in reserve, so to speak, within each of their developments. And they were very useful. Nice anonymous buildings. Great security. Top-class privacy. Nobody to see him come and go once he was inside the tall walls.

Plan A would be first prize. He still had a lot to do here. Two new developments to complete. Another twenty million or so to pocket on each one. He wasn't ready to go yet, but if he had to—well, it was all sorted.

Plan B was flawless. Across the border into Namibia. From there into Zimbabwe. And from there, a fake passport to take him out of the country to wherever he wanted to go. People were running away from that crackpot nation all the time.

Nobody would suspect a wealthy man on the run from a dangerous country. A tobacco farmer perhaps, resourceful enough to have got his money out with him, starting a new life somewhere more stable. He didn't know where. America, perhaps. He had connections there who could get him a green card. He could retire early. He was wealthy enough to park on his chunky ass in a luxury mansion and watch cable TV until his brain rotted away. The problem was he liked to keep busy. Whiteboy had an excellent work ethic. However, he was the first to admit that the type of work he thrived on was not what the authorities had in mind when they issued green cards to foreigners.

"Plan A is what we aim for," he told his trusted contact.

"Of course."

"We'll need to do it soon. It annoys me to have to duck and dive like this."

A dry chuckle. "Not your style."

"No," snapped Whiteboy. It was all right for his contact. He wasn't the one who had to look left, right and left again before reversing out of his damn garage, in case the Scorpions were jumping over his wall. He wasn't sure if the cops were up to speed with the situation yet. He hoped that the emergency precautions his other contact had taken would have quashed the investigation before it had moved any further in his direction.

On the bright side, it wasn't as if Whiteboy's photograph was stuck up on the wall with a caption "Wanted Dead or Alive."

As he had discovered, most white people in South Africa wore invisible blinkers that prevented them from being suspicious of anyone the same color. It made his job laughably easy. Although he was probably not the most savory looking guy they'd ever seen, with his goddamn ugly skin they could tell a mile away that he was white. And that made them trust him, even on a dark night, even when they were alone.

All he had to do was pull over, climb out and stroll towards them, and every single one—so far—opened their window to talk to him. The next—and last—thing they'd see was the barrel of his gun. He owned three different Colts, not counting the one he had recently sacrificed in Diepsloot, a Z88 and two Berettas. All kept scrupulously clean and oiled, in prime firing condition. Unlike the average thug on the street, Whiteboy couldn't afford to miss a shot. But he didn't want the ballistics people linking up too many of the shootings, if he ever lost one of his weapons. Better for everybody to think there were hordes of criminals out there, trying their hand at hijacking with an endless supply of guns. Well, that was no lie. There were.

Cell phones and wallets provided a useful excuse for a shooting. He changed his MO every time. Sometimes he broke gate motors in advance, other times he cable-tied them shut to get the owners out of the car and into the open. Occasionally he'd go for a completely different scenario, like a house robbery.

There was other stuff, too, that he had found helpful. One guy had half a kilogram of hash stashed in the cubbyhole of his BMW. Whiteboy had been careful to leave traces of it in the car when he removed it. As a result, the evidence gathered by the oh-so-slow police force had sent that particular investigation limping off in the wrong direction.

So he wasn't too worried about hiding out. If he obeyed the traffic rules and didn't get caught in any police roadblocks, he'd be fine. Till tonight. When they could get moving and end this goddamn problem once and for all. He hadn't been able to get the girl earlier. Truth be told, he had been reluctant to kill her when capturing her would be so much more fun. He smiled, remembering the furious pursuit. His contact had been right. She was spunky. All the more to look forward to later.

Now she was in hiding, he supposed. There wasn't time to flush her out or track her down from wherever she might be. But he wouldn't need to. He had a foolproof plan in place for getting her to the party. Better, really, than his original strategy.

He smiled. More than one step ahead. That was the way to play it. He'd stay put until the afternoon. Then he had a few errands to run before the fun could start. He jingled his keys in his hand. It wouldn't be long now before he climbed in his car and set off to pay a surprise visit to the broken-kneed Graham Hope.

36

By late afternoon, Jade had the information she needed. Her back was sore and she was stiff from hours of driving through traffic-clogged roads. Her head hurt where she had hit it on the roof of the car. But these were minor worries.

Robbie was a more major worry. She'd called him while she was stuck in a queue of traffic and demanded her gun back. He told her he couldn't return it just yet.

"I'm very busy, babe. I'm catching up with the creep who sold us out. I'll keep you posted, OK?"

"Robbie, I need it now. For God's sake, it's my weapon. I paid you for it. Use one of your own guns."

"I can't. They're all out with my staff at the moment."

Jade would have laughed if she hadn't been so angry.

"Have you found out who quashed the Hirsch case yet?" she asked him. "Who the corrupt cop is?"

"Well…" Robbie drawled. "It's not as easy as it sounds. There's different levels of corruption, you know. I've got contacts in the police service who pass information to me. In theory, they're corrupt. But they don't know who quashed that case. I'm asking around, babe. I'm asking. Don't panic, be cool."

Back at Annette's place, she concealed her car behind the house and hurried inside. She pulled her cell phone out, and started dialing the first of the numbers before the door had closed.

Her first conversation was with the previous owner of what, today, was Sun Valley Estate. Set in a gorgeous part of Jo'burg, it overlooked a wooded hill whose trees had not yet succumbed to the developers' chainsaws. The homes inside had looked spacious and elegant. Enough room to swing a large cat. Perhaps even a leopard.

The woman who spoke to her informed her in brisk tones that her husband had been shot and killed outside the property shortly before she made the decision to sell. Jade detected a hint of a British accent in her voice. Probably, the woman was concealing her heartbreak behind a businesslike manner, as the British seemed to like to do.

"He was parked at the gate," she told Jade. "He was waiting for it to open. I always told him he should never park in the driveway. He should wait parallel to the road, so that he could pull off if anyone came along."

"And he didn't do that?"

"The car was facing the gate when they found him. His window was down. He must have opened it. Stupid, stupid." She sighed. "Perhaps they pointed a gun at him and said they'd shoot him through the glass. I don't know what happened."

"Did they take anything?"

"Cell phone and wallet. The police thought he must have threatened or insulted them. Perhaps he refused to get out of the car. But that wasn't like George. He always said he would cooperate with hijackers, if it ever happened to him."

"I'm sorry," Jade said.

"They told me criminals are getting bolder nowadays. They'll shoot to kill, so that there are no witnesses. He said I was lucky they didn't come down the driveway and attack me. It's a frightening thought. I was in the house. The gate was open. The doors were unlocked. They could have walked straight in from the road."

"You sold soon afterwards?" Jade asked.

"I always wanted to sell. I felt the house was too big for us. And security wasn't good. I live in a flat now, in Cape Town. I feel much safer." She laughed, a short, sorrowful laugh. "Our land was a prime spot, apparently. It's sad to think that if George had sold when the developers approached him, this might never have happened."

"Just to get the situation clear," Jade continued. "You were approached by a number of buyers, but you didn't sell. Then after this happened, you sold up immediately."

"Yes. It was my husband who wanted to hang onto the house. Not me."

Who would have known that, Jade wondered. She looked at the sheet of paper. There wasn't much space left on it.

The woman continued. "We had offers regularly. Agents on our doorstep all the time."

"Anyone in particular?"

She laughed, a brittle sound. "Everyone in particular."

"Who did you sell through in the end?"

"The developers handled the sale directly. White & Company. Their agent was excellent. Mark, his name was. Very charming. And persistent. He was helpful after it all happened. Kind. Supportive. I was falling apart at the seams, of course. So he handled everything. He wanted to get me out of the house and put the sale through as soon as possible. I remember he told me that when the house had been knocked down and they'd built over it, the bad memories would fade. I think, somehow, he was right."

"May I ask you what they paid you for the land?"

She sounded vague. "A reasonable amount, I suppose. He said the shooting had affected property prices in the area, which was unfortunate for me. There had been a few other crimes there recently. Another good reason why I wanted to get out as soon as possible."

"You didn't consider negotiating with another buyer for a better price?"

The woman's voice sharpened. "No, dear. My husband had just died. I had more important things on my mind."

Touché, thought Jade.

"My apologies," she said. "I understand."

37

It was home time for most people in Johannesburg, but not for David. Because he didn't have anywhere he wanted to go. He couldn't go back to his room above the garage. He couldn't spend the night there, knowing that Jade was next door. She had betrayed him. She was involved with a gangster. He didn't know why, or what the extent of the involvement was. And he didn't want to know.

The other option was to go back to his house in Turffontein, where he had spent the previous night. That was equally unappealing. Naisha had welcomed him in delight when he had arrived. But when he'd told her he would be sleeping on the couch, she had broken down in tears. She felt rejected. Didn't he want her? Did he think she had picked up a disease from her lover? Because she hadn't. She could ask a doctor to confirm it, if he liked. Which left only one question for her to ask, the one he was now hoping to avoid. Didn't he love her any more?

He sighed as he remembered their mind-numbingly endless argument, conducted in hushed voices for the sake of

Kevin, who had been doing homework in his room. Eventually she'd stormed off to the bedroom and he'd fallen asleep on the couch with Kevin, who had stopped doing homework as soon as the bedroom door slammed and sneaked into the lounge to watch TV with his dad.

He didn't think he could take another round with Naisha. Last night's had worn him to the bone.

So here he was, sitting in a bar where he had been since lunchtime. His interview with Home Affairs had been a disaster. He'd sat through an hour-long interrogation by a twenty-year-old manageress. He could tell she didn't like his attitude. He wondered if she knew the feeling was mutual. A series of questionnaires and forms had taken him another hour to complete. All for the dismal prospect of a low-grade, paper-pushing job he was absolutely certain he didn't want.

David called the barman and ordered another Coke. He'd started with beer but stopped after the third one. He felt quite sober now. More sober, in fact, than he thought he had ever been before.

Hunched over the wooden counter, he was only vaguely aware of the noise of the traffic—the honking of taxis, the rumble of engines, the faint sounds of sirens as the emergency services rushed to sort out yet another collision.

He knew he should take the unmarked back to Johannesburg Central. They'd already phoned and demanded its return. Then he wouldn't have a car. Or a house. Because Naisha drove his car. And lived in his house. Where to go? Catch a taxi and shack up in a motel room for the night?

Images of Jade flashed into his mind. Fast asleep, her legs in a warm tangle with his. Smiling at him across the table, her green eyes promising mischief. Telling him a story in the car, something frivolous to make him laugh. Damn it, she was everywhere in his head, and right now he didn't have the defenses to fight her off. Why had she done what she did?

The ringing of his cell phone provided a welcome distraction. He was less pleased when he discovered the caller was Graham Hope.

Graham spoke rapidly. "Superintendent. I hope you don't mind me phoning. I called the station and they gave me your cell number."

David supposed he could thank bureaucratic inefficiency for that. No doubt the front desk hadn't yet been informed of his suspension.

"Mr. Hope. What can I do for you?"

"I need help urgently, sir." The man sounded shaken.

"What's up?"

"I've just got home. My gate's wide open and my front door looks like it's been forced. I locked everything up when I went out this morning."

David opened his mouth to tell the man he should contact the flying squad, but before he could, Graham continued. "My neighbor phoned me while I was on my way home. He said he'd driven past my house and seen the gate open and an unfamiliar car nearby. A black Mercedes without plates. He called to make sure I wasn't being hijacked."

David sat bolt upright. "Where are you now?"

"I'm inside. In my car. Parked in the driveway."

"Are you hooked up to armed response?" What a question, David thought, coming from a police detective. A ridiculous admission of the way things were in South Africa.

"I am. They're not very reliable, though."

"Call them now, quick. See if they're in the area. Ask them

to come round and keep an eye on the place for you. And in the meantime, stay in your car and lock the doors. Drive out of there immediately and go round to your neighbor, or somewhere else nearby where you'll be safe. Your life is more important than your household possessions."

"I'll do that."

"Give me your address. I'll come round and check things out."

Graham Hope's house was a short drive from where he was now, although the wealthy suburb of Houghton was a world away compared to the run-down area of northern Yeoville, where he was attempting unsuccessfully to drown his sorrows in a public bar.

Nelson Mandela had a house in Houghton. He had heard somebody talking about president Thabo Mbeki making plans to retire there, too. David wondered what his security precautions would be like. Probably the house would be so well guarded he wouldn't even bother to lock his front door in the evenings.

David paid his bill and left. He didn't like coincidences. He didn't think a simple housebreaking had anything to do with the case they were working on, but the presence of a dark Mercedes was troubling. He believed Mr. Hope was a busybody who'd been poking his nose into the investigation wherever he could. Perhaps his actions had alerted Whiteboy. He would have to question Hope in more detail as soon as he got there.

David called Moloi as soon as he was on the road. He asked him to send armed backup over to Hope's address immediately, because the man could be in danger. Moloi was a good officer. He didn't ask unnecessary questions or waste valuable time asking David why he was still giving orders when he'd been officially suspended. He just said yes and got off the phone to get it done.

David reached Hope's house in evening semi-darkness. The gate was wide open—a solid structure lined with huge wooden and metal panels. He pulled into the gateway fast and roared down the long drive. He stopped and jumped out, service pistol in his hand.

A white Lexus was parked at the bottom of the driveway, headlights on and driver's door open. He could hear the faint sound of the radio. The keys were in the ignition. He took a quick look inside. The car had an automatic transmission. And on the passenger seat was an envelope addressed to the Deeds Office. Hope was nowhere to be seen. There was no sign of the security company either.

"Shit," David breathed.

He called Hope on his cell. The phone was turned off and David found himself listening to a recorded message.

He hurried towards the open front door. It was framed by two tall plants in pots. A delicate spiderweb stretched between them, silvery in the gleam of his headlights. It was at the level of David's cheek. Most people would have been able to walk underneath it. Ahead, the hallway was dark. He ducked under the strands, reached for the light switch and flipped it on.

The hallway was empty apart from a polished wooden table, which looked antique and expensive. He saw a padlock key in a porcelain bowl.

"Graham?" David called.

He heard nothing.

What the hell had happened? Had the man been abducted? David stood, momentarily indecisive. What should he do?

This situation was downright weird. The sensible reaction would be to return to the car and wait for backup. He turned back towards the door. As he did, he saw something at the foot of the stairs, in the darkness beyond the hall. He whirled back again as he realized what the shape was. A pair of crutches, lying on the floor.

He walked over silently and stared down at the metal objects. They lay at an angle, half on the floor and half on the bottom stair. He didn't think a man with a gammy leg would drop his crutches at the foot of the staircase. Unless he'd been forced to.

David saw a brief flicker at the edge of his vision and spun around again. There was nothing to be seen. Only the shadow of the plants, backlit by the glow of the headlights, moving in the chilly wind that had started to blow.

Where was Hope now? Had he been dragged up the stairs?

Against his better judgment, he turned back again and climbed the stairs, his shoes quiet on the carpet. If this was a trap, he'd already walked into it. But Graham's life might depend on what he did now.

The first door at the top of the stairs led into a palatial master bedroom with an en suite bathroom that had a giant sunken bath. The bedside lamp was on, but the room was empty. Felt empty. David hardly bothered to check the cupboards in the walk-in dressing room.

He checked three other bedrooms, three other bathrooms. Nothing except for tasteful furnishing in dark wood and polished brass and a silence that echoed in his ears.

He walked downstairs again, past the discarded crutches. His palms were sweaty and the gun felt slippery. He gripped it more firmly and checked the ground-floor rooms.

Still no sign of Graham Hope. The house seemed prepared for show day. It looked as empty as his heart felt.

David hurried back to the hallway. There was no time to lose. Hope had been kidnapped, and he had just wasted five precious minutes searching the house. Now he needed to alert the control room, and fast.

As he reached the front door, he saw the figure of a man standing by his unmarked.

His heart suddenly accelerated and his gun hand tensed.

"Put the gun down, policeman," a voice called.

David took a slow step forward through the doorway. The spiderweb stretched and snapped and the broken strands drifted over his face.

"Put the gun down. Or your friend dies."

Graham Hope was in front of the unmarked. He was leaning back against the passenger door and his hands were tied behind his back. His legs were tied too, at the ankles. The cast was more of a hindrance than a help. Hope was obviously having difficulty supporting his weight on his good limb.

Whiteboy stood behind him, using him for cover.

"Would you like me to prove I have a loaded gun?" he called. "It would be so easy to shoot this cripple's other leg, you know. Then it would be wheelchair time for him. And the next shot he gets will be in the head."

David lowered his weapon and placed it on the ground.

"Walk forward now."

He walked onto the grass, towards his car.

As he approached Graham he saw that the man had been tightly gagged. He gazed at David in a silent plea for help.

"Thought you'd be all night in that house." Whiteboy smiled at him out of the shadows. The cold air had brought two slashes of crimson to his pale face. His scarred skin looked bloodshot and irritated. He was holding a Beretta fitted with a silencer and it was trained on David's chest. David wasn't wearing any Kevlar. The winter wind blew his shirt against his skin. The fabric felt cold and flimsy.

"Thought you were thinking of buying. Or squatting." He smiled again. "Anyway, you're out now. Time to go."

"Go where?" David squared his shoulders. Bravado was useless, he knew. But at least it would delay the inevitable. By a second or two.

"Wherever I tell you. Seeing as I have the gun."

"This is stupid. I'm telling you upfront. You'll be caught."

Whiteboy regarded him with a cool stare. "By the time anyone gets caught, I'll be long gone. Now pick him up."

David quickly assessed the situation. Whiteboy was standing too far away to try and get at him, past his gun. And too close for David to make a run for it. His army training showed in his stance and in the confident familiarity with which he held the Beretta. David knew that Whiteboy was a killer who wouldn't hesitate to shoot. And in any case, it wasn't only himself he had to worry about. Graham Hope was unarmed and immobilized. There was no way he would be able to run, even if David tried to help him.

David shrugged. "Your choice."

He glanced up the driveway. The backup car should be here any time now. All he had to do was survive the next few minutes and Whiteboy would be trapped.

The gate at the top of the driveway had been closed.

It was massive. Like the surrounding wall, it was topped with three double strands of electric fencing. Through the tiny gaps between its inlaid steel panels, he could see the flicker of headlights as a car pulled in from the road and honked loudly.

"Pick him up." Whiteboy's smile didn't falter. "Or I shoot him in the leg, right now. Then you in the leg. I'll shatter your kneecap."

What the hell was the man playing at with the police right outside the gate? Was he trying to create a hostage situation? If so, what did he want to bargain for?

He bent forward and hooked one arm under Hope's knees and the other under his back. He straightened up with the man's full weight in his arms, holding him like a sleeping child. The cast made both Graham's legs stick out at an awkward angle, which made carrying him more difficult. The ties around his ankles would be impossible to undo or break. Graham's breath was snuffling out through his nose and the fabric of the gag was biting deeply into his cheeks. His body was tense and unwieldy in David's arms.

"This way." Whiteboy kept the gun trained on them.

David staggered ahead. Years ago, when he started in the police force, one of his first arrests had been a knife-wielding teenager who had been threatening to stab his girlfriend. With more bravado than experience, David had aimed his weapon at the young man and had ordered him to move away from the terrified girl. While he watched the boy drop the knife and back away, he'd wondered how it would feel to be powerless and unarmed and at the wrong end of a gun.

He was finding out now.

Whiteboy directed him to a paved path that led through the garden. It led away from the lights at the top of the driveway. He heard the car honk again, but the noise was more distant now.

Walking was difficult with Hope's full weight in his arms. David was strong, but Graham must have weighed eighty kilograms. His arms were trembling and his muscles had begun to burn. His breathing sounded as rough as Graham's and he was seething with frustration. He couldn't believe that help could be so close and yet so bloody unobtainable.

"That's the problem with security in the new South Africa," he heard Whiteboy say behind him, as if reading his mind. "These automatic gates and walls and electric fences. They're wonderful if the criminals are on the wrong side, but they're a real bitch when you want your backup to get in."

"They'll get in eventually."

"I'm sure they will. It won't matter though."

"You planning on killing yourself as well as us, then? There's no way you're getting out of this situation."

"Turn to your left here, please, Mr. Policeman."

The ground was uneven and sloped down a steep incline. David stumbled in the gloom and felt his balance go. Hope's weight yanked him forward, impossibly heavy in his arms. They were going to fall. He would be OK, but Hope would hit the ground with David's entire weight behind him.

He took another giant step forward, fighting to regain his balance. He heard Hope cry out, a small helpless sound. As his right leg hit the ground he threw his weight backwards, bracing and twisting against the downward pull. His runaway momentum slowed, but at the same time his foot bent to the side and a white-hot pain lanced through his ankle, sending agonizing daggers straight up his leg.

He brought his good leg under him and stood panting, limbs quivering. He didn't know if his ankle would support his own weight, never mind the extra burden in his arms, but he had no choice. He took a tentative step forward. Perhaps it would be fine. Perhaps he could even play up his injury, let Whiteboy think he was more incapacitated than he was.

He almost collapsed. His ankle had no strength in it.

Behind him, he heard Whiteboy laugh.

"Don't even have to waste a bullet on you," he said.

David heard a humming noise, and a wooden garage door obscured by an overgrowth of ivy began opening up. Inside was a black Mercedes, its body gleaming even in the dim light. It had no front number plate.

Whiteboy walked past him and pulled a back door open.

"Put him in there."

David lurched towards the car. "You're crazy. You won't even get out of the gate."

"Don't let it worry you. Just put him in there. Across the seats."

David leaned forward, hopping on his left leg as he tried to maneuver Hope into the car. He lowered the man's shoulders down and pushed. The seats were leather, more slippery than fabric, which made the job easier. For a moment, their eyes met. David stared back at him helplessly.

Over the car door, Whiteboy still had the gun trained on him.

"Close the door."

David slammed the door shut. The sound was heavy and loud in the concrete-walled garage.

"Open the trunk."

David obeyed.

Whiteboy's smile widened. "Get in."

David stood his ground. "No."

Whiteboy indicated again with the gun. "In."

"No."

"Don't stall, Mr. Policeman."

"Stalling or not, it's game over."

Whiteboy shook his head. "Not at all. This particular property is what's known as a Rand lord's house."

"What's that got to do with it?"

"The people who originally bought land here in Houghton were extremely wealthy. Most of them had made a fortune on the mines. There aren't many houses left like this one. They're double-sized. Whoever this Rand lord was, he liked his space. So you see, it actually has two gates. One opens onto River Road, where your intellectually challenged colleagues are trying to work out how to get in. The other one opens onto Fifth Street, which runs parallel to River. I'm sure it's conveniently free of the police."

David watched Whiteboy's gun hand. It was rock-steady. The man wasn't panicking. The police were at the gate and he was making wisecracks. He was supremely confident.

"I'll give you a count of five," Whiteboy said. His lips drew back from his teeth, and his voice changed abruptly from calm and amused to furious. "You're lucky I'm giving you a chance at all, you dumb piece of shit. I'll shoot you right here, right now. It won't slow me down for a second."

David started to climb into the black-carpeted trunk. He was dealing with a madman. Better to stay alive for a while longer. He could make a plan, he could try to attract attention as Whiteboy was driving.

The trunk had a shallow rim. To get in he had to lift his legs and bend his knees and duck his head. It would have been a simple maneuver if it wasn't for his damn ankle. He had to lift it over the lip with his right arm and then roll over it. He half-fell inside and landed on all fours. It was the easiest thing in the world for Whiteboy to do what he did next. As quick as a snake, he whipped his arm forward and whacked David's head with the butt of his gun. It was a solid blow, and so fast that David had no time to react. He saw the Beretta flash towards him and then his head jerked sideways, bouncing off the metal lid before he slumped down onto the carpet.

His world blacked out in an instant.

38

White & Co had developed Fairway Lodge after the grieving owner had sold them the family home. His wife had been shot and killed outside the house while leaving for work one morning. Lake View Manor had been started when the residents sold their place after the next-door neighbors were brutally tortured and murdered in a house robbery. White & Co had killed two birds with one stone on that particular project, because the woman who lived at the end of the road had sold to them too. That beautiful piece of land then had forty luxury cluster homes erected on it and became Sandton Ridge.

Jade scribbled notes on her paper and ended her final call. She couldn't believe it. In every case, the surviving homeowners had sold to White & Co in a panic, traumatized by recent violent events. They had all unquestioningly accepted Mark's assurance that property prices had been adversely affected by the current crime wave and that they needed to move somewhere safer as soon as possible, so that their bad memories could start to fade.

All the survivors had told her how charming Mark was, how he had worked hard for the sale. How he visited them many times before the tragedy occurred. They'd regarded him as a friend.

The operation was as slick as any Jade had seen. Mark would gain the trust of the victims. During his conversations with the families, he would discover who wanted to sell and who didn't. Whiteboy would "remove" the reluctant partner, or orchestrate a nightmare crime scenario close to home to nudge the potential sellers into a "favorable" decision. Then the sale was as easy as taking candy from a baby. Easier, Jade thought, because in her limited experience babies and candy tended to form sticky combinations.

She was also sure that if any other developers decided to go up against White & Co for a particular property, Whiteboy would find very effective methods of making them change their minds.

She frowned, gazing out of Piet's kitchen window at the rolling hills, with the trees and fences and barn silhouetted against a tangerine sky.

There was only one problem.

She was still no closer to discovering why Annette had died.

If Mark, like Whiteboy, was a complete psychopath, she could have understood why he murdered his pregnant wife. Just. But Annette? Had she died because she was trying to prove that Ellie had been murdered? If so, how had she known about Ellie?

She hurried back to the lounge where the faxed copy of Ellie's friends and contacts that Bill Scott had provided lay on the coffee table. Jade's notes crawled around the edges of the photocopied text like ants around a sugar bowl. She only had one piece of paper. And there had been a lot to record.

Jade scanned the list, hoping to see Annette Botha listed as one of Ellie's friends. Perhaps she'd tried to catch up with her after a long break and panicked when she couldn't trace her.

Ellie's list of contacts read like that of a spoiled teenager. Her father had done his best. She thought he must have racked his brains to help her and David. He'd remembered names of riding instructors and dressage instructors, which was presumably different from normal horse riding, although Jade couldn't see how. She'd had riding friends and dressage friends. She'd had tennis friends and cycling friends and golf friends. Friends from school. Ellie had more friends than Jade could believe. No wonder she was smiling in the photograph that stood on her father's polished cabinet.

She was so intent on searching for Annette that she almost missed a familiar name. She carried on past it, and then she frowned, went back, and read the name again.

"Adrian Muller. Golf Coach."

Annette Botha hadn't known Ellie Myers. But her brother Adrian had. Well enough for her father to have added his name to the list.

Jade raised her head. She wished that she had her timeline in front of her. She'd forgotten to add one name to it. The name of Adrian Muller, who'd died five years ago, stabbed during an ATM transaction.

Ellie had died five years ago, in February. When had Adrian died? Were their deaths connected?

Jade went into the kitchen, turned on the light. She walked over to the boxes containing Adrian's sporting equipment. Packed and labeled by Annette before her move. She found a spoon in the sink. Using the edge of the spoon, she sliced down the center of the packaging tape of each box.

In the biggest one, she found golf clubs. More golf clubs. Golf bags. More golf bags. How many did a golfer need, she wondered. Other boxes contained golf shoes, shirts, trousers, tailored shorts. Umpteen caps. Plastic items which after a moment's confusion she identified as tees. Gloves, all for the left hand. She couldn't find any right-handed ones. Perhaps golfers only wore gloves on one hand. There was an entire gym bag crammed full of golf balls.

And one tennis racket.

Jade turned off the light and looked out at the early evening sky. Her eyes were automatically drawn to the dark bulk of the barn, framed by the tidy rows of wooden fencing. A brand-new horse barn, never used. Why had it been built? Adrian was a golfer. He had won trophies for his sport. He didn't own any breeches or shiny riding boots. There was no tack in the boxes. No whips or gloves or big padded helmets. Clearly, Adrian hadn't possessed any riding gear, or owned any horses. But Ellie had. Ellie was a horsewoman who practiced the mystifying art of dressage.

Ellie was three months pregnant when she died.

Jade shot back into the lounge and grabbed her cell phone.

✿

Reality returned to David in a gray, dizzy haze. For a moment he wished it hadn't. His hands were fastened together behind his back. The cable ties around his wrists were digging into his flesh. His legs were tied. His head was pounding and the bump on his temple burned every time the car turned or slowed. Bile churned in his stomach. At least he wasn't gagged. If he threw up, he wouldn't choke to death. Although in the heavy, solid trunk of the car, his voice was of no use to him.

David thought about Graham Hope tied up on the back seat. He couldn't hear the man, couldn't sense any movement from the car's interior. Hope clearly wasn't struggling. David supposed that, at night, there was no chance that anybody would notice him through the deeply tinted windows. Even if he made faces or tried to smash the window with his head, as David would have done.

Or perhaps wouldn't have done. Not if Whiteboy had been in the driver's seat with a loaded gun.

And then he heard a familiar, persistent noise. His dulled brain took a while to register what it was. His cell phone, ringing in his jacket pocket. Whiteboy obviously hadn't bothered to take it away from him. He must have thought that a sharp blow to the head, together with the cable ties, made it unnecessary.

After a short, intense and painful struggle, David realized he was right.

He slumped back down onto the carpet. Wasting his energy wouldn't help him now.

He could feel his cheek resting on the sharp edge of something small and shell-shaped. In the dark he couldn't see what it was. But he wondered if it might be the missing fingernail, the one that had torn away from Dean Grobbelaar's hand moments before he was tied to a tree to meet his bloody fate.

❁

Jade phoned Piet first. His phone didn't even ring. It went straight through to voicemail. Then, on reflex, she called David just to see if he would speak to her. No reply.

Jade called Johannesburg Central. She needed to know when Adrian Muller had died. She was sure that Piet would remember.

She knew David wouldn't be there, so she asked for Captain Moloi. He sounded tense and abrupt. Jade supposed that was because he was talking to her. Williams must have briefed him. She'd probably been labeled as a traitor, a turncoat. A career-damaging person.

Jade didn't care.

"I need to ask Piet Botha a question," she said.

"He was released just now. Williams told us to let him go. No reason to keep him any longer." Moloi seemed guarded.

"Oh." Jade paused, confused. She had assumed that Piet would call her as soon as he was released. "Did you give him back his cell phone? Because I haven't been able to get hold of him."

"Yes, we did." Moloi answered patiently. "All the usual procedures were followed."

"Do you know where he went?"

"I've no idea, Jade. Perhaps you could ask the sergeant at the front desk. He might have asked to use the phone there, if his battery was dead."

"Thanks."

A minute later, Jade was speaking to the sergeant. She informed her that yes, she remembered the man with paint on his face. He had passed by her desk after his release. She told Jade that Piet had met the person who had come to the station the other day. The man who had been using crutches. The one she had fetched a chair for.

"Piet got a lift with him?" Jade asked.

"Yes, I think so. He was standing in the doorway when Piet went out. I saw him speak to Piet. Then they walked away together."

So Graham Hope had picked him up. She was sure the insatiably curious estate agent had been eager to get the latest news from the holding cells. What better way to do this than giving the former suspect a ride home in his car?

She tried Piet's number again. The phone rang straight through to voicemail a second time.

Jade thumped the table in frustration. She needed her case file. For a crazy moment she wondered whether she should risk driving back to the cottage to get it. Because now she needed to contact Graham Hope urgently, in order to speak to Piet. She thought of the solidly packed queues of traffic between Johannesburg city and the northwestern suburbs. They could be another hour getting here. And there was no guarantee that Graham wouldn't whisk Piet off for a bite of supper, to squeeze more information out of him before he took him home.

Graham Hope's business card was in her case file in the cottage. His number wasn't stored on her cell.

She had one remaining option, and her chances of success were fading as fast as the evening light. With a sigh, Jade picked up the phone and dialed the number for the estate agents board.

The phone rang twelve times before it was answered. The woman sounded annoyed. Jade was sure she'd been on her way out of the door. She'd probably forgotten to turn on the answering machine and had only answered the call so she could have the satisfaction of telling the caller that her computer was turned off so they'd have to ring back tomorrow.

"It's me again. I called you earlier," Jade said.

"Yes. You did. Twice. Well, I'm on my way home now. Anything you need to ask will have to wait until morning."

There was no other choice. Jade would have to grovel.

"Please. I'm a private investigator in the middle of a vitally important police investigation. I'm sorry I took up so much of your time today. There is one final piece of information I need from you now. It's incredibly urgent and if you give it to me I promise I'll get off the phone and never bother you again."

The woman sighed loudly. Jade felt a glow of triumph. She was going to cooperate.

While she was listening to the faint sound of the computer starting up, Jade wondered why she hadn't ever tried to negotiate with David in the same way. Perhaps it would produce better results. Perhaps she should try it sometime.

Jade drew a pattern on the last blank corner of her paper, outlining a box for the number. It was a nice thought. But she knew she never would.

"What do you want?"

"The cell number of one of your estate agents. A Mr. Graham Hope."

She heard the woman repeat the surname as she searched the database. "Hope, Mr. G. Yes. We do have one for him," she said. Jade wrote the number down, thanked her profusely and said a hurried goodbye.

She dialed the number. He answered at the other end of the crackly cell phone line. Jade couldn't hear what he said at all.

"Hi there, Graham. It's Jade. Is Piet with you?"

More crackling.

"Piet Botha. Is he there with you?"

"No. This is Graham." His voice sounded deep and grainy, distorted by the poor line.

Jade sighed. She hoped he was heading into a better cell

reception area, because otherwise this was going to be a long conversation.

"Graham, I know it's you. I need to speak to Piet. Is he with you?"

"Piet who?"

"Piet Botha. You picked him up from jail earlier today. Or at least, you saw him there."

"From jail?" He sounded as if he was speaking underwater. She lost him again for a couple of seconds.

Jade sighed. Either Graham had amnesia, or the sergeant at the front desk of Johannesburg Central had been hallucinating.

"Is Piet not with you?"

Suddenly, magically, the line cleared. She could hear him.

"I'm sorry," he said. "I don't know what you're talking about."

She wondered for an awful moment if the lady at the estate agents board had given her the wrong number by mistake. She hoped not. Because she'd rather stick pins in her eyes than have to speak to her again tonight.

"I'm Jade," she said. "Remember? We met the other day at Annette Botha's place. The property you originally sold to her brother, Adrian Muller."

"Yes," he said, in a surprisingly harsh, grainy voice. "I remember selling Adrian that property. Out in northwestern Johannesburg. But I have no clue who Annette is. I have no idea who you are. And I'm not selling properties in Jo'burg any more. I moved down to the Natal Midlands in the middle of 1992."

Jade felt her fingers go cold. She nearly dropped the phone. This couldn't be happening. Not now, not when so much else had already gone wrong.

"You're definitely Graham Hope?"

"Always have been," he assured her.

She put the phone down and sat looking at the photo of Piet and Annette on the wall unit. Graham Hope lived in Natal; he had never met her. Or Piet. Which begged the question: who was the friendly, charming, plausible man claiming to be Graham, who had handed out business cards and won their trust? Who had kept track of the investigation and picked Piet up from the police station a short while ago?

Who she, in her innocence, had called earlier on today, to tell him she had discovered the existence of White & Co.

Jade thought she knew. They had been outwitted. Tricked, deceived and outmaneuvered by an enemy who had been two steps ahead of them the entire way. But now she had no idea what to do about it. Or where to start.

While she sat paralyzed with indecision, her cell phone rang. The noise was deafening in the silent house. There was no number identification for the call.

She pressed the button. "Yes?" she said.

"Jade." The voice was deep, unfamiliar, confident. "You don't know me. But I've got a good friend of yours here. Two friends, actually. We'd like you to come along and join the party."

Jade walked out of the living room and into the kitchen. She stared blankly out of the window. The sun had set. The sky was completely dark.

"Whiteboy," she said.

His mocking laugh was all the response she needed.

39

Whiteboy had abducted Piet. She knew that for sure. And with a dull thud of despair, she realized he must have David too.

Now he wanted her.

Jade's throat felt dry. She was scared to speak, in case her words somehow jeopardized their safety. "Why do you want me there?" she asked.

He laughed again. "Personally, I think you'll improve the party. Although that's just my opinion. But let's talk business now. If you don't join us within a certain time, I'm going to kill your friends. The short man and your cop partner. One by one. I hope your phone's battery is well charged, because I'll call you first before I start, so you can listen while I do the job. I think you'll find it entertaining." He paused. "If I can't get hold of you, then don't worry. They'll die anyway. The only question is this, Jade: which of the two will you choose to die first?"

Jade gripped her phone. Her hand felt suddenly slick.

"How do I know my friends are with you?"

"Now, now." His voice was reproving. "Are you implying I'm a liar?"

She swallowed. "Just requesting proof."

Whiteboy's voice was cold. "Call Johannesburg Central police station if you want proof. If you're a good investigator, you'll be able to get the answers from there."

She dared to bargain with him one more time. "I meant proof that they're still alive."

Now his voice was soft and icy. "You'll know they're still alive when I phone you again. And you listen to me killing them."

Jade touched one of the cardboard boxes. Even in the gloom, she could see Piet's elegant writing, smooth and dark against the grainy surface. He had sat and mourned as he packed his dead wife's possessions away. Annette had meant everything to him, and he had lost her. Now his own life was in danger. She closed her eyes for a moment. She couldn't even let herself think about David. The thought of him suffering, the thought of him dying, was too painful to bear.

"Where are you?" she asked.

"Good." Whiteboy sounded brisk and businesslike. "You're a sensible woman, Jade. Drive out on the M1 highway south, past Johannesburg city. Then take the Vereeniging road, the one that goes past Southgate shopping center. Are you on track here? Do you know where you're heading?"

"Yes." She walked back to the coffee table to write the directions on her crammed piece of paper. "Then where?"

"Then I'll call you again. In one hour. Make sure your phone is on. Make sure it's charged. And I'm sure I don't need to tell you, no cops. No backup, no help from anybody else. You arrive alone and unarmed."

"Right." Her throat was dry again.

"Look forward to it." The connection went dead.

Jade checked the time on her phone. Seven p.m. Whiteboy would be expecting her on the Southgate road at eight. The battery was half empty, but she had no time to charge it. It would have to do.

She hurried back to the kitchen, turned on the light, and ripped open the cardboard box that said, "Adrian— Personal." Adrian was stabbed after withdrawing money from an ATM. So his bank statements would show the day he had died.

In Adrian's personal box, she found more than bank statements. She found a brown envelope labeled simply "Ellie Myers." She glanced inside and saw a sheaf of cards, notes and letters. Records of a secret affair. She was sure that when Ellie fell pregnant she'd told Mark she was leaving him. Together with Whiteboy, he had planned a hasty revenge on the two lovers.

Jade imagined Annette preparing for her move to Cape Town, sorting through her brother's personal particulars that, perhaps, had lain neatly packed away in a cupboard since his death. Finding the envelope. Reading the letters. Wondering who Ellie was, why she had not known about her, where she was now. Where her child was, because she was sure Ellie had referred to her pregnancy.

Family was important to Annette. Piet had said so. Important enough for her to contact a private investigator to find out what had happened to the woman her brother had loved and planned to live with. And in doing so, she'd sealed her own fate.

Jade imagined Grobbelaar trying to trace Ellie from the pink-highlighted sheet in his car. Finding no record of her, he must have decided to locate Mark, who would have realized instantly that his well-kept secret was finally out. She was sure Whiteboy had helped Mark with his clean-up campaign. Kill the detective and torch his office. Shoot Annette at her gate. Locate and destroy her computer. And create a plausible scenario for each one. For Grobbelaar, make it look like a brutal revenge job. For Annette, a hijacking. For Yolandi, a house robbery. Who would ever connect three such different crimes in crime-ridden Johannesburg?

Jade closed the envelope and opened the file containing

the bank statements. Annette must have added the final one to the top of the pile. Adrian's last cash withdrawal was made on 22 February 2001. He had been murdered on the same day as Ellie Myers.

Jade scribbled a swift explanation on the back of the final statement. What had happened, where to look for evidence. Where she had gone. She added the date and the time, tore it out of the file and left it on the coffee table. If she didn't come back, somebody might find it. And it would lead them to the truth.

She remembered the case notes painstakingly written by her father and placed in his briefcase on the last night of his life. Nobody had read those notes after he died. She hoped that somebody might read hers.

Jade checked the time on her phone. Quarter past seven. She would have to run. She grabbed her keys and hurried out of the house, locking the door behind her.

She reached Southgate Mall at five to eight. The Vereeniging road was a two-lane highway, dark and arrow-straight. There were a few traffic lights along the way, largely ignored by most of the motorists traveling this route after dark.

Her phone rang at three minutes to eight.

"Jade."

"Yes."

"You're alone?"

"Yes."

"Good. Go through two traffic lights after the Southgate turnoff. After the second one, you'll see a sign for Grasmere. Turn right onto that road."

"Then what?"

"Then I'll call you again."

On her way, Jade noticed a couple of other cars on the highway, speeding along with their headlights on full beam. The Vereeniging road was dangerous. But probably not as dangerous, she thought, as what was waiting for her when she left it.

She turned right at the sign onto a wide dirt road lined with overgrown bushes and grass. Jade was sure that wherever Whiteboy was, he could now see the headlights of her car.

Her phone rang.

"This is my last call. Drive another half kilometer. On your left you'll see a small two-track lane. It's overgrown, so look out for it. Drive down the lane and stop when you see the black Merc. You know what it looks like. You won't miss it. Turn off the lights and get out of your car. Lean over the hood, hands on the windshield. Palms flat. Do anything different, your friends die." He paused and she heard him breathe heavily. "Don't make your own rules."

Jade's hands were trembling on the wheel and her feet threatened to slip off the pedals. She drove slowly, but even so she nearly missed the turning. It was dark and narrow, like a cave mouth in the dry, yellow growth surrounding it.

Branches swished over the roof of her car. She saw the Mercedes. It was parked ahead, lights off.

The lane widened into a clearing. In the arc of her headlights she saw David and Piet. They were lying on the grass, hands and feet tied. Graham Hope was standing over them and he had a gun aimed directly at David's head. His metal cast was nowhere in sight. It had been a prop, Jade thought, like his wedding ring. Part of Whiteboy's strategy of deception.

Jade cut the engine. She climbed out of the car and walked

round to the front. She bent over. The hood was warm but the windshield was icy cold. She spread out her hands and placed them on the glass.

Graham Hope looked up, as if he had only just noticed her there.

"Evening, Jade," he said cheerfully.

"Evening, Mark," she replied.

He laughed. "You're a smart girl, all right."

"Were you involved with Whiteboy before he helped you murder your wife?" Jade asked. "Or did you only turn bad afterwards?"

David twisted his head round and lifted it off the grass. He started to say something, but Mark shifted his weight and smashed a heavy boot into his head. David dropped to the ground, face first. He lay prone for a moment and then struggled onto his side again, choking and spitting sand out of his mouth. Jade saw Piet curl into a ball, bending his knees and trying to shrink down into the long grass.

Her fingers were pressed against the windshield so hard she could feel her nails scraping the glass like cheap chalk on a blackboard.

"We've got a few house rules here. Rule number one is no speaking. These boys aren't gagged because Whiteboy wasn't sure if you'd make the deadline. And then, as you know, you were due for an interesting phone call." Mark looked down again and frowned. "We might have to do it now, if they're going to get out of line." He turned back to Jade with a pleasant expression. "You know, you can tell a person time and time again that there's no point in shouting or screaming, because a gunshot is going to be louder in any case. But do they listen?" He shook his head. "Never."

"Where's Whiteboy?" Jade asked.

"Here." The voice came from directly behind her. She twisted her head round, her heart pounding. Huge hands grabbed her hair and forced her head back down onto the glass. She closed her eyes and clenched her teeth as she felt him touch her, patting and squeezing her from top to bottom. He removed her cell phone from her jacket pocket, turned it off and tossed it into the Mercedes.

"Stay there," he told her. He walked over to her car and pulled open the door. He checked the front and rear seats and popped open the trunk. He completed his circuit of the car and then stood behind her again.

"Good girl," he said. "You listened."

She could hear him breathing, loud and rough, almost panting.

Then he grabbed her by the shoulders of her jacket and flung her down onto the ground.

Jade rolled over, feeling dirt and stones and tussocks of dry grass underneath her. Whiteboy grabbed her again, under her arms, his hands closing around her shoulders. Then he dragged her away, out of the clearing and into the dark shadows of the undergrowth. She heard David shout in protest and saw Mark give him another vicious kick to the head. Then the long grass obscured her vision and Whiteboy let her go. She fell backwards sprawling onto the dry ground, rocks bruising her flesh.

"At last. We're alone together," Whiteboy said. She couldn't see his face as he stood above her, but she was positive he was smiling.

David tried to blink the stinging grains of sand out of his

eyes. His head was ringing and his vision was still blurred after the impact of Mark's boot. Whiteboy had dragged Jade away, and he had no doubt what the man was going to do to her. None at all. He strained against the bonds holding his hands behind his back, knowing that his struggle was useless. With a loaded gun aimed straight at his head, he wouldn't survive long enough to draw breath even if he did manage to break the ties.

Mark nudged him with his foot, more gently this time.

"Stop wriggling. It won't help." He spoke more softly, his voice dropping to a conspiratorial whisper. "He's totally insane, you realize. Insane but brilliant. He's made me wealthier than I could ever have hoped to be. Sorted out all my personal problems, too. That's why I humor his odd little quirks." He gestured with his head in Whiteboy's direction. "He wanted to do this right here, in front of you. But I think he realized that you could close your eyes and you wouldn't see a thing. So he's gone off to find a more private place. Of course, you'll still be able to hear. Difficult to close your ears with your hands behind your back. He wants you to listen. I think that's the plan."

David listened. He didn't want to. In the quiet night he could hear every noise they made. Each one felt like a dagger slicing through his heart.

He heard the sounds of a struggle in the dense undergrowth near the road. Jade was gasping for breath. She made tiny involuntary noises as she struggled. Leaves crunched and rustled. Whiteboy grunted and moaned. Occasionally, David heard a breathy snigger. A branch cracked. He thought he heard the breaking of glass. A choking, gagging cry from Jade. Then a soft, throaty gurgle of pleasure, a deep exhalation. The bushes rustled again, shaking in time to a frantic, pounding rhythm. Each sound painted a picture in his mind more shocking and dreadful than reality could have been. David forced his eyes shut, shoulders shaking, tears wetting his cheeks.

Then his eyes flew open as he heard a choking scream. He sat up, trembling as the primal sound of agony and despair echoed in the stillness.

Jade screamed again, coughing. This time, the sound was weaker.

"No, don't do that! No! Don't kill me, please, not like that, don't squeeze my neck! Don't squeeze my…"

Her spluttering cries cut off abruptly. The bushes rustled again and then they were still. Silence crept back like a fog over water.

David's heart felt as if it was erupting from his chest.

"Bastard," Piet shouted, in hoarse, broken tones.

Mark kicked him in the head.

40

Jade lay sprawled on the grass with Whiteboy standing above her. She still couldn't see his face, not even when he dropped down onto one knee and placed a hand on her arm. She heard him breathe and smelt the faint odor of old cigarette smoke as he bent forward.

Systematically, he began to rip away her clothing.

She struggled with the strength of despair, knowing that however hard she fought she had no chance against his power and bulk. That he was enjoying the chase as much as he would savor the kill. That David was a short distance away, hearing every movement, listening to every sound.

He ripped off her jacket, squeezing and groping her, sniggering in a way that made her want to spit in his face. He held her down with one meaty hand while he tore open the buttons of her jeans, yanked her shoes off and tugged the jeans down her legs.

Jade resisted every step of the way. She pushed his hands away and bent her knees. She kicked and thrashed and tried to bite, hearing the panting and sobbing of her own breath in the stillness. Whiteboy pushed her backwards until her head jammed against a large rocky outcrop. His strong arms overpowered her. His fingers bruised her thighs. Jade clamped her legs together. The denim bunched around her ankles and Whiteboy snickered again, using both his hands to tug the jeans off. Jade windmilled her arms in the surrounding grass, hoping to find a sharp stick or a stone that she could fight him with.

Her fingers closed around something better.

A discarded beer bottle made from heavy glass. Tossed into the bushes by one of the pedestrians, the poor people, the ones who walked alongside the roads. Faceless, nameless, unseen and unnoticed by the drivers staring ahead in their big fast cars.

Tossed into the grass by somebody who had inadvertently given her the chance to save her life.

Thank you, Jade thought.

She grasped the slim smooth head of the bottle like a lifeline. She had one chance and she would have to take it immediately, because if Whiteboy got hold of her arms again there was no way she'd get free. Jade raised the bottle and brought it down with all the force she could muster, onto the rock behind her.

Glass shattered around her head and she saw Whiteboy's shadowy form whipping towards her again. Jade sat up and thrust the jagged-edged weapon into the darkness like a spear, guided by the sound of his rough breathing.

She felt the glass slice through his flesh, felt cartilage and tendons rip and tear as the razor-sharp edges slashed them apart.

She'd stabbed the broken bottle directly into his throat.

Whiteboy made a final desperate grab for her. His fingers closed around her neck and squeezed. Jade felt the blood pound in her head. She gagged, struggling. Then his grasp grew weaker and his fingers slipped away. She felt, rather than saw, the blood pouring from his severed arteries. He folded onto the ground. His final breath gurgled in his lungs. He twitched, and was still.

Jade took a deep breath. He was dead. She felt weak with relief. But David and Piet were still in danger. She had to help them fast. With trembling hands, she felt around for her shoes and slipped them on. Whiteboy was on top of her jeans, so she would have to do without them.

Jade remembered Whiteboy's strategy. Deception and surprise.

She grabbed the branch of a tree and swung it violently back and forth a few times to mimic a struggle, feeling a rain of dry leaves falling around her. Then she screamed.

She picked up one of the pieces of broken glass from the rock and crawled out of the undergrowth onto the road. She screamed again, choking, gagging, begging him not to strangle her. Then she cut the scream short, and kept quiet, praying that the noise hadn't put David and Piet at further risk.

Jade crept back towards the clearing, trying to stay in the

shadows on the other side of the path, because her legs were so damn pale they would show up like flares if there was any light around.

Keeping silent. Moving carefully and slowly. Trying to keep her burning impatience under control. Trying not to let herself worry about everything that could still go wrong.

She heard Piet cry "Bastard" and then the sound of a boot hitting a skull. She edged forward, feeling the grass slowly yield to her shifting weight. Poor Piet.

Silence again. Now she was behind her car. It was lighter in the clearing. She would have to be very careful.

"Whitey?" Mark called. "Hope he hasn't gone to sleep," he said in a conversational tone. "It's not easy to keep him awake after he's had a good time." He called again, louder. "Whiteboy?"

Jade crept a few steps further. Now she was behind the black Mercedes. Mark wasn't looking in her direction. He was staring ahead at the bushes near the road, wondering what had happened to his friend.

She saw him move forward cautiously. He took the gun with him, but he didn't take David or Piet. He walked through the grass, stepping slowly. He held his cell phone up and used the light of the screen to see where he was going.

Jade hoped he would take a little while to find the corpse in the long grass using only a cell phone. As soon as he had stepped into the undergrowth, she sprinted across the clearing to David and Piet.

David stared at her as if she had returned from the dead, his eyes wide and his jaw slack with shock. Half undressed, with a bloodstained shirt and grass in her hair, she thought she probably looked as if she had.

She crouched down beside them and used the glass shard to cut through the cable ties. She freed David first, then Piet. They sat up, rubbing their wrists and ankles.

"Dead," she whispered to Piet. "The guy who killed your wife."

Piet leaned forward. His knotted fingers closed around her hand and held it gently for a moment.

"Whitey?" they heard Mark call.

David jerked his thumb. "Over to the car," he whispered. "Better cover."

Jade had to help him walk; he'd hurt his ankle so badly he couldn't bear any weight on it at all. They had almost reached the car when they heard Mark shout, "Shit."

Footsteps pounded back through the undergrowth towards them.

She was sure she would find a gun in the Mercedes. But there was no time to look. The three of them huddled together behind the dark, gleaming bulk of the car. Jade heard Mark run into the clearing. Then his footsteps stopped abruptly. She imagined him staring, astounded, at the place where his prisoners had been.

Jade heard the beeping of his phone, and saw the dancing shadow of the screen through the tinted glass of the car. Mark was hunting with his cell phone again. He wasn't as bright as Whiteboy, she thought, but even so it wouldn't take long for him to realize he could search far more efficiently if he used the car's headlights. He was armed, and ready to use his weapon. She was half-naked, David was half-lame, and Piet looked half-stunned. Could they overpower him before he fired a shot?

They didn't have a chance to find out. Jade heard the rumble of a car approaching on the road. She saw the beam of headlights, and above them, the reassuring signal of a bright blue light.

The car drove past the gap in the trees. It skidded to a stop and she heard it reverse. Then the headlights swung towards them and tires crunched as the vehicle stopped behind Jade's hired car.

She glanced at Piet and David. Their expressions were as blank as her own, lit up in shadowy white and blue. Across the clearing, she saw Mark Myers spin round and aim his gun at the vehicle.

The driver opened the car door.

"Put the gun down," Jade heard him say. "I won the South African police pistol-shooting championships five years in a row and I haven't gone a day without practicing since. So if you're looking for a shootout, forget it."

The voice belonged to Williams.

Jade and David glanced at each other and stood up. Jade brushed the soil off her bare knees. Beside her, Piet struggled to his feet.

Mark bent down and lowered his gun to the ground.

"That's better," Williams said. "Now put your hands in the air. You're under arrest."

He turned to David. "Superintendent, I thought I suspended you from duties."

"I can explain everything, Commissioner."

"I'm sure you can. But your explanation will have to wait. There's a pair of handcuffs in the trunk of the car. Get them out and then let's get this gentleman in a situation where he can't cause any damage."

Jade helped David stagger over to the police vehicle. Williams opened the trunk and David rummaged inside.

"There's everything here except the bloody cuffs," he said, pushing aside reflective jackets and kit bags and traffic cones. Jade bent across and helped him search. She wondered how Williams had known where they were. She'd have to ask him when Mark had been restrained. The sooner this was over, the sooner they could go home. The adrenaline had ebbed out of her. She felt as weak as a kitten. She wanted to sleep for a hundred years. Where were the damn cuffs?

Jade was reaching under a pile of papers when she heard a sound. A small sound, like a puppy might make if it was left outside the door in the cold. She straightened up to look.

"David," she whispered.

Williams had grabbed Piet in a headlock. His service pistol was pushed against the defenseless man's temple.

Williams nodded to Mark. Jade saw he had picked up his gun again.

"Go ahead. I'll take this one. You take the others."

The police commissioner stared at Jade, his eyes bright in the gleam of the headlights.

Piet looked strangely calm in Williams's grip, and as Jade watched him she suddenly knew what he was thinking. His wife's killer had died. He was finally at peace. He could face his own fate.

She watched Williams's finger tighten on the trigger, and as she heard the deafening crack of the shot she closed her eyes.

41

David yanked her down behind the car. Mark fired over the roof, running towards them. The sound of gunfire shook the air. David's hand was tight around her own.

No time to run or hide. She was unarmed. They couldn't fight back. The crack of another shot exploded in her ears. This was it. Game over. She was going to die here with him. For a fleeting moment she thought of her hastily written notes on the paper in Annette's house. Her final efforts had all been for nothing, just like her father's. Almost certainly, Williams would be the one to find it.

She braced herself, waiting to feel the hard punch of a bullet in her flesh, hoping death would be instantaneous.

Then the gunfire stopped. She heard a heavy thud as Mark keeled over. The clearing was quiet, apart from the ringing in Jade's ears.

"What on earth?" She let go of David's hand and scrambled to her feet. She looked over to the place where Piet's body had fallen. Except Piet wasn't slumped lifelessly on the ground. He was stepping gingerly over the body of the police commissioner, blood on his shirt and confusion in his eyes.

"There you go, you son of a bitch. That's what you deserve."

Jade spun round. Robbie stood at the edge of the clearing, holding her Glock. He was glaring at the crumpled body of Commissioner Williams.

He took a step forward. "I found the fucker, Jade. That's the guy who set us up. The one who phoned me for the hit on Viljoen. That bloody head cop turned informer on us. He's as bent as a wire coat hanger. Oh, and he quashed the Hirsch case, by the way. My connections eventually came through with the info. Then I followed him, tailed him here. I don't know who that other asshole is." Robbie jerked his thumb at Mark's lifeless form, turned and winked at Jade. "Nice legs, babe. Well, I'd better be going now. Verna's waiting. And don't look at me like that, Superintendent." He spread his hands, dangling the Glock from his index finger. "I shot him in self-defense."

❋

The following evening Jade was busy in the cottage garden. She'd discovered a plantation of spinach next to the shelter of the fence. Since she'd just renewed the lease on the place for another six months, she felt she was entitled to ownership of some of the garden produce. She'd picked enough leaves to fill a plastic supermarket bag when she heard David shouting her name outside the cottage gate. She looked round. He stood there, balancing stork-like on his left leg.

She buzzed the gate open and he hopped inside.

"You could get a crutch, you know," she said as he bumped heavily down onto a kitchen chair.

"I don't need a bloody crutch," he said. He stretched his leg across to the opposite chair. She fetched him a beer.

"Cheers," she said, clinking her wine glass against the bottle.

"Good health," he responded.

Watching him, she saw a vulnerability in his gray eyes that hadn't been there before. Something about the way he looked at her was making her awkward and happy and nervous all at once. With a firm effort she suppressed the feelings. Things might never work out between them. There was too much about her he might never be able to approve of or accept. Too much that she realized she couldn't change, not for David, not for anybody, because it was part of who she was.

But it would be worth playing the percentages, giving it her best try. Jade was certain of that. She was looking forward to it.

David took a gulp of beer and then wiped his mouth with the back of his hand.

"Jadey," he said.

"Yes?"

"What happened with Viljoen?"

Surprised by the question, Jade opened her mouth to speak but decided against it. She needed to come to terms with the situation on her own first. She'd never realized the extent of Williams's ambition, the depths of his greed. The crooked cop had seen the money-making opportunities that had presented themselves with the end of apartheid and the restructuring of the police service. But with Commissioner de Jong heading the team, he'd never been able to reap the rewards of corruption.

He'd tried to force her father into early retirement by sabotaging the high-profile Viljoen case. When that didn't work, he'd bribed Jacobs to set up the accident. His attempt on Jade's life hadn't succeeded. When she shot Jacobs, Williams had to think fast. He deliberately misinformed her by saying that the Viljoen brothers had organized the hit on her father. Then he'd waited to see what she would do when she returned to South Africa, maintaining contact with Robbie so that he could use the gangster's greed as bait.

She shivered to think how close she had come to murdering Viljoen, with Williams poised to close the jaws of his trap around her. How she now believed that Williams had been on Whiteboy's payroll as an informer, a trusted inside police connection. No wonder he had been unhappy when David was promoted to the higher ranks of his team and was assigned the investigation into Annette Botha's death.

She wanted to talk to David about it. And she would. But not now.

"I'll tell you sometime soon," she said.

He craned his neck. "What's in that plastic bag?"

Jade had been planning to steam the spinach for supper. Instead, she tied a knot in the top of the bag and put it in the fridge.

"Nothing." She turned back to look at him. "Are you still going to live next door to me? Are you still a detective in the South African police service?" They weren't the real questions she wanted to ask him. But she was sure he understood.

David grinned. "I'll tell you sometime soon, too." He took another gulp of his beer. "So what's for supper?"

Jade opened the fridge and took out two thick and tender pieces of fillet and a small bag of potatoes. There was no point in cooking any other vegetables, she knew. They would have to wait for another day.

"Steak and chips," she said.

"Great," David said, swinging back in his chair and nudging her with his elbow as she turned to the stove. "Cop food."

Turn the page for a sneak preview from the next
Jade de Jong investigation

Stolen Lives

I

October 14

Detective Constable Edmonds saw the running man just a half-second before the unmarked car she was travelling in hit him.

A slightly built man, dark-skinned and dark-clad in a tight-fitting jersey and a beanie. He burst out of the shadows behind a flyover and sprinted straight across the A12, fists pumping, head bowed against the gusting rain, splashing through the puddles on the tarmac as if he were running for his life.

"Look out!" Edmonds shouted from the back seat, but Detective Sergeant Mackay, who was driving, had seen the man, too.

"Hang on, people."

A shriek of brakes, and then the car reached the puddle of water that had pooled on the tarmac and went into a skid. Edmonds' seatbelt yanked hard against her chest, squeezing the breath out of her in spite of the regulation Kevlar vest she was wearing under her jacket. She grabbed the seat in front of her, and a moment later her hand was squashed into the padded fabric by the larger, tougher palm of bulky Sergeant Richards, who was also bracing for the crash.

The car slewed sideways, and Mackay swore as he

fought for control. Through the spattered windscreen Edmonds saw the running man look, too late, in their direction. He flung out a hand in defence, and Edmonds' heart leapt into her mouth when she heard a loud metallic thunk that seemed to shake the car.

The man stumbled heavily and went down, sprawling onto his side. But before Edmonds could even conceptualise the thought—is he hurt?—he got up again and set off at a shaky jog. He scrambled over the crash barrier on the opposite side of the road and disappeared from sight.

He didn't so much as glance behind him.

The tyres regained their purchase on the road and Mackay slowed to a stop.

"Jesus," Richards said. "What the hell was that all about?"

Nobody answered. For a moment the only noise was the ticking of the hazard lights, which Mackay had activated, and the flick of the wipers. Water splashed up as a car drove by in the fast lane, the motorist oblivious to what had just occurred.

Then Richards looked down and saw that his hand was covering Edmonds'.

"Oh. Sorry," he said, and removed it.

Mackay pulled over into the emergency lane, and two of the men climbed out and shone a flashlight into the darkness where the running man had vanished.

"He's nowhere in sight. Must have gone into that park over there." The detective who had been sharing the back seat with Edmonds and Richards climbed back in, and once again Edmonds found herself squashed, sardine-like, between the car door and the warm bulk of Richards' thigh.

"He's lucky you were wide awake." The detective sitting next to Mackay shunted the passenger seat forward for the second time that trip, in an attempt to give Edmonds a couple of inches more leg room.

"Lucky anybody is at this hour," Mackay said. "And that it's so quiet tonight." He let out a deep breath, then checked his mirrors and pulled onto the road again.

"But we hit him," Edmonds said. She could hear the unsteadiness in her own voice as she spoke, and she hoped the other detectives would put it down to reaction after their near-accident, rather than nervousness about what lay ahead. "Do you think he's all right?"

Mackay nodded. "He'll have a sore arm tomorrow, I should think. Nothing we can do about it now. I'll write it up when I make the report."

"Better hope you don't have a dent in the bonnet, or you'll be writing that up as well," Richards observed, and all the men laughed. Another clicking of the indicator, and they turned right off the A 12, heading east towards Stratford.

In the three months since Edmonds had been promoted to the Human Trafficking team in Scotland Yard, she'd been surprised to discover that most of the operations they tackled did not take place in central London, but in the middle-class and respectable-looking suburbs. Like the one where they were headed now.

As they drove down Templemills Lane, Edmonds stared at the tall wire fences and enormous crash barriers that lined the road. The headlights flickered over the stiff mesh, ghostly silver in the dark, as high and solid as a prison fence. But the area protected by the fences and barriers was no prison. It was the construction site for the 2012 London Olympics.

"That's where they're building the athletes' village." Richards pointed across her, to the left. "More than twelve thousand people will be living there. Not all of them will go back home again, if our last Olympics was anything to go by. They'll stay in the UK and claim asylum. About a thousand, probably. Mostly from Iraq, Nigeria, Somalia, Zimbabwe."

Edmonds peered into the darkness at the endless wire fence and the solid concrete barriers flashing past, but she found she couldn't get the image of the man out of her head. Fists clenched, head bowed, seemingly oblivious to the fact he was running straight across a major arterial road.

Running towards something, or running away?

For a troubled moment, Edmonds wondered whether the near-accident with the man was a sign that the police operation tonight, her first-ever raid, was going to go wrong.

Then she shook her head and told herself not to be so superstitious.

The crash barriers came to an end and, suddenly, they were in suburbia. Ranks of small, unremarkable-looking, semi-detached houses and flats, with shops and businesses lining the narrow high street.

"This is where you'll find the kind of places we're after," Richards had told her during her training. "Not in Soho and the West End. There, they work in pairs. One girl and one maid in one flat. That's legal. But what you'll find out here often isn't."

A police van was parked by the side of the road, waiting. Mackay flashed his lights at it as he passed, and it pulled out into the road behind them.

Peering through the rain, Edmonds made out a pub, a launderette, a fish and chip shop, and another business with a large sign written in lettering she couldn't understand—Turkish, perhaps. All dark and locked up, because it was already after midnight.

The unmarked car slowed as the establishment they were here to raid came into sight.

At street level, the place looked innocuous—a black-painted door with a small number six painted on it in white. Upstairs the windows were shaded by dark blinds and a sign hung, small and discreet, from a neat hook in the corner wall.

"Sauna? Yeah, right," Richards remarked drily.

The police van following them pulled to a stop behind their car.

"Right, everybody," Mackay said. "Let's get this operation going."

Heart pounding, Edmonds wrenched the door open and jumped out, slipping and almost falling on the wet, uneven pavement. Richards caught her arm.

"C'mon love. Round the back."

"Love"?

But there was no time to bristle at the word that Edmonds was sure, in any case, was unintentional. Time only to follow the plan which had been discussed in detail the previous day, to sprint round the back of the building with two of the uniformed officers and head for the fire exit.

She ran up the fire escape, the metal vibrating under her fleece-lined boots.

"Get in position." Richards was behind her, already out of breath.

Ahead, a solid-looking grey door.

As she reached it, Edmonds saw the handle move. Someone was opening it from the inside.

The door swung open and a middle-aged man hurried out. Tousled brown hair, furtive expression, busy buttoning his shirt over his paunch.

"'Scuse me, sir." Edmonds stepped forward.

The man glanced up, then stopped in his tracks when he saw the two uniformed officers behind the plainclothes detectives.

"I'm not . . ." he said. He whipped his head from side to side, as if wondering whether turning and running would be a better option, but there was nowhere to go.

"Please accompany the officers down to the police vehicles, sir," Edmonds said, aware that she sounded squeaky and not nearly as authoritative as she would have wished. "We need to ask you a few questions."

Footsteps clanged on the fire escape as the two officers escorted the unhappy customer downstairs.

Then a red-haired woman wearing a black jacket and a pair of dark, tight-fitting pants burst through the exit, almost knocking Edmonds off her feet. The policewoman grabbed at the railing for support.

The woman's skin was sickly pale, a stark contrast to her crimson hair. She looked older than Edmonds had expected; in her fifties, perhaps. Too old to be a sex-worker? Edmonds had no idea. She smelled of stale ciga-rettes and perfume, the scent musky and heavy.

The woman was past Edmonds before she could recover her footing, but Richards, standing a few steps further down, managed to grab her by the arm.

"Let me go!" She struggled, shouting at Richards in accented tones, but he had a firm hold on her.

"Nobody's going anywhere just yet, ma'am. Are you in charge here?"

"Me, no." The woman raised her chin and stared at him fiercely. "I am nobody, nothing. Forget you saw me."

"We can't do that, I'm afraid," Richards said, with heavy irony. "Who are you, then?"

Defiant silence. Then the woman snaked her head towards Richards, and for a bizarre moment Edmonds thought that she was going to kiss him. Before the big officer could stop her, she sank her teeth into the exposed strip of skin between the collar of his waterproof and his beanie.

Shouting in pain, Richards let go of her arm. He snatched at her head with both hands, grabbing her hair in an effort to pull her off him.

"Kick her!" Edmonds shouted, but in his panic, Rich-ards seemed to have forgotten his basic self-defence training. Her stomach clenched. God, this was it. She'd have to take the woman down. Fumbling for the canis-ter of pepper spray on her belt, she leapt forward, ready to tackle her, feeling the fire escape rattle as one of the officers below came running up again to assist.

Before Edmonds could act, the woman twisted away

from Richards' grasp, leaving long strands of hair dangling from his hands. Edmonds had a brief glimpse of her mouth, bloodstained lips curled back in a snarl, and her gut contracted again because she looked just like a vampire.

To her astonishment, the woman then hooked a leg over the handrail and jumped. Edmonds saw her red hair fly out behind her as she landed on the tarmac below on all fours, like a cat.

"Grab her," Edmonds shouted, and the fire escape vibrated yet again as the officer on his way up did a hasty about-turn and made a hurried descent.

Edmonds thumbed her radio on. "Escaping suspect," she yelled. "Back entrance. Red-headed female. You copy?"

She glanced down again, just in time to see the woman dart into the shadows and disappear from sight. She was limping heavily, favouring her right ankle, which must have twisted when she landed.

The radio crackled in reply. "We've got the two main streets cordoned off. She won't get far. Over."

Edmonds turned back to Richards. He was swearing, breathing hard, his fingers pressed to the wound on his neck. He took his hand away and stared down at the sticky smear of blood.

"Bitch!" he hissed through clenched teeth. "Bloody bitch. Can't believe she did that. God knows what she's given me."

A strong gust of wind wailed eerily through the gaps in the fire escape's supports. Blinking rain out of her eyes, Edmonds saw the woman emerge from the shadows, then bend and fumble under her trouser leg before she set off half-running, half-limping, towards the young constable standing by the parked police cars.

Edmonds grabbed her radio again. Through the worsening downpour, she thought she had seen the gleam of a knife in her hand.

"Watch out! She's armed!" she shouted, directing her voice into the radio and also towards the uniformed officer manning the cordon.

The officer didn't hear her warning. He moved confidently forward to intercept the fleeing woman, obviously thinking, as Edmonds had done at first, that she was one of the trafficked victims trying to escape. There was a brief scuffle, and then he cried out and stumbled backwards, clutching at his stomach. In the bright beam of the police car's headlights, Edmonds saw blood seeping through the young man's fingers.

Kevlar offered little protection against a sharp-bladed knife.

Firearms were not commonly found in brothels, as there was always the risk that they could fall into the wrong hands. Because of this, the police didn't carry guns during raids.

Right now, Edmonds wished she had a gun.

"Officer down!" she screamed into the radio, staring at the scene in horror. "Call an ambulance. We've got a man injured on the street."

Another pair of high-beam headlights blazed in the darkness, and Edmonds saw a sleek black car speeding down the street towards them. It skidded to a stop a few metres away from the police blockade. For a moment the lights from one of the police cars shone directly through the windscreen, allowing Edmonds to glimpse the driver, a sunken-cheeked black man. Then the passenger door flew open, the red-headed woman dived inside, and water hissed from under the tyres as the car spun round in a tight U-turn and disappeared down the Leytonstone Road.

Two other officers sprinted over to the fallen man.

"Shit!" Richards had wadded a tissue onto the wound in his neck and was also staring at the departing vehicle. "That was an Aston Martin. Looked like Salimovic's car."

"The brothel owner?" Edmonds' eyes widened. She'd heard Mackay on the radio earlier, communicating with the team that had been on the way to his house to arrest him.

Now it seemed that despite their careful planning and preparation, he had managed to escape.

"Shit," Richards said again, inspecting the wet and bloody tissue. "How do these bastards always know?"

"Well, it wasn't Salimovic at the wheel," Edmonds said. "I saw the driver. He was black."

The radio crackled again and Richards jerked his thumb towards the door. "Don't worry about what's happening down there. They'll sort it out. We're going in now. Room-to-room search. Keep your pepper spray handy in case there's trouble inside."

Edmonds tripped over the ledge in the doorway and almost sprawled headlong into the corridor. Great going, girl, she thought. Look good in front of your superiors, why don't you?

She moved forward cautiously, glancing from side to

side. It was gloomy in here, lit only by a couple of low-wattage bulbs. The walls were dirty and the floor was scuffed, the lino cracked and uneven. She caught another whiff of the unpleasantly musky perfume which she now realised hadn't come from the escaping red-head, but from the interior of the brothel itself. Underlying that was the stench of old dirt and another pungent odour that Edmonds suddenly, shockingly, realised was the smell of sex.

Pop music was coming from somewhere, piped through invisible speakers, but as she noticed it the sound was turned off. Now she could hear the voices of the officers at the front of the building.

"You three take the top floor."

"Bag that price list, will you?"

"Christ, it stinks in here."

"Oi! Where do you think you're going, sir? Hey! Someone grab him." Then there was the sound of running footsteps, followed by a brief scuffle.

She came to a closed door on her right. Aware of Richards behind her, she pushed it open. The room was gloomy; a purple lantern illuminated a single bed in the corner with a figure huddled on a stained mattress.

"Somebody here," she called, hearing the quiver in her own voice as she approached the bed.

A black girl lay there, eyes wide and terrified. She was on her side, her slender arms wrapped tightly around her legs, and Edmonds saw with a jolt that she was naked. She glanced around the room for something to cover her with, but there was nothing suitable in the small space. Nothing at all.

"Are you all right, miss?" Edmonds leaned forward. Now she could see the puffy swelling on the girl's left cheek, where the dark skin was mottled even darker with bruising. She could also see the massive, crusted scabs on her lips.

The girl flinched under Edmonds' concerned gaze.

The police officer breathed in deeply, suppressing her anger. Who had done this? The owner? A client? That middle-aged bastard who'd tried to wriggle out of the back entrance?

"Who hurt you?"

No reply. She whispered something in an almost inaudible voice, but it wasn't in a language that Edmonds could understand.

"I don't know if she speaks any English," Edmonds said aloud.

She reached out and gently took the black girl's hand in her own cold, damp one.

"Are you all right?" she asked again.

The girl looked up at Edmonds in silence, her eyes full of tears.

2

October 25

They came for him at night.

Eleven p.m. on a summer evening and Terence was in bed, propped up on his black continental pillow, fiddling around with something on his laptop. She was watching *Idols* on the big-screen TV, lying naked on the bedcovers, her hair spread over the pillow, listening to some teen-ager butchering a Mango Groove song.

Then, a noise. Loud, hard, frightening, cutting right through the hum of the laptop's fan and the screech of the South African *Idols* contestant's high notes.

He snapped his laptop shut and sat bolt upright. She raised her head from the pillow and stared at the window, as if she could somehow see all the way through it and down to the dark garden below.

"What was that?" she asked.

"Don't know." He pushed back the covers and climbed out of bed. "Turn the TV down, will you?"

He pushed back the curtain and peered out of the window. She felt around for the remote, nearly knocking the bedside lamp over. Where on earth was it? She fumbled in the folds of the duvet, checked under the pillow. Her heart was pounding, her hands trembling. What had made that noise? It was impossible that anything could be banging outside like that. But it hadn't sounded like a banging noise in any case. It had sounded like . . .

. . . like somebody knocking hard on the front door.

Which was even more impossible, because they were the only people on the property. It was well secured, as all the homes in this wealthy Jo'burg neighbourhood were, surrounded by a high wall and a five-thousand-volt electric fence.

She glanced across the bed. There it was, of course. On his table. It had gravitated to the man's side, as remotes invariably do. She stretched across, grabbed it and stabbed the mute button with nail-breaking force.

The teen's quavering voice cut off mid-wail.

"Can't see a thing," Terence muttered, turning away from the window.

Then they heard the noise again. It sounded louder in the silence.

Bam, bam, bam.

"Shit," he said. He hurried to the cupboard, flung it open, rummaged among the clothes.

"What is it?" she asked.

"How the hell should I know?" He pulled on a black T-shirt and grabbed his jeans. Searching through the cupboard once more, he took out a small silver gun. He did something to it that made a metallic, ratcheting noise.

She sat up and stared at him, wide-eyed, clutching the duvet and worrying it between her fingers. He turned around and regarded her coldly, as if she were a complete stranger, as if they hadn't been making love earlier that evening and sharing a jacuzzi an hour ago.

"Put on some clothes," he snapped.

Suddenly her own nakedness wasn't sexy or appealing. It made her feel vulnerable, afraid.

She leaned down to retrieve the outfit she'd worn earlier, now discarded on the floor. Short black cocktail dress, lacy panties, gold sandals. Hands shaking, it took her three tries to fasten her push-up bra. By the time she'd got the dress over her head, Terence was on his way downstairs.

She heard his footsteps on the tiles. Then nothing. She waited, perched on the edge of the bed, straining her ears. Was that the front door opening? She didn't know. It was too far away for her to be sure.

She waited for what felt like an eternity, expecting to hear a shout, a gunshot, something.

She heard only silence and the soft trilling of a cricket outside.

"Terence, are you OK?" she called.

More silence.

"Terence?" She tried again, louder this time.

She waited a few more fearful, stomach-clenching minutes. What should she do? Eventually she crept down the stairs, slowly, cautiously. Who would be waiting there? She didn't know. She needed a weapon, but what could she use?

Stopping at the foot of the staircase, she lifted an ornamental wooden spear from its resting place next to the painted Masai shield on the wall. It wouldn't be effective against a gun, but at least it was something. Its polished shaft felt comforting in her hand. She held it in front of her and cautiously made her way down the hallway.

The lounge was quiet. The hall was empty. There was no sign of Terence, no sound of anyone.

Ahead of her she saw the front door, gaping wide open. Beyond that—she froze, grasping the spear more tightly, feeling her heart hammer a panicked tattoo in her throat—the electric gate stood wide open, too. Wide open to the dark road outside.

The house was unguarded, vulnerable, its defences breached.

Terence was gone.

OTHER TITLES IN THE SOHO CRIME SERIES